Until September

by

Harker Jones

Memory. Without that, time would be unarmed against us.
— John Steinbeck

PROLOGUE

I was so young when it all began that the blame hardly feels like mine. But no matter how minor a part I played, mine was the most pivotal. In the end, it was a decision I made.

So though there are many stories I tell, this is the one I've never shared. I can't bear to think about it, except in my most submerged recesses, releasing it in the deep deep dark of night, when it will not be evaded.

How many years would you have to go back to change your destiny? That question plagues me. Because if I can think in terms of destiny, I can afford myself a slight reprieve, a misguided waft of air in a stagnant, decaying well. If I can think in terms of destiny, I can believe that I did what I did because I had no option. It had been predetermined and I'd only acted out my role.

But destiny is the weak man's conception. To believe in destiny is to take no responsibility for your choices.

And I won't allow myself the luxury.

I learned a little from Trent that summer, but not enough to open the eyes of a self-involved, spoiled, jealous 17-year-old. Then, later, years later, I ran into Dana. We had drinks, both of us smoking too much, talking too much, drinking too much, wondering if the other was glossing things over. I saw a subtle loneliness in her eyes that I recognized only because it was in mine, too. She knew. And she knew that I knew. It's scary, that loneliness, because you want so much to have someone alleviate it, yet the only people who can are those who know it, too. And when you find one of those people you're terrified that that person can see through your carefully wrought facade, and you realize you're naked in front of a virtual stranger, so you just run.

Run.

I learned most of it from Kyle. The details. The things I couldn't have known. Those things pursue me. Those and the things Dana told me happened after. After I passed out of the picture. I was able to spend some uncomfortable but pleasant time with her until she told me. That was when I had to flee. I had to escape. That was when the running became all.

I'm still running.

Just as Kyle is still chasing.

Neither of us will succeed—me in escaping or Kyle in capturing.

We know this.

We don't stop.

Someone once told me that tears water the soul. I do not believe this. If it were true, my soul would be fertile and verdant. But it is stunted and gnarled and withered and cracked.

Which is something I could live with.

If Kyle's had been spared.

Kyle would say this is Jack's story. But, just as this is the only story I can never share, this is the only one Kyle will ever be able to tell.

So I think of this as Kyle's story.

MAY

Kyle first saw the Boy at the shore.

He and his friends were coming over a dune in the hazy white midmorning sun in the summer of 1966, carrying magazines, towels, umbrellas. The Boy sat a hundred or so yards away, facing the sea, reading a book. Approximately 16, his body long and thin, he sat gracefully, his honey-colored hair cut into a pageboy that nearly touched his collar. His skin was brown and though his tan was not deep, it was even, offset by the brilliance of his white, loose-fitting shorts and button-down. A pair of gold, octagonal glasses sat atop his nose. He was so beautiful he was shining. He looked like a sand angel.

Kyle, carrying a cooler, stopped, transfixed; his friends, oblivious, continued on. He didn't breathe. It was like he had never needed to. His heart ached with sweet, terrifying longing that felt like despair.

The Boy was all.

"New kid, I guess," Claudia Fairweather said, coming up behind Kyle, tying her blond mane into a ponytail.

"Yeah," was all he could say.

"Come on." Claudia's voice was soft as she took one end of the cooler. She started forward and, reluctantly, Kyle followed to where their friends sat. Dana Weiss, in a powder blue bikini, was already supine on a beach towel, eyes closed. Trent Santangelo and Carly Salenger were unpacking. The day was warm.

But weren't they all then?

"See the new kid?" Claudia asked, as she and Kyle set the cooler in the sand.

"Bo-ring," Dana sang without opening her eyes.

"And if Dana says he's boring…" Carly fluttered a beach towel before her.

Kyle glanced surreptitiously at the Boy. He was the only other person on the entire expanse of beach. Absorbed in his novel, he was unconscious that he was being observed.

"I bet his parents bought the house next to you, Trent," Dana said, her eyes still closed.

I wonder what color his eyes are, Kyle wondered as he situated himself on a towel.

He made himself wait until he had opened a soda before braving another glance at the Boy, and that was when the Boy looked up from his book and turned directly to Kyle. Kyle stiffened in the incongruent bliss and horror of being caught, before he turned, guiltily, away.

He'd arrived only the evening before.

Like he did every summer when they returned to the beach house, Kyle Ryan Quinn caught his breath when he turned the key in the lock and the door swung open with its haunted house creak. As the stagnancy of the past rushed by him, like the house exhaling, liberating Kevin's spirit, Kyle braced himself for a swell of emotion and horror. But it never came. He thought he'd feel the shock of it most of all in the place where it happened. And if he didn't, what did that make him?

The house was moist and dark and cool as he stepped inside, expecting he didn't know what. He and his mother opened blinds and curtains, dispelling the gloom that had permeated the building in their absence. It was paneled darkly in wood with a large fireplace in a living room that overlooked the sea. A bi-level balcony trimmed the shore side of the house, so that it let into the living room, as well as their bedrooms upstairs. Though there were modern appliances, the place had a feel of something older. There were copies of magazines, twenty and thirty years old, bad watercolor seascapes on the walls, and unpretty, hand-knit afghans thrown over the sofas in the living room and basement. The house was well-loved, as well-loved as any of the characters who had taken refuge in it over the years. Rife with the generations that had preceded Kyle in summering, there were ghosts of barbecues and swimmers and damage withstood. There were silent cries of "Dry off before you come in the house!" and "Let's collect lightning bugs!" and murmurings of "I love you."

On the second level, he unpacked in the bathroom adjacent to his room: toothbrush, comb, tanning cream. When he unsheathed his straight razor, its blade was so fine he could feel its silvery sting. His father had shown him how to use it when he was thirteen. Kyle had been so daunted by it, he'd respected its power, thus it had never betrayed him.

He put it in the medicine chest, finished in the bathroom, and had placed only a sweatshirt in the chest at the foot of his bed before the roar and fall of the surf drew him to the balcony. A late afternoon breeze smelled of salt and sun. A large willow let on to the reeds and the sand. The water was green and magnetizing. It had an allure he had always felt but never understood or questioned. He inhaled deeply of the briny air, allowing the pull of the undulating sea to wash over him, drag him under, release him, clean.

He was glad to be back.

Kyle's first memory took place at the beach house. He remembered the lonesome cry of a gull, a swatch of blue sky, and, having just emerged from the water, the breeze cool against his flesh. His beach towel was too big for his four-year-old body; it draped his shoulders, drooping to his knees. Water welled in his nostrils and ears. His hair was so blond it was almost bright white as he stepped through the sliding glass door, Kevin, eleven, behind him, brown as toasted pecans. The living room was chilled and inviting. His mother came down the stairs in a blue one-piece, a towel over her arm, her hair, then long, around her shoulders. *Having fun?* she asked. And Kevin told her, *We're golden.* Kyle smiled. His mother squatted, opening her arms to him, and he ran to her, laughing. Kevin stood behind, water dripping from his earlobes in tiny, hesitant drops. Then Kyle began to sing. Kevin had taught him the song as they lay on the beach, making sand angels. *Frère Jacques, frère Jacques. Dormez-vous? Dormez-vous?* His mother smiled, then leaned in to rub noses with him. She was so proud. It was his first memory and it was what he remembered happiness to be.

He was just pulling a windbreaker over his head when he heard a horn from the other side of the house.

Trent and the girls were there.

"Don't be late," his mother said as he came down the stairs. Ann was a slender woman who looked like a '40s film star, with a pretty, heart-shaped face, short dark hair and a pale loveliness. She had been a figure skater before she'd met Kyle's father, and it had lent her a comfortable grace she bore even under the dense burden of life. She sat on the sofa with a straight spine and the slumped shoulders of a resigned princess.

"I will be and you know it." He leaned in to kiss her cheek.

She smiled. "I'll leave the porch light on. Be careful of deer." They were the same things she'd said since he was old enough to go out without her. It seemed to comfort her.

Like it was a protection spell.

Not that she'd be awake when he returned. She'd take her pill and slumber until dawn.

That and her protection spell got her safely through every night.

There was a boisterous reunion when he got to Trent's car, a Mustang convertible so dark blue it appeared black in the waning light. The girls kissed him. Carly squealed. She had been in Hawaii for Christmas and hadn't seen him since last summer. Trent threw him a bored smile because they'd seen each other only last week at school. Dana held Kyle's hand in the back seat where he was sandwiched between her and Claudia. Trent put the car in reverse and backed out onto the road in the dusk.

In the summer, there was a surplus of deer, so the seasonal speed limit was 45. But being invincible, Kyle and his friends—save rational Dana—steadfastly ignored the limit, cruising 80 in the rain. Trent's tires squealed when he put the car in drive.

"Look what we have," Carly said, turning around from her position in the passenger seat with a wide, even smile. She held up a bottle of vodka, draping her fingers down its side like a game show hostess, then presented a bottle of rum, her titian hair flapping around her face.

"Yo ho ho," Kyle said.

"Courtesy of Simon and Brenda," Trent said. Claudia's parents bought them alcohol, let them smoke, and sometimes even got stoned with them. Thusly, they were the cool parents.

"There are so many stories," Carly said, still turned around.

"When aren't there?" Claudia retorted.

"They're all going in my book." It was something Dana always threatened.

Though all of them had houses on the sea, they preferred to find an empty stretch of sand to be together. They thought of their summer hideaways almost as a secret club, though none of them ever spoke of them as such. They were exclusive, not open to parental scrutiny or outside interference.

They had a favorite spot, about four hundred yards from a mass of boulders that blocked them from a turn in the shoreline, with endless beach in the opposite direction. Trent drove them there without asking, parking among the reeds, fireflies dotting the dusk. The sun was setting with a slash of deep violet on the horizon as they unloaded the car and carried their items down to the shore, single file: Dana, Trent, Carly, Kyle and lastly Claudia. It was the way they always went.

Carly unfolded a blanket she'd been bringing every summer since Kyle had known her. It was so worn the oranges and reds and blacks and yellows of the plaid were muted. Beside it, Dana set up a transistor radio that Trent kept in his car solely for their nights on the beach. They had been doing the same thing for so long there was never a time when they forgot a towel or a magazine or a soda. Packing for the beach was second nature.

Kyle went to gather driftwood but it wasn't long before he was drawn to the dark, pregnant sea. Behind him, he heard Trent say, "I gotta play a lotta volleyball to help me practice for that tournament next month."

Dana turned the radio on and the dulcet strains of *Summer Wind* wafted on the gentle air. Only two radio stations were receivable on the island, an all-news station and one that played only pop standards and big band. Kyle liked to fantasize that they were caught in a time warp and that it was the '40s, and each night when, on the all-request show, he heard faceless women (almost always it was women) phone in and ask for *Someone to Watch Over Me* or *The Man That Got Away,* he wondered if they weren't pining for some GI fighting in Europe, if those voices weren't really echoes from another time, simply a repercussion in a story he couldn't know.

"You okay?"

He turned to find Trent proffering a drink.

"Yeah. I'm golden."

Trent and Kyle were blood brothers, confidants, partners in crime. They went to the same tony prep school, joined the same clubs, spent summers and holidays together, and would both be attending Princeton in the fall. They understood the honeycomb of each other's lives.

But, like with fraternal twins, there were subtle and significant differences: Trent's hair was thick, and wavy, and black like coal, where Kyle's was fine, and straight, and soft like cocoa; Trent's mouth was strong and square, his smile warm and wanton; Kyle had a gentle mouth, a girl's mouth, his smile wide and accessible; Trent's eyes had luster and were dark, like ink, giving him the bearing of a stallion; Kyle's, brown, and sad, were limpid and vulnerable, like a colt's, or a deer's. And where Trent was a god, Kyle was merely a prince.

"I always wonder who's looking back at me," Kyle said, taking the drink. "Who?"

He motioned to the horizon. "From Europe. Think about it. Someone is standing on the opposite shore of this same ocean looking back at us. And someday I might be on that shore in their place."

Trent just looked at him for a moment, determining if he was serious. Then he said, "Baby, that's the mainland."

Kyle blinked, determining if he was serious. Before he could respond, they heard a scream and turned to see Carly capering from a wave. Dana had a shoe off and was submerging a toe in the ocean. "It's freezing!" Her voice carried along the water's edge.

"You guys!" Claudia called. "Come start the fire so we can make our first toast."

Making toasts was one of their traditions, something begun in summers past with their parents. Those made on the first and last nights of the summer were the most important, the most special. The first was like Christmas Eve, heavy with the promise of unimaginable delight, while the last was like New Year's Eve, ample with melancholy at the passage of time.

But then—then the summer still stretched boundlessly before them.

The wind that night was not strong, but it was brisk and sure enough that after he and Kyle had gathered wood, Trent had trouble lighting a match for the fire. Finally Carly knelt beside him, cupping her hands so that when the match came to with a breathless rasp, the wood caught fire and smoke began quivering toward the ocean.

They lifted their cups.

"To love," Kyle suggested.

Carly gave him a look as if to say, *Oh, for crying out loud.* "To summer."

"To truth," Dana said.

"I feel like superheroes," Kyle said.

"Or dwarves," Claudia said. "To Grumpy."

Trent ignored them, his voice full and resonant. "'Drink wine, it's what remains of the harvest of youth—the season of roses and wine and drunken friends. Be happy for this moment, this moment is your life.'"

"We studied Omar Khayyam this year," Kyle explained. "He rehearsed."

"Better than that carpe diem bullshit," Claudia said.

They drank.

And it was time for synopses.

The girls went to three separate schools and, though they oftentimes came together at Christmas, they didn't have as much time to catch up until summer. So they had the entire school year to relive. And the first night they shared the biggest of their stories. Another tradition.

Claudia was lissome with powdery blue eyes, her nose small and upturned with a sprinkle of freckles, her temper mercurial. "I'll go first," she said, pushing her blazing blond hair over her shoulder. "I won the state track championship for the school. I mean, it was a group effort, but I'm the one who pulled through." She wasn't the type to embellish.

"Wow," Kyle said. "You're such an athlete."

She pushed her right sleeve up to her shoulder and flexed. Her arm was lean and hard like the rest of her body. Trent made a muscle next to hers, easily eclipsing her, quipping, "You've almost caught up."

"I won the best column of the year award at the newspaper," Dana said.

"Wow," Carly said. "Everybody won something."

"What was the column about?" Kyle asked.

"My broken heart." Dana looked coolly at him across the fire. She was the most laidback of the group. Not the everything-will-be-all-right type, but the we'll-get-through-it type. Only her broken heart had nearly broken her.

"I was voted Homecoming King," Trent said.

"That's what your mother was saying," Claudia said.

Carly proceeded to tell them about her date with a frat boy from a neighboring university and how he had gotten violently drunk and she had had to escape and hitchhike home.

"How did this happen to you?" Dana asked. "Nothing like that has ever happened to me."

"These things only happen to me," Carly said, not without pride.

"So, Kyle," Claudia said as Trent mixed him another drink. "What happened to you this year?"

"I got a poem published in the school quarterly."

The girls oohed and aahed. "How sensitive," Claudia said.

"He's going to be Jack Kerouac and I'm going to be Neal Cassidy," Trent said.

"And I'll write the true story after you're both dead," Dana told them.

"Recite it!" Carly exclaimed.

"He had to recite it to the whole school," Trent said.

"It was awful." Kyle smiled, surprised at how bashful he was.

"Recite it, baby," Trent urged.

"I don't have it memorized."

"Oh, my God," Carly said. "You are *such* a liar."

Kyle laughed. "No, I'm serious. It's long. I can only tell you parts of it."

"There was something about a blue jay," Trent said.

"No! You make it sound stupid out of context!" He cleared his throat and looked into the fire. "It went something like this: 'Spring came with its humid, sultry days / You watch me from the front porch as I make my way across the lawn, the rain pouring in the sunshine. / I want to ask you how long it's been, / but I have it down to the day / and I stop, and we look at each other and laugh. / You run to me and spin me around in your arms, laughing. / We have the illusion that we are going somewhere.'" He met their eyes again, indicating he was finished.

The others applauded. Kyle bowed from his sitting position.

"You really *are* sensitive," Claudia told him.

"You're going to be my writing adversary, I see," Dana said.

"Never been prouder," Trent said.

The major stories out of the way, they segued into stories of Dana's spring break in the Virgin Islands and Trent's father's attempts at building a fallout shelter and Carly's Christmas in Hawaii ("'Hoku' means star," she had learned).

They were best friends. It was the way it had always been and the way it would always be. Sex had never entered the picture. Kyle figured it was due to the fact that they'd grown up together, as they'd been summering on the island all their lives. And he was grateful for that as it had kept him free from the pressure of sleeping with one of the girls. The time with them on the island was innocent. They drank, they smoked, they swore, but above all, they were friends, and that was all.

And, despite there being other summer people their age, they had always been a select group. They approached no one and no one approached them—not because they were more beautiful or smarter or richer than anyone else, though those things were true as well, but because of the way they didn't need anyone but each other at a time when their peers needed approval and acceptance from everyone. They, as a group, were so wrapped up in each other, you wanted to be wrapped up in them, too. You wanted to know their secrets and you wanted them to know yours. But how could you hate them for not inviting you to a place you didn't belong?

That was how it was every summer.

"The fire's almost gone," Dana observed, before observing that her drink was, too.

"Who's going to get more wood?" Carly asked, clearly intimating that it wasn't going to be she.

Trent leaned over and tagged Claudia. "You're It."

"You're cracked." Kyle played with a gold ring that hung on a gold chain around his neck. The ring was solid and had a large *K* inscribed on it, with the engraving *Belle Epoque—The Pretty Time*—on the inner circle. He thought of his life as the pretty time. Things weren't as pretty as they'd been, but he had it better than most.

Claudia went off in search of wood. Kyle began to mix a drink for Dana. Trent turned the volume up on the radio and, standing, began to sing. *It Was A Very Good Year*. It was the only song Trent favored. He sang out in a loud baritone, his voice a smarmy Frank Sinatra imitation. "*When I was seventeen...*"

Kyle and Dana smirked at each other. Carly rolled her eyes, but she was smiling. Trent went over to stand before Kyle, who squatted around the cooler, and put out a hand toward him as he sang. Kyle just grinned.

"*When I was twenty-one...it was a very good year...*"

"Every year's a good year for you." Kyle closed the cooler and went to sit by Dana, giving her the cocktail. When the song wound down, Trent joined them, smiling. "God, it's good to hear that again," he said.

Carly, paying no attention, giggled to herself. Her laugh was intimate and buoyant like she was sharing a joke on herself with herself. Kyle and Dana gave each other questioning looks. Trent, eyes narrowed, leaned toward her and said fluidly, "Carly." Beat. "Truth or dare?"

She opened her eyes and let out a squeak. Trent always, without fail, knew the precise moment to start the game. When each of them had had just enough to drink, was feeling just relaxed enough to be taken off guard, he'd lean forward, his devilish, charmingly sexual grin in place, and say, "Dana— Truth or dare?" or "Kyle—Truth or dare?" and an electric current would glimmer through the others and the person in question would smile deliciously before choosing his or her fate.

It was a game they'd played since they were children, and they had shared so much over the years that there was very little they didn't know about each other. This made them comfortable asking and answering just about anything. "No secrets" was something they often said.

There were very specific rules by which they played.

First, the name was spoken, then the challenge stated.

The one challenged had to choose.

No dare could be given that the challenger him or herself would not see through.

If anyone in the group felt the challenger would be unwilling to fulfill the dare him or herself, they could call the challenger to task, but if the challenger saw the dare through, both the person being dared and the person disputing the dare had to match it. This was a rule not often used.

No dare could be to answer a question because that would be a truth.

No question could be asked if the answer was already known.

And once the question had been asked or the dare stated, there was no hiding. The dare had to be seen through. The truth had to be disclosed. They had a code of honor that each kept intact. None of them had or would forsake that.

Kyle was surprised they'd never asked him about his sexual preference. He'd never expressed interest in a girl, but his orientation had never been questioned. And if it ever came down to it, he would tell the truth.

He'd have to.

It was one of the rules.

Now, as Dana lay down, placing her head in Kyle's lap, Carly grimaced, as if she were in a bit of pleasurable pain. "Truth," she said like she meant it.

"You told us about the frat boy who frightened you," Trent said. "You told us how drunk he was and how he wouldn't let you leave his room. You told us how you had to make a break for it and hitchhike home."

"Thanks for the summary," Dana cracked.

"But did you have sex with him?" Trent finished.

There was silence except for the rhythmic lap of the water and the soothing music from the transistor. Firelight sought their faces like tentacles. Dana looked up at Kyle and they smiled at each other, enjoying the suspense.

"Come on," Trent said. "No secrets, remember?"

Carly finally capitulated. "So what if I did?"

Kyle and Dana roared with laughter.

Carly looked up as Claudia rejoined them with two more pieces of driftwood. "Claudia," she said. "Truth or dare?"

"Must we start this tonight?" A shower of sparks shot up as she carelessly dropped the wood on the fire.

"We have eight months to catch up on," Trent told her. "There's no time to lose."

"And I'm It and I choose you," Carly said.

"Dare," Claudia said sitting down again.

Kyle let cool sand sift through his fingers. Dares weren't as interesting as Truths.

"I dare you to finish all of your drink in one gulp," Carly said.

"You're cracked," Kyle said, not even looking at her.

Claudia did so without flinching, then turned her gaze on Trent. "Trent. Truth or dare?" Her eyes were narrowed just slightly so that it was apparent she wanted a Truth.

"Dare."

Kyle smiled to himself. Claudia was the one you didn't want to cross. She was tenacious and patient as a cat and had the capacity to be vicious. Trent had taken the easy way out, but she would bide her time until she got the answer she wanted.

Trent fulfilled his dare to run into the ocean and the game continued to the tinny, faraway sounds of forsaken lovers.

Trent asked Kyle a question.

Kyle gave Carly a dare.

Carly asked Dana a question.

And when Dana asked Claudia a question, Claudia looked to Trent again. "Trent," she said levelly. "Truth or dare?"

Instead of prolonging things, Trent chose truth.

She was ready. "Which girl did you hook up with last night?"

Trent shot a look to Kyle because he hadn't had time to tell him yet. "Veronica Blythe."

"Which one is she?" Carly asked.

The island girls all blurred together.

"She works at Olympus," Dana said. Olympus was an Italian restaurant in town. They'd never understood why an Italian restaurant had taken the name of the home of the Greek gods, but as they'd pretended to be gods and goddesses when they were younger, they had always thought of it as their place.

23

That prodded Kyle's memory. Veronica had lusted for Trent for years. And, as the group normally stayed away from the islanders even more than they did the other summer people, he wondered what had made Trent lower his standards.

The game continued until Dana, head still in Kyle's lap, looked up at him and said his name, then, "Truth or dare?"

He chose truth. He always chose truth, though he couldn't have said why. He sometimes wondered if it wasn't the thrill of the gamble. If he chose truth there was the chance that he would be asked the one question that mattered. He would *have* to come clean. So he willingly placed his head on the block.

And so far he'd come away intact.

Then Dana took aim. "Did you get a girl this year?"

He did feel like a washout for being the only one who was perpetually single. But there were no secrets. Except for one. So he said truthfully, "No."

"Oh, Kyle," Carly said. "You have to start experimenting. We don't want you to be lonely."

"He's just choosy," Trent said. "He could have had a lot of girls. They were throwing themselves at him."

"Girls always throw themselves at you two," Claudia said. "But you," she said to Trent, "take advantage of them, while Kyle is cavalier."

Kyle, stroking Dana's hair, said nothing.

Kyle abandoned his magazine to the sand. The sun was working its subtle spell of warmth, and his eyes were drooping. Trent had already fallen asleep and Kyle wanted to spread out next to him and take a nap. Instead, he braved another glimpse of the Boy under the pretense of scanning the beach, and was shocked to find him gone. He jerked, cracking his wrist against the cooler in his surprise.

Claudia, stretched on her own towel, shielded her eyes and looked up at him. "What's wrong?"

He had the absurd urge to run to the road to see if he could see the Boy. Instead, he settled himself on his towel and said, "I had a bad dream." It sounded cracked even to him.

She gave a quizzical look but lay her head down anyway.

He scrutinized the beach again with the irrational fear he might never see the Boy again. What if he were only visiting? What if today was his last day on the island? What if he never learned his name?

His heart pumped in abject terror. He had never had so many conflicting emotions. It made him want to cry.

Instead, he lay back on his towel and tried to slow the thunderous beating of his heart, hoping the others wouldn't notice he had changed.

He remembered mild summer nights when he had taken his bath, his hair still damp, his cotton pajamas downy against his sensitive skin, the summer wind breathing through the house, providing gracious harmony to the lull of the sea. He would lie on his parents' bed, watching his mother ready herself for the night, attentive, content, secretly anticipating the moment she would produce the charms that would adorn her wrist and that beguiled him: the petite Eiffel Tower, the miniature Golden Gate, the tiny crown that he yearned for, but would never have—for he was not to be king.

And the swan. There was a planter in the shape of a swan that sat aside the walkway to the beach house. It was the essence of elegance. Thus, the delicate bird that hung from his mother's chain came to symbolize to him the beauty of their lives, there, in the place he loved most, in his princedom by the sea.

As he awaited their presence, his mother, in her slip, the clean, dry smell of powder in the air, would go to her closet, whisk through her collection of dresses, and ask which he thought best suited her.

He had always had a sense of sweet, perfumed longing. A bittersweet feeling for what he had, a poignancy sharpened by the idea that his safe happiness might one day end. It wasn't melancholy because nothing had yet been lost.

No, melancholy would come later.

The outfit that most often, but not always, brought about that longing was a sleeveless, powder-blue cocktail dress. His mother assumed it was his favorite, and, though he tried to explain that he had no favorites, that this just happened to be the one that made him feel the most, his lack of vocabulary made clarification impossible. She would just kiss him, rub noses with him, and tell him he was such a serious little boy. Yet, without fail, she would abide by his word, which made him feel grand and important.

So she would lay the dress (the powder blue, the mauve, or the peach) across the bed, the nighttime scent of Emeraude in the air, then sit in her dressing chair and talk to his reflection while she readied herself, vases of flowers—asphodels, clematises, cinquefoils—contrasting their plainness with her grace. She'd tell him of the fabulous party she and his father were going to, of the funny people they would see, the games they would play, the dances they would dance. It was all so romantic to Kyle. The music and the laughter and the summer. His parents went out a lot then. To dances. To parties and to barbecues.

They didn't go out so much anymore.

And he knew this was the price they were finally paying for that happiness he once found in the night.

The island and its community were small and devoted chiefly to fishing and the summer people. The main street, Park, began at a park in the center of town, hence the name, and ended at the marina. Somewhere past the horizon was the mainland.

When Kyle and Ann ran errands a couple of days later, they found banners strung across Main Street trumpeting both the upcoming volleyball tournament and Founder's Day. At the latter there were to be music and food and games, and, at night, a dance. Kyle had done them all so many times they had become tedious.

He was so caught up in thinking of the Boy as they came into town that he didn't even realize when his mother parked the car in front of the supermarket. The day was warm and gray, the water steely. After getting out, Ann poked her head back through the window.

"Are you coming?"

"Of…course." He slipped out of his seat belt and out of the car. Ann gave him a worried look across the roof of the Mercedes.

"What?" Kyle asked.

"You're just…different. Off."

"I'm just me," he began stupidly, but then, past her, he saw, coming from the movie theater up the street, the Boy. He had sought him from the passenger seat of Trent's car, at the beach, in the park. At every instant he had been aware of everyone and everything around him, yet he could not find the Boy.

He couldn't probe his friends for information, because he was afraid they would figure him out. He had an awful, heart-stopping image of casually asking if anyone had seen the new boy and Carly or Dana suddenly exclaiming, "I knew it! You're in love with him!"

Unable to tell anyone, he had borne his secret like the weight of a threat. He felt flattened by it. By the questions, and the longing, and the churning hope and drowning desolation. He'd withdrawn, hiding inside himself, and he was aware others were starting to notice.

He had lived in suspense since that first day on the beach, and now, there he was, the Boy, as simple as love.

He watched as the Boy came up the sidewalk, then stepped into the bookstore on the opposite side of the street.

What luck! Kyle's mind screamed. *What luck!*

"Kyle?" Ann still looked at him from the other side of the car.
"I'll be a minute. I have to get something."

The bookstore was dark and cool. Kyle grabbed a magazine from just inside the door, then hesitated so his eyes could adjust and his heart could start again. Nothing moved, within or without, no whispering of pages, no shifting of light. But then, as Kyle's pupils dilated, the Boy, cool and dry as flour, materialized at the mystery section overlooking the street. His cheekbones were weightless, his lips, soft, like rain. His golden-white hair fell in fine straight lines. His skin was smooth, as if he'd never shaved. And his eyes— soulful, sad eyes, rimmed in gold—were eyes that betrayed his years. A vivid cornflower blue, time had not dimmed their brilliant luster of childhood.

Kyle gawked.

Dust motes streamed between them like comets.

And then the Boy looked at him.

Kyle gasped lightly, not at being caught, but at the Boy's magnificence. He wondered if he'd ever be the same.

Then the Boy slipped by him with a suspicion of sandalwood and was gone.

Kyle followed to the stoop, oppressive heat bearing down like guilt after the shadowed hush of the store. He watched the Boy cross the street and head inland before passing to the park and disappearing in a stand of trees. He wanted to breathe him in, kiss his fingertips, protect him so he could never get broken.

He would have settled for knowing his name.

It wasn't until he'd joined his mother that he realized he still held the magazine. Ann looked at him with concern. He smiled, though he wanted to cry, to reassure her.

She wasn't reassured.

The sun came out just in time for it to set. Kyle joined his friends at Dana's. Trent and Carly played tennis by the house. Dana walked by the shore. Kyle and Claudia sat in the sand, knees drawn to their chests.

She watched him for a full minute before asking, "What's wrong?"

Slowly he came back from his place on the purple horizon where he'd been thinking of nothing. "What do you mean?"

"You're so wistful. You sure you didn't leave a young lover behind?"

He gave her a glum smile. "Just dreamy, I guess."

"Come here." Claudia moved so she was seated behind him and began to massage his shoulders. His muscles were tightly wound and she had to work. "How can you be so tense and dreamy at the same time?" she wondered.

He laughed and leaned back into her. She slid her arms around his chest. He felt safe.

JUNE

The days were endless, and with timeless hours spent idly idealizing the Boy, Kyle needed something to distract him. So one day he came to stand in the doorway of the beach house and looked out at his mother kneeling in her garden, a sunbonnet on her head, rooting around amaranths like coagulated blood. Where in past years she and Kyle's father had spent time at parties and dances, Ann now passed her time nurturing a blaze of color: reds and yellows and purples and blues; amaranths and hyacinths, bellflowers and begonia, pansies and poppies, daisies and daffodils, gentle morning glories, cruel marigold. Kyle couldn't keep count as they bloomed and waned throughout the summer.

Ann had no formal experience in gardening. It was a hobby she'd begun when she was alive. It had given her satisfaction to nurse something to fruition; it had been done with loving and purpose. But now it seemed to Kyle that she did it because she had done it for so long that she no longer knew different.

He stood, leaning against the doorjamb, crimson and purple lilacs on either side. The swan planter sat beside him, filled with benevolent bluebells. It had been at the beach house longer than he had. He felt nostalgic just looking at it.

"I couldn't kill these amaranths if I uprooted them," Ann said.

He smiled. "Need some help?"

She gave him a quizzical look. "Sure. I'm just pulling weeds. You can start over there." She gestured to the opposite side of the walk.

He knelt on the grass and began weeding through the tulips, yellow, red, variegated, his back to her. She watched him, fully aware something was wrong, as she had been since they'd arrived. The offer to aid in the gardening was the strangest thing yet. "You okay?" she asked after a moment.

He turned to her. "Yeah. Why?"

She shrugged. "You've been...reflective since we got here."

She and his father were so attuned to the variant shades of his moods. "Should...should I be concerned?"

He hated himself for hurting her, making her doubt, making her wonder. She'd lost so much and now he was picking at those wounds without even meaning to. But how to explain the upheaval of emotion he was experiencing? He gave his own shrug. "Just taking some down time before throwing myself into summer, I guess."

She nodded, accepting but not believing.

"You going to Simon and Brenda's barbecue?" he asked.

"It depends how tired I am," she said, which meant, *No, but I'll put you off for a bit.*

He nodded, accepting but not believing.

He'd expected as much.

When he was a child, Kyle liked to fantasize about being abandoned. His parents had usually deserted him because they were wanted by a faceless, nameless military agency. Then, naturally, special agents went after him in order to entrap his parents. So his life on the run was filled with intrigue and excitement.

He had other fancies, too. Sometimes he and the group pretended they'd been in a plane crash and had to make lives on their deserted island. Sometimes he assumed the role of a film star, sitting by the pool and granting exclusive interviews about his upcoming projects and current romantic staytus. And sometimes they—he and the group—posed as gods and goddesses, waging war on Titans, earthlings, and each other.

But always he returned to the concept of being deserted. Of being alone. It excited him in the way a debutante might be by the prospect of an affair with a drifter.

All that changed, of course, after Kevin.

After Kevin, his parents swooped down, lifted him to a position from where he knew he could not fall, from where they would not let him fall. They asked "Are you happy?" and told him "We love you," and again "We love you." They talked to him as an adult, as an equal, asking for his input and valuing his voice. They listed for him pros and cons, without forbidding or condoning, so that he could make his own decisions and they could advocate whatever they might be. They were open and supportive and trusting and giving so that he'd grown up confident, yet not arrogant.

He never took advantage of that position. He preferred to look at things as fairly as possible so that he could make the best judgment: He hadn't selected Princeton based on the beauty of its campus, but upon the strength of its reputation. Given the choices of an adult, he chose as an adult.

So he grew up seeming older and somehow sadder than the rest. He liked the fact that he was self-assured, but, from a place he didn't yet recognize in order to acknowledge and understand, he resented that he was different, because it gave him a tender heart.

The next day it poured. Relentless boredom set in. Kyle sat with the group in Claudia's damp, cold basement, not reading the magazine in his lap. Trent and Carly played War with a deck of cards. Claudia stood at the sliding glass door watching the rain pelt her reflection.

"What're we gonna do?" Dana asked from the sofa, a blanket pulled around her legs.

"Well, we can't practice for the damn volleyball tournament," Trent said.

"Like you need practice," Carly responded.

"What do you want to do?" Claudia asked, not turning.

Dana shrugged. "Anything but sit here."

Carly let out a scream as Trent took a pile of cards to his side.

"This rain isn't going to let up," Claudia pronounced.

"Let's go to the movies," Dana said.

"Nothing's playing." Carly slapped a card on top of one of Trent's.

"Yeah, there is." Kyle came back from his faraway thoughts of the Boy. "Some musical."

Claudia looked at him. He hadn't spoken in so long that it stood out that he finally had. They made eye contact, and Kyle wondered what she was seeing, what pieces of the puzzle she was attempting to assemble.

"Let's do it," Claudia said. "I'll drive."

They didn't realize they'd forgotten umbrellas until they were in town, so they were soaked when they reached the theater. They burst into the empty lobby in a cacophony of voice, then shushed each other as they made their way up the aisle in the dark, their shoes squishing on the carpet. Carly and Dana giggled at the back of the group. Trent snaked up an aisle toward the front. By the time they were seated, the film had begun and their conversation had petered out.

Seated between Claudia and Carly, who was on the aisle, Kyle held a bucket of popcorn between his legs so the three of them could share. Water from his hair trickled distastefully down his neck. He leaned over to Claudia and whispered, "I'm making up the rule that whoever drives has to drop us off and pick us up at the door if it's raining."

The movie had been playing for twenty minutes before he became uncomfortable. His butt had fallen asleep. Also, his legs hurt, so he stretched them over the seat in front of him. He glanced at Carly who was enraptured by the film. Aware of him, she murmured, without looking away from the screen, "This is nice."

Then, beyond her, something caught his eye.

A glimmer of white in the dark.

The Boy.

Kyle's hand instinctively came out of the popcorn, his fingers oily and glistening. He felt sick. All of the swirling emotions he'd been submerging came raging forth. All he'd wanted was to see the Boy again, but now that he was presented with that chance, he was overwhelmed with insecurity. And panic. And he was desperately sad. And he wasn't even sure why.

He had the ridiculous urge to shout *Fire!* but realized he could be arrested. Then, with dread, he realized he had to wait until the movie was over before he could do *anything*.

Time crept by. Carly cried. Claudia sniffed at Carly. Kyle sneaked surreptitious glances at the Boy, terrified Carly would notice and even more terrified the Boy would.

To take his mind off his anxiety, he tried to rehearse what to say to the Boy, but every line rang false. How to start a conversation that meant so much when he had nothing to go on? When he didn't even know the Boy's name? How to form a word, let alone a coherent sentence?

Twelve thousand years later the film ended and the lights came up. Kyle stood quickly, afraid the Boy might exit before he did. But the Boy didn't move. Carly languorously stretched in her seat, so Kyle jostled past her, saying, "I have to go to the bathroom."

He went to the lobby and stood against one of the walls just outside the theater door. His friends appeared before the Boy did, but with the rain still coming down, Claudia dangled her keys in his face and said, "Guess I'll go get the car," alluding to his new rule. Dana went with her. Trent and Carly went to the bathroom.

And Kyle remained against the wall, sweat tickling his sides, afraid to breathe on his surprisingly borrowed time. He could hear nothing but his heart. It echoed in his ears, making him feel lightheaded. The lobby warped and became garish. He had never been more afraid in his life.

He jumped when the Boy came out of the theater, holding a book, his feet angled out a bit. He walked with a reconciled slump to his shoulders so that he looked a little lonely, like he was walking home from school alone in the rain. Kyle watched him pass, and would have let him walk out the door, too awed to act, but, instead of leaving, the Boy went to stand against the same wall Kyle was, closer to the entrance, leaving a scintilla of sandalwood in his wake.

Kyle was alone.

The Boy was alone.

This was it.

But instead of moving, Kyle simply stared.

Neither of them moved for many moments.

Then the Boy looked into the rain, chin up, pensive.

Kyle nearly bolted at the suddenness of the movement. Looking at the back of his handsome head, he thought, *I want to know what he's thinking this very second.*

It was so important.

And his fear transformed in that second into energy. It was his only chance, and he had to put his self-doubt at bay in order to take advantage of it. And so he did. He became the Kyle the rest of the world knew, confident and well-spoken, not the anxiety-riddled shell he was in his head.

He started forward, wet shoes squeaking. His usually agile body felt gawky and slow as he traversed the lobby; he felt dirty and savage when he stopped before him, achingly voiceless…

The Boy looked at him with those eyes, those amazing eyes, so big and so bright, like they were lit from within. Kyle felt himself start to slide, inundated by their color, immersed in warm, comfortable light. But he couldn't lose himself yet.

The Boy was looking at him.

And he didn't know what to say.

"Hi," came out.

And nothing followed.

He had an almost undeniable urge to flee.

"Hi," the Boy said, his voice quiet.

Kyle's heart sang. They were chatting!

The Boy stood with comfortable grace, like that of minor royalty. He wore a white shirt and white linen shorts. His hands were large, his fingers long, his shoulders broad. He was quite thin, his nose a little long, forehead streaked with pimples.

He was flawless.

Kyle was so mesmerized, he was unable to offer a smile. He became transfixed by the Boy's chest, that virgin expanse and all the secrets it encased. The possibilities of who and what the Boy was were limitless.

Finally, manners stirring, he extended his right hand. "Hi, I'm Kyle Ryan Quinn."

The Boy took the hand into his own, and, for an instant, all Kyle could think was how easily the Boy's hand enveloped his, how his cool, dry fingers whispered along the sensitive underside of Kyle's wrist. "Nice to meet you, Kyle Ryan Quinn. I'm Jack Averill."

Jack!

Jack.

He looked like a Jack.

Jack Sprat.

Jack.

"Is this your first summer on the island?" he asked, his heart rejoicing.

"Yes. We just bought a place. We usually rent a cabin in Minnesota for the summer."

A steep silence descended. Kyle thought he would buckle under its weight. He could think of nothing to say. The hush threatened to swallow him.

Then the Boy saved him. "Did you enjoy the movie?"

Of course! They were only standing in a theater lobby!

He recalled very little of the film, but he thought it was best to be agreeable, so he said, "Yeah. Did you?"

Jack's eyes glittered. "I loved it. I've seen it eight times."

Kyle gulped, a real gulp, loudly. "Eight?"

"It's only playing for a week so I thought I should see it as many times as I could. Tomorrow's the last day. I have this fantasy of going to the Eiffel Tower and singing like they did in the movie."

Kyle cloudily remembered the Eiffel Tower, but he certainly didn't remember anyone singing at it. "Wow." He could think of nothing else to say. "Sounds fun." *Cracked.* His eyes came to rest on the book that was clutched in Jack's hand. "What're you reading?"

"Oh." Jack raised the book in an embarrassed gesture. "Just a cheesy thriller."

"No way! I love cheesy thrillers." He was magnificently beautiful *and* they had something in common! "May I see it?"

"I'm reading *The Beautiful and the Damned,* too," Jack said, practically apologizing as he handed over the paperback.

But Kyle hadn't heard. "I've read this."

"Yeah?"

"Yeah. The butler did it." He smiled, kidding.

Jack smiled back, a shy smile.

And that smile made Kyle heedless. "Do you want to come over tonight? I mean, I have some books. That you could borrow. If you'd like."

There was a flash of heated anticipation before Jack could respond.

Then, suddenly, Trent was there, arms around Kyle's neck, pulling him backward, and Kyle was thrilled. Now Jack could see how fun, how important, how loved he was. He could see him in his element. He could see who he was. Kyle didn't question why all this was important. He just accepted that impressing the Boy, Jack, was all.

"You don't want pizza, do you?" Carly was there, too.

"Tell her you're starving and pizza's the only thing that will satisfy you," Trent said, laughing.

Carly laughed, too. "Damn you, Trent." She kicked his foot lightly. "Let him answer." She looked to Kyle. "He just wants to flirt with Veronica Blythe. And I'm damp. I want to change my clothes."

"I thought you liked being damp," Trent said.

She gave a mock-horrified expression and swatted him.

Kyle gave a helpless, what-can-I-say-these-are-my-friends look to Jack, who cocked his brows. Kyle was so caught up in the moment that it took a second for him to catch the sadness in Jack's carriage. It made him want him more.

"We can get pizza tonight," Carly said. "We can take it to the beach." She nodded like she was convincing a dog to go outside.

The burst of energy from Carly and Trent gave Kyle the confidence to say, "Well, that depends on Jack."

He said it casually, but Trent's grip loosened around his neck and Carly stopped giggling. Kyle suddenly felt foolish trapped in Trent's arms, so he struggled free and looked at Jack.

Claudia and Dana pulled up in front of the theater, and Carly started, slowly, toward the exit, looking back to see who would follow. Trent took a couple of hesitant steps after her. She stopped at the door, a hand on the bar to push it open, watching, and waiting.

"That's, um, Trent and Carly," Kyle explained, a little shyly, to Jack. He nodded in the direction of the street. "And that's Claudia and Dana. They're—we spend our summers together."

"How romantic."

Kyle knew the others were waiting, but he couldn't pull himself away. He wanted to kiss Jack. Then he realized what he'd just said. "What?"

Jack smiled. "How romantic you spend your summers together."

There was another flash of heated anticipation, this time before Kyle could respond.

Then Trent was there again, arm around Kyle's neck, pulling him away.

"You are so cracked!" But Kyle was laughing.

"For Christ's sake!" Carly exclaimed. She was back, too. "Let him choose!"

Kyle had his hands on Trent's iron-like forearm as he was dragged away. "Jack!" he shouted. "Come at eight!" He gave his address. "Okay?"

Jack smiled a warm, genuine smile, teeth white as the glare of exposed bone, and there was a flutter in Kyle's chest. "Does that mean you've chosen?" Jack asked.

As Trent pulled him through the exit, Kyle watched Jack watching him until Trent released him on the sidewalk and he turned to get into Claudia's car.

"What's up with the new kid?" Claudia asked as she pulled away from the curb.

"I was just getting to know him," Kyle said. He sat in the back seat between Carly and Trent who had one proprietary hand on Kyle's leg. Now that he had done it, approached the Boy, Jack, and it was over, he felt like collapsing, just curling up and taking a nap. He was exhausted.

"He's sorta homely." Carly spoke like she was quipping something over her shoulder. That was how she always spoke.

"Aren't you gonna come with us tonight?" Dana asked.

Kyle was uneasy because for the first time, save family engagements, he was pulling out. It was for just one night, he reasoned. But he was so uncomfortable he couldn't even bask in the residue of his encounter with Jack. It was already losing its potency. He grasped at the insinuation of sandalwood.

"Maybe not," he finally said. "The new kid—er, Jack's coming over to exchange some books." He wondered which would offend them more—inviting Jack over or not inviting the group to join them.

"Well, that shouldn't take long. What—fifteen minutes?" Carly looked at Kyle, then past him to Trent, then back to Kyle. "Right?"

"Well, we'll probably hang out for a while, too," Kyle said, resenting having to spell it out.

"You sure move quickly." Claudia met his gaze in the rearview, she daring, he defensive.

"It's not like Trent didn't ditch us when we first got here," Dana said, turning to the backseat. Apparently this was of more interest than the new kid.

"What do you mean?" Kyle asked.

"Before you got here," Claudia said, "Trent indulged in carnal pleasure with one of the islanders."

"Veronica Blythe." Kyle thought this had already been covered.

"She's another one," Dana told him.

Trent just smiled guiltily.

"Come on," Carly said. "No secrets, remember?"

"Trent." Claudia was decisive, the rain loud on the car. "Truth or dare?"

"Oh, no!" Dana turned back toward the front and propped her knees on the dashboard. "Claudia pulls out the big guns."

"Fine." Trent exhaled. There was no getting around it. "Betsy Branigan. The next day when I went into town, she was positively mooning."

"You're breaking her heart," Claudia said, laughing.

"I can't believe you didn't tell me about this." Kyle was both insulted by the omission and, as always, envious that Trent was having sex with so many others than himself.

To which Trent responded, "It wasn't exactly something I was bursting to tell anyone, baby. She's just an islander."

"No secrets," Dana said, which made Kyle feel like a hypocrite. How could he berate Trent for not telling him about Betsy Branigan, when he had an even bigger secret himself? He felt guilty and a little dirty.

Then, as if to warn him, Dana turned back and added, "Remember?"

The person Kyle had been that morning was no more. He found it unsettling to be so new. When he was toweling off after a shower, the sight of his naked torso in the mirror snagged him. He looked different, though he couldn't say how. He leaned in and probed his pupils, like through a keyhole, to see what there had changed. He peered until he realized he was staring back at himself.

He'd never looked closely before.

He didn't know if he was beautiful.

When he went downstairs in a burgundy silk shirt and shorts, he was shaky and scared. His bravado from the afternoon had fled. And he wanted to cry. Not because he was afraid, or insecure. The emotions were just too much. They needed an outlet.

He stood at the sliding glass door looking out to the sea, attempting to control his feelings. He hated being the emotional one. He longed to be Trent, who sailed through life never doubting himself, never wavering.

Tears slipped out as he stood there, comporting himself with as much dignity as he could.

He jumped when he felt Ann's hand on his back. He swiped angrily at the tears, but didn't turn to her.

"You okay?" she asked, concern quavering her voice.

"I'm fine…"

"But you're not."

"But I am. This isn't like before. I promise."

He couldn't look at her, so he went out onto the balcony, greeted by the roar of the surf. The sun was shooting roses and oranges and greens across the water. The tenderness of lilacs coalesced with the savory sea air. The willow's branches swayed gracefully. His shirt billowed around his body, smooth and cool in the wind, which dried his tears. He leaned on the rail and inhaled deeply, so nervous his teeth were chattering.

Then he heard his name.

He went to the stairs to find Jack standing on the sand, books in hand. He was a vision in white linen shorts and a white silk shirt. (Kyle took the fact that they'd both chosen to wear silk as being significant.) His hair, just beginning to curl under, twisted in the breeze.

Kyle devoured him. "Hi," he breathed, and he didn't know if the word was lost in the wind.

"Hey," Jack said, his eyes the size—or at least it seemed to Kyle—of suns.

Kyle wanted to say something clever or sophisticated—intelligible even—but, as he descended the stairs, all he could do was stare. That was why, two steps from the bottom, his ankle twisted and he fell, rolling into a sitting position on the sand, horrified at his gracelessness.

Jack gaped at him in surprise.

Kyle went into autopilot. There was too much at stake to lose it all because he was emotional. So he flipped a switch and stood, attempting urbanity. "Don't worry," he said. "I know how to fall." He felt like a fool, but Jack smiled, a humble, enchanting smile, and Kyle knew then that he'd jump through hoops of fire to make Jack smile. "I'm glad you came," he said, with soft, hopeful eyes.

"Of course," Jack said gently, and Kyle felt stupid for having doubted. "How could I not?"

They climbed the stairs back to the deck and went through the sliding glass door into the living room. "This place is beautiful," Jack said. "It's so old. You can feel the history." He went to a model ship that sat on the mantel among a variety of shells and photographs. "This is cool," he pronounced.

Kyle wondered if Jack's lack of nervousness heightened the perception of his own terror. "My grandfather made it," he said.

"He made this?" Jack peered around the ship, taking in details, not presuming to pick it up.

"Yes," Kyle said, but Jack had moved on to one of the photographs.

"Are these your ancestors?"

"Um—yeah. I guess so." He'd never thought of it that way.

"Wow." Jack moved to a second photograph, staring hard at it for many seconds. "I like to try to figure out what people were thinking at the precise moment their photo was snapped. It's one spark of what made them up, and the only clue to who they were." He looked at Kyle. "Especially your ancestors. Because without them you wouldn't be here. That spark in this photo is you."

Kyle was still thinking of a response when Jack said, "Am I being weird?"

"No," Kyle said a little too quickly.

"I photograph everything."

"Oh. Why?"

Jack looked at him, seemingly surprised Kyle didn't already know, the answer was so plain. "So I won't forget," he said. "You have to know now what will mean something later."

Kyle was surprised at how familiar that was, but before he could process it, Ann came in from the kitchen, yellow jonquils cradled in the crook of her right arm, her sadness over Kyle muted, and Jack turned to her, clearly taken by her simple, understated beauty, her grace.

He was seeing her as Kyle had as a child.

When they went up to Kyle's room, Jack sat at the head of the bed and proffered his books. "These are for you." Kyle took them, and Jack turned, plucking novels from the shelf above Kyle's bed, trying to look at four of them simultaneously. Then, when he looked up, delight in his face, Kyle knew he was lost to it. Whatever was happening was more powerful than he was.

He grinned stupidly.

"These are great!" Jack exclaimed. "I mean, I've never heard of them, but they sound great!"

There was a sudden rush of—ardor? rapture? love?—and Kyle longed for him with the desperation of every cell. Parts of him he hadn't known existed ached with yearning. He was afraid he would die of it.

"They're yours," he said.

"I wasn't hinting!"

"Really. Keep them." His voice was gentle.

"Thanks," Jack said. "That's really cool."

Kyle grinned, blissfully, foolishly happy that Jack was happy.

Jack looked at the books again, then set them on the shelf and looked to Kyle. "These can wait," he said. "Now there's us."

Kyle decided he'd better sit before he fell. He situated himself at the other end of the bed, their bare knees touching. He could feel the hair on his legs stand up. He had no idea what to say. So he said, "Tell me."

Jack took his glasses off and, leaning the side of his head against the windowsill beside the bed, asked, "What would you like me to tell?"

Everything, Kyle thought expansively.

"My favorite color is blue."

Blue! "Mine is violet." They were quiet. Then he asked, "When's your birthday?"

"July twenty-first. I'm a Cancer. Barely."

Kyle nodded. "Mine's April eighth. I just turned 18. None of us have summer birthdays. Me and my friends."

Jack said, "I'm still seventeen. I don't even have my driver's license yet."

"You don't have a driver's license? How do you get around?"

"In the city, you don't need a car so much."

That made sense. "Do you have brothers or sisters?"

"No, it's just me."

"We—me and my friends—we're all only children, or the youngest."

"It's nice you have each other."

"It is. We're our own family." He wanted to include Jack in that family just because he was so ready to fall, but he knew it was still too soon. He didn't know if there would ever be a time for that kind of proclamation. He sighed. "What's your middle name?"

"Sheridan. Can you believe it? Soooo pretentious."

Jack Sheridan Averill. Kyle let the name roll around on his tongue. Jack Sheridan Averill. It was enchanting. Almost melodic. To be blessed with such a poetic name.

If he doesn't want me? How much will I cry?

Then Jack asked, "Who's your favorite writer?"

"Fitzgerald."

"Me, too!"

Kyle didn't know what to say. Then palpable silence invaded and he had to strangle down a primal scream of horror. He smiled, then wanted to die.

"This is nice," Jack said. "Just hanging out. It's…"

"What?" It was so important.

"I don't know." He fluttered his hands. "You're going to think I'm a fruitcake."

"Never."

Jack smiled, grateful. "There's something familiar about you. Like you're a long-lost friend I hadn't been aware I'd lost. But you're new, too. And that's weird."

Kyle was so taken aback he needed time to form a response.

"You *do* think I'm a fruitcake."

48

"No! You just—" Mesmerize, hypnotize, entrance and enchant me. "—surprise me."

Jack looked at him, judging his sincerity. And then, assessing Kyle was genuine, he did the most amazing thing of all. He opened his mouth and began to talk.

Kyle listened with subdued reverence as magical, lyrical, glittering words fell from Jack's mouth. He leaned forward, as if held up simply by Jack's flow of speech, spellbound by his light, mellifluous voice, captivated by his lips.

And then, when Jack hesitated, searching for the right word or pausing for impact, Kyle would feel himself start to fall. His fear would come rushing back, and he'd start to crumble. He didn't know why but it mattered more than anything that Jack love him.

Then Jack would start to speak again, and color would rush back into the world, just in time to keep Kyle upright.

Jack—Kyle's heart still swelled when he thought his name—was hoping to spend the summer reading and sunning and photographing. He was serious, serious about things no one else was serious about, so he'd kept mostly to himself through school. Despite having a small number of friends, he had never felt like he fit in. "I'm sure you've never felt that way," he concluded.

Suddenly Kyle felt as transparent as a primer. Because he realized he and Jack had even more in common than he'd realized. "Actually, I always feel that way."

Jack leaned forward, surprised and hopeful. "Really?"

Then Kyle thought for a second. "Well, except for Trent. I mean, he's not like me, but—I don't know. He's cool. Sometimes I think he'd like to be *more* like me. I don't know." He'd never had to sum Trent up before and it was difficult. "He doesn't treat me like I'm different," he concluded. "And the girls are cool."

"So you do fit in," Jack pointed out. "With a lot of people."

"But I've never found anyone who was like me."

"But you have a place."

"But I'm still alone."

Their banter had reached a crescendo, as though they were arguing, Jack that they were different, Kyle that they were alike. And as soon as the words were out, Kyle realized how true they were and how pathetic it made him sound. He had never thought about it so simply.

"That's sad," Jack said. "Because it's what I've always wanted, and now you're telling me it's not enough."

Kyle didn't think that was what he meant but suddenly wasn't sure. It was a moment before he heard Jack say, "What's your favorite season?" and he was grateful for the out. It showed him that things were still okay.

"Autumn," he said.

"You're so tragic."

"But there can be beauty in tragedy. The struggle is all the more glorious because you know all is lost." He fluttered his hands, wondering if *he* sounded like a fruitcake. "What's yours?"

Jack was ready. "Summer." He smiled down the length of the bed. "What's your favorite summer memory?"

There was only one option. "The nights with Trent and the girls. On the beach."

"You've got memories of a thousand summers. I'm envious."

Kyle reached out and touched Jack's knee. His flesh was warm. "I bet you've got tons of stories." When he took back his hand, Jack's heat tingled on his fingertips. He beheld them, resisting the urge to inhale them, and there was nothing but the moment.

Then he realized Jack was watching him, and their eyes caught like they were looking into a mirror.

Kyle couldn't blink to save his life.

But he was charged enough to say, "Tell me some of them."

Jack was charged, too, aware something had passed between them. He told of his first experience drinking ("Apparently, I was the life of the party"), of playing the triangle in the band ("Can you believe I was the guy who played the triangle?"), of his father's diagnosis with diabetes and how he, Jack, had had to learn to administer injections, of how he was going to the University of Michigan in September. And when he got to the punchline of a story, he'd say, "Can you believe it?" with a wide-eyed, open face. Like, "She was missing for two weeks, and then we found she was with a friend in Paris." Beat. "Can you believe it?"

Clearly, it was unbelievable.

Kyle was hypnotized by the words that were making Jack more complete, more real, imagining how he'd have held him through his hangover, the concentration with which he must have played the triangle, how diabetes must have affected the family, how he wanted to withdraw from Princeton to attend the University of Michigan so they could be together, all the while resisting the urge to place his hand on Jack's knee again. He wanted to take one of Jack's hands, kiss the fingertips, intertwine their fingers and then, simply, hold it.

That would be enough.

When Jack finished it was nine o'clock and long shadows fell across the room. Their eyes met in the semi-darkness, Kyle's lids heavy with longing.

Neither spoke.

The conversation had ceased as quickly as it had begun.

"I've rambled," Jack said. "I don't even know how I got started. I never feel this comfortable."

"I'm glad you do."

They were silent again, then Kyle sat up, suddenly remembering etiquette. "Oh, shit! Do you want a soda or juice or something?"

"No. Um. But I have to pee."

Oh.

"Of course. So sorry. It's right down the hall."

Jack stood and drew close to the dresser and a small gallery of photos. "I've been trying to figure out who these people are."

Kyle went to him and pointed to the supporting characters in his life, trying to keep from shaking with nervousness. "That's my grandfather. The one who made the boat downstairs. And that's my mom. She used to ice skate. And that's me, Trent, Carly and Claudia." He pointed to a photo of the four of them on the beach. They were in windbreakers and the wind was whipping their hair around their faces. It had been a cold, damp night. The photo was unframed and wedged into the border of his mirror.

"Where's the other girl?" Jack asked.

"Dana was taking the photo. We've never gotten a photo of all five of us at the beach, because it's always only the five of us."

"That's too bad. Who's this?" The subject was a boy, about fifteen, with dark hair, dark brown eyes and a wide, confident, carefree grin that was all teeth.

"A friend," Kyle lied.

Jack nodded at the photo, studying it, then headed for the door. He turned, about to step into the hall. "I've had *Autumn Leaves* in my head ever since we talked about autumn. So annoying."

And then he was gone.

Kyle went to the door and saw the bathroom door shut before bounding back to the bed and picking up the pillow Jack had been sitting on. He lifted it to his nose and inhaled the residue of Jack's heat, his scent of sandalwood. He held the pillow to his chest, arms around it, chin on top.

Jack liked him. Jack Averill, the most beautiful boy in the world, *liked* him. The fact that Jack Sheridan Averill, in all of his lanky, straight-haired, bespectacled magnificence, wanted to be friends with him made Kyle glow in the dying rays of the day like his popularity and athletics and grades had failed to do. His heart had never been so full and yet he'd never been so afraid. Instead of vanquishing his fear, somehow his triumph had accentuated it.

"I can't believe I talked so much," Jack said, reentering the room.

Horrified, wondering how long he'd been standing clutching the pillow, Kyle flung it onto the bed and turned, hiding his hands behind his back. "I—was just, um—fluffing! The pillow!"

Jack stood in the doorway, cleaning his glasses on his shirt. "Sorry I smooshed it."

"No. God, no. It was already—smooshed."

In the remaining sunlight Jack's skin glowed translucently, a nimbus of fiery color about his head.

"Would you—" Kyle said with a smile that came out goofy because he was drunk on Jack's overpowering presence, and more than a little lovesick. "Would you like to get some ice cream?"

He remembered the house Jack's family had bought. Uninhabited for as long as he knew, it had two especially large windows facing the sea. They were so big he had often wondered how small someone on the inside would look. They always seemed cold to him, those windows, like hardwood floors. From the beach, they looked like eyes, reflecting the sky, blue and pink and white. He remembered lying in his bed at night, wondering what the house might be thinking to cause its eyes to turn murky blue or metallic gray. Yet, though he thought of the house as having eyes, a mind, he could never quite imagine it being alive.

When they came down the stairs, Ann was sitting on the balcony looking at the sea. Kyle went to the screen door behind her. "We're going to town. For ice cream."

"I'll leave the porch light on. Be careful of deer." She didn't turn to him.

"I know, Mom. Have you taken your pill?"

"Of course. I'm just enjoying the night air."

He lingered for a moment. "Of course."

She said nothing else, so he turned to Jack and they headed outside, his thoughts turning from his mother's sadness to his own insecurity.

When he and Trent had turned sixteen their parents had given them convertibles—navy blue for Trent, deep magenta for Kyle. Everyone was impressed. Girls wanted to ride in them, guys wanted to drive them.

So, unsure about his own beauty, his own appeal, Kyle was certain his car would impress Jack.

Consequently, as he and Jack passed the swan planter glowing like snow in the moonlight on their way to the driveway, he didn't let on, using the element of surprise as a bargaining chip in impression. Yet, when they got to the car, all Jack said was, "What a nice shade," and got into the passenger seat. And there was nothing Kyle could do or say without obviously fishing for a compliment or a reaction, which was not the point. He didn't care about the car as much as he did about Jack.

So he said nothing.

Kyle's vain anticipation over the sensation his convertible would cause energized him, so he drove too quickly. He didn't notice until Jack said, "Aren't you worried about the deer?" Kyle didn't know what he was talking about and took so long figuring it out that Jack finally said, "You're going too fast." Kyle felt reprimanded, so he slowed down and began to babble to cover his discomfort. He told Jack about his family and friends. About the girls, and Trent, and their dorm. About Princeton in the fall. Jack listened until they were in town. When Kyle was done, he said, "So it's official. You're a popular boy in disguise."

Kyle wasn't prepared for that, so the smartest thing he could say was, "In disguise as what?"

Jack looked at him, his hair turning in the breeze. "I don't know," he said. "What're you hiding from?"

Kyle was spared answering when he found a parking spot outside Olympus, the Italian restaurant on Park Street. But getting out of the car, he realized he'd walked into another minefield.

Veronica Blythe stood on the sidewalk smoking a cigarette beside a stand of foxglove. She wasn't a beautiful girl, but she was pretty, and she had spirit. She was of average weight with long dark hair and eyes, darker even than Trent's. She wore a pair of jeans and a red apron that was dusted with flour. She was one of the island girls.

She called Kyle's name as he and Jack were about to cross the street. Kyle reached a hand out to Jack's to stay him. They turned but did not go to her.

Instead, she went to them, her face alight. "How was your winter?" she asked in an easy drawl.

"It was nice," Kyle answered automatically. He didn't want to prolong the conversation, so he didn't inquire after her own. He turned to Jack and introduced them.

"Where's Trent?" she asked, her hand slipping from Jack's. Her eyes glittered with a queasy lovesick glint Kyle feared his own did. "You two are always together."

"He's—with the girls." He touched Jack's back and they started to cross the street.

Behind them, Veronica said, "Tell him to give me a call."

55

The inside of the ice cream parlor was bright and shiny. Jack went to stand in line, and Kyle followed, gliding, sliding, slipping down the sleek sweep of Jack's neck, unable to catch himself, save himself.

Then Jack turned. "They have praline crunch!"

It was a small gesture, but Kyle had to blink twice to see straight.

"It's my favorite." Jack's smile lit the room or, at least, Kyle's world.

Kyle felt bliss radiate from within, and he shivered, goose bumps pebbling his flesh. He gave a nervous smile and said, "Guess someone walked over my grave."

Jack's joy dissolved to distaste. "What does *that* mean?"

Kyle felt himself dim. "It—just—you know—means someone in the future walked over your grave, and it causes you to shiver in the present."

Jack just looked at him.

"Cause it's kinda weird," Kyle supplied.

Then Jack grinned. "You're interesting."

Kyle couldn't help but grin back. "That's good, right?"

"Most boys aren't," was all Jack said, and then they were at the counter.

While Jack went to get napkins Kyle ordered two cups of praline crunch and two Cokes. He loved the contented feeling he got from taking care of Jack. But when he grabbed their order and turned from the counter his sense of balance tipped.

Trey Shaw, another summer boy, stood there, inexplicably holding two yellow hyacinths. He was leaner, more confident than he had been last summer. His mouth was long, the ends turning up in a boyishly sexy half smile even when he wasn't smiling. His black hair was straight, except the bangs, which curved around his face like stage curtains, his eyes green and glittering, as if he had a secret.

"Kyle!" he blurted.

"Trey. Welcome back." Kyle took a step past him in an attempt to avert further conversation, but Trey reached out and lightly grasped his arm.

"I'm glad I ran into you."

"Yeah?" He looked from Trey to Jack, who was sliding into a booth. Already Trey was in the way.

"Yeah." Trey gave a consciously nonchalant shrug. His sureness had given way to the awkward insecurity he'd had the summer before. "I wanted to get together."

"That's great," Kyle said without thinking. It wasn't what he meant, but he was flustered, afraid Jack would see them and introductions would become obligations.

"How was your winter?"

"Great. It was great." He had to break free. He started to walk away but Trey spoke.

"Kyle?"

He stopped. He didn't turn. "Yeah?"

"He your friend?" He spoke of Jack.

"Yeah. He is."

After a moment, he heard Trey sigh. "Is he why you can't see me?"

"I didn't say I couldn't see you, Trey." It was his turn to sigh. "I'll see you around."

He knew Trey from his summers on the island. They had always been on friendly terms, but Kyle had had his circle, and Trey wasn't part of it, so there had been a line. Trey couldn't cross it, and Kyle wouldn't. Then, last summer, they'd run into each other in town and begun talking. Somehow afternoon became evening, and they found themselves on a dark street lined with latent lilac trees. They strolled through the shadows to the last house, where the neighborhood gave onto the strand, and they walked, the sea on one side, a barricade of reeds on the other, eventually taking a seat by the water, looking toward the horizon. Kyle was startled but not surprised when he felt Trey's hand on his thigh. He *was* surprised by how quickly it led to kissing, and then exploring.

It was good.

It was great.

Trey's body was warm and hard and alive.

After that they met two or three times a week at an abandoned house. Every time it was the same. They would make small talk until Trey was brave enough to touch Kyle, and when they were through, Kyle would lie on the floor of the porch overlooking the sea, his eyes on the dusty windows, the cobwebs in the corners, the cracks in the ceiling. Anywhere but at Trey. And Trey would lie too close, talk too much, try too hard. He would look at Kyle with a beseeching expression and sigh, and Kyle could never tell if the sigh was born of hopelessness or boredom.

Trey wanted to join Kyle's circle of friends.

But no one joined the group.

And Kyle feared the others would somehow know or find out what they did together.

So Trey, powerless, learned to be content with what he could get, and they reached a sort of medium, though neither was particularly happy.

Kyle had forgotten about him since.

The night was warm and deep as a kiss. Kyle and Jack walked for a time through shadowed, hushed neighborhoods, breathing deeply of the sea air, Kyle pointing out places of note, relating adventures, revealing history. It helped him get out of his head to play tour guide. He hardly had time to think of Jack, let alone his own troubled heart.

They had been strolling a while before Jack said, "What's your pendant?"

They stopped, and Kyle fished the ring out from under his shirt.

"It's beautiful," Jack said. He fingered it, the large inscribed *K.* "Where'd you get it?"

"From a friend." He'd told the lie often but still wasn't comfortable with it.

"Well," Jack said. "Mysterious *and* tragic."

Kyle looked down, away, flattered, flushed, self-conscious. "It's just personal," he said.

Jack smiled. "I wasn't pressing. I wouldn't expect you to divulge all your secrets tonight. We have to save some for tomorrow."

Kyle grew warm at talk of the future.

"What does *Belle Epoque* mean?"

"'The pretty time.'"

Jack looked at him openly. Then he said, "You're so romantic," soft as lilacs.

Kyle forgot the simple function of speech.

"Most boys aren't romantic either," Jack told him.

That was the exact moment Kyle fell in love. He knew it as it happened. He could only breathe, "Trent's gonna love you."

Jack smiled a small, surprised smile. "He means a lot to you."

"He's my brother. I can't even remember life without him. He's smart and cool and he cracks me up and—yeah. I don't know. I love him."

"I can tell by the way you talk about him. There's so much affection."

"Yeah," Kyle said, thoughtful. "I guess there is."

He steered Jack down a side street that dead-ended at the beach. Aromatic, abundant lilac trees—pink, white, lavender, blue, magenta, violet—lined the sidewalks, petals carpeting the street as if awaiting a bride.

Jack looked up, his face beaming. "It's not real!"

"It's all real. And it's all for us."

"What do you mean? Do you mean to steal?"

"We do it every spring."

"And you don't get caught?"

"Of course not. We're golden. Come on." Kyle led Jack to a tree that was bursting with purple blooms and reached up, snapping off a stem. Petals rained down on them like glitter. Jack gave Kyle a spirited smile, blossoms in his hair, on his nose, on his glasses, and Kyle wanted to kiss him, right there, in the fragrance and the moonlight.

They made their way to the next tree, and the next, ripping clusters of color from the air. There were no cars, no pedestrians, no intruders on their dream, so their arms were laden when they reached the end of the road where they stopped so Jack could look back on the street they had pillaged. "It doesn't even look like we touched it," he breathed, his Adam's apple swelling.

How can no one else be struck dumb by your beauty? Kyle wondered. *How can someone look at you without shielding their eyes?*

Jack turned and gave him a gentle, penetrating look. "Thank you for tonight. For the ice cream and the lilacs and everything. For taking the initiative."

"Beauty is fleeting so it's only just that we revel in it," Kyle said, not sure if he was talking about Jack or the lane of lilacs. He felt like he was teetering at the edge of a precipice. Even though the consequences could be horrific if he lost his balance, self-destructively he craved it. The prize if he survived was worth the chance he might have to pay a price. It was worth the death of everything he'd previously been.

"Join us tomorrow," he said. "Me and Trent and the girls."

Jack pushed hair behind an ear. "I don't want to tag along," he said, without appealing for mollification.

"If you weren't there, I'd be wondering where you were."

Jack looked at him in hesitant surprise. "You like me enough to break your circle." A statement.

A thousand times, yes. "You'd be enlarging it."

"I could bring my camera. I could get a photo of the whole group."

"I was so hoping you would."

Jack looked away then, out into the ancient darkness, toward the sea. He inhaled deeply, and the flowers, cradled in his arms, surged, as in reverence. "Most people don't bother getting to know me," he said. He released his breath, not quite a sigh, and when he turned back, Kyle couldn't see for the brilliance of the sun. He was unable to put up his mask quickly enough. Jack saw, but said nothing.

"I'm different," Kyle said, meekly.

When he dropped Jack at home, Kyle said, "So you'll join us?"

The motor of the car hummed as Jack thought. "Will they mind?" he said after a moment.

Yes. "They'll love you."

Jack rapped his knuckles against Kyle's jaw. "Knock wood. I'll just leave if everyone's uncomfortable. Deal?"

"We'll both leave if it's uncomfortable."

"Kyle."

"Jack." Then Kyle was laughing. "I mean it."

Jack touched his arm, causing the hair on it to stand up. "I feel like you're watching out for me or something."

The place where Jack's flesh met his own was so alive it was painful, the nerves screaming at attention. Kyle wanted to pull his arm away because it was too much. "Maybe I am," he said.

And then the fingers were gone, and Kyle could breathe.

Jack got out of the car, closed the door, and looked in through the open window. "So I'll meet you at the same place I saw you before?"

"You saw me that day, too?"

"How could I not? You were like a caravan or something. I was waiting for the camels."

Kyle smiled.

"Okay." Jack tapped his knuckles on the door twice. "See ya."

And he was gone.

By the time he was home and turning off the porch light, Kyle veered between wanting to run barefoot singing through the streets and curling up naked in a corner. What kept him from siding with despair was the knowledge that he'd be spending the next day with Jack.

No matter what was to come, that could not be changed.

So he nodded off, savoring the warm, welcoming buoyancy of memory and anticipation.

He could think of nothing clever to say, so Kyle opted for, "Hey," when Jack opened the door the following day. The morning was as breathless as Kyle felt.

Jack smiled like he'd been hoping Kyle would come.

"I thought I'd, um, come by and get you." He hadn't wanted Jack to have to face the group on his own the first time. He'd realized in the night how much more closed they'd be if he showed up alone. And it saved him the suspense of whether Jack would show up at all.

"This way I can't get lost, right?"

"Something like that."

Kyle waited on the porch while Jack gathered his things, then, as he backed onto the road, he said, "You know, they may seem a bit aloof at first, but that's just how they are."

"How they are, huh?" Beside them, the turquoise sea contrasted with the bleached earth of the shore.

"Don't worry. We're all pretty basic. As WASPy as it gets. Except for Dana."

"You're so—vigilant," Jack said. "I feel like you've been appointed to be my friend or something."

Kyle had wondered if he weren't trying to buy Jack's friendship. But looking at him in his white shorts and tank top, he knew it was more. He wasn't aiming to procure Jack's affections so much as prove the depth of his own.

"You're sort of freaking me out," Jack said then.

"I'm freaking *you* out?"

"Yes! I'm like, My God, this man is *cool. And* he likes me."

Scorched by the soulful expression on Jack's face, all Kyle could think was, *He thinks I'm a man.*

They looked at each other, openly, for many seconds, and the space between them was charged.

And then they were laughing, loudly, relieved that the raw moment had been there and also that it had passed.

Claudia was the first to see them coming from the road, beach gear in hand. She was spreading a towel under an umbrella. Kyle was unable to read the look on her face. It made his anxiety skyrocket. Not only was he nervous about Jack accepting him, he had to worry about the group accepting Jack. He didn't know which was less likely...

"Hey," he said when they came abreast of her.

She looked from him to Jack, appraising. "Hey."

"This is Jack Averill." Kyle said his name like it was important. "Jack, this is Claudia Fairweather."

Jack extended his hand. "You have a beautiful name."

"Thank you, but I hate it. It makes me sound like a fairy or an optimist or something. It's nice that you could join us today." She said it pointedly, with just enough stress on *today* for Kyle but not Jack to notice.

Carly and Dana gave them curious looks from where they stood in the sea. Trent, farther out in the water, hadn't caught sight of them yet.

Kyle and Jack unloaded their things and were setting up an umbrella when Carly and Dana came to assess. He caught the glances the girls shared, none of them sure she approved.

"Jack's new to the island," Kyle said, as if anyone would care.

"We know," Carly said. "We saw him the same time you did."

"He's a photographer." He held up Jack's camera, still hanging from its strap around Jack's neck.

"Intristing." Carly, along with Dana, settled on her blanket and closed her eyes, tirelessly bored.

Kyle, not knowing what to say, reached for his tanning lotion.

They fell silent. Claudia, who was closest to Kyle and Jack, leaned back and closed her eyes. The girls receded into the background like paper dolls. After a moment, Jack said, "I forgot my suntan lotion. Can you believe it?"

Claudia opened an eye.

"This is where vigilance comes in handy." Kyle pulled a tube of his own lotion from his bag.

"Good thing I have a sentinel."

"Hey."

He turned to see Trent, his hard, brown body dripping water. "Hey." He introduced Jack, unable to read Trent's expression. "We saw Veronica last night. She said to give her a call."

"That'll happen," Claudia sniffed.

"She could become annoying." Dana repositioned into a cross-legged stance and stretched a brush toward Trent. "Brush my hair, please."

Trent took his place behind her and began working through wet, matted snarls. Kyle realized the girls saw Jack as an intruder; Trent, as an adversary.

"It's too hot to be at the beach," Carly said. The sun was cruel.

"We just got here. It's only going to get hotter." Kyle handed Jack the lotion, self-conscious now that the paper dolls had come back to life so quickly.

"You should have heard her before you got here," Dana quipped.

"Some days are just too hot for the beach," Carly said. "We're sitting here roasting like…like… Well, like something that roasts."

"God, you're eloquent." Claudia laughed.

"Let's set up the volleyball net, Kyle." Trent handed the brush back to Dana. "I have to practice for that tournament."

"What about my hair?"

"It'll just get messed up when we play," Trent said, standing.

"It's too hot to play volleyball," Carly said.

Trent crouched, the pole of the volleyball net between his legs, while Kyle twisted it into the hot sand. "So you really hit it off with this kid." A statement that awaited justification.

"Yeah." Kyle wanted to sum up his feelings about Jack, yet seem blasé, and there was no word he knew that encompassed it all, so he said, "He's cool."

"He seems to like you."

Kyle grinned, hoping. "Y'think?"

"Would he have come if he didn't?"

There was a hard surface about a foot below the surface of the shifting sands and the pole would go no farther. "Was it a mistake to bring him?"

"I don't know." Trent looked at him, his eyes screwed up in the glare of the sun. "Was it?"

Kyle thought, then said simply, "I'm not sure yet."

They worked at the pole for a minute more, then Trent squinted at him again. "What's going on?"

Shit. "What do you mean?"

"You've been lost in your thoughts since you got here and now this? Are you okay?"

No. But what could he say? He hadn't expected a straightforward confrontation. "Of course."

"You'd tell me?"

"Of course."

Trent thought for a minute then touched the volleyball pole. "This isn't going any farther. Let's just play."

"I'm really bad," Jack said to Kyle, who squatted beside his towel.

"So's Dana. Don't worry. If they laugh at you I'll beat them up." He smiled, but Jack looked at him with concern. "If you really don't want to play, you don't have to," Kyle said.

"Do you want me to?" Jack asked.

"Only if you want to."

"Jack." Trent stood a few yards away, holding the volleyball. "You're on my team with Carly."

The game started well. The ball volleyed predominantly between Trent on one side and Kyle and Claudia on the other with Dana. Kyle was glad Trent chose Jack for his team because Trent was by far the superior player of the group, and that way Jack had to do less. After a few minutes, Jack even began laughing.

Once they had been playing for a spell, Carly, arms akimbo, asked "What are we doing tonight?" of no one in particular.

"We could troll town," Dana suggested.

"I've got some weed," Trent said.

"When don't you?" Claudia quipped.

"Let's do that," Carly confirmed.

All in agreement, they collectively turned to Kyle. "What about you, baby?" Trent said.

It happened so quickly it felt like they'd rehearsed a script. Kyle didn't want to commit until he was sure what Jack wanted to do. How to be both noncommittal and appeasing?

"Sure," he said, not sounding very sure at all and unable to mask his resentment.

"Great!" Claudia readied to serve the ball.

"It's too hot to play volleyball," Carly grumbled.

"I need to practice for the tournament," Trent reminded her.

"It's too hot," Dana said. "Let's wait until the sun starts to set."

Trent wasn't happy, but he acquiesced, and he and Claudia went into the water, the others taking their places below their umbrellas. "Are you comfortable?" Kyle asked Jack.

"Yeah."

"Do you want to swim?"

"Oh. Um. I can't swim."

"How can you not swim?" Carly said. "Don't you roast?"

"Yeah," Dana said, with a throaty laugh. "You know, like something that roasts?"

Jack was a little embarrassed they'd overheard the conversation. Taking note, Kyle murmured, "Do you want me to teach you?"

Jack's tank hung on his frame, billowing like a flag of surrender. He gave Kyle a vulnerable look. "The truth is, I'm afraid of the water." He glanced over Kyle's shoulder to be sure Carly and Dana hadn't overheard.

"I won't let anything happen to you," Kyle said.

"That's very sweet. But that's not what it's about."

Kyle didn't know what to say, so he looked away to see Claudia curiously watching them from the water's edge. They looked at each other expressionlessly for many moments, and when he looked away he felt like he'd given in.

Later they gathered for a photo. Waiting for them to situate, Jack zoomed in on Kyle, who was telling Dana that she should be in front.

"Why do I have to be in front?" she wanted to know.

"Because I do, too," Carly said.

Claudia saluted. "Kyle Hitler!"

"Don't be a bitch," Kyle said. "I just want this to be good because it could be the only one we get."

"Honey, you're always the organizer," Claudia told him. She was kind.

They arranged themselves, following Kyle's directions, consciously or not, Carly and Dana before the others. Once placed, they smiled, posing, as Jack focused the camera. He was about to shoot when Trent broke form and tripped Kyle from behind, and they fell to the sand, grappling and laughing.

"For Christ's sake!" Carly exclaimed, but she and Dana were giggling.

"Y'all sure are good friends," Jack said, lowering the camera.

"We're very close," Claudia said, with or without intimation. Kyle couldn't tell from his position on the sand.

"Come on, you big homos!" Carly poked them with a foot. "You can jerk each other off later."

"You never let us have any fun," Trent groused.

They got up, sand clinging to their legs, their hands, their backs, and stood, their arms around each other's shoulders. They were so familiar with each other's bodies, with their chemistry, they moved fluidly, fit instinctively. Kyle was never more himself than when he was with Trent.

"Are you sure you're ready?" Jack asked.

"Of course," Dana said. "We've been waiting on you."

Jack aimed the camera again and as he was about to shoot, Carly said, "Say cheese."

"Muenster." Trent and Claudia spoke at the same time, then turned to each other in surprise. Kyle jerked forward, laughing. Dana smiled pertly. Carly put forth mostly teeth.

And Jack snapped the photo.

When they lay down for naps, Jack whispered to Kyle, "You guys actually do this all summer?"

"I guess it's the kind of fun you have when you don't notice." Kyle propped himself on his side, the gold ring on his chest flashing in the sun. "You okay?" He tried to keep from doting, but he was a happy slave. And the fact that Jack had been somewhat welcomed by the group had heartened him.

"Sure." Jack shrugged.

"What are these?"

Beside Jack were two stones, one flat and green, one white and round. Kyle reached out and picked up the white rock. It was almost translucent.

"I collect stones each summer," Jack said.

"Souvenirs, huh?"

He pushed hair behind an ear. "Want one?"

"I wouldn't take one of your souvenirs."

"It'd mean more if you took it."

"Which one?"

He laughed. "Whichever speaks to you."

Kyle kept the white stone in his hand. He was already planning to save it forever.

Jack dozed off, his glasses on the ground between them. Kyle, still propped on his side, let his eyes wander down the length of his body: the chest with the round, brown nipples, the abdomen with the capricious covering of sand, the legs with the golden hair. He had an almost uncontrollable urge to place the palm of his hand on the smoothness of Jack's stomach.

But Trent and Dana were still awake.

And Jack would have a heart attack.

So he contented himself with a lingering look, before taking Jack's glasses in his hand so they wouldn't be crushed in their sleep.

Turning onto his back, he lay still trying to control his breathing.

Over the summers, they had spent countless days migrating from house to house. It was easy to go a week without seeing their parents, simply because there were so many other places to go. Their younger years had been filled with choruses of Miss Mary Mack, grilled cheese sandwiches, and the construction of houses of cards. That all passed upon the discovery of alcohol, attainment of drivers' licenses, and the realization that Kyle could cook. When Kyle developed a skill in food preparation, the group's eating habits changed forever. He was good. And he enjoyed it. Everyone benefited.

That day, after the beach, they went to Trent's. His parents were in the city for the week. Carly and Dana had purchased fresh lobster that morning.

"We only have five," Carly said to Kyle as they unloaded the convertible. "We didn't expect a guest." Her words were tart.

"He'll eat half of mine," Kyle said. "So you can stop being a cunt."

And that was the end of that.

Once the lobsters were boiling, Kyle and Trent stood in the kitchen sharing a cigarette while Jack sat on the counter. Kyle and Trent were dusty, shirtless and shoeless. Already they were more accustomed to being without shirts than with them. Carly referred to them as natives.

Trent stubbed the cigarette out and nudged Kyle. "Let's go get the beer, baby." The beer was in the basement and they had a tradition of getting it together and, while they were there, downing a bottle or two.

"You okay for a few minutes?" Kyle asked Jack.

"Yeah," Jack said, but his voice was quiet.

"You sure?"

"Jack." Trent stood at the top of the stairs. "Want a beer?"

Jack smiled. "Yeah. I think I would."

That was the Trent Kyle knew and loved. Not the prep-school partier. Not the all-star quarterback. Not the serial heartbreaker. But the man who would rise above his friends and shine, not only when it was needed but when it counted.

"That was good of you," Kyle said, once they were downstairs. The refrigerator was in the laundry room and he sat atop the washer. "To offer Jack a beer, I mean."

Trent shrugged. "He's a guest. I'm the host." He retrieved two bottles from the refrigerator and gave one to Kyle. Around them were shelves filled with canned goods and preserves. The Cuban Missile Crisis had spooked Trent's father, so he'd stocked both their primary home and their summer home with supplies.

"I know. But the girls haven't been exactly warm to him."

"They don't mean to be hard. There's just never been an outsider."

"So they resent him?"

"Wouldn't you?"

"Do you?"

"I don't know. He seems like a nice enough guy."

"But you resent him."

"I didn't say that, Kyle. I think the girls would agree we really can't be ourselves. It's not like we can play Truth or Dare with a stranger around."

Kyle didn't know what to say, so he just said, "Yeah."

"Let's drink a toast. And we'll chug these."

"To group photos. *Finally.*"

They touched bottles.

As they headed upstairs, Trent in the lead, each carrying a six-pack, Kyle said, "Thanks for being honest with me. And for being good to Jack."

Trent stopped at the top of the stairs, facing the closed door. "You don't have to thank me," he said, affronted. "You should expect it." Then, without looking back, he pushed the door open and ascended to the next level.

After, when it was dark, they sat in the living room, drinking, smoking, talking. An overstuffed white sofa and loveseat met at a cherrywood end table, on either side of which sat Jack and Kyle. The day's sun and alcohol were making Kyle sleepy. His lips were salty from the water, and he could feel grains of sand in his shorts. His stomach made a pleasant rumbling noise. Giving half his meal to Jack had left him a little hungry, but the sacrifice had been such an honor, he bore the hunger pangs like medals.

Leaning his head on his hand, he gazed at Jack, who was sipping his third beer and looking rather tipsy as he listened to Dana and Claudia debate whether the statue of *David* was in Rome or Florence. Before them Trent and Carly were building a fire.

Kyle had allowed himself to relax as the evening progressed, had allowed himself a sliver of hope. Maybe Jack did like him. Maybe his friends would like Jack. Maybe Jack would like his friends. He began to imagine there was a scenario in which everyone could win.

He gazed at the Boy until the fire warmed the room and Jack's skin began to glow, his eyes to droop drunkenly, comfortably. This was his Jack.

"When I was in Florence," His Jack suddenly said. "*David* was there."

Claudia responded, but Kyle didn't hear. He was feeling such a rush of pride he was practically swelling. But then he remembered it was a secret. And his rush of pride turned to a howl of loneliness.

"What's wrong?" Jack looked at him across the expanse of cherrywood.

He panicked at having been caught in such a private moment. "Why do you think something's wrong?" he asked without lying.

Jack smiled knowingly, almost suggestively. "Oh, I've got you figured out, Kyle Ryan Quinn."

Before Kyle could grasp that, Trent stood from the fireplace, watching them for a second, then took a seat beside Kyle, vaguely territorial. For the first time it felt like boys against girls. Something it had never been.

Then, being just the three males, none of them knew what to say. Kyle had never felt uncomfortable in Trent's presence in his entire life. Finally Trent turned to the girls. "What're you talking about over there?"

"That baseball game Kyle won," Dana said.

"How embarrassing there's only one," Kyle said to Jack. "With Trent we'd have to say 'Which one?'"

Jack gave a sweet smile. He had won none.

Trent turned to Jack, feeling the need to illustrate their history, their bond. "It really was crazy. Bottom of the ninth, two outs, behind by three. Kyle comes in and nails a triple."

"And *then*," Carly said taking a seat on the floor beside Dana, "he steals home to win the game."

"It really wasn't so exciting." Kyle spoke low to Jack.

"Sounds like it was," Jack said.

"It just sort of happened."

Observing this, Trent hooked an arm around Kyle's neck and gave him a loud, wet kiss on the cheek. "Never been prouder, baby."

"Trent," Dana said. "Will you get me a beer?"

He looked at her, a trace of unusual annoyance on his face.

"Get me one, too, please," Carly said.

"Claudia?" Trent queried, standing.

"Since you've offered…"

He scowled, but went into the kitchen.

Kyle and Claudia caught each other's eye and smiled, shrugging away Trent's mood. With their recent friction, Kyle liked feeling like conspirators.

When he turned back, Jack jerked his eyes up, as though he'd been caught at something. "I was—looking at your ring," he said awkwardly. "It's beautiful."

Kyle gave a quick, hollow smile. "Thank you." But he looked away.

Jack became aware that Claudia was observing them. They gazed at each other, coolly, for a moment, without speaking. Then, without looking away, he called out, "You're a great volleyball player, Trent!"

"Thanks," he said from the kitchen. "Kyle's my luck."

Kyle loved that they were having a conversation. It seemed so simple, but it was more than he'd allowed himself to hope for.

"I understand luck," Jack said. "I have my beliefs, too."

"What do you believe in?" Claudia asked, and Kyle couldn't tell if her intent was malice.

"Fate. What do you believe in?"

A moth bumped against a screen.

"Circles."

They looked at each other without daring.

"I believe in fresh drinks," Trent said returning with beers for everyone and effectively ending the conversation.

When they left, Carly had already gone up to sleep in one of the guest rooms and Dana was dozing by the fire. Trolling town had been postponed. Claudia didn't move from the sofa but she waved and said, "It was nice to meet you, Jack. Maybe we'll see you around."

Kyle was so surprised and his senses so dulled by alcohol, he couldn't respond. Her words were civil, bordering on polite, but her tone flawlessly conveyed the fact that he, Kyle, was part of the group, and that they, the group, might collectively see Jack sometime because he, Jack, was clearly not part of the group.

Kyle wanted to belt her.

He was glad when Jack chose to not respond but turned and walked away.

"Do you see what I'm talking about?" Jack said, once they were on the road. "You tried so hard for them to like me."

Kyle wanted to take Jack's hand and squeeze it so he would know how not alone he was. But he didn't know what to say.

"I feel like the new kid in school trying to break into a clique I don't even care about."

"They don't dislike you," Kyle said. "They just resent you."

"Thanks."

"I don't mean it that way. They'll get used to you."

"No. They won't."

Kyle felt a tingle of anxiety, like suspense.

"We'll still hang out," Jack said. "Just not with them." Then, returning to the first subject, he added, "It doesn't really bother me. It just strikes me as odd."

"I don't know how people don't beat themselves up to be friends with you."

Jack looked over at him in the moonlight. "You really mean that," he said after a moment.

Every sound, every syllable, every word. I'm hopelessly, helplessly, breathlessly, wonderfully, terrifyingly in love with you. Kyle wanted to park the car at the side of the road and swallow him, be swallowed by him, right there, with the wind in their hair, the essence of burning oak in their clothes, the shore murmuring beside them.

But he refrained, his aloneness roaring at the idea that Jack might go away. It gnawed bloodily, hungrily, emptily—for it was only sated when it was empty—leaving his eyes tearing, his flesh wanting.

He said nothing.

Kyle didn't call Jack the following day for fear he'd seem overeager, stewing instead in his trepidation over whether his friends and Jack would gel, and the dread over what he would do if he had to choose. So by early afternoon, an enormous sadness weighed heavily and with such concentration on him he wondered if it might still his heart.

As he helped his mother chop vegetables for dinner, his mind was still muddied. He tried to lose himself in the mindlessness of the carrots and the celery and the onions, but instead he was lost in uncertainty. So he didn't notice when Ann leaned against the counter, watching his anxious face.

It took him a beat to become conscious of her. Then he said dully, as if coming out of a stupor, "What?"

"You're preoccupied. Something is happening."

"I'm just tired." After it was out he realized it wasn't necessarily untrue. He was tired in the absolute no-energy way that a fleeting, yet taxing experience leaves one almost unable to stand.

"You're not tired. You're sad."

"No." He didn't look up, tried to focus on the celery he was slicing. "Just thinking."

"Please tell me it's a girl."

"Everyone always thinks it's a girl."

"That's because it usually is. Is it Claudia?"

"No. I mean, there isn't a girl."

"Claudia's adorable."

"Claudia's a bitch."

"She's one of your best friends."

"I don't see that you're disagreeing with me." He looked at her and wondered how she'd react if he told her the truth. His parents had been so good to him since the incident. (He never knew what to call it. All they knew was that it hadn't been an accident.) But this. Would they draw the line at this?

"Please just promise me you'll tell me if something's wrong."

"Mom. Of course."

She looked at him long and full in the face. "I've never seen you like this."

He gave her a quick, frightened, fluttery smile. It was too big for him to hide. "I've never been like this," he said, and his voice was small.

He was in the upstairs bathroom flossing when he heard the phone ring and his mother call, "It's for you!" He half expected it to be Trey, who had left two messages already, but then she added, "It's Jack!"

His mouth literally dropped in surprise.

Jack.

He rinsed and went to the extension in the upstairs hall. He took a deep breath before picking up the receiver and saying, "I've got it, Mom." He waited until he heard her hang up, his hand going to the white stone in his pocket, before he said, "Hello," almost hesitantly.

"Kyle."

The word was a breath, and Kyle felt tension he hadn't realized he'd been holding drain at the sound of Jack's voice. He wondered if Jack, too, was relieved to be connected again.

"Jack."

"I'm surprised you're in. I thought you'd be out with the group."

"I stayed home today." *I love you.*

"What did you do?"

Think of you. "Nothing."

"Me neither."

A silence fell, and Kyle had to repress a scream of horror. Silence was the worst thing of all.

"So," he said. *So what?!* his mind shrieked.

"Did you want to get together tonight?" Jack blurted.

Kyle sat on the chair beside the phone stand. How was he supposed to say he couldn't? When all he wanted was to be with him? "Jack—"

"I'm sorry I called. I feel stupid."

Kyle laughed. It was nice to know Jack was unsure, too. "It's just that Trent's going to pick me up any minute. Can we do something tomorrow? Just us?"

"Would you show me around the island? I want to know where to explore with my camera."

"Of course!" He heard his mother downstairs and looked through the banister to see Trent standing just inside the door. "I have to go."

"Oh. Um. Okay."

"I don't want to," Kyle said, heedlessly, turning his back to the rail.

79

"Oh, Kyle," Jack said with such emotion Kyle shuddered. Every time Jack said his name there was such depth, such definition, such majesty to it that he realized he'd never been aware how beautiful it was.

"I'll pick you up," he said, his voice viscous. "Is ten good?"

Jack allowed himself to exhale. "Perfect."

There was another pause.

"I'll, um—see you tomorrow then," Kyle said.

"Okay. Um. Okay."

"Jack."

"Kyle."

Neither wanted to let go.

"Good-bye, Kyle."

Kyle paused, then said sparingly, "Good-bye."

The night was palpable and still. The group, in shorts and sweatshirts, stalked through the park in the center of town, coy fireflies winking around them. Kyle couldn't stop grinning because Jack had called. The note of desperation in his voice made him wonder if Jack didn't feel the same, if Jack didn't miss him, too. Then creamy hope would begin to churn until he'd realize how unlikely his chances were, and he'd despair for a second before remembering that Jack had *called.*

Dana put an arm around his neck and they walked in step to the gazebo, where they sat, Kyle leaning his head back over the rail. The sky swam because he was drunk on the summer, the sea, Jack. When his head stopped spinning, he saw there were myriad stars. Their presence comforted him. It was relieving to see they were still there, despite being perpetually outshone by the lights of the city.

He wondered what Jack would think.

Trent brought out a joint and, after lighting it, sent it around the circle. Kyle looked over at him, his thighs splayed, hands dangling between his legs. Trent met his eye, his own glazed, and gave him a relaxed smile. Kyle grinned back, happy. For all the emotional chaos he'd endured over Jack, he was free for a bit.

They smoked without speaking for a few rounds.

Then, bursting with idealism, Kyle said expansively, "These are our halcyon days. We must treasure each one."

"You're in a better mood," Claudia said.

"Baby," Trent moaned. "Don't get sentimental. It's so morose."

Kyle was about to explain that being sentimental wasn't about being sad, that it was about being happy, but before he could, Claudia threw a shell at him, and when it missed by a good four feet they both roared with laughter.

"You two are messed up," Trent said, lighting a cigarette.

"Let's get a pizza," Carly said.

"My God." Claudia wiped her eyes. "A big pizza pie sounds *amore.*" This sent her and Kyle into fits of giggles, and they ran ahead, doubled over with laughter, through the darkened park toward the street. When they came to the sidewalk, they stopped to wait for the others, and that was when they saw Trey Shaw coming.

Shit, Kyle thought.

When they were close enough, Claudia said, "Hey," still partially out of breath from running and laughing. Trey exchanged pleasantries with her then looked past her to Kyle. "You didn't call me back," he said, and Claudia turned to look, too, and Kyle knew she was thinking, *What other strays are you going to bring around?*

"I didn't know you called," Kyle said, knowing that Trey knew he was lying.

They regarded each other, then Trey said, "I saw your friend today. He seemed...available." The word was chosen with purpose.

Kyle felt rage and jealousy to the point that his vision blurred. He had never felt such fury. He had to consciously restrain himself. Claudia became aware something was going on and immediately stepped beside Kyle as the rest of the group appeared on the sidewalk behind them.

"See you around," Trey said, as he started forward again.

Kyle knew the worst thing would be to react, but he couldn't help himself. His foot shot out between Trey's legs and tripped him to the ground.

"Shit." Claudia had a dazed smile of shock and admiration on her face.

Trey looked up at Kyle with hurt eyes. There was no more cockiness in his expression; he was so wounded Kyle was instantly regretful. He reached down and offered him a hand. "Sorry." He *was* sorry, but part of him still wanted to punch him in the throat. He helped Trey to stand, brushed his chest with nimble fingers.

"That's all right," Trey said because he was supposed to.

"No. It's not." Kyle could only imagine how horrified his mother would be. He smiled wanly.

"Is it all right if I give you another call?" Trey asked.

Kyle was annoyed and disgusted at Trey's opportunism. And he didn't want to say yes with all his friends there because his primary concern was getting them to accept Jack, but what could he do?

The first thing Trent saw when they entered Olympus was Veronica. She stood behind the counter, a long floury red apron protecting her black shirt and blue jeans. Her face kindled when she saw them approaching.

Trent gave her a warm smile. "Hel-lo. We need a table for five."

Kyle wondered if Trent noticed the disappointment that flickered her smile. She seated them against one of the front windows, and the girls immediately made for the bathroom. She sat menus at each place and said explicitly to Trent, "Can I get you anything?"

Trent looked across to Kyle, who was smoking a cigarette and looking out the window to the street, still charged over the confrontation with Trey. Deciding for the group, Trent ordered three pitchers of beer.

Veronica gave him a dubious look. "Are you old enough?"

"I'm old enough for everything."

Kyle had tuned them out and sat seething. Had Trey and Jack really run into each other? Had Trey said anything? Had he tried to come between them? He felt sick with suspicion.

The only way to find out would be to ask Jack.

But to ask Jack might be to unveil both his true feelings as well as his history with Trey. His cocoon of happiness had been riven, and he was teetering on the precipice of panic again.

When Veronica left, Trent leaned in and said, "What happened back there?" He looked stung, like he'd failed because Kyle had dealt with the situation before he'd been able to help. Like he was unnecessary.

Kyle relived the incident, and when he was done, Trent said, "So he was saying Jack's queer?"

"I guess."

"That freaked you out enough to take out Trey?"

"Wouldn't you want me to do that if it was about you?"

"But, Kyle, you've only known Jack for a couple of days. And you *never* get violent."

"I didn't take time to examine my motives and options. I just reacted."

"You're always so sensitive."

"Maybe I'm sick of being the sensitive one!" His tone was sharper than he'd intended.

"God. Relax. Some people would take that as a compliment."

"I'm sorry. I'm still worked up." He fingered a white rose that stood in a vase between them. He couldn't let on how jealous he really was. He had to get a grip. He made a conscious decision not to tell Jack. He was ashamed of his behavior.

"You're not the same," Trent said. "We've all noticed. It's like you're not really here. Earlier, you were like the old you. Now you're someone different again."

"I'm fine."

"Is it Kevin? Did something happen?"

"Everything's not about Kevin. Sometimes it's just about me."

"Then what is it?"

"Nothing!"

Trent sighed, deciding not to pursue the topic. "So, is he? Jack?"

"What?"

"Queer, Kyle. What were we talking about?"

"No. I mean, as far as I know he's not." Which wasn't a lie. Then he had to say what he did next. "Would it matter?"

"It wouldn't matter to me. I mean, we're cool with Perry Parker at school, and he's pretty queer. I wouldn't tell everyone, though. If he is, I mean. He'd be lynched."

Kyle had an image of townspeople with torches.

Then Veronica was there with the beer, and Trent was asking when she got off. "In a half an hour," she said. "Maybe I can join you."

"I was thinking maybe I could join *you*," he said, deftly deflecting her from the group.

"We'll see," she said, meaning yes.

Jack's mother was a thin woman with dark hair and a warm face that beamed through the screen door of her beach house. "So," she said. "You're Kyle." She held the door open, extending her hand. "I'm Violet Averill."

Kyle shook her hand, saying, "It's nice to meet you. Mrs. Averill." She was in a greenish-brown housedress. And she was older than he had expected, perhaps in her mid 40s.

He stepped into the cool shade. There were so many wonders to behold, so much to be learned, from that woman, that house. The furniture was dark. On the balcony there was an easel. There were daisies on the mantel.

It was Jack's life.

Along the base of the stairs was a bureau covered with framed photos, and Kyle felt a thrill, hoping to see Jack as an adolescent, a child, an infant— the Jack he hadn't been able to know. And it was then that he began to understand the search for the past in photographs.

"My husband, Sheridan, is out on his boat," Violet said. "It's his toy."

"Wow," Kyle said, stupidly, awed.

"It's nice to be able to put a face with the name," Violet said. "You're all we've been hearing about since we got here. 'Kyle says this.' 'Kyle says that.'"

"Mom!"

That was when Kyle became aware that Jack stood on the stairs. He looked luminous in the dimness of the house, glowing in his white. "Don't worry," Kyle said without averting his gaze from Jack. "My friends are sick of hearing about Jack, too."

And then Jack looked to him and they met each other's eyes.

Kyle drove to a lagoon on the other side of the island and parked the car where the reeds met the sand. A coral reef glittered in the azure two hundred yards out. A lazy breeze meandered in from the clinquant sea. Jack sat with a look of wonder for a minute, then turned his wonder to Kyle. "This is beautiful," he breathed. "We're like the Lost Boys."

Kyle's smile owned his face. He hoped he wasn't glowing, because he felt like he was, which only made him smile more radiantly. "I hoped you'd like it."

"You know, it always made me sad that Wendy grew up."

Kyle understood. "Me, too." Then, feeling bold, he blurted, "I'm glad you called last night."

Jack blinked slowly at him. "I am, too."

It was the only time they alluded to the charged emotion they'd felt the evening before.

They took their things down to the sand, and Jack stood for a moment looking out to the reef and the sea, Kyle looking at Jack.

Finally, Kyle said, "I brought a flask," holding it forth. "Not sure if you'd be, you know, interested."

"I'm not as innocent as I look, Kyle Ryan Quinn."

He took the flask and swallowed twice, and when he gave it back, his lips were shiny. Then he took his camera out and said, "Tell me when you're ready to go. I figure you'll be bored in twenty minutes, but won't say anything for an hour."

Kyle dismissed him with a wave of his hand, then took his shirt off and went to stand by the water. He lingered there for a while, the sand squishy between his toes. The reef looked like a crown bobbing on the ocean. He'd never noticed before.

Contemplating it, he drifted out to where the ocean topped his knees. He was so high on Jack that he forgot to be nervous, forgot his fear that he would always be alone, that he would scare both Jack and his friends away. He felt solid. For the first time in what felt like forever.

When he looked back, he found Jack standing at the water's edge, taking photographs of him. Kyle didn't know what to do, so he just stood there. Jack continued shooting for a bit, then stopped, lowering his camera, swallowing hard, and they beheld each other.

Kyle wanted to run to him, kiss him, openmouthed, a coral crown beckoning, prismatic layers of light glinting off the water like a kaleidoscope, shattering their dream into myriad renderings, but he just stood, regarding him, Jack's eyes bright even at that distance.

Jack slung his camera around his neck and waded in to join Kyle. As the water crept up his calves, he wavered but didn't stop. When he was close enough, Kyle reached out a hand, and Jack took it, rushing the last couple of steps so that they stood close.

"Hey," Kyle said.

"Hey."

"You okay?"

"Yeah." He held Kyle's hand for a second, then released it and looked to the reef. "Too bad we can't get out there."

"We can. The water's that shallow."

A look of doubt crossed Jack's face.

"Do you want to?" Kyle asked.

Jack thought for a second, then nodded, as if to himself. "I want to try."

They inched forward, but as the sea began to lap at Jack's thighs, he hesitated.

"You okay?" Kyle asked.

"I'm not sure."

"Jack." He was earnest, leaning in close, so close he could see the pores in his skin. So close his eyes were two worlds. So close he could have kissed him. "Do you want me to carry you?"

Jack laughed, his hair lighter and smoother than corn silk. "Absolutely not."

"You can't weigh more than—what? 110?"

"124, thank you very much."

"I can lift Trent and he weighs 170."

"I can't think of anything that would make me more uncomfortable."

"Then I'll walk ahead of you. So you can see how deep it gets. It won't go above my waist. Cool?"

Jack smiled uncertainly. "Yes."

"Do you trust me?"

This time Jack didn't falter. "Yes."

Kyle began walking backward toward the reef, his gold ring flashing like a beacon in the sun. The water crept up to his pelvis then stopped rising altogether. "See?"

When he got to the reef, he held his hand out to Jack, who paused, deciding, then began to slowly cross the distance between them. When he got there, Kyle helped him get steady footing on the coral, then joined him in looking out at the sea. The sun was hot on their heads and blinding on the water.

"Nothing to it," Kyle said.

They looked at the horizon for a few moments, then Jack said, without turning from the view, "You're the first person who's made me feel like I'm not different."

And Kyle said, "Maybe that's because you're not so different."

"How long will you be here?" Kyle asked, suddenly realizing he hadn't a clue. They lay next to each other on the sand, having eaten the lunch Kyle had packed.

"Until September."

"We're always here until September. It's the end of vacation, the end of summer. I used to cry when we had to leave. Our last day, we'd have already packed our things, and I'd go sit by the water and just contemplate it."

"You were tragic even as a child, huh?"

They grinned at each other. Kyle had to fight the compulsion to clasp Jack's hand, survey it, note every line, every crease. *I love you,* he thought. *I love you.*

Jack looked at him seriously. "Are you okay?"

Kyle blanched. He thought he'd hidden it so well. But could he hide anything from Jack?

"Of course. I'm so happy." It sounded cracked even to him. He sat up and looked to the water. Facing Jack, he was afraid all would be revealed in his countenance.

"I poke fun at how 'tragic' you are, but…sometimes you really seem sad."

Kyle took a deep breath and released it. "We all have our moments, I guess."

Jack seemed unconvinced but how to rebut? "Just… I don't know what's come before, I'm new, but—I'm here."

Kyle focused on the horizon, not sure he could control his emotions. He could only squeak out, "Okay."

Jack didn't know what to do either, so, sitting up and looking out at the water himself, he awkwardly sang a snatch of *Moon River* to segue into something else. Anything else.

Kyle's heart gasped. "What made you sing that?"

"Just sorta popped out."

Kyle remembered his parents dancing in the beach house one twilight a few years back, no music, just his father singing the sweetest, saddest melody he'd ever heard. It made him aware how alone he was, with just the three of them.

He'd blocked it out immediately.

He was silent so long, he finally became aware Jack was staring at him, his eyes squinched in the sun.

"It's just sad," Kyle offered.

"Well, maybe you'll be my Huckleberry friend."

"I'm hopeful."

Jack realized he'd hopped from one sad subject to another so he hopped again, this time with feeling. "You know what I want to do? Make a sand castle! I haven't been to the shore forever."

"You've been here how long and you haven't built one yet?" Kyle hadn't built one himself for years. Not since Kevin.

"It's not fun by yourself," Jack said.

So they built one, Kyle sculpting, Jack fetching water. It turned out to be big and lumpy and crumbling, but Jack was happy. "It doesn't matter how it looks," he said. "It's ours." And it had snapped Kyle out of his mood.

"It reminds me of a song my mom used to sing to us," Kyle told him.

"Sing it for me! I bet your voice is sweet." He feared he sounded a touch manic trying to keep the energy up.

Kyle laughed. He could deny Jack nothing. So he took a deep breath and sang with a tremulous delivery:

"Do you love me, Prince Kyle, Prince Kyle?
How much do you love me, my darling Prince Kyle?
A penny's worth, a nickel's worth,
Even, perhaps, your princedom's worth?
Oh, do you love me, Prince Kyle?"

"Awwwww. She made this up for you and Trent?"

"No. Just me."

"You said she sang it for 'us.'"

Oh. "I'm used to speaking in the plural. Always being with the group and all." To change the topic, he said, "You know what we used to do?" He leaned back in the sand and began sliding his arms and legs back and forth.

Jack leaned over him excitedly. "Sand angels!" He fell back and did the same as Kyle. When they were done, Kyle's was bigger, but Jack's had more grace.

"I haven't done that forever either," Jack said, propping himself up on an elbow.

"I'm glad I was able to spark your nostalgia."

Jack studied him, squinting in the glare of the day, like he was deciding. Then he said, "I've got something to show you."

The room was under the stairs in Jack's house. Kyle stood, bathed in a sharp red glow, watching him mix fluids in a tray, using tongs to submerge paper.

As he moved, Jack's hand flirted with Kyle's, his jaw tight with concentration. It was a shock to Kyle's system. Ardor sped from his groin to his heart and onward until his fingertips and toes tingled. He wanted to inhale his heady musk, draw in his moistness to maintain the electricity. He closed his eyes and breathed in gently, apprehending nothing but the scent of chemicals.

Then Jack turned, taking him off guard. He reacted but Jack didn't notice. He just clipped another print to a string that hung beside them.

Attempting to cover, Kyle asked, "How did you learn all this?"

"I take so many photos it seemed like a logical step. It's a lot easier when you have an interest."

Hanging from the string, there was a sequence of images from earlier that day when Kyle had been standing in the water looking back at Jack on the shore. His face so vividly expressed his feelings he was horrified. Was he really not able to hide better than that? Could Jack not see the lovesick glint in his eye?

And worse, Kyle could see his sadness. He had never been able to hide his emotions, but he hadn't realized just how clearly they were telegraphed. It made him nervous.

Jack began hanging up a series of Kyle and the group as they situated for their group shot. Claudia's Nazi salute. Trent tripping Kyle. Carly kicking them on the sand. "I had no idea you were taking all these," Kyle said, marveling.

"The candids are often more fun than the poses," Jack said.

"What about you?"

"What about me?"

"What about photos of you?"

"I'm the man behind the lens." He smiled, amused, and hung up another print.

"Let me take some of you." The camera sat on the table. Kyle grabbed it.

At the first *click*, Jack looked up and his amusement turned to horror.

Click.

But then he smiled again. "Kyle."

Click.

"Kyle." Jack put a smooth hand over his mouth, shy.

"What? You think it's fair you have photos of me and I have none of you?"

Click.

Jack dropped his hand, his face lowered, eyes sparkling up at the camera and at Kyle.

Click.

And then Kyle understood that no one had ever made Jack feel special.

He stopped and let the camera hang loosely in his hand.

"What?" Jack said. "Did I break it?"

"Of course not." Kyle's voice was gentle. "You're golden."

That was the first night Kyle's father was on the island. Graham was a tall man with brown eyes, a soft smile to match his voice and dark hair that was beginning to recede. He was one of those people who seemed to get younger as he got older. He embraced Kyle warmly when he came home, fresh from his visit with Jack.

"How are you?" Kyle asked, heading into the kitchen.

His father followed and leaned against the counter, a glass of white in hand. "Busy. This time of year always is. How about you?"

Kyle nodded. Then he said, "Good," like he'd had to decide. He smiled, not at Graham, but at Jack's memory, and then he was reminded how alone he was, and that the closer he got to truth, the further he seemed to be, and then the smile seemed to filter until only the impurities remained and he focused on something beyond the kitchen wall.

"You sure?"

Slowly he came back to the present. "Um… Of course." Thinking of nothing, his eyes gazing out the window over the sink, looking on to the front lawn, he realized something was askew. But before he could place what, his father continued.

"How are the girls?"

"Good. Great. Claudia won the track tournament." He squatted before the refrigerator, reaching into the vegetable drawer.

"She sure is a fighter, that Claudia," Graham said.

"Yeah," he said. "A fighter." He still knelt before the refrigerator.

"Kyle?"

Kyle looked up as if just remembering his presence. "Yeah?"

Graham searched him, looking for evidence. Then he turned away. "Nothing."

After they'd eaten an early dinner, Graham poured each of them, Kyle, Ann and himself, a glass of wine, and they retired to the balcony. The late afternoon was heavy and sticky. The willow's switches were restless.

Kyle went to the rail and looked out at the roaring sea. He couldn't stop thinking of Jack's reaction to having his photo taken. Kyle wanted to be the one to make him finally see how special he was. But he wasn't sure how, or if he'd ever get the chance. And then he was wondering if Jack missed him like he missed Jack. Without him, every moment was steep with suspense, breathless with longing.

"I have a surprise," Graham said behind him, pulling him out of his reverie.

Ann situated herself on a chaise longue. "I love surprises."

"I take it it's a good surprise?" Kyle turned back to them.

"It's wonderful. I've been thinking about it for a while, but I didn't want to tell you until I was sure it was viable."

Ann looked to Kyle then back to Graham. "So?" she said, impatient.

Graham grinned. "I'm going to buy a villa in Italy."

"Oh, my God!" Ann exclaimed. "I can't believe you didn't tell us about this!"

"Dad," Kyle said, too surprised to think of much more. "Wow."

"We had such an incredible time when we were there, I thought we'd like a home of our own." He paused. "The only thing is…we'd have to sell this place."

"We have had this place for a long time," Ann said.

Kyle's ears burned red. "I don't want to leave," he said simply, abruptly.

"Well, we'd stay the rest of the summer," his father said. "I just thought that since you'll be off to college in the fall you'd enjoy spending summers in Europe. You're at the age where you can appreciate things as an adult."

Europe. The things Kyle had seen there—the Eiffel Tower, the Sistine Chapel, Stonehenge—didn't rival Jack's beauty let alone rouse Kyle's spirit, inspire him the way Jack's presence, the knowledge of his existence did. And the island might be the only connection he would ever have to Jack. "I don't want to leave," he said again, feeling childishly on the verge of tears. "This house has been in the family since the turn of the century. I want to summer here when I'm old."

Ann looked at him with understanding eyes. "You always were sentimental."

That was when Kyle realized that being sentimental meant he felt more than other people, and he was left wondering whether that made him stronger, or weaker.

He walked along the shore to Trent's at dusk. Gulls rode the breeze over the water. The final rays of the day had turned it gold, buttery sunlight flashing off the sea and dancing lambently across Kyle's features like diamonds. He got to Trent's and climbed the steps to the deck. Through the sliding glass door he could see Carly and Claudia in the living room. Claudia was lifting up her hair and Carly was applying cold cream to a blistering sunburn on Claudia's back. Claudia winced as the coolness of the cream touched her skin. The temperate sounds of *What Now My Love* wafted from the stereo out onto the deck. He heard a chuckle and that was when he became aware that Trent was sitting sideways in a recliner, legs thrown over one of the arms, his back to the deck and Kyle.

There fell a lengthy, comfortable lull that Claudia interrupted by saying "Goose bumps," sending all of them into fits of laughter. Kyle gathered it was an inside joke and, for the first time, he was on the outside. He had the sudden, consuming sensation that it might be better if he just went away, went home. Though it had been only a day since he'd been with them, he feared he might not belong anymore.

That was when Dana came into the room, her black hair pulled into a ponytail. She saw Kyle and stopped, causing the other three to turn to the deck.

Kyle slid the screen door open and stepped inside. "Hey."

"So," Carly said. "The prodigal son returns."

"Where's your familiar?" Claudia asked.

He'd expected as much and, somehow, it assured him that things were all right.

"Where've you been, baby?" Trent asked.

"Just hanging out. You know."

"With Jack?" Claudia queried.

She was such a bitch. "What's your point?"

"I'm just asking," she said. "You don't have to be cross."

Maybe he *was* being peckish. "Yes," he said. "And with my parents."

"We saw Trey today." Carly continued rubbing cream on Claudia's back.

Kyle had no idea how to respond. "What did he say?"

"He said you'd better be out of town by sundown," she said, and they all laughed.

And that was when Kyle knew that things were still all right. Because right then, at that moment, they were still able to go through the motions.

The next morning Kyle knocked on Jack's door at 8:52. He hadn't been able to wait a minute longer. He'd woken up feeling not sad, but solid. Excited instead of anxious. He had the whole summer to show Jack how special he was. And he wanted to dive in.

Jack, eyes still puffy from sleep, appeared two minutes later wearing the powder-blue bottom to a pair of cotton pajamas. "Hey." A smile stole across his face before being devoured by a yawn.

"Were you sleeping?"

"Well…it's not even nine."

"Sorry. I thought I'd take a chance and see if you were free today."

Jack held the door open. "Of course I'm free today. I'm free every day."

Kyle stepped inside, saying, "I hope I didn't wake anyone else up."

"My dad's probably out on his boat. I don't know where my mom is." He turned as Kyle shut the door, then said, "Let me get dressed," and headed for the stairs.

Kyle was caught by the sudden, joyous surprise of Jack's back and it was a moment before he got his bearings. "If you're still tired, you can go back to sleep. I can come back or wait for you down here or something." *Cracked.*

"Like I'm going to make you wait."

Kyle watched him go up the stairs, then went to sit on the sofa. He sat there for a few minutes before he became aware of the undistinguished watercolors on the walls. Then he remembered the easel he'd seen on the balcony the day before. He wondered who the poor artist was. Then he recalled the bureau—and the photos atop it—that ran along the base of the stairs. He went to it, feeling illicit.

There was a picture of Mrs. Averill, fifteen years younger, hair longer, very pretty, standing beside a tall, handsome man. The backdrop looked like a foreign city. A honeymoon? He picked the photo up and examined it, noting a resemblance between Jack and his father. They had the same straight hair, the same high cheeks, the same full lips. But there was something intrinsically dissimilar about them that he couldn't ascertain.

Beside a vase of purple phlox was a photo of a strong girl with dark hair and a spray of freckles. Wearing a blue one-piece, she was on a ladder emerging from a lake onto a small boat.

Then there was Jack. Around age four, he sat on a picnic table in a pair of olive shorts, no shirt, an unlit cigar in his mouth as he looked at something above the camera.

The next photo, too, was of Jack. He was about seven, in a white suit. There was something about the closeness of the camera that had warped the image. He'd been thin even then, his limbs like dowels. He looked tired and irritable. His eyes were so big, so deep, giving him the impression of maturity.

How much more could you see with those eyes? Kyle wondered.

"Piecing together my past?"

He looked up to see Jack descending the stairs in a pair of crisp white shorts and a white polo shirt. He felt terribly primitive wearing only dirty denim. "I'm trying to figure out what you were thinking at this very moment." He held up the photo as Jack came closer.

"It was my birthday party," Jack said. "I'd just gotten a red plastic tractor that I could ride around the lawn. I couldn't wait to go plant beans or something. My mother was holding up a stuffed parrot I'd gotten, saying, 'Say cheese, Say cheese,' and I was looking at her thinking, 'Why would I say cheese? Polly wants a cracker.'"

Kyle could do nothing but grin. Then he said, "Why do you wear so much white?"

Jack grinned back. "Because I like it. Why? Did you expect some big, bad secret?"

"Maybe." He couldn't stop smiling. But at least Jack was smiling with him.

"So what did you want to do that you got me up so early?"

Be together. "I don't know. Hang out. Maybe go back to that lagoon. Whatever you want to do I thought we could just talk." One sentence.

"Maybe we'll see some mermaids out at that lagoon."

"Are you sure?"

"You already got me up, Quinn. Let me get a jacket."

"You won't need a jacket."

"What if it rains?"

"It won't. The sky is blue until forever."

"Shouldn't tempt fate. It tempts back…"

&

Kyle took a shortcut across the island, past boundless meadowlands and farms, the top down, the air already humid. Where the dirt road joined the main road to the shore they found a stand selling ears of corn. "Those are everywhere in Minnesota," Jack said.

"Miss it?"

Jack looked at him for a moment. "I haven't decided yet."

"What's your favorite song?" Jack asked midmorning. By the time they had gotten to the lagoon, the morning haze had burned off, so they lay on their towels, eyes shut to the radiance of the sun. The day was warm, and it made them lazy, so they had both drifted off. Now, Jack squinted over at Kyle, then reached out and peeled a scrap of skin from his shoulder.

A swell of desire lit Kyle from within. He swallowed raggedly over the compulsion to grasp Jack's hand to his shoulder so that they could remain touching. "*My Funny Valentine*," he said, and his voice was thick with yearning.

"Why?" Jack, unaware, settled back on his towel, eyes shut to the sun.

"It's sad."

"Oh, of course. The tragedy."

Kyle pushed him gently on the arm. "Yeah, the tragedy. Even though the girl he loves doesn't think she's beautiful, the singer does. And, really, isn't that what it's all about? Even if he loses?" Kyle glanced over at him. "Is that good enough? Or did you expect some big, bad secret?"

Jack smiled, enjoying being teased. "I like how you think, Kyle."

That meant more to Kyle than if he'd been voted the most beautiful man in the world.

The rain woke them.

They jumped up, hastily assembled their belongings, and bolted to the convertible, already sopped. Jack sat in the passenger seat as Kyle put the roof up. "This is why you don't tempt fate!" he called, laughing.

Once the roof was in place, Kyle jumped behind the wheel, his face and chest shiny with rain. Their breath was hard and loud under the torrential rain. He looked at Jack and a broad smile broke on his face. Jack's hair hung in strands around his shoulders. He held his wet, fogged glasses in one hand. He was so beautiful and Kyle was so happy that when "Sleep over tonight" came out, Kyle surprised even himself.

"Okay," Jack said simply.

The rain hammered the roof, seeming very close, yet far away.

And then it stopped.

Just like that.

The sudden silence was louder than the thunderous downpour had been. They both looked out the front window in surprise, then turned to each other, smiling.

"Weird," Kyle said.

"Creepy," Jack said.

On the way back, Kyle stopped at the vegetable stand they had passed earlier. "Just to make the transition a little easier," he said, before jumping out to purchase a dozen ears of corn.

When they got to Jack's house, the sun was shining. Jack stood beside the car, eyes as bright as the sky. After a moment, he gave up and turned to Kyle who was watching him. "I'm looking for the rainbow," he explained. "I feel cheated."

Jack's father, Sheridan, was a lean, warm man, about Violet's age. He gave Kyle's hand a hearty shake and invited him into the living room while Jack went upstairs to pack a bag. "I'm excited you and Jack have hit it off," he said, going to the bar behind the sofa. "Drink?"

"Sure." Kyle sat on the sofa, wondering what sort of impression he was making, shirtless, wet, disheveled.

"Where are you headed to school this fall?"

"Princeton, sir."

"Jack's going to the University of Michigan."

"A great school. And I hear Ann Arbor is a wonderful place."

"Do you have a girlfriend?"

Kyle smiled. "No." *But I'm in love with your son.*

"Do you have other friends on the island?"

"My four best friends are here. We come every summer."

"What do you like to do?"

"Do?"

"You know. Sports, girls, music?"

Oh. "I like music, sports," Kyle offered weakly. He was beginning to feel like he was being interrogated.

"Great! Which ones?" Sheridan gave Kyle a small glass of Scotch and sat beside him on the sofa.

"Thanks. Um, different ones. Baseball. Volleyball." He hoped his shorts wouldn't dampen the couch. He resituated himself.

"Great! Maybe you can get Jack interested in some of them."

"Jack doesn't like sports." There was something about Mr. Averill's eyes. They weren't particularly beautiful—they were a dark, murky brown, like a shallow mud puddle—but they caught his attention.

"No, he doesn't. I always did, but I've had poor health my whole life so I couldn't play. I had hoped that Jack would do it for me."

"He has lots of other interests."

"I think part of it is that he's so small. I keep telling him he should get some meat on his bones. Don't get me wrong. I love Jack. I just wish he were more like you."

Kyle was disquieted and wasn't sure how to respond. "Sir," he said, "you don't even know me."

"You're what I would have been if I'd been healthy. That's what I know."

Kyle didn't think it polite to protest again, so he said, "Thank you."

"I'm glad you two are friends."

"I'm glad we are, too." Kyle took a quick swallow from his drink and the Scotch scorched its way down his esophagus.

"I started to worry that he was going to be a loner all his life," Sheridan said. "I was afraid he would be lonely."

Kyle felt a little lightheaded from the alcohol and thought Mr. Averill's sentiment was lovely. "He'll never be lonely, sir," he said, feeling almost patriotic.

"He thinks a lot of you, so I'm glad to know you think so much of him, too."

Kyle grinned, finally relaxing. "Yeah."

"Kids at school called him queer."

Kyle almost laughed out loud at the horror of being confronted so abruptly.

"I never understood that. Just because you're bookish and slight doesn't mean you're not a man."

"No, sir, it doesn't."

"Please don't call me 'sir.'" Sheridan laughed. "I'm trying to be your friend here. It's very exciting to talk to one of Jack's buddies. He's brought home so few."

That was when Kyle realized that Mr. Averill was trying to understand Jack through Kyle. He was moved that Mr. Averill loved his son enough to work at understanding him.

Before he could think of an appropriate response, Jack came into the room with a handful of photographs and a small bag. He'd changed into a dry pair of white shorts and a white shirt, his hair still damp. "You shouldn't be drinking!" he exclaimed, and for a second Kyle thought he was the one being addressed. But Jack spoke to his father. "It's time for your insulin."

Chastened, Sheridan said, "I was just being sociable."

And that was when it hit Kyle. Both Mr. and Mrs. Averill had brown eyes. Jack's had skipped a generation.

He stood. "Are you ready to hit the road?"

"As soon as you are." Jack walked over and took the drink from Kyle, handing him the photos. "Really, Dad. Alcohol?"

"I'm just excited about meeting him," his father said. "We've really hit it off, haven't we, Kyle?"

Kyle glanced at the photographs. They were the ones he'd taken the day before of Jack in the darkroom. "Famously," he said.

"Trey called." Ann didn't turn from the issue of *Life* she was reading on the sofa when the boys came through the door. She spoke in her I-disapprove-of-your-behavior-and-you-should-know-better tone. "He's called a number of times. Hello, Jack."

"Hi, Mrs. Quinn. Unreturned phone calls are an etiquette faux pas."

Kyle smacked him on the arm for kissing up and they ran upstairs.

Then, as Kyle was pulling a shirt over his head in his room, Jack asked, "Why don't you call Trey back?"

"It's hard enough for me to get Trent and the girls to accept *you*. I certainly can't do it for someone *I* don't even want there."

Jack smiled. "That's too bad. About Trey."

Kyle grinned back. "Yeah. Poor Trey."

Graham knocked on the door before sticking his head into the room. "Kyle. Can I speak to you for a minute?"

The sun was setting in a white sky as Kyle hopped up on the rail of the deck. Graham studied him in the final brilliance of the day for many moments before saying, "God, you're handsome." Kyle smiled, self-conscious. "And I'm not just saying that because I love you. I'm thrilled my son is this good-looking. Must be from your mother's side of the family."

They both chuckled, and Kyle said, "Cracked."

In the haze of dusk their likenesses were enhanced and they appeared almost brothers. Graham leaned against the rail and looked out to the whispering willow, to the water. "We're not selling the beach house," he said. "You know, don't you, that we would never do something like that without your consent? Your vote can veto a decision just as mine or your mother's can. You do know that?"

Kyle felt relieved tears burn his eyes. Things were so emotional that summer. He smiled, but it came out lopsided. "I didn't. I thought so, but I didn't know."

"This place is as much yours as it is ours."

"I love it here."

Graham laughed. "I guess I hadn't realized how much. You said no to Italy for this place!"

They fell into easy silence. Kyle's eyes meandered over the balcony to the front of the house. And without even wondering, he comprehended what was different, what he'd only subconsciously noticed Graham's first night on the island. The swan planter was missing. It was gone. Stupidly, dramatically, Kyle felt his heart jerk. He went to the side of the balcony and looked over the garden and as much of the front lawn as he could see, but he couldn't find it.

Before he could ask, Graham spoke again. "I know this might not be the best time to talk about it. But your mother's noticed your mood."

Kyle felt the protective happiness Jack's presence had draped over his sadness rent. His sorrow rumbled inside of him, the beast awakened. He reached for the white stone in his pocket as he turned back to face his father. "Actually, I'm happier now than I've ever been." He didn't mention that he was also unhappier than he'd ever been.

"I just need you to know that she's noticed. And that even though I'm not here one hundred percent doesn't mean you can't call me anytime you need to. I'm always here for you."

"I know." He gave a pained smile.

"We can't help if we don't know what's happening."

"Honestly?" Kyle said.

"Yes."

"Honestly, you couldn't even if you knew."

Graham searched his face for answers that weren't there. "You used to come to me," he said. "I suppose this is your time to pull away." He was sad. "But I'll miss you."

Kyle didn't know how to make it better—for his father or for himself. So he said nothing.

Meanwhile, Jack and Ann were in the kitchen, Ann preparing a casserole, Jack observing while the lush fragrance of lilacs drifted through the windows. Ann liked how awkward the delicate boy was. He seemed self-conscious, like he was uncomfortable in his own body. But he was sweet. And she couldn't help but admit, she liked how he looked at her with adoring eyes. She hadn't had a fan in a very long time. "What do your parents do?" she asked, slicing an onion.

"My mother doesn't do much. She likes to paint, but she isn't very good."

Ann glanced at him for a second. "What about your father, Jack? Has he taken the summer off?"

"Yeah. He's been sick lately, so the doctors told him to take a break. We normally go to Minnesota, but this year we came here instead. What about you?"

"Me? I don't do anything. I mean, I take care of the house—"

"Which is a lot."

"Yes. It is a lot. But with Kyle away at school most of the year, and headed to college this fall—he's going to Princeton, you know." She was so proud.

"Yes," he said. "I know."

"It hasn't been as much work in the past few years. The house stays cleaner without children. And Kyle's a far better cook than I am." She looked up from her onion. "What are you interested in, Jack?"

"Books," he said. "Books and photography."

"Any sports?"

"No." He smiled humbly. "I'm so small."

"There's nothing wrong with a slight stature." They were silent for a moment, the small talk seemingly having exhausted itself. Ann finished with the onion and dropped the pieces into a bowl.

"Kyle said you used to be a figure skater."

She gave him a dubious look as she picked up a cucumber. "I dabbled."

"You have a lovely garden," Jack said then.

She turned to him with a wanting-to-believe smile. "Really?"

"It's beautiful. You can tell you work at it."

She'd never had a boy notice. She couldn't remember Trent even mentioning it. "Do you have an interest?"

"These are harebells," Ann said pointing to the tiny blue clusters. "These are prince's feathers. And these—" She knelt beside a small group of scarlet blooms. "—are pheasant's-eyes. They're part of the Adonis family. I like the name Adonis better than pheasant's-eyes." She felt almost girlish she was so excited to share her love.

"I do, too," Jack said. The perfume of the garden was heavy in the mild, humid twilight.

"I like the lilacs, too, but they're so fleeting."

"That's what Kyle said, too. That first night. When we went to town."

"Kyle's very sensitive to things like that."

"I'm sure he gets it from you."

Ann smiled, pleased.

"He told me you grew up in South Carolina. Did you have a big garden?"

"As a matter of fact we did, but I didn't pay a whole lot of attention to it. I was too busy running off with boys." She smiled. "I wish I'd gotten some tips from our gardener, though, let me tell you."

They went and sat on the porch steps. From around the corner they could hear Graham's and Kyle's voices between the rhythm of the waves. And over the sound of the water and the wind they could hear the tinkling of wind chimes.

"Did you go out a lot?" Jack asked.

"My, yes. All the time. I was the wildest of the girls. I have two older sisters. They thought I saw too many boys. But, naturally, I figured you needed to see as many as possible to determine who was the best of the bunch."

"Did it work?"

"Did what work?"

"Were you able to determine who was the best of the bunch?"

She sighed, a soft, scented sigh. "Well, once I met Kyle's father I knew."

"Must have been romantic."

"Yes," she said. "But the years turn commonplace things romantic, so sometimes it's hard to remember what's real."

"Yeah, I can see that."

She wondered if he really could. She didn't think he'd yet been damaged enough to understand. And she felt an uncommon flare of envy for his tenderness.

It was then they heard the men moving about the house. Ann's mind shifted from Jack's innocence to her son's sadness. And as much as she enjoyed Jack's company, she would never lose sight of what was truly important. She stood, wiping off the bottom of her dress. "Well," she said. "I suppose it's time to get back to the real world."

Later, after they'd eaten and the dishes had been done, Graham set a card table up in the living room and they sat to play Hearts, Jack and Kyle against Ann and Graham. After the first hand had been dealt, Ann said, "Are you and your family going to the Founder's Day dance, Jack?"

"They've talked about it. I'm not really sure, though." He and Kyle smiled at each other across the table as if simply understanding how nice it was to smile.

"There's a gambling tent, too," Ann said.

"Oh," Jack said absently, "I'm not much of a gambler."

She looked at him with a comradely smile and that was when she noticed she didn't have his attention. She was surprised and unused to losing attention to her son. "I call hearts."

Kyle was so captivated by Jack that it kept his sadness at bay. Jack laughed and talked with his parents like they were friends at a sleepover. He was respectful, yet never treated them like they were separate. He was charming them. And Kyle could think of nothing but him.

Once, under the table, Jack's foot innocently bumped Kyle's, and all Kyle could concentrate on was the small point of pressure. It seemed terribly intimate. Hot energy coursed through his veins, stimulated his cells, kindled his passion. He and Jack both looked up. Unable to keep from smiling, Jack muttered, "Sorry," and kicked him again, before moving his feet safely under his own chair. And Kyle wanted to throw his cards down in joy, push the table aside and fall at Jack's feet.

They lost the first game. Then they lost the second.

"Kyle, this is your fault," Jack said, only teasing.

"Don't worry." Kyle hadn't given a thought to the game. He picked up the cards he'd been dealt. "I'm concentrating now. We're sure to win."

"You tempt fate even after this afternoon."

"You'll have to teach me the particulars. I'm just a novice at superstitions, you know."

"What happened this afternoon?" Ann asked. "Pass."

"We just got drenched because Kyle said it wouldn't rain. Pass."

"You spoke too soon, son," Graham said. "Pass."

"See?" Jack smirked at Kyle. "Your father gets it." Then, "It's your turn."

Kyle just gaped at him, hanging there, suspended, until Jack turned to Graham, and Kyle felt like he was going to fall forward onto the table, his support removed, until he was able to eke out, "Pass."

"Did Kyle tell you we were thinking of buying a villa in Italy?" Ann asked.

"No! That sounds wonderful! My mother's parents have a house in Portugal. They like that it's not overrun with tourists."

"We've decided against it," Graham said.

"We'd have to give up this place," Ann said. "And none of us are ready to do that."

Jack looked from her to Graham and then to Kyle, on whom his eyes remained. "That's beautiful," he said. "To realize that what you have is what matters."

"You sound like Kyle," Ann said.

Jack smiled at her while considering her son. "I guess that's because we think alike."

And Kyle was happy, with just Jack and his parents, there, in the place he loved most. But the happiness was sharp and poignant and reminded him of sadness, because he couldn't share it with anyone, let alone Jack, the lone person who did understand, without fearing losing him.

So he lowered his eyes so he didn't have to feel his layers being pulled away like premature scabs under Jack's gaze.

They lost the third game, too.

They went to bed about midnight.

While Jack readied himself in the bathroom, Kyle hurriedly put on a pair of white cotton pajamas for the first time since he left school.

He spread out sleeping bags and pillows on the floor between his bed and the door.

He flicked on a small lamp.

He turned off the overhead light.

He went to the screen door where he could see his parents' shadowplay on the deck from their room.

He half closed the sliding glass door, thinking it might get too cool for Jack.

Then he went to his bed and closed the small window beside it.

He closed the sliding glass door entirely.

Then, satisfied, he jumped on the sleeping bag farthest from the door, leaned against the bed, his ears burning red, breathlessly afraid Jack would catch him before he was in place.

And he waited.

He ran fingers through his hair.

He resisted the craving for a cigarette.

He returned to the sliding glass door and opened it a crack.

And it was still another two minutes before Jack came in. His face was scrubbed, hair brushed and shining. He wore the same pair of light blue pajama bottoms Kyle had seen him in that morning but now he had the top on, too. "Jesus," he said, closing the door behind him. "I can't believe you use a straight razor. Doesn't that creep you out?" Then he laughed.

"What's so funny?" Kyle demanded, smiling. How could he not smile when Jack was laughing?

"It's nice to know you wear pajamas, too. You just seem like a boxers kinda guy. And I had this feeling I was going to look old-fashioned. You know?"

Kyle looked at Jack and could think of nothing to say. Jack was there. In his room. He could ask for little more. "I—didn't know which sleeping bag you'd prefer."

"Why don't you sleep in your bed? You don't have to sleep with me."

"I just thought it'd be easier to talk this way."

"I'll take this one then." Jack settled on the one closest to the door, leaving Kyle the one he was seated upon.

"Do you need anything?"

"I'm set," Jack said. "Or golden, as you would say." He laughed, then suppressed it, a hand over his mouth. "I hope I'm not keeping your parents up…"

"My dad could sleep through Armageddon. And my mom…well, she has help."

"Good. Because I'm not quite done with you yet." He fumbled in his bag for a second, then pulled out a book and held it up for Kyle. *The Little Prince.* "Because of that song. Prince Kyle. You've probably read it a million times. I got it at that bookstore in town. It's my favorite. The book, not the bookstore."

Kyle took it from him and flipped through the pages, glancing at the illustrations. A gift from Jack. It was the most precious thing he'd ever owned. Next to the gold ring he'd inherited.

"It's sad," Jack said. "I think you'll appreciate it."

"Because I'm so tragic?"

Jack smiled. "It's deeper than that."

"Thank you. So much. You don't know." Kyle held the book close and gave him an open look. "Jack?"

"Yeah?"

"I'm sorry we got wet today."

Jack laughed again. "It added to the adventure."

"Adventure, huh?"

"Everything with you is an adventure."

Kyle felt like a New World explorer. Then, partly to change the subject and partly because he couldn't not say it any longer, he said, "I like how you said we think alike."

"Don't you think we do?"

He didn't know what to say. Whatever came to mind was either too explicit or didn't even come near the mark. "It's just—nice," he said. "You know—that you're here." Then he felt naked as Jack grinned at him, and, unexpectedly, he became aroused. He was horrified and raised a quick knee to tent himself, grateful he had on the PJs.

Jack didn't notice. "You're like a godsend, Kyle Ryan Quinn. You just drop into my life like you've been here the whole time and I just never looked over to notice you. Why can't more people be like you?"

Kyle beamed stupidly. "Then I wouldn't be special."

"I'd love to stay up till the wee hours discussing how special you are, but someone got me up early today." He started to slip into his sleeping bag. "And I don't mean to be rude, but I'm turning my back on you because it creeps me out to sleep on my left side."

"Your left side?"

"It sounds weird, but that's the side of the body the heart is on and it creeps me out to know that gravity is pulling everything else on top of it."

Kyle couldn't speak for a second he was so surprised. "I can't believe you ever thought of such a thing."

"I figured it out when I was six. G'night." He rolled onto his right side, back to Kyle, and was asleep. Just like that.

Kyle placed the book on the nightstand and turned the light off before lying on his own right side, head resting in his hand. In the sudden darkness, he couldn't see Jack's slumbering form at first. Then, abruptly, it became visible, the rise and fall of his torso even and slow.

For a few moments, Kyle gazed at the silhouette of the Boy whose beauty caused him so much pain. Then, closing his eyes, he listened to his breathing, sure and sighing, for a long time before he allowed himself to drift off.

He awoke with a start in that hour that's not night and not morning, the hour that doesn't belong anywhere, the darkest hour. He'd been sleeping so soundly that for a full five seconds he couldn't shake the sensation of falling. And, unused to being on the floor, it took another five to figure out where he was. When the world had righted itself and he was finally able to focus, he found Jack's face only inches from his own. He had turned over in his sleep. His heart th-thumped at the proximity. He couldn't breathe for fear of awakening him. So he lay still, trying to control his heartbeat.

The next day when he and Jack were leaving, they passed Ann on her knees in the garden. She looked up at them from under her sunbonnet, secateurs in hand. "Headed out?"

"Time to adventure," Kyle told her.

"It was a pleasure having you," she said to Jack. "I hope you'll come back soon."

"As soon as Kyle invites me."

"Oh, don't wait for that," Ann mock-scolded. "You stop by any old time the notion takes you. I always leave the porch light on."

"I'll do that," Jack said and headed for the car.

Ann and Kyle watched him go. Kyle was just about to ask where the swan planter had been moved when she said, "I'm glad we're keeping this place," and turned back to the amaranths. "I feel closer to him here, you know."

Kyle felt a sudden surge of sadness and love and wondered if there was a difference anymore. "Yeah," he said. "I know."

There wasn't a specific image that came to mind when he thought of Kevin. But that song, that melody would come. The words would run through his head in a loop like numbers on a gas pump. The refrain would chase him, mocking, so that he would actively seek to absolve himself. He would turn on the radio or place an album on the turntable, immersing himself in violins and drums and oboes and horns, all worked into uncountable arrangements with innumerable layers and rhythms and melodies and lyrics, with the hope that one of them would catch.

And when he was finished, he would have ephemeral freedom.

But then, like Prometheus's liver, the lullaby would return, plaintive, pleading, provoking.

He wondered how his parents had been able to shake their grief. Or if, perhaps, no matter how heavily they weighted it, how often they sent it plummeting to the depths, sure it was gone for good, they were astonished to find it bobbing gaily, sardonically, malignantly, every time they turned for shore.

The next night was humid. Lightning flickered on the horizon. The clouds blocking the moon were tumid with rain. As Trent and Kyle drove to Veronica's, the wind cut sideways through the car. Kyle looked at the water, watching the mirror-lightning, pretending he was looking at the storm upside down. Then Trent pulled away from the shore and Kyle saw a deer dart into the undergrowth as they became enclosed on both sides by trees, the wind rushing in the leaves.

He hadn't wanted to come. But he had devoted the day to Jack. They'd gone hunting for mussels when the tide was out, squatting over tidal pools with a bucket. And then they'd walked, far, following the shoreline, passing summer homes, rock formations, the beachfront country club. They'd gone to Kyle's, and he'd prepared the mussels for dinner before Jack had to return home. He hadn't been back for two days.

So Kyle had delivered him and was looking forward to an evening with *The Little Prince*.

Then, Trent.

"You have to come with me to Veronica's," he'd said from the opposite side of the porch door. "She's getting me grass, but she'll never let me get away if I'm by myself. And you haven't been around to help me practice my volleyball…"

Kyle had felt guilty. He hadn't seen any of the group for a couple of days, to play volleyball or anything else. Hell of a friend he was.

So he'd acquiesced.

Trent found a still neighborhood on the other side of town and, after turning down a side street, pulled into a driveway. The homes were all one-level, brick and situated on small, well-tended plots, each with an aluminum garage. How Trent had been able to find Veronica's with such ease made Kyle wonder how often he'd been there.

Trent got out, and Kyle called after him, "Do you want me to wait here?"

"No!" Trent stage-whispered. "Come with me."

"Figures."

After Trent knocked, they stood quietly. A mist of mosquitoes hung over the yard. Fragrant catchflies flared forth from beside the steps. There was a swing to their left that was cumbersome in the smallness of the porch.

When Veronica answered the door, Kyle could see a glimmer of unadulterated happiness on her face before she concealed it behind a smug smile. "So," she said. "You made it."

"Yeah," Trent said. "I told you we'd be here before nine-thirty."

"Want a drink?"

"We really have to get back. The rain's about to start."

Her camouflage slipped. "Sure."

When she turned inside, Trent murmured, "She's pitiful."

"No thanks to you, right?"

Trent didn't respond.

A moment later, Veronica returned with a plastic bag. She held it just out of Trent's reach for a second, until his eyes wavered, obliging her with the small gesture of subservience she craved. Then she dropped it into his palm and he gave her three bills. "You're a doll," he said, flashing one of his rakish smiles and turning for the car.

Veronica looked after him, her smile dropping by degree.

"Thanks," Kyle said, uncomfortable.

That was when she noticed him.

He gave a small smile. He felt pity for her because he understood.

Kyle and Jack spent that languorous stretch of mid June together, close as brothers with an intimacy usually exclusive to lovers. They went to the lagoon in the mornings, Kyle swimming and Jack wading or tanning or photographing. Then, in the afternoon, they'd lie next to each other, the heat rising in a shimmering wave, the sun turning them brown as wet sand. Sometimes they'd read, and when one of them found a word or sentence or passage he found particularly striking, he'd sit up and read it aloud. Kyle loved to listen to Jack read, his voice full of life, eyes glittering like sapphires. Sometimes they just drove, with the top down, the radio on, singing along to the songs they knew, talking, or not—when they would just look at the sea and the trees and the farms in a panoramic blur. They became lazy like young people in the summer do. The days were long then, the possibilities boundless, their destinies defined.

Sometimes, when Jack was showering or helping his father or retrieving fresh clothes for a sleepover, Kyle would draw himself away to watch Violet paint on the deck. Standing inside, viewing her through the screen, he didn't observe what she was painting; he observed her. The way her mouth drew down to the left when she couldn't get something, a flourish or a hue, just so. The way she mixed the paint mercilessly until she had muddy puddles dotting her palette. The way she genuinely tried despite her stunning mediocrity.

He wanted more than anything for her to offer to paint him. To be important enough to have the memory of his presence commemorated on canvas became a real hunger, as real as the one he had for her son.

Then one day, as he stood observing her through the screen door, he realized that he was inside Jack's house. All those years he'd imagined the house watching him on the beach with those empty eyes. And, finally inside, instead of seeing what those eyes saw, understanding the house's mind, apprehending what it was thinking, he wondered what he looked like from the outside.

Did he have a small countenance?

Was he murky blue, or metallic gray?

Did he appear to be alive?

Where Violet had her painting, Sheridan took to Kyle, exulting in him as a father would, living vicariously, since he did not choose to through his son. And, though Kyle didn't think his life was of interest, he liked being the center of attention. Trent had always been the one with the glory, and Kyle had never envied that, but he came to understand how seductive it could be. So he told of his friends and his parties and his dances and his travels. He told of his golden life. And when asked about girls, he proffered Trent's stories to satiate.

          Spending so much time with Jack, Kyle was able to observe him administering Sheridan's insulin injections. Sheridan needed to have a shot every morning approximately thirty minutes before he ate. The first time Kyle took in the procedure, wanting to be part of every aspect of Jack's life, he nearly passed out. He got past the fulfillment of the syringe. He got past the choosing of a site and the pinching of the skin. He even got past the puncturing of the flesh. But as soon as Jack's thumb began deflating the plunger a wave of white passed over him and he sat, hard, on the sofa.

"You okay?" Sheridan asked.

"Yeah." But Kyle was still seeing white.

"I know, it's awful. I can't look myself. Thankfully I have Jack."

"You get used to it." Jack removed the needle and placed an alcohol swab over the hole. He was methodical almost to the point of being mindless. "What's gotta be done's gotta be done. You know?" He looked over at Kyle and winked.

All the time with Jack meant there was less for the group. But when he did join his friends, it was with Jack in tow. At first, Claudia made snide comments. Carly sniffed air. Dana let silence voice her disapproval. Trent, of course, treated him like a prince.

After a few visits, though, the group began to be more accepting, and if Jack wasn't greeted warmly, he wasn't unwelcome either. They came to rely on him to have his camera, and that became his niche.

So they would laugh and talk and drink like old times. But they weren't like old times. Kyle felt like an outsider. For his benefit, the others would recount the adventures that had befallen them, but that would only make him feel more separate.

His friends were different.

Or maybe he was different.

He didn't know.

He *did* know, regardless, that it was the price of having Jack.

And while he was happy to pay it, it made him sad there was a price at all.

"It's about time you helped me practice for the tournament," Trent said one blistering day when they met the others on the beach, and Kyle knew he was only half kidding.

"Cracked," he said.

The sun was so glaring it hurt.

They played volleyball to spite it, Trent, Carly and Jack against Claudia, Kyle and Dana.

"So what are you going to do about the Veronica thing?" Dana said as she served the ball.

"Really," Carly seconded. "What *are* you going to do?"

Trent was easy. "Why must I do anything?" He dove for the ball but missed.

"You're lucky you weren't here two nights ago," Carly said to Kyle. "She came around *drunk*."

Kyle grinned. He missed these times already. "I told you you were going to break her heart."

"How many nights have you spent with her, anyway?" Dana asked.

"I already told you. Two." Trent served the ball, and Dana went to hit it, but she, too, missed, and it bounced into the water.

"What are you talking about?" Kyle said. "I know for sure you've been with her three."

"Guess I miscounted."

"Like you'd forget," Carly said, as Dana went to fetch the ball.

"Trent," Kyle said. "Truth or dare."

Trent looked at him, an irrepressible smile of surprise breaking across his face. "You son of a bitch."

"I knew it!" Kyle shouted.

Trent was laughing. "You son of a bitch."

Jack stood behind him, saying nothing. Despite being accepted, he still had no voice.

"Come on, Trent," Carly said. "No secrets, remember?"

Trent just looked at Kyle. Finally, he said, "Truth."

"How many—"

"Nine."

"Nine!" Carly shrieked as Dana returned with the ball.

"No wonder she thinks you're engaged," Claudia said.

It was then that Dana caught on. "You slept with Veronica *nine* times?"

"I can't believe you weren't going to tell us," Kyle said.

"I would have told *you,* except you were never around." Trent spoke lightly, but it came out sounding resentful and accusing, and his words hung between them like betrayal.

Kyle was taken aback, but he wasn't offended. The remark only intensified the white lump of guilt that had been growing since he'd first seen Jack. In that moment the balance had shifted, and Jack had begun to take precedence.

"Baby, I didn't mean that the way it came out," Trent said. "I meant it…not viciously, you know?"

Kyle smiled. "Yes." Trent didn't say things with malice. But the fact that it came unbidden said a lot about what Trent wasn't saying at all. "Really. Let's just play."

Later, as the day began to lose its luster, they gave up the game and reclined on the sand. Claudia lit two cigarettes and gave one to Kyle. "Would you like one?" she asked Jack.

"No. Thank you."

She withdrew, and Kyle turned to Jack. "You don't mind if I do, do you?"

"Of course not."

"Jack."

They both looked up to Trent who stood over them. "Come with me to get some firewood."

All five of them looked at him in surprise. No one spoke until, after a lengthy pause, Jack said, "Okay."

They started up the shore, the white sun muted by the haze of early dusk. A hundred yards or so down the way, Trent stooped for a long piece of driftwood. Still squatted, he looked up, spindrift cooling them in gasps and wheezes, and asked, "What's wrong with Kyle?"

Jack looked at him uncertainly. "What do you mean?"

"His parents came to me. They're concerned. They want me to talk to him, but he doesn't seem open to me right now."

"I think it'd be good for both of you to talk."

"Do you know what's wrong with him?"

"I know he's depressed."

Trent stood with the driftwood and they continued without speaking. Then, as they turned a bend so they were no longer in sight of the others, he said, "He's always been happy, you know."

When it was clear there would be no embellishment, Jack said, "That's what I gathered."

"He's golden," Trent said, using the driftwood as a walking stick. "People are drawn to him."

"Does that make you jealous or envious?" They were no longer looking for driftwood. They were just walking.

"I was never afraid they'd like him more than they liked me. I was afraid *he'd* like *them* more. I didn't want anyone to take him away."

"So: jealous."

"I need him more than he needs me. I don't know if he knows that."

Jack knelt by the water's edge to pick up a conch. Their footprints led back around the curve of the land to the group. He stood and they resumed walking, Trent with his staff, Jack with his shell.

"I always protected him, you know," Trent said. He so needed to prove his worth to someone. "But now there's something going on I may not be able to control."

"This is really big of you," Jack said. "Appealing to me like this."

"I'm only telling you in case he's talking to you. You don't owe me anything, so if you do know something you're not telling me... I want you to be able to go back to him with these things. I want you to know." A gallant plea. He looked away from Jack, then dropped the wood, letting it harmlessly dent the sand. "Let's head back," he said. "Maybe we won't have a fire tonight."

One day at early dusk when he came down the stairs on his way to pick up Jack, Ann stood from the sofa and turned to him, clasping her hands before her heart. He stopped in the foyer at the look of apprehension on her face but said nothing. She stepped forward, then stopped.

"Kyle."

He sensed what was happening, what was coming, and though he wanted to be glib and sail out the door, he hadn't been expecting a confrontation so it brought all of his emotions to the fore in a thunderous, paralyzing crash, so he stood, rooted for what was to come.

She smiled at him, brightly, kindly, her face crinkling. "What's wrong?" Behind her, a bouquet of vivid purple clematis mocked her with garish insolence.

Kyle could feel his sadness in his throat like a cancer. He was weary. "I'm fine."

"We don't know what to do." She spoke quickly, as though she couldn't contain the words, spitting them forth and seeming to regret them immediately. When she spoke next, her voice was ghostly. "We're terrified."

Silence entered.

Then she began again, speaking with difficulty, her words slow and thoughtful. "You're at an age where you might feel you can handle things by your—"

She broke off suddenly and Kyle heard the surf crash.

"I have to try," she finished, composing herself. "At least that. I have to try."

"Mom." Then his voice was coated, and he had to clear his throat, though the imperturbable sadness remained. "Please, don't."

And Ann turned from the gentle flower she was into a woman enraged. "I have to!" she cried. "Do you think I can stand here and let you fade away? Do you?!"

He looked at the ground, shamed. "You can't help."

She crumpled.

They were silent for many moments, facing each other without looking at each other, a bloodless showdown. Then she said, "Talk to Trent. To Jack."

"I can't."

"Why!?"

And then he was shouting, fed up with the questions, both voiced and unvoiced, the fear, the not knowing, the energy it required to remain alive. "Because this is about me! *Me!*" And then his face pursed up like he was about throw back his head and howl. He hated his sadness, his insecurity, his despair. He hated how the weakening was so familiar, so comfortable, so gratifying. He felt like an alcoholic leaping off the wagon, despising himself for welcoming the slippery slide into the arms of his beloved.

He turned away, too embarrassed to face her, too weak to walk away.

Kyle wasn't always sure which memories of Kevin were real and which had been stitched together from images and other people's recollections and impressions of feelings he thought he recalled. But he did remember a golden day with him on the island. He had been five, Kevin twelve. They had been at the summer house for over a month and had yet to build a sand castle. So they went down to the water's edge midmorning when the sun was still mounting, and became so involved in the conception of their palace, Kevin creating, Kyle fetching water, that neither noticed the horizon brewing until the climate abruptly turned icy. They looked up to see violent black clouds cleaving the blue. The squall would be on top of them in seconds. "Run!" Kevin shouted, and they had. Up the sand, past the reeds, past the willow tree, racing the tempest. And then Kyle had to brave a look back. He stopped and turned his face to the sky, so black the world was cast in the eerie glow of an eclipse. He was so overcome with fearful awe he just gaped. The wind sang past him, thunder shook the ground beneath him, electricity crackled around him. Then Kevin was gripping him around the waist and he was being carried to the house. As the malevolence overtook them, Kevin slid the deck door open and set Kyle down inside, his bottom lip quavering, eyes flashing like full moons with the damp of imminent tears. Seeing how spooked he was, Kevin squatted before him and touched his cheek. "My little prince," he said. And then he did the only appropriate thing.

He laughed.

Kyle smiled tentatively, and then he laughed, too.

With a gesture, Kevin had brought back the sun.

That was how Kyle knew the world could be right.

Because it once had been.

The next day when he was expecting Jack, Kyle was surprised to find Trey on his stoop. They regarded each other coolly through the screen, before Kyle, feeling a combination of guilt and annoyance, said, "Hey, Trey," then smiled at the rhyme.

"You're home."

"Yeah."

"What have you been up to?"

"Lots. It's a busy summer."

"Good."

"Yeah."

The conversation lulled, and Kyle was pissed off about it. If Trey had something so important to say, then by God, Trey had better say it. Kyle was not about to take responsibility for upholding a conversation he hadn't started. Unable to mask his frayed patience, he said, "What do you want, Trey?"

"You know, Kyle—I looked forward all winter to seeing you." Trey looked at him, beseeching.

And Kyle felt like an asshole. But looking into those emerald eyes, at that long, sensual mouth and its eternal smile from which he'd swallowed so many kisses, he felt nothing. Trey was beautiful. But that was all.

"I just don't know what to think anymore," Trey said.

That was when they heard the screen door to the deck open and they both looked to see Jack stride into the living room, an empty soda bottle in hand. "Hey," he said, beaming. He stopped and tossed the bottle into the trash can in the kitchen where it fell with a simple and clear thud. Then he saw Trey. "Oh." His expression dropped in comic surprise and he glanced at Kyle, then back to Trey. "Hey."

Without taking his eyes from Jack, Trey said, without rancor or self-pity, "I guess I do know what to think." Then he turned and walked away, his footsteps hollow going down the porch steps.

Jack went to Kyle and looked out at Trey getting into his car. "What was that about?"

"Nothing." Kyle couldn't explain the jealousy Trey felt without explaining the reasons for it. So he simply said, "He just doesn't like me very much anymore."

When Kyle and Jack came out of the movies that night the air was warm and heavy with moisture. Teenagers were cruising the streets and crowding the sidewalks and as Jack and Kyle headed up the block toward the car they had to pass through a large, unruly group. Coming out the other side, Kyle realized he had lost Jack. And then, above the sounds of the town, the traffic, the people, he heard one distinct word. *Fairy.*

Before he could react, Jack stumbled out of the throng. Kyle strode toward him, glowering. "What did they say?" he demanded.

"Nothing," Jack said, embarrassed.

"What did they say?" Kyle looked past Jack to the group. Two sullen boys glared back at him.

"Nothing," Jack said.

"Did they say that to you?"

"Kyle. It's all right."

"No. It's not." He started to step beyond Jack. "I'm going to talk to them." But he wanted to beat the shit out of them.

Then Jack spoke with sudden venom. "God damn it, Kyle. Can't you tell I'm humiliated enough?"

He walked away, ending the conversation.

Rebuked, Kyle swallowed his outrage. They were in the car and headed home before he could hold back no longer. "I didn't mean to make you uncomfortable. It's just that no one's fucked with one of my friends before. I mean, never anyone who couldn't defend himself. And I was pissed off in your honor. So it never—"

"Stop explaining yourself," Jack said curtly. "You're driving too fast."

Kyle wanted to apologize again but refrained. Instead, he took his foot off the gas pedal, and that was when he realized how low the tank was. He considered turning around, but wasn't sure how Jack would react, so he remained quiet.

Heat lightning flickered from the direction of the water. After many moments of pregnant silence, Jack looked across the expanse of seat to Kyle and asked, "Why does Trent call you 'baby'?"

Kyle didn't respond at first, wondering if he was being baited. Then he said, "I don't know."

"Do you mind?"

He hadn't thought about it before. But he knew the answer. "No. Not everyone loves you enough to give you a pet name."

Jack was thoughtful before he said, "Okay."

Kyle was grateful an argument had not erupted. He'd either navigated himself well or Jack's irritation was waning.

They entered a forest where the static of wind in the leaves was dramatic. They had been driving for many minutes before, without preface, Jack said, "You know, I hate when one of your friends hurls out, vicious as a taunting child, 'No secrets, remember?' As if being part of the group means giving up your right to privacy. There's something unconscionable about the calculated coldness of baring open the hides of peers for fun. As if you're bored by everything but the sacrifice of one of your own. 'No secrets.' Those are the dues one pays. I don't know how you can stand them."

Kyle was so surprised by the stinging monologue, he had no idea what to say. He certainly couldn't argue Jack's points as they were valid.

Then it happened. The car's engine died. Kyle felt his heart freeze as they lost momentum. He put the car in neutral and tried to restart it. The engine clicked and coughed but didn't turn over. As the car rolled to a stop, he glanced at Jack, who sat in the passenger seat, his lips in a fine, tight line.

"What the hell is happening?" he demanded.

Kyle's voice was meek. "I think we ran out of gas."

Jack didn't respond, so Kyle continued. "We can push the car to the side of the road and walk to my place. My dad has some gas for the lawnmower in the garage."

Jack didn't speak.

"I'm really sorry," Kyle said.

And then Jack got out of the car and began walking with long, sure steps into the stage of headlights.

Kyle sat up on the back of his seat. "Jack!"

Jack didn't answer and he didn't stop. Kyle felt a chill scuttle through him. The scene was playing out so quickly. He hopped over the door and caught up. "What are you doing?" he asked, their features dimming as they moved out of the light.

"I'm going home."

"We can get gas. I said I was sorry. You don't even have to come back with me. You can go to bed."

"Fuck you, Kyle! I don't want to go to your house!" His beautiful features were warped and grotesque. He was so enraged, Kyle feared he might strike out. "You tempt fate and you get fucked every time!"

"What!"

"You don't get gas, you drive too fast. You're going to get us killed sometime! And I can't believe you joke about someone walking over your grave!"

Kyle didn't understand, but he didn't ask. "Okay. But I can't let you go by yourself. Let me turn the headlights off."

But Jack wasn't stopping walking. Desperately, Kyle grabbed his arm. Jack spun toward him, pulling free with a jerk. He was standing at the edge of the blacktop and when his arm came loose, he took a step back, his foot half on the road, half in the dirt, and he lost his balance, falling with an undignified thud on his rear.

Kyle just stood there, too shocked to speak. The fall had brought about such an awkward break to the argument he was afraid if he so much as exhaled, Jack would explode.

Jack sat on the ground, profoundly confused, looking from side to side, searching for the gnome that had tripped him.

Kyle slowly extended a hand, but Jack ignored it, standing on his own.

"Jack—" Kyle began.

"I'm going home." Jack's emotions had leveled or at least been checked.

Kyle wanted to say, "Let me give you a ride," but he had no car. Instead, he said, "I'm sorry."

They looked at each other in the shadows, Kyle's face drawn, Jack's tight.

"So am I," Jack said and walked into the night.

Kyle was diffident to follow. It might piss Jack off more. So he just watched his diminishing form in the dark, alone with just the wind and the unthreatening, ethereal heat lightning.

Kyle didn't call Jack the following day.

Or the day after.

He didn't see the group those days either. He hardly left the house. Graham was gone, so it was just him and Ann, who spent most of her time in the garden or the basement, where it was cooler. Which meant that Kyle had the run of the house. He cooked a lot, forgetting himself in teaspoons and spices, casseroles and vegetables. The chopping and slicing and measuring and mixing was so mindless it was the only way he could lose Jack, even for a moment. Because he was in utter terror that he would lose him forever. That his only chance at love was gone. He was gutted. He felt weak as paper. It was all he could do to keep from just blowing away in the wind. He was so afraid he couldn't even cry.

Ann noticed but said nothing. She watched from a world separate from the one he inhabited, afraid to attempt contact, frightened she might put more distance between them. So she pretended that her 18-year-old son's haunting was as expected and natural as her heartbeat.

In Jack's absence, Kyle took to poring over the photographs he'd taken of him with his bashful eyes in the darkroom. The images ripped at him, but he could not stop looking. Part of him feared they might be all he would have to remember him by.

That was when Kyle found time to read *The Little Prince*. The story moved quickly and Kyle found himself laughing a little and smiling a lot. But by the end his heart was heavier than it had been, and he stared at the last drawing for a long time. He wanted more. More than that barren landscape and solitary star. He eventually went out onto the deck, looking up to the sky, hoping for consolation.

But he saw no stars.

His sadness deepened when Jack did not call on the third day.

At twilight he stood in the living room, looking through the screen door to the shore and the sea beyond. The arms of the willow fluttered lackadaisically in the breeze. Over the water, the sun was shooting orange, yellow and violet arms into the sky to pull the night down. The sunset was resplendent, but beyond wondering what Jack would think of it, it didn't call to him. The colors only emphasized his paleness.

It was a moment before he felt Ann's arms circle his waist from behind, the side of her head resting against his back. She couldn't ease his pain, so she just held him.

The country club was on a rise overlooking the ocean. The day of the Founder's Day celebration, tables had been situated around the dance floor. On top of each table were white linen tablecloths, silver candles and gold glitter that also dusted the floor. At one end of the sunken terrazzo floor a platform had been set up on top of which were Sadie Burroughs and Her Orchestra, playing big band hits. Sadie was a tall, dark-haired woman in a red dress and shockingly red lipstick. Opposite the stage, past the dance floor, were four sets of open French doors that opened onto the shore, giving the room an airy feel. Against the far wall was an open bar and a buffet table with vegetables, crackers, cheeses, olives, canapés and punch. Beyond this were four more sets of open French doors that let onto the yard and a lane that led past the swimming pool to a pavilion where the gambling had been set up on the tennis courts. Against the near wall was another bar. There were roses everywhere: white, red, yellow, pink, damask, coral, musk, burgundy. They were on tables, on the buffet, climbing trellises that had been constructed in the four corners of the dance floor and that met in the air over the crowd. The room was semi-full with men in tuxedos and women in evening gowns, among whom moved black-attired waiters and waitresses with drinks atop silver trays.

This was the scene when the Quinns arrived, Kyle and Graham in tuxedos, Ann in a kelly-green evening dress and a gasp of Emeraude. Kyle's face held only traces of his anxiety about whether Jack would show, but the suspense was so intense in his heart that the event felt harrowing. Playing with the white stone in his pocket for luck, he scanned the room, consciously concentrating on each person in succession to determine it was not Jack.

After they found a table on the opposite side of the room, Claudia, in a white taffeta dress, her hair pulled back in a chignon, descended. Ann looked up hopefully. She still harbored aspirations that Kyle was in love with her, despite, or because of, the fact that he was sad. "Claudia!" she exclaimed with a bit too much enthusiasm.

"Hi, Mrs. Quinn. Hey, Kyle." Claudia nudged his shoulder with the back of her hand. "You're supposed to stand when a lady approaches."

He smirked up at her. "I will."

Underneath his dry humor, both knew there was something pointed in his words.

"Let's get a drink," she said.

ଛ

"I can't believe I was the first here this year," she said when they were standing in line at the bar.

None of the group liked to be the only one in such a situation. If the situation had to be dealt with, they at least wanted to be with one of their own.

"How long have you been here?" Kyle asked dutifully.

"Forty-five minutes. I've seen, done and talked to anything and anyone worth doing. You missed Mrs. Barnett stumble down the stairs. She was drunk. It was weird. She suddenly looked old."

"Remember when we were at the age where everyone here was perfect and magic just because they were adults? And now they're just people. And you wonder if they changed or if you did."

Claudia gave him a mock-scolding smile. "You're always so romantic," she said, almost like an accusation.

He wondered that that didn't make her envious.

Their drinks arrived and they tilted their glasses, but before a toast could be made, Carly appeared. She was in a silver silk flapper's dress and looked fussy. "There are swans in the pool."

They headed to the pool on a path strewn with red rose petals. Two swans crossed in front of them. Two more were in the water.

"Is that strange or is it just me?" Carly asked, indicating the floating birds.

"It's just you who's strange," Claudia retorted.

Kyle thought of the planter that had disappeared from outside the house. He kept forgetting to ask his mother where she'd put it.

"Wanna hit the gambling tent?" Carly had moved on from the swans.

"Let's just go back to the dance," Claudia said. "Gambling's boring."

"So's the dance," Kyle pointed out.

"But it's got drinks."

He conceded to Claudia's point.

ℒ

When they returned, Trent and Dana were standing just inside the doors, Trent in a tux, Dana in a periwinkle velvet dress that made her skin look muted and lackluster. They were already consumed with ennui. It wasn't that the dance was so bad. They all just enjoyed being bored by it.

Claudia lit a cigarette with a gold lighter. A dot of gold was on the height of her left cheekbone. Kyle felt a little high from the champagne as he wet a forefinger and removed it.

"What's up with all this glitter?" Carly asked rhetorically, her lips cast in a mild pout.

Sadie Burroughs began crooning *Out of Nowhere*, and Trent and Claudia went to dance. The other three took flutes of champagne up a few steps to stand just inside the French doors that opened onto the veranda with the shore stretching beyond, so they could look down upon the crowd. They watched the other summer people, dancing, drinking, laughing. The scene was colorful and convivial, but it seemed to be imbued with melancholy, and Kyle couldn't tell if it was really there, or if he was projecting his own emotions. "Who here's happy?" he said, surprised to find himself speaking aloud. They didn't know what had happened, so they didn't notice, or didn't understand, his trembling hands, his darting eyes, his pallor.

Carly pursed her lips at him. "We are, silly."

And that was when Jack and his parents came through the main door. Jack, holding a single red rose, was in a tuxedo, and Kyle, in his most fantastic imaginings, hadn't dreamed he could be so beautiful. He had a new stature, a self-confidence that made him appear sturdier. His hair shone under the lights. And even from the distance at which he stood, Kyle could make out those shimmering eyes.

Any composure he'd had fled. He wanted to bolt in terror. For the first time he was seeing Jack not as a boy, but as a man.

And he wondered if he were enough.

The Averills were greeted by a stout man and his brassy wife. Jack touched his hair absently, almost superstitiously. Then Violet leaned in, said something in his ear, and pointed, and they both looked up to where Kyle stood. Jack's expression turned from a polite smile of introduction to a mixture of relief and joy, and Kyle wanted to run to him, his sadness and fear forgotten.

They pushed their way through the crowd, past sequins and linens and silks. The bodies seemed to recede, lose dimension, until they were only cutouts from a stage set, their voices and laughter coming in slow recorded warbles. When Kyle and Jack met halfway, they were alone in a sigh of sandalwood.

Kyle didn't know what he wanted to say. He hadn't thought. His only objective had been to get to Jack. And he certainly couldn't think straight once they were so close. It was all he could do to remain upright.

"Hey," Jack said.

"Hi." It was a breathless sigh. All Kyle could see was Jack's face. Gentle strains of violins floated past them like butterflies and sunbeams, the only other beings in the room, maybe the world.

And Kyle began to speak, not caring who was near. "I'm sorry about the other night. I only wanted to—"

"You don't have to explain yourself." Jack was kind.

"I guess," he said, "I'm trying to say I missed you."

Jack just beamed at him. "I know."

They went to the balcony with champagne, the setting sun turning a majestic cloud formation and the glinting sea a brilliant shade of orange sherbet. Dusk had pared down its edges so that the world was tender. From inside the club, Sadie Burroughs turned sorrowful with *Autumn Leaves.*

Jack proffered the flower.

Kyle accepted it, the thornless rose, mindlessly, hardly noticing. The only thought he could form was, *He's stunning,* and it came out a sigh. He had never really meant it of anyone before.

Jack tapped the smooth oak rail as a swan passed between them and the shore.

"Why are you knocking wood?"

"Sometimes I guess I'm just afraid of being too happy." His hair blew around his face like they were in the convertible. "You're the best friend I've ever had, Kyle Ryan Quinn."

"Really?" He was thrilled.

"I'm sorry I flipped out on you. I was afraid you'd still be mad."

"I was afraid you'd be *furious.*" He had an I'm-so-high-I-can't-stop-smiling look. He pulled the stone out of his pocket. "I held this the whole time."

Jack grinned then said, "I didn't call because I thought you might need some space."

"Me, too."

"But I don't want to mess this summer up."

"Me neither."

"Will you teach me to drive?"

"Of course!"

"I want to spend every day together. Even if I have to spend them with your friends. This is my classic summer."

"There are going to be so many more."

"Look at you. Always so romantic." A compliment. Points of light caught in his magnificent eyes so that they flashed, as if lit from within, and for an instant they appeared dimensionless, like a cat's, so that Kyle could see into them, into him.

And then they were simple jewels again, and Kyle could think.

"I loved *The Little Prince,*" he breathed.

"I knew you would."

"It bothered me."

Jack gave a compassionate smile. "It's supposed to."

The nearness of him drowned out everything, the orchestra, the people, the sea. Kyle was so in love he wanted to die of it just so he wouldn't have to endure it any longer.

Jack's hair shifted in the wind. "Look," he said, pointing to the slowly darkening sky.

It was the first star burning through the kaleidoscopic rush of sunset. Kyle closed his eyes and made a wish like he was in a pop song. And then something tickled his nose. He opened his eyes to find gold glitter floating around them like radiant dust in the sun. Jack had his mouth open in surprise. They both looked up to see two young boys leaning out a second-story window, dropping fistfuls of gold into the wind. They heard a shout from above, and the boys scurried inside, apparently caught.

Jack held out his hands, palms up, like it was raining, and laughed aloud.

Through the doors Sadie Burroughs and Her Orchestra segued into *I've Got a Crush on You*. It made Kyle realize how badly he wanted to dance with Jack.

"I guess this time we're really golden," he said, the glitter fading around them.

Specks of gold were in Jack's hair, on his nose, on his glasses. "What'd you wish for?"

"How did you know I made a wish?"

"Because I did too."

"Well, I can't tell you or it won't come true."

"I knew you'd say that."

"Yeah?"

"I see who you are. I just worry that you don't."

Jack looked at him so guilelessly, Kyle didn't feel vulnerable. There was no point if Jack already knew everything. All it could do was empower him. "I guess no one like you has ever been around to bring it out," he said.

Jack grasped one of Kyle's forearms. "Well, now you're free."

If Jack had been a girl, Kyle could have kissed him. Just to show where things stood.

But things were not so simple. And Kyle was afraid Jack could see his anguish.

"I should find my parents," Jack said. The undersides of the big, puffy clouds were lit deeply pink by the departing sun.

"I don't want you to go."

"I don't either. But I have to." He raised his glass. "But first, a toast."

Kyle raised his own glass. "A toast."

"To tomorrow."

They clinked and drank.

"Tomorrow," Kyle said.

"And the day after that."

Kyle's smile deepened. "And the day after that."

Jack backed toward the open French doors, smiling. "We've got every day until September."

And he turned and was gone.

Later, Kyle walked through the quickly fading lilac dusk from the gambling tent, where he'd watched Trent lose two hundred dollars, to the dance. He was giddy, still coming down from Jack. He found Carly inside and they joined the throng on the dance floor. She was replaced by Dana, who was replaced in turn by Carly, who complained about a boy who was attempting to ply her with alcohol. "As if I couldn't drink him under the table," she scorned.

Kyle drank more champagne. He ate canapés. He visited with Dana's parents, who roped him into a tedious conversation on socialism. They were nice people, but stodgy. So, feeling guilty as he, light from wine, still clutching the rose Jack had given him, considered ditching them, he sat, Mr. Weiss's cigarette smoke in his eyes, and watched as Jack interacted with people Kyle had been on nodding acquaintanceship with his entire life. When Jack began waltzing with some of the summer girls, Kyle could see that he was a graceful dancer, making even the most doltish girl appear poised.

And Kyle felt cruel envy. He didn't see how it was fair to be robbed of such simple pleasures as a dance, a kiss, the grip of a hand—things most people took for granted. All his life he'd seen his friends flit off to flirt and make out, and he'd always been left wanting, trying to not look like he felt left out.

It wasn't until Claudia led him to the dance floor that he could feel the bubbles that danced in the tawny wine begin to jitterbug in his brain. He searched for Jack as both he and the bubbles spun. He spotted him dancing with Wendy Wennechuk a beautiful girl he had seen precisely eleven times, every summer at the Founder's Day dance. He felt a flash of jealousy but tempered it with the memory of his and Jack's reunion. Wendy was beautiful, but she was a coquette. Jack would never be attracted to her type. He craned his neck, spinning Claudia fast, then slow, so he could keep Jack in his line of sight.

He saw his mother dancing with Claudia's father, and she waved, giving him a relieved smile, which he gathered was because he was with Claudia. Overly sentimental from the wine, he was suddenly taken aback by her beauty, the beauty he alone, as her son, could see. It reminded him of when she had been the most beautiful woman in the world. He raised the rose to her.

When the song ended, Claudia asked if he wanted to continue dancing, but he declined, also declining the offer of more wine. The alcohol was suddenly making him massively tired. He sat at an empty table on the far side of the room, facing the dance floor and Jack. After a few minutes, Claudia joined him with both a drink and Trent, who tugged at his tie peevishly. Kyle was about to bum a cigarette, when he heard, above the crowd and in the lull between songs, Jack's name. He reacted like it had been his own. Then he saw Trey Shaw motioning to Jack as he left the dance floor with Wendy.

Kyle was immediately blinded by a jealousy that bordered on hatred. He felt frantic. Wendy disappeared in the crowd and Trey and Jack approached a table on the opposite side of the floor, yellow roses awaiting them, Trey looking dapper in his tux. He was only doing this to get to Kyle. Of that Kyle was certain.

Unless.

Unless he was trying to steal Jack.

He was about to go over to beat the shit out of Trey when he felt a hand on his shoulder. "Don't," Trent said.

Kyle remained seated, becoming more enraged and more insecure by the second. His heart hurt as he watched His Jack entertain Trey.

And then he felt sick. He stood suddenly, unsure whether he should dash for the bathroom.

"Kyle?" he heard Claudia say behind him.

He didn't move, awaiting another swell of nausea or the abatement of the first. Then the second came, and he was moving, across the dance floor, among swirling taffeta and velvet, broad black backs, gold glitter that made him dizzy. He rushed past Jack and Trey, up the stairs into the foyer, feeling better to be away from the tightness of the crowd. He passed the nearest bathroom and headed down a hall for a more private one. It was empty, and he stood inside for a moment, letting the cool of the room calm his roiling stomach and spinning head.

And then he was sad and the alcohol magnified his sadness, making him maudlin, and he started to cry, quietly and fiercely, like the sneezes of kittens. He wasn't even sure why he was crying.

Then he was horrified to hear a meek voice.

"Kyle?" Jack stood just inside the door, uncertain.

Wanting to laugh at his numbing humiliation, instead all that came out was another sob. He gave a sad, pathetic smile. "All I want to do is cry," he said, and it sounded like a question, as if Jack might be withholding the reason why. "Please. Leave me alone."

"Do you want me to get your friends? I mean…they know you better."

Kyle gave a short, humorless laugh, because Jack was so wrong. Then an enormous sob that was bigger than he, but not quite as big as his sadness, erupted, and he bolted into one of the stalls and threw up in sick, jolting spasms, still clutching the rose Jack had given him. The porcelain was cool to his face and hands. The stained water mocked him.

Then he felt Jack's hand stroking the hair at the back of his neck. "I'll stay with you," Jack said.

Kyle wanted him to stay. Of course he did. But he was so ashamed, he reacted like he'd been struck. "Can't you just go?" he shouted, a blob of vomit in the crease of his mouth. "Go!"

Jack stepped back. The wounded look on his face branded Kyle, but he made no entreaty for him stay.

Jack backed out into the hall where Trent and Claudia stood waiting.

"What happened?" Trent flicked the ash from his cigarette onto the carpet.

Jack was unable to meet their eyes, wondering if they'd heard, feeling like they were secretly deriding him for being shunned. "He wouldn't talk to me," he said sadly, evenly. "I was hoping one of you might know."

"We don't seem to know anything these days," Claudia said. "Thanks to you."

Kyle felt better after he threw up. Still, he had to get away. He told his parents he'd walk home, along the beach, looking forward to the time alone after the required sociability of the dance. Dana had already gone, so he said good-bye to the rest of the group, who were concerned and suspicious.

Then he approached Jack, who looked at him warily. He touched his hand, and Jack gave him a wounded smile, a smile of the attacked.

"I'm sorry," Kyle said, berating himself for destroying the intimacy that had been between them earlier.

"I know."

Kyle didn't know what else to say.

"Will I see you tomorrow?" Jack asked.

"Of course." He attempted to sound gracious and warm. "And the day after that…"

He trailed off, but Jack didn't play along. Instead he gave a tight, guarded smile and said, "I'm glad."

He was already at the sand's edge when he saw a couple by the water, holding hands. He regarded them with a humph and was headed in the opposite direction when he heard his name. He turned to find Trent running across the expanse of beach with a bottle of champagne, fireflies flashing like sequins in the dark. "I'm coming with you."

Kyle wanted to be alone, but with the way he'd been treating Trent, he couldn't very well tell him to get lost. "You're ready to leave?"

"Hell, yes." Trent loosened his shirt and tie then half squatted, the bottle between his legs. "I just have to open this." He struggled with the cork until it gave way with a startlingly loud *pop!* Kyle ducked as it rocketed past him toward the water. Trent offered the bottle, foam overflowing onto his hand. "Bubbly?"

The landscape was silvered by the brightness of the moon. Kyle tried walking with his head back so he could see the host of stars, but the motion made him dizzy, and he collided with Trent, their legs tangling. Trent pulled himself out of it without tripping. They took their shoes and socks off and for a while walked right where the water broke, not talking, Kyle still holding the rose Jack had given him. Holding the bottle to his lips, he looked at Trent sideways, smiling. "Where'd you get this, anyway?"

"A friend of Veronica's."

Kyle wiped his upper lip. "You and your connections."

Trent surprised him when he said, "You want to go swimming?"

They stopped, and Kyle looked to the dark sea, then up and down the empty length of beach, debating. Then he was unbuttoning his pants.

As they stripped, he was unable to keep his eyes from Trent's body. He knew that body better than he knew any other save his own. He knew every mole, every freckle, every scar, the breadth of the shoulders, the length of the fingers, the height of the brow. He knew when Trent had first gotten an erection, masturbated, French kissed. Just as Trent knew everything about Kyle—everything but the tiny yet significant fact of his homosexuality. Trent had always been, next to his parents—and, of course, Kevin—the most important person in Kyle's life.

But that night, as they undressed by the cold light of the moon, Kyle realized that Trent had been eclipsed. And all he felt looking at him was a minor void because he wasn't Jack.

They waded out to where the cool water touched their thighs, then dove in, the coldness surprising their hearts. Submerged, they cut through the murk, scarier because of the night, to where it was deeper, and Kyle could hear his heart beating.

It made him feel strong.

Thoughts of Jack, the dance, the bathroom echoed dully in the underwater chamber of his head. They were hard to pin down despite seeming to come more slowly than he was thinking them. He tried to focus on them, process them, his experiences and his reactions to them, when suddenly it seemed he'd been immersed forever and the ticking clock of his heart was winding down. He became frantic, fearful his lungs would burst, and he struggled to the surface, breaking into the atmosphere with the desperation of one caught in an undertow, the taunting thoughts and his painful breath releasing simultaneously. He panted for air, swiping at his eyes, trying to orient himself. When he got his bearings, he saw that Trent was already cutting through the surf with sure, even strokes toward the shore.

By the time Kyle reached the sand, Trent had seated his naked butt by their clothes and was trying to find his second sock. His lips were pursed and he didn't look up as Kyle approached.

"What's going on?" Kyle came to a stand before him. Their skin was fraught with goose bumps in the suddenly crisp night, their hair matted with saltwater, locks pasted to their foreheads.

"Fuck you." Trent glowered. He ran a hand through his sopping hair then took a long swallow from the champagne that sat beside him in a niche in the sand.

"Trent?" Was he too drunk to catch it, or was Trent too drunk to relate it?

"Kyle," Trent said firmly, implying the unspoken, *Don't push me.* He sighed quickly then looked away, handing the bottle upward, offering.

Kyle drank, the fizz biting his throat. He waited, expecting…something. He didn't know what. Finally, he said, "What's up?"

"Fuck you." Trent glared sullenly.

So. He was going to have to drag it from him. He plopped into the sand, and they sat for a few moments, passing the bottle without looking at each other, their bare legs touching.

"Why?" Trent said finally. "Why did you choose this summer?" He cocked his head to look at Kyle with an open, pained face. "This was going to be the best one of all. And you went and screwed it up." The bottle of champagne sat between his legs, his right hand loosely draping it.

"You're not making sense to me," Kyle said gently.

"This is our last summer before college. You knew how much we were all looking forward to it. And then you go and desert us. Desert me."

Kyle said nothing.

"I miss you, baby," Trent said, drunk.

Kyle started to speak, but Trent cut him off. "I don't want you to stroke me. That's not the reason I'm doing this. I'm doing this for me."

Kyle sighed.

"You know the girls are resentful." Trent's shoulders fell for a second then he drank from the bottle, his frame weary. Then he admitted reluctantly, "I am, too." He looked at Kyle. "But not like they are. I—"

Kyle was surprised to hear Trent's voice crack. He hadn't realized how upset anyone but himself might be.

"I hate losing you," Trent said. "I've never been without you." His face and voice were contorted with overemotion. "I don't know anymore what—what to think anymore." He brought his knees up and hugged them to his chest, biting his bottom lip, hard, suddenly crying, his tears opalescent in the moonlight.

Kyle didn't know what to think anymore either, let alone what to say. He put an arm around Trent's shoulders, and Trent leaned into his chest, and, like a little boy, put his arms around Kyle's waist and wept.

After his cries ceased, he looked up and said, "I'm sorry," like he had been commissioned by his mother to apologize. "Don't resent me." He was remarkably and abruptly coherent.

"I could never do that," Kyle said. Then he thought, *I should be the one asking for mercy. I'm the one indulging myself.*

Trent stood, his emotions seemingly having run dry, and began to dress. Kyle did the same and, as he pulled his clothes on, he watched Trent, wondering what else he'd wanted to say or if he was satisfied. Trent caught him looking, and he smiled an embarrassed, self-conscious smile and said, "Don't look at me. I feel stupid."

They finished dressing without speaking.

It wasn't until they were headed home that Trent was ready to conclude. He stopped and said, "Kyle."

Kyle turned back to him, the night wind off the sea stiff, cool.

The empty bottle dangled from Trent's hand. "Truth or dare."

Kyle's shoulders sagged. After everything that had happened that night Trent wanted to play games. The alcohol, his breakdown and Trent's confrontation had taxed him, and Kyle felt very alone and very much aged.

But there were rules to be obeyed and choices to be made.

"Truth," he said, resigned, still holding the rose.

Trent's voice was thin. "Are we still best friends?"

Kyle knew he couldn't dispute the validity of the query because he had already justified it relentlessly, but he was still absurdly pissed off, demanding, "How can you even ask me that?"

Trent just said placidly, "You can't answer a question with a question."

Kyle looked at him, hating him and hating himself. And then he was crying with such force he could hardly breathe. He hadn't cried so hard and so often since he was a child. And there was no longer any Kevin to make things right. "Of course we are!" he shouted. He continued up the beach, feeling like they were players acting out roles, saying and doing things they didn't mean because the script had already been written.

"I had to ask!" Trent wasn't following. He couldn't rebut because, as they believed, the answer was truth. "Because the way you've been this summer, I can't tell!"

Kyle stopped but didn't turn back. "We've always had our own lives," he said. "Why is this different?"

"I don't know! That's what I want you to tell me!"

"I don't know, okay!? It just is!"

They fell silent. Even the sea grazing the shore was quiescent. Then Trent said, "That's the confirmation I needed." He dropped the bottle in the sand and began the long walk home.

Kyle looked after him, spent, then followed.

He was too young when it happened to feel the soulless grief his parents did. His horror was overcome by curiosity. He wanted to know why. Not like his mother who collapsed at the memorial service, nor his father who carried the note with him for months afterward (and perhaps still did). No, Kyle was curious in a detached way.

The enigma haunted him still.

I've awakened.

It happened in January. The winter was harsh. The winds of a freak blizzard were tearing at the beach house when the three of them flew down, unsure what they hoped or expected to find.

Kyle was eleven, and he made the discovery in the basement. He was quietly surprised as he approached his brother's cold, unmoving body in a heap on the floor. Kyle knew he was dead. His skin had lost its pinkness and been replaced by a tinge of blue, with darker rings around his lips and eyes. He lay half on his right side, half on his back, head lolled to the left. His eyes were closed. Before him lay a sheet of white paper, folded once, in half. He'd been there for four days.

Kyle, still in his coat, approached. Above, he heard the voices and footsteps of his parents. He didn't call out. Not yet. He knelt before the body, knowing it was Kevin but unable to reconcile the pile of blue flesh with his brother. He leaned in so that he could look directly into his face, his breath, in such close proximity, rebounding off the cold corpse.

From somewhere in the past he heard *Frère Jacques* begin, muted, as if he were standing outside a theater during a concert.

It got louder as he rocked back on his feet, squatting.

He heard his mother say to his father that she was going to check the basement.

The song became a clamor.

He took Kevin's right hand and pulled, pried, using his fingernails to try to separate gold from flesh.

His mother opened the door at the top of the stairs and began to descend.

The song roared thunderously, until he felt dizzy and terrified like there was not enough air.

The threat of shame if he were caught overwhelmed him.

155

His mother reached the foot of the stairs.
Melody became cacophony.
The ring came off in his hand.
And warmth abandoned their world.

The day after Founder's Day was the volleyball tournament.

Jack went to Kyle's house, and, finding him still in bed, leaned over his stubbly face and poked a forefinger into his cheek. When his eyes fluttered open, Kyle smiled, content.

Then he remembered.

"Hi," he said, his mouth sticky. He'd passed out as soon as he'd gotten home and slept for eight hours. His limbs ached, and his throat was raw from crying and vomiting. His head throbbed with champagne residue. He didn't think he could lift it from the pillow, let alone stand.

"It's ten. What do you wanna do?"

Cry. "I'll get in the shower and leave that up to you." It was the least he could do. "The tournament isn't until two."

Jack went downstairs to find Ann sitting on the sofa in a pair of blue shorts and a white blouse. Beside her was a spray of harebells. She hadn't been there when he'd passed through the first time.

She stood. "Hi, Jack. Where's Kyle?"

"He's showering."

"Good. Join me on the balcony."

"Do you know what's wrong?" she asked when they stood at the rail. She took one of his hands into hers and held it tenderly.

"Wrong?"

"With Kyle. I need to know what's wrong."

Jack only looked at her.

"I don't want you to forsake any secrets." She squeezed his hand hard, afraid they wouldn't have enough time, afraid he would deny her. "But you have no children of your own yet. You don't know what it's like to hear them cry. His sadness atrophies my heart."

Jack gaped at her, his eyes like saucers. "Mrs. Quinn."

"You can't know what they're thinking." Her voice was heavy, urgent. She wasn't the fairy tale she'd been that night in the garden. She was a suddenly gray butterfly.

He looked at her for a long time before he said, "He doesn't talk to anyone about it."

She searched his eyes, determining his sincerity. And when she saw that he was truthful, she didn't cry. She squeezed his hand so tight that both felt pain.

But she didn't cry.

They were late.

They'd headed, at Jack's suggestion, to the lagoon. They'd reclined on the sand, watching seabirds scavenge, talking lazily about nothing, actively ignoring last night, the sun ascending. The next thing Kyle was aware of was Jack shaking him awake. "We're late! We're late!"

As they sped toward town Kyle could only imagine the wrath of his friends. He felt sick with dread, his hangover pounding a dull, pressing reverberating rhythm, like a tribal drum, in his head. "I am so fucked," he said. "Trent will never forgive me this." This would totally undermine the conversation they'd had the night before.

When they arrived twenty minutes later, Jack was climbing out of the car before Kyle had even turned the engine off. They made their way through the small, crowded parking lot to the beach where a stand of bleachers had been erected facing the sea. On the sand was a volleyball net where two teams were playing. Noisy gulls circled over the spectators. Kyle and Jack stood at the nearer end of the stands and searched the throng of mostly young, tan people for the girls. Finally Jack pointed to Carly, sitting alone nearly two-thirds down.

As they passed in front of the crowd at the bottom of the bleachers, Jack whispered to Kyle, "There's Trey."

Kyle looked up to see Trey in the crowd, watching them, then he stopped, letting Jack pass ahead of him, one hand lightly draping the small of his back, so no one but Trey would understand. That made Kyle feel so much lighter, he forgot his anxiety about being late until they approached Carly, sitting halfway up.

"Where the goddamned hell have you been?" she demanded as they sat down, Kyle in the middle.

Kyle could hardly look at her without his head cracking with pain. He had never had so wicked a hangover. "We were delayed."

"You are all Trent was counting on." Carly was unable to resist casting an accusing glance at Jack before turning back to Kyle. "He worships you. What don't you understand about that?"

"What's happened?" Kyle looked to the court, bright even through his sunglasses.

She shook her head in disgust. "He was disqualified twenty minutes ago."

They arrived at Trent's after dark, Kyle in his school jacket, Jack in a navy windbreaker. Trent had avoided them at the tournament and escaped before Kyle could catch up with him.

He wasn't sure they'd be welcome.

"Am I coming between you?" Jack spoke in the stillness after Kyle turned off his car.

Kyle was so surprised by the question, he said, "No," but then wondered if he'd spoken too quickly. "I don't know."

"I don't want you to resent me."

"If my friends and I grow apart, it's because it's time."

"You might not feel that way someday."

Kyle let them inside. The sound of the surf from the balcony took Jack into the living room. Kyle went into the kitchen, where he watched Trent mix a drink, wishing he could take back any hurt he had caused.

It was the only time he flickered in his quest for Jack.

"I'm sorry."

Trent didn't even look up. "I'm over it." He screwed the cap on a bottle of rum.

"Don't be flip."

"I'm not." Trent handed him a drink then reached for his own. "It's just volleyball, baby."

"Don't call me that!" Kyle's tone was sharper than he'd meant.

Trent looked at him, hurt. "You never minded before."

Kyle wasn't sure he wanted to go through the motions of taking it back, uncertain he wanted it nullified. "I wish I could explain it," he said.

"Jack?" Trent leaned against the counter.

"Yeah. He—"

"Kyle. Don't. You're only going to make it worse by trying to explain. Right now, as of this moment, we can pretend things aren't changing." There was a sadness around his mouth. He looked past him to their doppelgangers in the sliding glass door in the living room.

As he did so, Kyle saw there was something different about Trent's face. It was familiar as home, but the features were skewed so that he couldn't see what, precisely, had changed.

"A toast?" Trent raised his glass, and Kyle did, too. "To history?"

Kyle smiled, but he was so sad. "To history."

Claudia followed Kyle into the guest room where he placed his and Jack's jackets on the bed. "What is going on?" she demanded.

When he turned to her, he saw she'd shut the door and was leaning against it. "What're you talking about?" He motioned to the door.

"Don't worry. He's playing a drinking game." They both knew she referred to Jack. "You're the only person Trent counts on for support. And just like you have been all summer, you come around with your head up your ass. And I want to know what's going on."

"I knew I'd have to deal with you. I heard all this from Carly earlier, okay? Nothing is going on."

"What do you do all of this time with Jack?"

"Leave Jack out of it."

"I can't, Kyle. He's obviously part of it."

"It's not his fault." He was defensive.

"What's not his fault?"

Kyle sat on the edge of the bed, wondering why he was honoring her with time. He felt like he was being torn between two shores of a lake, Jack on one side, the group on the other, and he was terrified both would give up and he'd fall and drown. "Nothing," he said, and it had taken him so long to respond, it wasn't clear if he was answering Claudia's question or dismissing the entire conversation.

"We like Jack," she said, her tone softened. "But I wanted to let you know that you're not the same."

Like he didn't know. "Is that necessarily bad?" He looked at her with narrowed eyes.

"Of course not. But if you'd explain it maybe we could be more understanding."

"What do you want me to explain, Claudia?"

"Just what's going on." She went and stood before him.

"Nothing is 'going on.'"

"He's not like we are."

Before she could justify her statement, he stood and said angrily, "Maybe it's taken me all this time to realize I'm not either." He moved past her to the door.

"Wait!" she called.

He stopped, but didn't turn back. "You better stop now, Claudia, before you say something untakebackable."

"I know a way you can help Jack out."

He spoke to the door. "What do you mean?"

She approached him from behind. "Dana's got a crush on him. I told her I'd talk to you about it."

As she spoke her voice receded until it sounded like she was whispering from a cave at the other end of the world. He knew she was lying, yet he'd never known such raging jealousy. He hadn't adapted to loving Jack yet, let alone to the idea that he might someday lose him.

Without responding, he went to the kitchen where the others were playing cards. Jack regarded him through drunken, hooded eyes, and his smile was so genuine, it told Kyle he'd been having a fine time, but now that he, now that Kyle was there, he was going to have a brilliant time. His simple gesture released a large portion of Kyle's despair. No matter what was to come, right then, that second, Jack liked him best.

He sat, giddy with alleviation. He had the ridiculous urge to kiss Jack on the cheek simply for justifying his love.

"We're playing Man Overboard," Jack said. Then, lowering his voice: "I'm just drinking when they tell me to."

Kyle grinned, feeling protective. "I'll make sure they treat you fair."

They perceived each other for a moment, the rest of the world at bay.

Then, suddenly, and this caused them all to jump, Claudia snapped, "Kyle!" She stood leaning against the doorframe, arms crossed. Kyle became aware that the others had all been witness to his exchange with Jack.

"Need a refill?" Claudia asked smartly, knowing she'd scored a point.

He wondered if she even cared at all.

Then, when he looked into her eyes, he knew that she knew.

The others looked at him, expecting something. He took their anticipation as treachery so he chose to give them nothing. He pushed back his chair with a *scree* until it slammed into the counter, and walked out the door.

When he got to his car, he stood looking dumbly past it to the water. He wanted so much to succumb to his sadness that to fight it was like resisting anesthesia.

He could no longer remember a time before Jack. Every memory before that summer was tinted with his presence. It seemed that every decision, every betrayal, every idea that had transpired ever since the world began had or had not happened all so he could find Jack. All of it had been for them. And all of that time he had known it would come without ever being aware of that knowing.

He heard something from the house. Jack stood inside the screen door, holding their jackets. He appeared angelic with the light behind him. The image made Kyle's heart throb.

Jack flicked the light off and, letting the door slam behind him, went to join Kyle, placing their jackets in the backseat of the convertible. "It wasn't so much fun without you," he said. "Even though they *did* plead with me to stay."

When Kyle said nothing, Jack placed a hand on his back. "I didn't realize when I met you that you were so sad."

Kyle gave him a pained smile. "I didn't either."

"I can tell you only three things. The past is simply prologue; the future doesn't exist; the present is eternal. There are no regrets, because there is no past and there will never be a future. There's just now."

Kyle swallowed heavily. He wanted to say "I love you" and hope he wouldn't regret it since, apparently, there were no regrets. But he said nothing.

They went to the beach. Kyle drove the car onto the sand and parked twenty yards from the shore, large rock formations on either side of them, like sentinels silhouetted in the starlight. He slid over to the middle of the seat, so he wasn't closed in by the steering wheel and leaned back, legs spread so that they were just touching Jack's. He was glad they were away from the group. He was beginning to wonder why he would ever return to his troubled circle of friends.

They sat, passing Kyle's flask, their heads leaned back to a panorama of stars, sparkling and glimmering like a promise. Jack made a sound of contentment. "Look at all of them," he said.

Kyle looked at him, then to the water for relief.

"You ever think how the moon moves you?" Jack asked.

"Moves me?"

"Yeah. Your emotions."

"The *moon?*"

"Well, if it can move the oceans, just think what it can do to us. We're 60% water."

Kyle had never thought of it that way. It made him feel wildly less than.

They contemplated the constellations for a while before Jack asked, "Do you know your mythology?"

"We used to pretend we were gods when we were younger. Can you believe it?"

Jack laughed. The moon was reflected in the wetness of his mouth, on his golden glasses, in his eyes of azure.

"Recently it's been more about movie stars, though," Kyle said.

"Movie stars?"

"Trent likes to fancy himself James Dean."

"He seems more like a Kennedy than a rebel."

"A couple of summers ago, the girls were enthralled with Natalie Wood after seeing *Splendor in the Grass*. So they were always running off, being Natalie. And then, well, Dana be*came* Natalie over some boy, so the fun wore off. We've just been ourselves since."

"You can never be yourself again after having been a god," Jack said.

"It *was* cool. I was Apollo."

"The god of light and truth."

"Yes! He seemed happy. At least until Daphne."

"It doesn't surprise me that while everyone else was playing cowboys and Indians and cops and robbers you pretended you were gods. And you don't see why Trey wants to be part of you?"

That was hardly something Kyle expected to hear.

"You're the beautiful ones. And Trey is, too."

"Come on," Kyle said.

"I'm serious."

"Give me the flask, Averill."

"Quinn," Jack said, surrendering. "I've never drunk so much as I have this summer. You all are going to be alcoholics."

As he took the drink, Kyle was acutely aware that Jack's lips had just been on the mouth of the flask. "Is, um—is the rum too strong for you? There's nothing I can really do about it now but for next time…"

"It's better than beer, I'll say that."

"You don't like beer?"

"It's awful. But if your friends are going to include me, I can't very well say no when it means so much to you, you know?"

"You only do it for me?"

"That's the only reason I ever put up with them. It's the price."

They were silent again and Kyle felt warm inside.

And then Jack started, pointing to the sky. "Look!"

Kyle jumped, startled.

Jack looked at the stars, Kyle at Jack's cheek. He could see the curve of his lashes, the scruff of his beard just beginning to surface, the arch of his throat when he swallowed. He felt really drunk and his head wanted to roll back.

Then Jack turned to him and their noses almost touched, the energy between them charged. "I thought I saw a shooting star," he said, tentatively. His lips were parted and shiny from the drink. His breath smelled of rum.

Kyle's own breaths were uneven and quick.

He was acutely almost painfully aware of his and Jack's breath meeting, intermingling, becoming one.

And then he was leaning over, and he was kissing him, enveloped in the aroma of sandalwood. It was sudden and daring and Kyle could taste him, could understand him in a way he hadn't theretofore.

It was just a moment but to Kyle it felt like lifetimes.

And then he jumped back, aghast. What had he done? He wanted to cry and he wanted to run. "I'm sorry!" he said quickly. "I'm sorry!"

Jack's mouth was open, his expression dazed. "Kyle?"

Kyle wanted to look away, but he couldn't, trapped by those eyes. He felt sick. "I'm sorry. Don't hate me." He started to breathe hard. "Please, don't hate me. I'm so sorry."

"Don't be," Jack said. "I mean, are you?"

"Yes! I mean, should I be?"

"I don't know." Jack turned away, then back. He started to speak, then stopped.

It was only then that Kyle began to wonder. "Jack?" Jack's face jiggled with the beat of Kyle's heart. Tears of fear seared his eyes. The only thing worse than losing, would be never knowing. It was his moment of truth where all would be lost or gained. He had to know. "Can I kiss you again?"

Jack looked shaken and afraid. His voice was tremulous. "Do you want to?"

"Do you want me to?"

"Do you want to?"

Kyle sat up. He nodded once, twice. "More than everything."

He reached out his right hand to touch Jack's cheek, making sure he was sure.

Jack nodded, more with his eyes than his head.

And Kyle was leaning in, and it felt like he was crossing a canyon. He was so terrified and overjoyed he wasn't thinking until their lips touched and their mouths parted, and they were kissing again, swallowing. Jack's mouth was so moist and so soft and so sure, his breath so hot. The hottest Kyle had ever felt.

When they broke apart, Kyle rested his forehead against Jack's, still tasting him. He was feeling the most incredible colors.

"What's happening?" Jack whispered.

Kyle could feel Jack's belt buckle thrusting into his thigh, but it just reminded him that he was alive and that it was real. "I've thought of doing nothing but that from the second I saw you. I'm—I'm—really confused." He sat up decisively. "Yes. I'm really confused. And shaken up. Yes. I'm shaken up." Was he babbling? "I'm drunk."

"Don't be upset."

"I'm not upset," Kyle said, resenting being called on it. "I mean—I just don't want you to think the wrong thing."

"Which is?"

"I don't know." *I love you.* He had to restrain himself from saying it. The words wanted to fly from his lips. And then they were there. "I love you." They came as easily as the first lie. And they were so freeing he couldn't stop saying them. "I love you. I love you." And then he was trying to articulate it all, as though words could translate what he'd felt that summer. "I love your smile and how you walk. And you're funny. And you're romantic and you're smart. And I love how you're afraid of the water and I don't want you to be and I want to protect you from it. And you're so beautiful you're like an English poem. You're so beautiful I want to turn away. It hurts, like looking into the sun." He angled his face down, his eyes peering up in reverence. "Animals must bow in deference when you pass by," he said. "How could I not?"

"Kyle…" Jack breathed. "You don't mean that."

"If I were talented I'd write epics and poems and love songs about you. I'd paint you and sculpt you. But I have nothing to offer but myself…and I don't know if I'm enough."

Jack touched his temple. "My head hurts. You fight with your friends then bring me out here and kiss me and tell me you're in love with me." He looked like he was going to cry. "Are you fucking with me, Kyle Ryan Quinn?"

"I couldn't," Kyle said ardently, urgently. "Not about this. Not this."

Jack looked at him long and hard. Then he sighed and said, "Good. Because I love you, too."

Kyle leaned against him, suddenly too exhausted to remain upright, his forehead against the side of Jack's neck, that extraordinary neck. "I love you," he whispered. It felt so good to be able to say it, finally, he just wanted to keep repeating it.

Then they were together again, kissing, shy, probing kisses. When they pulled apart, Kyle put a hand to Jack's face, gently, his fingers touching his cheek, his jaw, his lips. His heart swelled so much it hurt. His eyes were as big as Jack's.

Then Jack was laughing. "Are you serious?"

"Are you?" Kyle hated to ask, but he needed to know.

Jack nodded. Before he could speak, Kyle met him with a firm, needy kiss.

When they separated, they just looked at each other for a few moments, digesting. Then Jack asked, "What do your friends think? This *has* to be affecting The Group."

"They don't know. They think I'm just ditching them. And Trent thinks you're my new best friend."

Jack beamed. "But I'm not."

"I knew that first day I saw you on the dune."

"You pursued me."

"Hell, yes, I pursued you. I was willing to scale mountains just to get you to look at me." He kissed him again, unable to help himself, renewing his taste. His face was flushed and hot. He was excited and happy and…happy. He'd never felt such bliss. "Is it wrong to love you?" he whispered into Jack's mouth.

And Jack said, "Not if I love you back."

When he went to pick up Jack the next day, Kyle didn't know what he was supposed to feel, let alone how he was supposed to act. He was torn between rapture and terror. What if Jack looked at him in broad daylight and wanted to run? What if he were ashamed? What if Kyle had brought about the ruin of all that was just and good?

But…he had kissed Jack.

And Jack had kissed him back!

Was that not worth the death of all that had been before?

When Jack answered the door, he was ready to go. They faced each other, on opposite sides of the threshold, lips swollen from kissing, eyes puffy from lack of sleep, both a little unsure.

Then Jack stepped past him and headed for the car.

When they got to the lagoon, they sat for a time in silence after Kyle turned the engine off. They didn't look at each other. Kyle thought he was going to throw up.

They went down to the sand, and Kyle lay on his towel, watching Jack stray into the shallows. He looked like art, his legs slender, waist tight, chest flat. He wondered if he'd ever be able to touch that body again.

"There's something to be said for wading!" Jack called then. Facing Kyle, he didn't see the swell coming. It crashed into him, thrusting him forward. He laughed with a child's abandon at the surprise of it, endeavoring to maintain balance against the force of the sea.

Kyle was electrified, but he hurt.

A few minutes later, Jack trekked back up to join him, taking his place on his towel. Kyle was glad Jack also chose to not speak. He wasn't sure what was appropriate. He wanted to verify the night before without seeming like he was verifying it. And more than that he wanted to know that Jack was okay with what had happened. But, to stay a possible execution, he just sat quietly, trying to keep from breathing too loudly.

It was many moments later when Jack asked, "Do you still love me, Kyle?"

Kyle hadn't expected something so forthright or so simple. Or clever! Without giving any indication of his own feelings, Jack had phrased it so that Kyle had to reveal himself before he, Jack, made any commitment. He wasn't sure how to tread, so he continued looking out at the water and said placidly, "Yeah. Do you still love me?"

Jack sighed like he was very tired. "Yeah."

Kyle gazed at him, leaning back on his elbows in his white tank top, facing the sea, and said, "I'm glad."

Jack rolled onto his side to look at Kyle. "Me, too."

Kyle cupped his cheek. He could see nothing but his face. The simplicity of it stole his breath.

They kissed.

It was different in the light of day.

Being able to see made it so much more real.

They lay on the beach for hours, kissing because it was so new, until their lips were chafed and sore. Kyle was astounded by Jack's body, his ardor, his heat, his firmness. And his mouth! His yielding, responsive, eager mouth. He didn't want to do anything ever again but kiss Jack.

"You have the most beautiful hair." Kyle pushed it back, out of Jack's face, reveling in the freedom he felt.

"People have always liked it long," Jack said. "It's the only thing anyone ever notices about me."

"What about your eyes?" He probed them, closer and bigger and more blinding than they'd ever been.

"What about them?"

"They're stunning. People don't tell you that every day of your life?"

Jack smiled. "People don't usually notice me."

That perplexed and saddened Kyle.

"This whole thing is strange," Jack said.

Kyle laughed, throwing his head back because it felt so good to be unshackled from his insecurity, his terror, his shame.

"I keep thinking you're gonna get up and go away," Jack said. "Back to your friends."

"That will never happen." Kyle looked away. "I love you, you know."

Jack smiled, hitting him lightly on the chest. "Why can't you say that while you look at me?"

Kyle smiled, too. "Because I'm afraid if you see how much I feel you might be scared away."

"If your friends can't scare me away, nothing can." Jack rolled on top of him in one smooth motion.

Kyle was immediately aroused. They wrestled, then kissed, their legs tangled, sand clinging to their skin. Jack breathed into Kyle, and Kyle inhaled, his lungs expanding with life. "Are you mine?" he demanded hotly. "Are you mine?"

"Forever," Jack said, their bare chests together.

"I was so afraid," Kyle murmured.

"Never."

"You've owned me since the first day."

"I love you."

"I love you."

That night they got pizza and headed along the coast. Birds chattered nervously in the moist heavy dark in anticipation of an oncoming storm. The white noise of wind rushed loud in the leaves of the forest beside them. A flash of lightning, like a serrated violin bow, sizzled across the sky. The world lit up like a darkened room by a flashbulb, and then they were cast into pitch again, their eyes tormented by specters of light, a furious overture of crickets playing around them.

Kyle turned down a dirt road and soon came to a large white house with mullioned windows on the second level, dormer windows in the attic and a wide porch that spanned the length of the house. The grass was long and uncontrolled in the yard, in the midst of which stood an enormous mulberry tree.

"We used to ride our bikes out here," Kyle said.

"Where are we?" Jack looked up at the house, its empty windows reflecting back the night. It looked gothic.

Kyle reached in back for a blanket and a lamp. "It's deserted. It belonged to the McAllisters at the turn of the century. No one knows where they went."

"Can't we get in trouble?"

"Not if we don't get caught." Kyle flashed a wicked grin, and they stepped out into the wind.

As they crossed toward the house, lightning illuminated the yard and an eerie white figure above the porch.

It vanished with the light.

"What was that?" Jack called.

"Just a statue! Hurry! Before the rain starts!"

They ran around to the back, Jack with the food, Kyle with the blanket and the lantern. There was a smaller porch there, and they climbed its steps so they were out of the force of the wind. Beside it was an entrance to a dirt cellar. Kyle opened an unlocked door and they stepped into a dark, dirty kitchen. "The front door is jammed," he said, lighting the lamp. "And there's no electricity."

"Just like the Four Seasons," Jack joked.

They started down a small walkway, past a pantry, toward the front of the house. As they were about to step into the living room, Jack stopped, touching Kyle's arm. "Wait," he said. "Do you hear them?"

Kyle listened for a second. All he could hear was the hollow wail of the wind. "Who?"

"Ghosts."

Kyle mock punched his arm. "You're cracked."

They continued to the living room where there were five dusty pieces of furniture: a sofa, a love seat, an armchair, a coffee table and an end table, all of which sat before a picture window that looked onto the front yard. Against the rear wall was a large stone fireplace, and beyond it, a staircase that led to the second level.

They set their things down, and when Kyle turned to speak, lightning lit up Jack's face or, maybe, Jack's face lit up the room, he couldn't tell. Words failed him. He had to turn away from Jack's eyes so that he could process thought. "I had the idea we might like someplace more private than the beach," he said. "Being together like we were today is tempting fate."

Jack grinned. "You're right. This is perfect."

Kyle took his hand and led him to a door past the fireplace, past the stairs, that wasn't visible in the light from the lamp. He opened it and they stepped onto a screened-in side porch, housing a black wrought-iron table, four matching chairs and a wood swing. Air sang through the screens, rattling a wind chime, creaking the swing, riffling their hair.

"I thought we could spend our time out here," Kyle said. "The house gets stuffy. Tonight's too stormy, of course." He pointed through the screen. "And the shore's right there. We've even got a view."

"You think of everything," Jack said.

At that moment, Kyle understood what Jack meant by fearing he'd tempt fate by being too happy.

Then Jack said, his voice soft in the dim, "What're you going to do about them, Kyle?"

The one thing shadowing his happiness. "I haven't had time to think about it."

"Would they understand?"

"What? The reason I spend so much time with you is because I'm in love with you?"

Jack didn't respond. Kyle could feel his slow, measured breath. "Say it again," Jack said then, hot and needing.

"I'm in love with you."

That was when headlights appeared from the driveway. Kyle crept to the front of the porch and peered around the corner. Trent's convertible was parked beside Kyle's. "Shit. It's Trent and Carly."

"What should we do?" Jack whispered.

"I don't want to see them. Today is for you."

They hurried inside and gathered their belongings, then Kyle took Jack's hand and led him to the pantry in the hall where the shelves were covered with dust and clutched at by cobwebs. Kyle blew the lamp out. They heard Trent and Carly enter through the kitchen.

"Kyle?" Trent called.

They went past the pantry to the living room.

"I'm going to check upstairs," Trent said. "Maybe he fell asleep in one of the bedrooms."

"Hellooo?" Carly sang out. "Kyle?" She pushed open the door to the side porch and peered into the darkness, the wind twisting her hair. The rain had not yet begun.

From upstairs she heard Trent. "Maybe he's not even here!"

"He has to be here!" she called as she went back into the living room. "His car is here."

Jack looked at Kyle. "Your car!" he whispered.

Kyle silenced him with a kiss.

As Carly passed the pantry, she said, "God damn you. We just want to talk."

A moment later Trent came down the stairs and joined her in the kitchen. "He doesn't want to see us," he said.

"He's really angry."

"No. He's hurt. Let's give him some space. We'll leave a note in his car."

"They want to apologize," Jack said, once they were gone.

"Tomorrow."

"I can't believe you kissed me when Carly was that close. It was so daring."

"I feel like I'm corrupting you."

"You're clarifying me."

Kyle's heart tremored. "Jack," he breathed. "What are we going to do?"

Jack took his hand. "Why must we do anything?"

The following evening at twilight, both in shorts and windbreakers, they joined the group at Dana's, the storm having cooled the island. They circled the house to avoid getting roped into a conversation with the Weiss' and found the group sitting around a fire to the side of the tennis court. As Kyle and Jack approached, the others looked up.

"Where have you been?" Carly demanded.

"Don't use that attitude with me," Kyle said testily.

"We looked for you all day," Dana said more diplomatically.

"I'm here." He sat between Trent and Claudia, Jack taking a seat behind him. "How'd you know where we were last night?"

"That's where we always go to hide," Trent said.

"First," Dana began, "we want to apologize. None of us were very adult the other night."

"Apology accepted." Kyle pulled his feet under him so he sat cross-legged.

"We talked a lot last night—" Claudia started.

"Don't. I said the apology was accepted."

"But—"

"No. I'm going to say to you what Trent said to me. You'll only make things worse by explaining. Right now, as of this second, we can still pretend things aren't changing."

No one said anything. Jack looked at the grass, Claudia at her feet, the rest into the fire.

Then Claudia turned her gaze back to him. "So you just get to drop in and give us attitude whenever you feel like it and we're just supposed to sit back and take it."

It was then that Kyle realized he was coming to hate her. "Yes," he said. "Because I've been taking your attitude for weeks, and I've been subordinate, apologetic and guilty. And after your outburst in Trent's bedroom, I decided I'm not feeling guilty anymore."

"Veronica's pregnant."

It took a second for what Dana said to register. Kyle looked at her across the fire. She nodded.

"That was the second thing we wanted to talk to you about," Carly said.

178

He turned, openmouthed, to Trent. "My god. Is she sure?" He could hardly breathe.

"She said she is and, well…" Trent shrugged.

"And chances are she is with the way you've been fucking her," Kyle supplied.

Trent tore blades of grass. He glanced up to see Jack watching him. Jack looked guiltily away like he'd been caught watching a girl undress. "Yeah," Trent said. "Basically."

Kyle gave him a disbelieving look, the smoke from the fire stinging his eyes. "What are you going to do?"

"Marry her," Trent said. "What else?"

Kyle inhaled sharply in surprise, and the smoke burned his lungs, bit his throat. He could hear wind rustling the leaves. Outside the warmth and light of the fire, he felt the darkness shift.

Trent laughed. "She's going to get rid of it, Kyle." He glanced again at Jack, who had been silent thus far. "Hanging out with you hasn't made him any less gullible, huh?"

"This isn't funny!" Kyle snapped. "What did she say about an abortion?"

"She disagreed with me. Vehemently."

"Wow." Kyle could feel Jack rubbing the base of his spine, assuring his presence. The comfort he took in that shook him. "This is so serious. So adult. I don't even know what to say." His mind roared at him. They had turned a corner. Nothing would ever be the same again. This was untakebackable. "What's going to happen now?"

Trent looked at him, humbly hopeful. "I need you to go with me to see her tomorrow."

They arrived at Veronica's at dusk. The neighborhood was still and beige. From nearby they heard a dog barking, the slamming of a screen door. Catchflies still blazed from either side of the porch.

When Trent opened the car door it was loud in the serenity. Kyle followed him up to the front door, and they stood without speaking after Trent knocked. They heard nothing from within. They didn't look at each other. Kyle felt awkward.

After several moments, Veronica appeared, wraithlike, dressed in white, and stepped outside. "Hey," she said. "Hey, Kyle." She fluttered her fingers coolly in his direction.

"Hey."

Veronica looked expectantly at Trent.

"We have to talk," he said.

"Yes. We do."

Kyle motioned to the porch swing. "I'll wait here."

Trent and Veronica went inside, and he took a seat on the side rail. There was a trellis entwined with morning glories and moonflowers. The morning glories were dormant for the evening; the moonflowers were in full, luminous bloom, surrounded by dark, heart-shaped leaves. Looking past them, he could see a neighbor's house less than ten yards away. From it he could hear the dreamy notes of a singer mourning *The Man That Got Away*. The keen, clean smell of cut grass was on the air. Kyle glanced at two boys who rode by on bicycles.

Then, hearing a sound from the house next door, he turned to it again. Through a bedroom window, he saw a thin, pretty woman with blond hair, pale skin and a cascade of freckles across her back lighting a cigarette. She stood in a pearl silk slip, her hands trembling lightly. She sang a few lines of the song under her breath, swaying her hips suggestively, dancing only for herself.

The music came to Kyle on a waft of cheap perfume as if over a hundred universes. *Is she one of those women*, he wondered, *who calls in requests on the radio? Does she have a man? Has he gotten away?*

He watched, observing the way her breasts rose when she inhaled from the cigarette, the way she closed her eyes when she exhaled, the way one hand draped over her stomach as she danced. Kyle wanted to know her story...

Suddenly Veronica's screen door crashed open against the wall behind him. He jumped and turned to see Trent storm down the stairs. Kyle, his heart pounding in fright, glanced back to the blond woman, but she was gone, and only the radio with its forlorn song remained.

He headed toward the porch stairs and was about to descend when Veronica appeared in the doorway. He turned to her, still dazed. She was weeping, her faced cloaked in despair. She reached out a hand to him. He could hardly reconcile her with the girl who had answered the door just moments before. Or had it been only moments?

He stepped back. He saw a wildness in her eyes that he found familiar but didn't think he actually knew, didn't actually remember. Yet he understood it, as he'd understood her longing.

It made him want to run.

She took a step toward him, hand still outstretched, fingers flexed, as if attempting to grasp.

He took another pace back, but he was at the top of the stairs, and he wasn't prepared to step down. He lost his balance, scrambling for purchase but then he was weightless, the world turning upside down, and he was spinning, falling.

"Kyle!"

Trent's voice was loud.

He heard himself respond irritably. "What?"

Then Veronica. "Are you okay?"

He opened his eyes and that was when he realized they'd been closed. He was on the ground, the grass cool against his exposed flesh. All he could see above him was darkness and it didn't strike him as particularly alarming.

Then Veronica's face came into view and terror pumped through him again. He scrambled up, arms flailing, stumbling over his feet to get away.

"Are you all right?" Trent asked.

Kyle backed toward the car, keeping Veronica in sight as if he feared she might materialize behind him if he blinked. She and Trent looked at him with concern and confusion. Once he'd climbed into the passenger seat, eyes still on Veronica, he said evenly, "Okay. Drive."

Trent looked back at Veronica then turned and got into the convertible.

"Drive," Kyle said again.

Once they were headed back to Trent's, where they'd left the girls, Kyle felt blackness start to cover his eyes, and he only realized his head was falling forward when Trent spoke. He jerked up, a dull pain throbbing behind his left ear.

"You sure you're okay?" Trent asked. "You fell pretty hard."

"I'm fine." But he felt woozy.

"The grace of God, I guess." He spoke gently.

Kyle touched his wound and he could feel the pulsing of his heart in his fingertips. When he pulled his fingers away they glinted with blood. "Yeah," he said. "The grace of God."

The girls were waiting at Trent's when they returned. "What happened?" Carly demanded as she and Trent helped Kyle to the sofa. Dana ran for a towel.

Kyle's mind was contorting around the edges. "I—I don't know." He looked to Trent. "You scared me when the door slammed open." He spoke slowly, like he had to catch the words in the air before he could say them. "And then… I don't know. I fell."

"So what is she going to do?" Claudia asked, sitting beside Kyle.

"She's going to have to get rid of it, because there's no way in hell I'm marrying her."

"Did you tell her you'd pay for it?" Claudia shifted on the sofa as Dana returned with a small towel and peroxide.

"Of course. I asked her if she knew a doctor who could do it, and that's what pissed her off."

Kyle winced as Dana dabbed at his wound with the towel, but somehow the pain cleared his mind. "She wasn't pissed," he said. "She's hurt. She's in love with you. Can't you treat her with a little delicacy?"

"Can she really be in love, though?" Carly queried.

"Yeah," Trent said. "She hardly knows me."

"Whether it's 'love' or not is irrelevant. You're hurting her."

"This might sting a little," Dana said, about to apply peroxide.

Kyle shrank back from the smarting chemical. He felt woozy. "I think I'd better lie down."

"No," Carly said. "You can't in case you have a concussion."

"Maybe we should take you to a doctor," Dana suggested.

"No. I've been hurt worse in football. But I'd like to go home. Can you call Jack? He's right next door, and he can help me get home." He recited the number and Carly went to phone.

Dana kissed him on the cheek. "You're set." She got up to return the towel and peroxide to the bathroom.

"We could take you home." Claudia stood and went to the fireplace.

"Claudia, don't start," Trent said.

"This way none of you are inconvenienced." Kyle's argument sounded weak even to himself, but after seeing Veronica he needed to be with Jack.

"That's fine," Trent said. "Kyle. You okay enough for a beer?"

"Yeah. Thanks."

On his way to the kitchen, Trent passed Carly, who was returning to the living room. "He'll be here in two minutes." She took a seat in a wingback chair and threw her legs over the arm.

"How would it be an inconvenience?" Claudia said.

"What is *with* you!" Kyle suddenly shouted. His head throbbed with the volume of his voice, but he couldn't stop himself. He felt lucky he was able to keep from belting her. He could feel the jolt of contact in his arm. "Why is it so important when I choose Jack?"

"Because you're choosing him over us," she said. "I'm the only one who'll tell you. Everyone else is afraid they'll alienate you."

"You're doing a fine enough job on your own."

Trent returned, handing a bottle of beer to Kyle. "Shut up, Claudia," he said, taking a seat on the sofa.

"If you don't want me around anymore, just say so," Kyle said.

"Given a choice between us and him, that's exactly what you'd choose, isn't it?"

Kyle leaned forward. "Is that an ultimatum?"

"It's a statement that awaits verification."

"Stop! Just stop!"

They turned to see Dana standing in the doorway to the hall. "This talk about whether Jack should have come or Kyle should have invited him or allowed him or warned us or *whatever* is so *boring*! I'm sick of all this arguing. We're friends for Christ's sake!"

"Every time I think it's behind us, Claudia brings it up again," Kyle said.

"Really, Claudia," Carly said. "Give it a rest."

"I'm simply being honest." Claudia was unflinchable.

"We weren't thrilled with Jack at the start either," Dana said. "But we know him now and he's nice enough and he's obviously important to Kyle. So there's no grief to be given."

"I'm not meaning to give grief." Claudia leveled her eyes at Kyle. "I just want the truth."

There was a knock at the door, tempering their emotions. Kyle stood and went to let Jack in with his shadow of sandalwood. "That was fast."

"I came as quickly as I could. Carly told me about your head." He smiled. "I thought you knew how to fall."

Kyle smiled back, but it hurt. When he turned to the living room again, he saw that Dana had taken a place on the loveseat. He looked at her for a moment then at Trent. "I'll call you."

As he and Jack turned to the door, he could feel it. Something in the night forewarned him that it wasn't over, but before he could process anything, Claudia spoke, her voice crisp, sure and daring.

"Kyle."

He and Jack both stopped. Neither turned. She spoke again and he could hear the self-assured relish in her voice.

"Truth or dare."

"Kyle!" Dana called from her place on the loveseat. "You know you don't have to do this. You just run along home, okay?"

"God damn you," Trent said to Claudia. "Why are you such a bitch?"

But they knew.

Kyle had to choose. It was their code of honor. And, after all, this was what he'd been anticipating—and fearing—for years. This one was for keeps.

"Truth."

Claudia smiled easily, having known he would not waver. Her eyes were cold as glass. "Are you in love with Jack?"

The room was so quiet they could have heard ice form. Kyle swallowed. The silence bore down on him until his shoulders sagged and his head burned. But when he spoke, his voice was as clear and confident as Claudia's.

"Yes."

Then he took Jack's hand and they went out into the night.

Once in the car, they breathed again.

"Uh…" Jack said.

"Tell me about it." Kyle put a faint hand to his forehead.

"Your bravery was astonishing."

"Was it?" He really didn't know.

"Yeah." Jack reached over and rubbed the back of his neck. "I had no idea I was in for fireworks when Carly called."

"Neither did I."

Jack took Kyle's right hand into his left. "You'll be okay."

"Will I? Right now I feel sort of sick."

"I feel like you stood up for my honor or something."

"I slew the dragon Claudia, huh?"

"Something like that." He stroked Kyle's hand softly. "I'd kiss you, but I'm afraid they might see."

"Why don't you do it anyway?"

Jack grinned then leaned over and their lips bonded, but then he pulled back laughing.

"What's so funny?" Kyle asked.

"Nothing. I just love you."

Ann prodded them awake the next day, Kyle at the head of the bed, Jack at the foot. Kyle opened his eyes to dazzling sunlight and his mother's delicately made up elfin face. "Time for church," she said. They went to church infrequently, but when Ann made up her mind they were attending, they attended.

Kyle nodded, mute, then watched her white folds of taffeta swish to the foot of the bed where she roused Jack before disappearing into the hall.

Kyle looked down at Jack and wriggled the toes that peeped beside his face.

"How do you feel?" Jack asked.

"Good. I feel—good."

"Good."

"I don't have to hide from my friends anymore." He gave a wry look. "If they're still my friends."

They arrived just as the bell was beckoning. The small, white church stood on a grassy hill, its slender steeple stark against expansive cerulean. Inside, Kyle was surprised to catch sight of Carly seated on the right with her parents. He hadn't expected to see any of them so soon. And there, in the bright, white real world, the enormity of his confession hit him.

There was no going back.

They sat midway up on the left, and as the service began he believed he could sense Carly watching him.

He was afraid to glance over to verify.

When they stood to sing, he shared a hymnal with his mother like he always did, but his hands trembled. He felt that all of the people around him could tell, that they were judging.

And for the first time, he felt dirty.

He cast an uncomfortable look at Jack, who smiled contentedly, his eyes half closed, satisfied, like a cat purring of its own accord. He appeared to be enjoying the service.

It relaxed him seeing Jack so at peace. It reminded him that they weren't dirty. That loving Jack was the purest thing he'd ever done.

So he rejoiced.

Outside, after the service, Carly's father, a tall, lean man with curly dark hair, approached Ann before Kyle could orchestrate their escape. Mr. Salenger said, "We haven't seen you much this summer."

Ann took his hand. "We've just been so busy this year."

Carly and her mother came up. Iris Salenger was a tall, thin woman with a beaked nose and thin lips. Carly looked at Kyle and Jack.

"Hi, Kyle," she said levelly.

"Hi, Carly," Kyle responded just as levelly, so she'd see how strong and unashamed he was.

"Hi, Jack." She looked to him beyond Kyle.

"Hi, Carly." Jack gave a quick smile, his glasses flashing in the sun.

Kyle hated that they kept saying each other's names. It was like they were trying to show they remembered each other. Carly was one of his best friends. Yet he could think of nothing to say to her.

"So what're you two doing today?" she ventured.

And that was when he could see precisely how things had changed. All summer he'd been torn over that lake, Jack on one side, the group on the other, pulling at him, keeping him aloft. And last night he had crossed over.

For the first time he was seeing them from Jack's side.

He didn't know who had changed. They or him?

"Nothing," he said in response.

They went to the McAllister house that afternoon. It was the first time Jack had seen it in the daylight. Dandelions were overtaking the yard. The mulberry tree was stately in its loneness. Above the porch steps was a medium-sized white marble statue of a man, draped with a sheet about the waist, one hand holding a finger to his lips, the other clutching a white rose. His face was cast in an expression of haunted mortal fear.

"Creepy," Jack said.

"It's Harpocrates. The god of silence."

"I guess that's the right god to protect us here then."

Kyle took his hand and led him to the back of the house, where Jack could now see there was an enormous lawn, overrun with grass and weeds and dandelions and encircled by a wall. And in the middle of it all was a tall and slender pear tree, bare until the upper third of its trunk, where an explosion of leaves, silver in the breeze, clustered in a head.

"Whoa," Jack said.

"We've never understood why it grows that way."

"It's bliss."

"No, you're bliss." He leaned in and kissed him gently on the lips.

Then he took his hand and led him through the kitchen and the living room, to the side porch. Jack saw willow trees just outside, beyond which lay the sea, the water curling and sparkling.

They set about creating their hideout. They removed cobwebs, scrubbed tile, wiped windows. They pushed the wrought-iron table against the wall, spreading a mattress and pillows and blankets on the floor. Over the course of days, Jack left a small radio, Kyle a lantern. They took clothes and toiletries and books, Kyle a pulp paperback, Jack *The Beautiful and the Damned*. Kyle began storing bottles of soda and beer in the cool dirt cellar behind the house. Jack brought in handfuls of dandelions from the yard. They took flowers from Ann's garden: magnolias, prince's feathers, bellflowers.

The house became theirs.

Soon they began spending all of their days at the McAllister house. Jack fretted that they were trespassing, that someone might come, but he never suggested they leave. Kyle didn't ask, but he sensed Jack was afraid they were tempting fate. He tried to reassure him without seeming like he was reassuring him by referring to the many times he and the others had been there.

He never mentioned the times he and Trey had been there.

Kyle's friends never called.

They never stopped by.

They made no effort of which he was aware to get in contact.

And neither did he.

One hot, humid night after they'd moved in, Jack and Kyle sat on the porch, reading. Myrtle was heavy in the air. Past the willows, heat lightning glimmered on the water. There was just enough breeze to keep them from being miserable. Kyle, sweaty and shirtless on the swing, turned a page, but he was looking at Jack on the floor: his disheveled hair; the way he comfortably chewed his cheek; the white tank that billowed around his slender form, affording a snatch of tan. Despite the moistness of the night, he was fresh and dry. Kyle drank him in.

Then Jack looked up; Kyle flushed at being caught.

Jack smiled. "Why don't you come sit down here with me?" He put Fitzgerald aside and patted the blanket beside him.

"I was just sort of zoning out." He was realizing he had no practice dating.

"I want you to, Kyle."

He decided it was less embarrassing to acquiesce than to protest, so they sat together, Jack snuggling close so their sides touched, Kyle looking out at the fireflies in the dark.

"You okay?" Jack had mulberry juice on his lips.

"Yeah."

"Miss your friends?"

Kyle hadn't thought so, but as he was about to say so, he realized that he did, desperately. "I guess I do."

"They need time."

"I guess."

"Maybe you should go to them."

"I'm not ready for rejection yet."

"They're your friends," Jack said. "And though I don't like them, I think there's something between you that is strong enough to overcome this."

"That's what I thought, too. But I guess I just assumed it, because this is the first thing we've had to overcome." He looked at Jack, finally, their faces almost touching. Over the water they heard a low touch of summer thunder. "You're worth it either way."

Jack averted his face then, toward the willows, toward the sea. "Did you know I needed to hear that?"

"No! Have you been struggling with it?"

"I don't get the dynamics of your circle, Kyle. Sometimes I feel like Nick Carraway, observing a troubled, privileged world I don't belong to or understand."

"Puss, you don't need to understand my friends. You understand me."

Jack turned to him, slowly, comprehending. "You really love me." It was all revelation.

"Yeah," Kyle said. "I do—" Then he smiled. "I do."

"Do what?" Jack grinned at making him say it again.

"You know…love you."

"Oh," Jack said. "That."

"I won't leave you, Jack. Ever."

It was then that he acted. He went to put his arm around Jack, but in doing so he bumped his glasses to a diagonal position on his face. They both laughed, and Kyle slid his arm around Jack, and Jack leaned into him, and it was so much more comfortable than being shoulder to shoulder.

Jack smiled, serious. "You're my first boyfriend, Kyle Ryan Quinn. So I might be a little insecure for a while."

Kyle laughed again. Why did it feel so good to laugh with Jack? "Yeah, well, you're my first, too. Sometimes I don't even know how to go about holding your hand."

Jack held up his right hand like Exhibit A, then took Kyle's right and rested them both on Kyle's thigh. "It's that simple."

That was the first night they made love, there, on the porch, by the sea. They joined in the house's chorus of creaks and sighs, and later, when they had fallen into sticky, satisfied sleep, their breathing fell into step with the house's rhythm.

JULY

Independence Day loomed as the temperature surged. On July third, his parents having gone to bed early to rest for the following day's festivities, Kyle sat on the veranda after sunset, the willow heavy in the humidity, the sky inky and deep and clouded, so that only one star was visible, an American flag billowing majestically against the blackness of the night from the rail of the balcony. He felt abundantly satisfied. Even his estrangement from the group was—in a sense—a relief, despite—in another sense—their silence—especially Trent's—being such a betrayal.

The thing that surprised him most was how little their absence bothered him. It seemed there should have been a bigger sense of grief or loss. As time wore on, the idea that he might never see his friends again began to creep into his mind, and though the thought was awful, it was hardly unbearable.

That should have made him sadder than it did.

"Why didn't you tell me?"

He jumped in surprise, then saw Trent, in a long pair of navy shorts, standing at the top of the stairs that led to the beach. "How did you know I was here?" He could think of nothing else to say.

"You live here." Trent crossed so that he stood over him. "Why didn't you tell me?"

He wasn't prepared. "I don't know. I didn't know how you'd react." He'd wanted them to come, but he hadn't imagined what he'd say when they did.

"Do you want to know how it is from my side?" Trent asked. "Do you want to know how *I* see it?"

Kyle looked at the drawn face of his best friend, surprised how good it was to have him there, and suddenly realizing how much he'd miss him if ever they were separated.

He nodded.

"From my side it looks like either you didn't love me enough to tell me or you didn't believe I loved you enough to get past it. And this past week all I've been trying to figure out is which would hurt less."

Kyle almost crumpled. What could he say to *that?*

In the distance a premature firecracker popped and echoed.

"I know you better than anyone," Trent said. "Did you really think I would turn from you?"

"I don't know!" Kyle said quickly. "...I was afraid."

"We made it through Dana's broken heart, and Carly's mom's affair, and my parents almost getting divorced, and Carly finding out she's adopted. It was only a matter of time until it was you or Claudia. Only, this time, since it's you, I'm afraid you'll change."

"*I've* always known. This isn't a surprise to me. I'm more me than I've ever been." But Kyle had to wonder if that was true. He'd changed since he'd arrived on the island. Knowing the truth hadn't prepared him for accepting and dealing with it.

He sensed that no matter what happened that summer he was going to lose something he loved dearly.

"Wouldn't it have been easier if you hadn't had to live with it alone?" Trent asked.

"It wasn't a burden. Until Jack."

"What *is* it about that boy?"

Kyle suddenly beamed. "It's so cracked. He's everything. Everything you hear about in songs and read about in books. If a thousand dreamers dreamed a thousand years, they couldn't have conceived of something so extraordinary. I knew the moment I saw him." He grinned at his giggly words, then became serious. "He's the sun."

"So all you've been doing is martyring yourself, armed with the clichés everyone else in the entire history of the world has already endured thinking they're exclusive to you."

"For once someone likes me best. Why is that so hard for you?"

"For Christ's sake. Everyone always likes you best."

Kyle was so surprised by how true Trent's words rang that he just looked at him. He could see the seventh-grade rugby player, the boarding-school bad boy, the heart-breaking scoundrel in the man who stood across from him, but he couldn't recognize the man. He couldn't find Trent. He looked so old. So ... adult. How could he have changed so much without Kyle noticing? A familiar stranger had taken the place of his best friend.

"You know what's always bothered me most?" Trent asked, smiling the saddest smile Kyle'd ever seen. "People think I'm stronger than you. But you don't need anyone. I've always needed you. And you've never needed me for anything." He gave a short, humorless laugh. "Not even after Kevin."

Kyle was horrified to know that that was how Trent perceived him.

"And whether you didn't trust me or need me or both… It just makes me realize where I must stand," Trent concluded.

And then Kyle was furious. He was so enraged he was shaking. "You even doubting that I need you breaks my heart," he seethed.

Trent smiled, satisfied, point made. "Now you know what I've lived with for eighteen years." He turned and descended the stairs to the beach, leaving Kyle with the dark roar of the surf and the dry jerking flap of the flag in the wind.

Normally Kyle and his parents spent Independence Day with the group and their families. After the confrontation with Claudia, however, Kyle had requested they do it with only Jack's family that summer. Ann seemed to take the solicitation with relief, like she had tired of entertaining years ago yet had said nothing. Her attempt to play down her alleviation came in the form of a feeble gesture of justification. "We'll see them all at the fireworks."

It turned out, though, that Jack's parents were taking part in the Independence Day aquatic parade that circled the island. Boat owners started from the marina in town and circumnavigated the entire island in a long line of yachts and speed and pontoon boats. So Jack came over alone that day with a package of hot dogs, joining Kyle, who was making macaroni salad, and Ann, who was forming hamburger patties, in the kitchen.

"What's wrong?" was the first thing he said, addressing Kyle. He gave the dogs to Ann, who placed them on a tray beside the hamburgers.

"Nothing." Kyle spoke without a smile. He had hoped to tell Jack the details in private. "I'm golden."

"No," Jack said from the opposite side of the counter, "you're not." His silk shirt, in the pattern of an American flag, rippled gently about him in the breeze from the ocean.

"Kyle's always chosen such outspoken friends." Ann gave Jack a hot flash of concern. She, too, of course, had noticed Kyle's mood.

"That's because we're used to getting what we want," Kyle said, insolent.

"At least you boys have passion." Ann placed a hamburger patty on the top of a pyramid she was creating. "That's what makes you stand apart from your peers."

"Thanks for the moving comparison," Kyle said dryly.

"'A boy's will is the wind's will.'" Her job done, she went outside to light the grill, taking along the platter of meat, not risking another look at Jack.

Kyle dried his hands on a dish towel, then leaned against the sink and crossed his arms over his chest before relating the story. Jack listened without interrupting.

"I'm afraid I'll see him tonight," Kyle concluded. "And I won't have decided what to do." He smiled. "At least you'll be with me."

"Carrying you if I have to."

The phone rang and they looked at each other, both thinking it might be Trent.

When Kyle answered, his disappointment and relief were visible when he said, "Hi, Trey."

Jack giggled and popped a piece of gum in his mouth, then went to lie on the sofa, legs over the arm closest to Kyle.

"I was wondering if you might want to hang out at the fireworks tonight," Trey said. "You are going, aren't you?"

"Um, well, actually we're not sure yet. We might be going out on Jack's parents' boat to watch them from the water."

"Oh. Okay. Um."

Nothing.

"But have a great Independence Day," Kyle said.

"Um... Is Jack there now?"

"Yes, Trey. He is." Kyle knew he sounded as exasperated as he was. "Which means I really can't talk."

"You really like him, huh?"

Kyle looked at Jack, who had propped himself up on his elbows, legs still over the arm of the sofa, blowing a big, pink bubble. Kyle couldn't help but beam. "Yeah. A lot."

"Okay," Trey said, and it was apparent he was pulling from his reserves. "I guess I might see you tonight if you come to the park."

"Okay."

"Um. Bye."

"Bye."

Jack stood and went over to Kyle who was hanging up. "He wanted to meet you at the fireworks?"

"Yeah. Can you believe it?" He put his hands on Jack's hips. "Now we have that to look forward to, too." He glanced past Jack to where his parents stood by the shore, the grill forsaken for the moment, watching a string of boats glide by, flags flittering in the breeze. Then he turned back to Jack, leaned in and kissed him once, twice, and then once again.

They joined Kyle's parents by the water and watched the boats float past in the brightness of the sun, waving at the people they knew. When Jack's parents came into view, Sheridan blew his horn, and they on the beach cheered. Violet flapped her hand, shielding her eyes from the sun.

And then they lost interest in the parade and turned to the food.

After lunch, when Ann and Graham went into the water, Jack stood near the willow, hands in the pockets of his white breeches, observing.

"I can't believe you have a flag shirt." Kyle came up behind him with a smile. "What? You get it out once a year?"

"Sometimes I get it out for Flag Day, too."

Kyle pulled his shirt off over his head. "Comin' in?"

"You think if you ask me smoothly you might fool me in?"

Kyle smiled. "My goal is to get you in before summer's over."

"Never happen," Jack said simply, watching Graham dive into an oncoming wave.

"Not even if I'm there to save you?"

"It's not about drowning, Kyle."

And with that he dismissed the entire topic.

The park at the center of town was crowded when they arrived at dusk, the scents of brine and beer and burgers carrying over the sea of people. Kyle, Jack, Ann and Graham made their way through the multitude, overstepping feet and drinks, touching the edges of cotton and quilted blankets. They passed an old man who sat on a wooden folding chair watching his son and daughter and their families ignore him. A young girl ran by with a sparkler, her cheeks puffed in excitement. From the pavilion on the hill came the sounds of an orchestra.

Finding a spot near the baseball diamond, Kyle and Graham spread out their blanket.

"We'll never find anyone in this crowd," Ann sighed, not too regretfully, as she settled in, her white sundress tucked beneath her legs.

"Oh, I wouldn't bet on that," Jack said. "My mother could find Amelia Earhart if she put her mind to it."

As if she'd been waiting in the wings, Violet alighted. Behind her stood Sheridan with a cooler. Kyle felt tendrils of anxiety tickle his stomach.

It was so important their parents got along.

"You have a beautiful boat," Ann said after introductions had been made.

"We'll have to have you all out on it sometime." Sheridan passed out bottles of beer as he spoke.

"We'd love it," Graham said.

"It's been a real pleasure having Kyle around this summer." Violet fanned herself with a hand. "In fact, we've seen so much of him, I'm surprised we haven't met before now."

"It's been sort of a quiet summer," Ann said.

Speak for yourself, Kyle thought.

"We haven't seen our friends much this year," Ann continued.

"Actually," Graham said. "They're all supposed to be here tonight, so we'd love for you to join us later up at the pavilion if you have no other plans."

"Please do," Ann said. "They have music and dancing and drinks."

"Sounds like my kind of place." Sheridan turned to Kyle and Jack. "Where are all of your friends?"

The first firework exploded and the crowd oohed collectively, saving Kyle from having to respond. He looked over to see Jack's face lit up with red, white and blue confetti. Jack smiled at him, placing his hand on the blanket so their little fingers touched.

Fireworks screamed and glittered overhead. Neon oranges and golds and reds painted the blackness from an electric rainbow palette. Silvers and violets and blues flashed and shimmered. Silent sparks rocketed into the dome of black sky above their upturned faces before exploding into brilliant flowers of whistling pinks and greens and whites, attacking the dark with booms and cracks and screes, wavering above them like charged specters before fading into dullness. The sky glimmered and danced and glowed in a glory of ephemeral sequins, lighting the eyes and throats and visages of the onlookers, who were as comfortable as a whole as they would not be again until the following year.

And when it was over, the night seemed darker than it had.

They sat for a moment before Jack said, "It's always so dazzling, but it's always so brief."

As the consequential smoke began drifting over them like regret, Ann prompted them with, "Shall we head up to the pavilion?"

The pavilion was crowded and warm, the scents of spirits and cigarettes, beer and bodies commingling. Picnic tables had been set up along three sides of the floor. On the remaining side, a stage had been erected atop of which sat an orchestra that was playing *America, the Beautiful*. This left the center of the floor open for dancing.

Immediately Graham saw, among the throng of people, Trent's and Claudia's parents, who had reserved seats for them. Neither Trent nor Claudia was with them.

Alice Santangelo waved them over, her long, narrow arms dark with freckles and the sun. As he approached, Kyle felt guilty. He'd seen Trent's parents so irregularly that summer he felt like a betrayer being with them then, after the fight.

"Trent and Claudia are off with Carly and Dana," Claudia's mother said, after introductions were made.

"Great." Kyle determined they knew nothing about the argument. "Maybe we'll run into them."

"I think they went to the gazebo," Trent's father said, unaware that meant they'd be smoking a joint.

Kyle and Jack sat down, but Kyle couldn't relax with the threat of Trent's return hanging over them. And observing the adults made him feel wistful. Graham came to the island less frequently. Ann had faded. Dana's parents had grown too old. Carly's too rich.

The force that had drawn them together was ebbing.

"Let's get outta here."

Kyle felt Jack's warm breath tickle his ear from behind, his silk patriotism whispering coolly against his skin. "You ready?"

"Yeah."

"You don't want to dance or drink or something?"

"I wanna get out of here."

Kyle grinned. "Why the rush?"

"Because you're not happy."

Had they been alone, Kyle would have kissed him. Instead, they stood and he leaned in over Mrs. Santangelo. "We're gonna go beat up some eight-year-olds for their sparklers."

They all laughed. Trent's mother touched his hand and said, "Oh, you."

"Actually, we're gonna head home."

"So soon?" Ann queried, and Kyle wondered if she weren't envious.

"I can get you guys some beer," Sheridan offered, half standing, waiting for the command.

"Thanks," Kyle said. "But we'll take a rain check."

"It's awfully early. We've hardly seen you all summer." Claudia's mother looked up at them hopefully.

Kyle hadn't realized they might miss him, too. "We're sorta tired. We'll probably just hang out at home, then go to bed." He looked at his mother. "Don't worry. I'll leave the porch light on. And we'll be careful of deer."

She smiled at him for teasing her.

The night was less oppressive once they left the lights of the pavilion. Most of the mob had dispersed, but there were still scattered groups lingering on the lawn. Children wrote their names in the air with sparklers, shooting stars captured for their fleeting felicity. The strings of the orchestra chased fireflies on the softness of the night. Firecrackers popped and boomed periodically from all over the island.

On their way out of the park, Kyle decided to stop at the restroom, leaving Jack to wait outside. The bathrooms were dark and dank and smelled pungently of urine and stale cigarettes.

Kyle went into one of the stalls, holding the door shut with his foot. Graffiti was hardly legible in the dimness, but one inscription stood out, big block letters in red magic marker: *V.B. gives V.D.* And below that, though he had to lean in to discern the black ballpoint, were the words, *And good head.*

He wondered if *V.B.* weren't Veronica Blythe.

He felt sorry for her.

Outside, Trey and an island kid stood in shadow, watching Jack clean his glasses, looking lonely, awkward, sorry. His visible surprise at their presence when he put them back on caused Trey a flicker of bitter satisfaction. A scintilla of electricity flashed between them.

Trey motioned to the kid and they crept forward.

"Hi," Jack said to Trey, appealing.

Trey didn't respond.

"Whatcha doin'?" the kid asked. He had dirty blond hair and a dirtier sneer.

"Waiting on a friend."

They glared at Jack, challenging. "Nice shirt," the kid hissed then, maliciously spiteful. There was something menacing in his demeanor, like he was looking for a fight, not because he was angry, not because he was drunk, but simply because he wanted to hurt something.

A slight coloring rose from Jack's chest to his neck. He swallowed, but didn't respond. "Like the fireworks?" he said instead to Trey.

Trey didn't rejoin.

The three stood for many moments, Trey feeling shining in comparison to Jack's dullness. He couldn't get his mind around the idea that someone as homely as Jack was touching Kyle in ways that Trey felt should be only his. A jolt of painful jealousy tore through him. "Why don't you go find your *boyfriend?*" he spat. In his words there was no implication of Kyle's sexuality, only that Jack was a sissy.

Jack inhaled slowly, with pain, as though something heavy had expanded in his chest. The kid took a quick step toward him, one hand outstretched as if to hit, and Jack flinched. The kid laughed, liking his power. The skin on Jack's cheek began stuttering. He reached up and touched his spectacles, smudging them, but did not remove them. Trey could see him despising them with a white purity, wishing he could throw them, break them, stamp on them.

Then they heard the flushing of a toilet. Trey and the kid stepped back. The kid pointed at Jack with an angry look, as if warning that he wasn't finished. They had completely receded into shadow again by the time Kyle came out, wiping his hands on his shorts.

From the dark, it leveled Trey to see the easy way Kyle touched Jack's hip, and his insolence gave way to anguish.

"You ready?" Kyle asked Jack.

Jack looked wearily into the dark, reached to remove his glasses, then stopped, there being no point. "Yeah."

The crowd in the pavilion had thinned. The orchestra was playing a slow, yearning summer song. Trent and Dana approached Trent's parents, Claudia's mother and Graham. They were flushed and smiling when they got to the table.

"We're heading to the beach." Trent wondered how stoned he looked.

"Kyle and Jack are at home," Graham said. "You might want to stop and see if they'd like to join you."

"He'll know where we are," Trent said.

Dana hung back, saying nothing.

"Trent." Graham turned to look up at his son's best friend. "I just wanted to let you know we've seen a big improvement in Kyle. He seems much better. Not like he used to be, but he's getting there. Thank you."

Trent wasn't particularly prepared for that, drunk and stoned as he was. His jealousy at no longer being the most important person in Kyle's life had been tempered by the marijuana, but Graham's sentiment brought it about in searing pinpoints in his chest. "That's great, Mr. Quinn," he said. "Fucking great. You might want to thank Jack for that, though. I didn't have any luck."

And he walked away.

Kyle drove the speed limit on the way home.

Jack was quiet.

He let Kyle hold his hand.

Once they were at Kyle's, Kyle turned on one of the lights in the living room. Jack stood in the center of the room, numb with shame.

"You okay?" Kyle asked, going to stand before him. He took Jack's hands into his own. Jack was trying to not cry, his eyes the frosty gray-blue of water just beginning to solidify. He didn't look at Kyle, instead gazing past him to the dark, pregnant sea. "You really don't like my shirt?" he asked almost inaudibly.

"Puss, that's not what I meant. I was only teasing. I thought you were teasing back. Flag Day and all."

"Really?"

"Of course. Jack, are you all right? Did you want to stay at the park?"

"No. Of course not." He finally looked to Kyle. "I'm glad we're alone."

Kyle didn't understand, so he put his arms around him, inhaling his scent of sandalwood, his tiny body smooth and cool and fragile and trembling. He said simply, "I love your shirt," into his hair.

They began spending less time at their lagoon because of the privacy the McAllister house afforded. They lay on their exclusive beach, letting the sun bleach their hair, turn their bodies brown as savages', their spirits easy. Jack waded, Kyle swam. They spent hours kissing—sometimes ardently, sometimes languorously.

One cool day, they boiled water in the fireplace and Kyle shaved Jack with his straight razor out on the porch, gray rain falling in a mist. Both of them shirtless, Jack sat in one of the wrought-iron chairs. Kyle stood behind, pulling the blade through the bristle of Jack's beard in long, slow, smooth strokes. It was the most erotic thing either of them would ever do.

They slept naked, spooned, on their right sides, Kyle behind, left arm around Jack, their fingers laced, as though each feared the other might disappear in the night.

They had no way of marking time there, so they took a big wind-up clock and set it on the wrought-iron table on the porch. Its ticking was so loud that Kyle could be standing in the kitchen at the opposite end of the house and still hear the minutes elapsing. It made him nervous. He found himself having nightmares about an empty house with a clock deep in its heart, counting down the days, the hours, the minutes, until September. He would run from room to room, searching for the secret door that would reveal the house's innards, that would allow him to still the clock, to stop time, to attain peace. He would find wristwatches, pocket watches, chronographs and metronomes, on tables, in drawers, behind doors, but it was never the one he sought. Eventually, he would find himself frantic, suffocating from the pressure of the time slipping away, the ticking coming faster and faster, louder and louder, and he'd awaken with a start just as the air in the house ran out and the ticking ceased, and he would get up and bury the clock under as many pillows as were free and put the entire pile on the stairs. And once he was back in bed, snuggled up next to Jack, he would wonder if what he heard was still the clock or only the harried beat of his heart.

One bleak, warm day the color of pewter, they rode their bikes to the center of the island to a majestic hill. Covered in purple myrtle, it sprawled toward the ashen sky, an amethyst in a prison. Dandelions dotted the hillside, their bright suns contrasting with the violet resplendence. Jack let his bike fall to the side of the path, his mouth agape.

"I knew you'd love it," Kyle said. "We call it the magic mountain."

They ran up the hill, through the myrtle, bees and butterflies flitting about, oblivious. At the top, the clouds were nearer and bigger and more tangible than they had ever been. The wind whistled around them, through their hair, in their ears and clothes.

"I feel like I'm touching infinity!" Jack exclaimed. He fell into the flowers, the gray blanketing him, and plucked a dandelion. Kyle lay beside him, looking into his face, at the sandy stubble of beard, the lips, puffy and chafed from endless kissing hours, purple petals clinging to his disheveled hair. With the dandelion stalk, Jack drew a milky, sticky streak across Kyle's cheek. Kyle caught the stem in his mouth, and they looked into each other, then Kyle kissed him, leisurely and deeply, for what seemed like minutes, but might have been hours, before he lay again at his side.

Jack grinned, then laughed. "This isn't real!" he called to the heavens, suddenly so close.

"We're the only thing that's real," Kyle said. "You and me."

Then Jack turned serious. "Why me, Kyle?"

"That's like asking why the sky is blue!"

"But there's an answer to that!"

"It's everything, Puss. Your smile and your glasses and your camera and your superstitions. How you breathe into me when we kiss. The way you say my name. It's your spirit. Your chemistry. Music sounds different since you. You make me feel immortal. I always had a golden life, but now…now I have a golden future again. I can never be alone again." His thumb stroked Jack's cheek. "Don't ever forsake me, Jack," he said. "I'd waste away for want of you."

"Oh, Kyle… Sometimes I believe that. But sometimes, when I'm alone, or after you've fallen asleep…sometimes I start to wonder what will happen when we get to the real world. And sometimes I wonder if you only think you love me because I'm here, now. And sometimes I'm just plain afraid to be happy, because the happier I am now the more painful it will be later, and

I know I'm insecure but I can't help it because I don't want someone to steal you away just because they think you're beautiful."

Kyle was surprised by the sudden turn of emotion, but he smiled. "How did you get to be so insecure?"

"I'm always insecure. I'm just usually too insecure to show it."

"You're cracked. Do you actually think someone can steal me away when I don't want to be stolen? What can I do to prove I'm yours? I give up everything to you." He held his hands up to show he was defenseless.

Jack took one of them and kissed his knuckles. "I'm just not used to being adored, I guess."

"I worry about losing *you*. People will fight me for you."

"Quinn."

And then Kyle's voice was soft. "I'm afraid because people go away. Even people who say they won't."

"Kyle."

"Then I wonder if I'm just a diversion. Or that I won't be enough." He smiled, trying to make light of his feared impotence. "But I don't know how to be more than I am."

Jack gave a mock-anguished-but-brave smile. "Whatever will we do?"

But Kyle was still serious, and he was driven. "We've got to start making plans. I'm going to withdraw from Princeton and go with you to Michigan."

"What! Maybe I don't want you to drop out!" Jack protested. "Princeton is a better school."

"Which is why I wouldn't have a problem getting into Michigan."

"Kyle."

"Jack."

And then Jack was moving, rolling so that he was on top of Kyle. Kyle, surrounded by violet blossoms, held Jack's hair back to reveal the moon of his face and the arc of his neck, that amazing, elegant neck. Then Jack was lowering his face so they could breathe into each other again. "How I love when you don't shave," he murmured into Kyle's mouth.

He thought about his brother a lot those days because he was the same age Kevin had been when he'd killed himself.

Sometimes he'd walk around the beach house, looking at the fireplace, or the view from the deck, or the bedroom they had shared, and wonder what Kevin had thought, felt, when he'd looked at the same things, knowing it was for the last time. How could he have been so insensitive as to go to a place where his loved ones would find him? And why leave such an enigmatic note? What sort of blackness led to that?

He pondered those questions, but he felt detached, like it hadn't happened to his brother, or to him, but to someone in a movie he hadn't even enjoyed very much.

Then he would turn his thoughts to Jack, who washed clean all things tainted.

One day Kyle and Jack ran into Carly downtown. The meeting was a little awkward as Kyle hadn't realized how ensconced they'd been until he saw her. It made him see how much things had changed in the past couple of weeks. He and Jack were practically one. He was nowhere near the person Carly had known. He was so different he was surprised she recognized him.

They looked at each other almost warily, unsure after the initial hellos. Then Jack said, "I'm going to run to the supermarket."

Kyle touched his hand. "We're gonna get some ice cream."

When they were seated with malts, Kyle looked across the table at her like she was a substitute teacher. He normally shared so much time with his friends over the summer he was unable to detect changes, but right then he could see how much lighter her hair was, how much deeper her tan. And there were more subtle differences he couldn't pinpoint.

"So," she said, the skin on her nose peeling. "Tell me what you've been doing."

"God." He grinned, looked away, then back again. How could he express how happy he was? "I've been so busy, but there really aren't any stories."

She sipped her malt. "It's always more about the little things that make up the days than about the days."

Behind her, against the back wall, a girl with a strawberry blond ponytail dropped coins into a jukebox. A moment later the melancholy sounds of *When the Wind Was Green* began.

"So what's up with you?" he asked. He craved a cigarette, and it took him a while to realize it was because he wasn't comfortable. He didn't ask if he could bum one.

"My father's thinking of taking us to Brazil for the second half of the summer."

"Carly! What did you say? That you couldn't because it was your last summer on the island before college?"

"Oh, you," she said, almost coquettishly. "I'm sentimental, but this is Brazil for Christ's sake. Besides—you wouldn't even notice I was gone." She said it only because it was true and, seeing that it was, for the most part, Kyle didn't dispute it. He averted his eyes.

"Veronica's coming around a lot," Carly said. "I can't believe she thinks Trent will marry her. I mean, it's rather apparent he wants to be a playboy when he grows up."

They smiled at each other, understanding, then Kyle asked, "How's Dana?" and as soon as it was out he felt queer. They'd never been separated for so long that he'd needed to inquire after one of them before.

"She's fine. We're having a great summer. You should come around. You could bring Jack." She fluttered her hands. "Or not. I mean, that never seems to work out. You know?"

"Yeah. None of us like that."

He remembered the summer Carly told them she'd seen her mother with another man in the city. She hadn't confronted her. She, in fact, never mentioned it to her. But it clouded the way she, and the group, looked at Iris Salenger. They had been fourteen, and it had bothered Carly more than she or they might have anticipated. She became quieter. She withdrew.

And none of them had looked at their parents the same way again.

Kyle wondered if they'd be able to look at each other the same way after that summer.

They finished their malts and went out into the sticky, still air. Carly turned to him. "We—" she started. Then, "I guess I'll see you around."

"Yeah."

They embraced, and for the first time it was forced and, hence, awkward.

Trey was in town that day, and when Jack came out of the supermarket, he literally ran into him. Trey looked at him, fully, expressionlessly, unwilling to give. Then he went to step beyond him, but Jack wouldn't allow it. "What's the matter with you?" he demanded.

"You got in my way," Trey said. "I tried to go around you. What did you expect me to do?"

"Why do you keep bothering Kyle?" Jack was strident.

"I'm not 'bothering' Kyle."

"I don't care what you do or say to me, but Kyle is off limits. Why don't you just leave us alone?"

"Because!" Trey suddenly shouted. "I'm supposed to be there!"

"*Where?*"

"With Kyle! With all of them. I was here first and you took my place."

Jack looked at him like he was a bright tenth grader who'd misspelled his own name. "I couldn't take your place, Trey. Because you never had one."

Trey's face crumbled, slowly, like resignation. Then he cut back with vicious contempt. "You're not their type." He saw the dagger slash effectively, the ends of his lips, usually turned up in a hopelessly sensual way, set in a malicious nongrin. He was sorry as soon as he'd spoken, but he was also glad.

Jack suddenly looked very tired. "If you mean I'm not beautiful enough," he said with just enough conviction to convince Trey he was trying, "it's not about beauty."

He turned away, and the breeze rushed past him into Trey's open face.

The next day when Violet took Sheridan to the hospital on the mainland for a checkup, Jack took Kyle sailing. Kyle had been on the boat several times, but never with Jack at the helm. As the golden thread of the shore disappeared and Jack brought the boat to a standstill, Kyle stepped away from the rail and went to stand behind him at the wheel, sliding his arms around his waist, placing his chin on his shoulder, fitting into him. "My little sailor," he said, proud.

"You're feeling amorous *now*?"

"I like when you're in control."

They laughed, and Jack turned into him, and they laughed some more, and then they were kissing.

After Jack dropped anchor, they lay without speaking, the late morning sun so hot and relentless that even with their eyes shut they couldn't block its glare. Their bodies grew oily; waves lapped woodenly against the boat; the sun and the sway of the water lulled them into lethargy.

They lay like that for a long while before Kyle decided to tell Jack about Kevin. He had never disclosed the story to anyone. The people who knew, knew. But he didn't tell. He didn't want there to be secrets with Jack, though. And Kevin was the only secret he had. And his truth was not something Kyle wanted to hide from.

He sat up and looked over to Jack. "There's something I have to tell you," he said decisively.

"Mmm?" Jack's eyes remained closed to the dazzle of the sun.

"It's about Kevin."

"Is he the love of your life who will haunt you forever?"

"No," Kyle said. "He was my brother." The breeze coming off the ocean was warm. "He killed himself."

Jack sat up.

And Kyle told him. When he was done, he reached for the ring that hung around his neck. "When I found him—I took this."

"From his body?"

Kyle fixed his gaze past Jack to where he imagined the island was. "Yeah."

"No wonder it's so important to you." Jack took the ring from Kyle's fingers and turned it so the *K* faced up. "And the *K* stands for Kevin." Goose bumps dotted his body.

"I wore it for a long time before my parents found out. My mom was pretty upset because they had looked for it, wanting to bury him with it. They decided it was my way of dealing with my grief. Which, I suppose, it was." He thought, his lips pursed, then nodded, to himself, and lay back on his deck chair. "Remember that song I told you about? Prince Kyle? Well, I was prince because Kevin was king." He reflected for a moment. "I've been thinking about that a lot lately."

Jack continued to look over at Kyle. After many moments, he lay back and said, "I guess that means you're king now."

The following week, on the veranda of the McAllister house, Kyle sat beside a slumbering Jack. He had found him in the attic earlier, looking through boxes of old photographs. "These have really sucked me in," he'd said. "I've been pondering the McAllister's secrets. Do you ever wonder what your parents' secrets are?"

"No," Kyle had replied, cavalier. "They have none."

"I could be one of yours someday."

"Jack. Never."

Jack gave him an open, soulful look. "But, Kyle, I already am."

Kyle hadn't been able to disregard the truth in Jack's words, and they had stuck with him. Just as he hadn't wanted Kevin to be a secret from Jack, he was ashamed that Jack was one he kept from his parents. He was coming to understand that he couldn't be free until his parents knew.

"Kyle?"

The voice came from inside the house. He gave a start. Jack hadn't awakened. Kyle jumped up and went to find Dana in the living room. She gave a self-conscious smile and pushed hair behind an ear. "Hi."

He sighed visibly. "Dana. I thought we'd been caught or something."

"Sorry. I wasn't sure where you were."

"We—" He gestured in the direction of the veranda. "We spend most of our time out there. It's, um, cooler." He had that springlike, fresh-fucked glow and a look of dazed, stuporous bliss and wondered if she could tell.

"Are you free?" she ventured.

"For what?" He was still surprised she was even there.

She smiled nervously. "Just to talk?"

Uhhhh… "Sure."

They sat on the sofa.

"I don't know what you've been thinking, but I want you to know what's going on." She was direct. "None of us care about you and Jack. In fact, it's better. It's okay to trade us in for someone you love, you know? Do you understand that?"

"Yeah," he said, just then realizing it. "Actually, I do."

"We were all shocked, but after it sunk in, we realized: everything makes sense."

"Do they know you're here?"

"No. I'm going to tell them tonight. We've been talking about it a lot, but we didn't know what to do. We were afraid you were angry. But we want you to come back. With Jack."

"Now that he's not a threat."

"Well, yeah. We're not in love with you." She gave a nervous laugh but didn't smile. Then she leaned in close and whispered, "Is he here?"

"He's sleeping."

She sat back, seemingly content with the response. "I guess I should say this, too."

"What?"

"You're going to have to understand that we're accepting and all, but it's going to be strange."

"I know."

"Because you're who you are and we've known you for so long—you know—it's like Jack's cool, no big deal, but with you—wow! With you we have to adjust. We have to resign ourselves to the fact that we can't have you."

She gave such a forced laugh Kyle wondered how long she'd rehearsed the line.

She cocked her head. "What's that sound?"

He listened for a second. "That's the clock."

"It's like the fucking Tell-Tale Heart."

Kyle forced his own laugh, then, trying to sound casual, asked, "How's Trent?"

Dana gave him an uneasy look. "He hasn't really been part of these conversations. He told us you had a fight."

"Yeah." Kyle didn't know if he was more nervous to find Trent hated him or that the girls knew what had transpired between them. It had been so raw, he still felt a tender blistering when he thought about it.

"He's been really moody," Dana said. "When he's around, that is."

"Where's he been?"

"Alone, I guess."

"Should I call him?" No, he shouldn't, and he didn't want to, and he couldn't believe he'd asked.

"I don't know. I don't know how the fight went."

That was one good thing.

"He's finally gotten Veronica talked into it."

223

"It?"

"The abortion."

Kyle put a hand to his hairline. "Christ."

"I wish it hadn't come to this," Dana said.

He wondered if she meant Veronica or himself.

Then they heard Jack in the entranceway. Dana stood. "Did we awaken you?"

Jack rubbed his eyes with balled-up fists like a child. "I hadn't meant to nap so long." He had a bit of sleep in the inner corner of his left eye.

"I should be going." Dana smiled down at Kyle, then over to Jack.

"Don't go on account of me," Jack said.

"No, no." She approached him, and she was only a little hesitant in reaching out her hand to take his. "Um." She took a deep breath and a small step back. "Kyle can explain, but we'd like you to join us." For a second it appeared she was going to hug him, and Kyle was so surprised he almost laughed, but then she stepped away.

"I'm glad you stopped by," Kyle said.

"I am, too." She smiled. "It needed to be done."

When she was gone, Jack leaned against the doorframe, his arms crossed. "What was that?"

"That was Dana Being Big."

"Was she for real?"

"Yeah. Can you believe it? The girls are okay with us. Or so they think."

"The girls?"

Kyle looked out the picture window. He could see the cloud of dust Dana's car had kicked up.

"He needs time, Kyle."

Kyle nodded, his gaze on the mulberry tree.

He was still sitting there, focused on it but not seeing it, when Jack went back to the porch and headed down to the water to splash himself awake, the screen door slamming in his wake.

He went to see her that night. Her street was hushed and mild in the humid early evening. When he brought the convertible to a stop in her driveway, he saw where he'd fallen. The demon that had terrorized him was not there.

When he climbed the steps to the front door, instead of knocking, and not knowing what he expected or hoped for, he crept to the side railing. On the trellis, the moonflowers were open and glowing like wraiths. The house next door was dark and quiet, its windows open to the tenderness of summer. He was surprised at his disappointment. Her presence would have soothed him.

He returned to the door and rapped on it, peering through the screen, surprised to find the house as neat as it was, not knowing why he'd anticipated that it would be slovenly.

Then Veronica appeared, drying her hands on a dish towel. "Kyle!" she exclaimed. "Hey!"

"Hey."

She looked at him expectantly through the screen door.

"You wanna take a walk?" he offered.

Neither of them spoke again until they were on the sidewalk. "Why are you here?" she asked then, and her voice was soft in the stillness of the neighborhood.

Why was he there? He hadn't bothered to wonder why. And he suddenly wished he could take it back. Finally he said, "I don't know."

"Did Trent send you?" Like Kyle, earlier that day, when he'd also asked of Trent, she was unable to mask the yearning in her voice.

"No. He doesn't know I'm here."

Her shoulders fell as hope fled.

"How are you?" he asked. He didn't know what else to say.

"Not good. How about you?"

They had come to the end of the block and turned the corner before he settled on a response. "It's been an odd summer." He could think of no other way of summing it up.

"You're telling me."

They walked in a comfortable silence, until, at the next corner, she sighed heavily. "Is there a purpose?"

He sighed, too, but his was thinner. All he could think to say was, "I'm sorry."

"For what?"

"For it all, I guess. The fact that you're getting a shitty deal. That you fell in love with someone who treats you like this."

She gave him a small, sad smile. "I could always tell you were the nice one. Jack's lucky to have a boy like you."

He smiled at her, sickly, his heart lurching. It was startling to hear someone outside his circle reference his relationship with Jack. "How—how do you know…?"

"Kyle. Come on."

Oh.

"We've got it scheduled for next week."

Again with the "it." "Do you think you're making the right choice?"

"I didn't realize I had one. I'm not going to raise a child on my own. I don't even have a car."

"Where are you getting it done?"

"A guy on the other side of the island."

"He's not even taking you into the city?"

"This guy's okay."

He wanted to say he was sorry again but realized how limp it was. Once they turned the next corner, he said, "Do you hate him?"

"Hate him?" She was incredulous. "If I hated him I'd have the baby," she said colorlessly.

"What is it you see in him?"

She thought for a moment. "It's how he kisses you… It's like he means it."

Were they talking about the same person? Trent was the type of guy who would expect a girl to give him a blow job, come in her mouth, and then not even thank her, as he heedlessly and consciencelessly ripped her world apart.

But he said nothing. He didn't want her to justify herself. It would make him feel like he'd helped her rationalize it.

At the last corner, she stopped, and that was when he saw her eyes had become glassy. "Will you tell him I love him?" she asked dolefully.

He was shaken by how much he understood her despair. If things had gone another way with Jack… "Of course." The grace of God.

When they came to her house, she stopped again, not turning to him. "I'm glad you came by. I had part of him with me tonight." She patted her stomach. "Well, another part."

The next afternoon, the weather gray and humid, Kyle and Sheridan went to town to purchase food for a barbecue. When they were in line at the supermarket, Sheridan suggested that Kyle run up the street for ice cream. "Strawberry and mint should do. Maybe some butterscotch."

"And praline crunch for Jack," Kyle said. "It's his favorite." He figured he knew more about Jack than Jack's parents did.

He was halfway down the street when he heard his name. Glancing back, he saw no one. He was about to continue on when he heard it again.

Feeling foolish, he called out, "Hello?"

"Kyle, I'm down here."

He took a few steps back and that was when he became aware of an alley between a hardware store and a seafood restaurant. In the alley stood Trey in a pair of khaki shorts and a violet and yellow rugby shirt. He put out a hand as if to keep Kyle from bolting, or attacking. "Don't..."

"Don't what?" Kyle demanded. "Don't beat the shit out of you?" Almost enjoying himself, he stepped into the alley, hoping he appeared menacing.

"I want to apologize," Trey said. "We were friends before, and I—I don't know why I acted like I did. I'm sorry."

Kyle felt himself deflating. He supposed that meant there wasn't going to be a confrontation.

"I hadn't realized," Trey continued more quietly, "I was in love with you."

"We hardly know each other." Kyle regretted saying it immediately.

"I know." Trey nodded, eyes on the ground. "But I was really hurt by your rejection." He gave Kyle a wistful expression. "So...can we be friends?"

The plea held the dubious promise of heat lightning. But he did look repentant. And though it would have been fun to make him suffer, Kyle knew he wouldn't be troubled by him if they were on good terms. So when he spoke, he didn't look away so Trey couldn't. "I don't think we'll be friends, but now we won't be enemies either."

Trey had wanted more, but he accepted the terms. "Tell me. ...Do you love him?"

It felt good to say "Yes," because he knew Trey could not harm them. But he didn't delight as much as he'd anticipated in the slowly numbing look on Trey's face.

Then Sheridan stepped into the alley, two brown paper grocery bags in his arms. Kyle turned, ready to walk away, to spare Trey the dignity of introduction. But then he decided that an introduction would show Trey just how close he was to Jack. You weren't with someone's parents unless you were part of the family. So he turned back and presented Sheridan.

Trey was almost bashful. "Hi, Mr. Averill. We met at the Founder's Day dance."

"Yes," Sheridan said. "Nice to see you again."

"Same here." Trey gave a respectful nod.

"We'd better get back so Kyle can get this chicken on the grill."

Kyle turned to Sheridan. "Yes. We'd better. Trey distracted me, so I haven't gotten the ice cream yet."

As they headed down the sidewalk, Sheridan said, "What's that kid's story?"

"Oh, Mr. Averill," Kyle said with confidence. "He's not part of the story at all."

Sheridan nodded as if Kyle had confirmed something. "That's good. He's too pretty. People who are too pretty don't have character."

The next day, Kyle drove to the center of the island, where the roads were dusty and they were surrounded by farmland. He brought the car to a stop, then turned to Jack, both of them shirtless. "I'm going to teach you to drive," he pronounced.

"Now?"

"What better time?"

"Here?"

"What better place?" He grinned.

Jack grinned back and leaned over and kissed him on the lips, lingering, fingers on his chest. "You're right, as always."

Kyle hopped out of the car and ran around to the passenger side while Jack slipped behind the wheel. A farmer, far out in his field on a tractor, waved, and Kyle waved back, sliding to the middle of the seat, so his bare leg brushed Jack's. Jack put a hand on his thigh and squeezed, then turned the key in the ignition until there was a grinding noise. Kyle reached over and clutched his hand. "It's already running, Puss."

Jack cocked his brows. "And so the lesson begins."

Kyle kicked off by explaining the gas pedal and the brake, how to signal, and how to adjust the mirrors, before moving on to the dashboard. "The speedometer is connected to a coaxial cable," he began. "Inside the coaxial cable is a hose that's connected to the transmission—"

Jack clasped his hand. "Love, I don't need to know how it works."

"Doesn't that help you understand?"

"The second you said 'coaxial cable' I completely dropped out of the conversation."

"But if you don't know how it works, who's going to fix my car?" he teased.

When the tutorial was complete, Jack had only one question. "Why can't I drive with both feet?"

"That's just the way it is."

"That's stupid." He put the car in gear and they started rolling forward, his right foot covering the gas pedal, his left, the brake. "Why not?" he shrugged. "It's more comfortable."

It took a few tries before he got the hang of braking, but as they passed through rolling farmland, he began to relax. He even began fiddling with the radio, though he never drove over 35. Kyle instructed him on how to make turns, reverse, and even how to pass a tractor. They waved at the farmer as they eclipsed him. The farmer honked and waved back.

Once they were clear, Kyle kissed Jack's silken shoulder. "You're doing great."

"Nothing to it."

The scintillating scent of Jack's warm, dry maleness surged immediately to Kyle's groin. His essence never failed to arouse him. He took his hand and put it over his own maleness. Jack whooped with surprise and grabbed his hand back. "I can't believe you distracted me with that!" he exclaimed joyously.

"Turn right at the next road. I want to have you out in the open."

They parked between two enormous fields of prospering goldenrod. Monarch and swallowtail butterflies meandered jerkily above the sea of gold, a shimmering palette of shifting oranges and blacks and yellows.

Before Jack could take the key out of the ignition, Kyle was kissing him. He grasped one of Jack's hands and placed it on his chest, over his heart, while angling back and leading with the other, spreading his legs, submitting. Jack reached down to liberate himself. Kyle caught his bottom lip between his teeth, grunting, as Jack, unfettered, positioned himself.

"It's all about you," Kyle panted, his breaths short and hot. "My beautiful Christopher Robin."

Jack breathed wetly, directly, into him, into his moist, wanting mouth, their chests sweaty and surging. "My golden king. The angels smiled on me the day we met."

"No, they smiled on me." Kyle beamed like a fool.

"Must you always argue?"

"I'm clarifying."

They laughed lustily.

Kyle had never felt so alive, so complete, so potent as he did in that moment, looking into the face of the boy he'd first seen sitting on that dune in his white. They took each other in, understanding, in a quiet moment of insight.

Then Kyle pulled Jack into him, their chests and abdomens and hips moving in a rhythm they'd conceived.

When they were spent, Jack lay his head on Kyle's heaving chest, and they were still. A monarch shuddered and trembled over their glowing, gratified bodies. They lay like that for so long, Kyle felt sleep closing in.

Then Jack breathed, "I wasn't real until you loved me, Kyle. I wasn't born until I came to this island."

Kyle kissed the fingers of his hand before moving to the underside of his wrist, his lips lingering on the sensitive flesh, the percolating code he had broken. "This is just purgatory," he murmured. "Our real life starts in September. That will be the pretty time."

They fell silent again, Jack's fingers on the flatness of Kyle's stomach. "I can hear your heartbeat." He hmmmed contentedly. "It makes me feel strong."

That night Kyle and Jack went to meet the girls for dinner at Claudia's. Insects bounced and danced around the porch light as Kyle knocked. Jack squeezed his hand. When the door opened, the first thing Claudia noticed was the fact that they were holding hands. Jack immediately dropped Kyle's and looked at her guiltily.

She gave a half-forced, half-sincere smile, but was unable to hide her surprise. "Don't worry," she said, regrouping. "We already know, remember?"

Jack smiled self-consciously, and Kyle found it endearing.

Claudia stepped back, letting Jack enter, and then she looked to Kyle. "Hi," she said uncertainly.

"Hi." He didn't smile.

"Do you hate me?"

"I don't know," he replied not untruthfully.

Before he could say anything else, she said, "I'm sorry," and she was.

He shook his head as though he could still hardly believe what a bitch she'd been. "You *were* relentless."

"Maybe I'm just as sentimental in my own way. And just as resistant to change."

He said nothing.

They hugged and it was clear their friendship would continue—albeit in a different form from what it had been.

"My parents are at Carly's," she said as they entered the dining room. Grape hyacinths sat in a vase on the table.

"But look what they left us." Dana held forth a golden key on the flats of both palms like it was the holy grail. It was the key to the liquor cabinet.

"Where're Trent and Carly?" Kyle asked, before remembering. "I mean—"

"Carly's in the kitchen," Dana said.

"Trent's probably with Trey," Claudia said superfluously.

Kyle couldn't suppress his surprise or hurt. He felt like he'd been pushed from a height on which he hadn't been aware he'd been standing. The girls looked at him and then away, verifying his nakedness.

"Trent's not 'probably' with Trey." Dana looked guilty, and Kyle wondered if that was because she had known about Trent and Trey the day she visited him at the McAllister house and had chosen to withhold the information. "Only possibly."

Kyle smiled, swallowing bile. "I'm going to join Carly in the kitchen."

&

Before dinner, Claudia gathered them in the living room. Curling her legs beneath her, she presented three thick joints. "The finest hemp in Havana," she said with a perfectly executed arch of her brows.

"We'll need it to enhance the flavor of the food," Carly said. "Because the three of us sure as hell can't cook."

Claudia lit one of the joints and passed it to Carly. When Carly went to pass it to Jack, he declined with the self-consciousness of someone who hadn't yet learned to accept a compliment.

"I've tried it before," he said. "It doesn't affect me."

"It always affects you." Kyle's stomach still roiled over the mention of Trey. "It just affects you in different ways."

Jack passed the joint to him, but when it came back around he said, "Okay, I'll try it."

"You'll be one of us yet," Claudia said supportively.

He took one drag and exhaled an enormous plume of smoke, suddenly gripped in a violent fit of coughing. Kyle held out his hand to take the joint so it wouldn't drop. Jack's face turned a ripe shade of violet before he was able to gain control. "I think I'm okay," he said through a close throat.

"You are so fucked," Carly said. "I wish I could take a hit like that."

As Dana took the joint from Kyle, she said, apropos of nothing, "Veronica's getting the abortion next week."

"I sort of think she should have it," Claudia said.

"The baby?" Carly asked.

"No, the tea party. Of course, the baby. Some people think of birth as an awakening."

"Yeah, well, some say that about death, too." Jack put a hand over his lips and sat back, giving covert, almost accusing glances at the others, his mouth dry as rust.

"You okay?" Kyle leaned in and whispered to him.

"My voice."

"What about it?"

"It sounds…stripped and bare and…I don't know. It's got a weird pitch. I'm not speaking anymore."

Kyle smiled warmly at him. "It's just the pot, Puss."

Dana said, "But both are coming into a whole new world…death …or life," as though she were very wise.

"What're we talking about?" Jack asked.

"About death being an awakening," Carly said.

"We're still talking about that?"

"Jack?" Kyle said.

"Yeah?"

"Hi."

"Hi."

"You are, aren't you?"

The girls roared, but Jack didn't get it. He said, "I just feel so… relaxed."

"That's the beauty." Amply emotional because he was stoned, Kyle stroked the back of Jack's neck, the place where his hair hit.

He was surprised back to reality when Dana said, "I want to be loved like Kyle loves Jack."

They all turned to her.

"You were ready to give up everything for him."

My kingdom, Kyle thought.

But before he or anyone else could respond, she stood abruptly and went to the kitchen.

Dinner consisted of a bland beef stew, hard green beans and harder rolls. Jack couldn't eat enough. "This is fantastic," he kept saying.

"It's only 'cause you're high," Claudia told him.

As she spoke, Kyle noticed how she was looking at Jack. And he realized that his friends were sizing him up. The night was a test and he hadn't prepped himself, though there was nothing he could have done. Friends were often harsher judges than parents, he knew, because friends had different interests to guard.

Then his life shifted.

"We always said love wouldn't come between us," Carly began, holding up her glass of wine for a toast, "always knowing that of course it would. Now we have our first test of friendship. And we won't know if we survived, not just this, but the way we grow, until we come out on the other side. Until we come back to summer with our own families."

There was a pause, then Kyle said, "That was beautiful."

"I only use that as a preface," Carly continued. She looked at each of them in turn, even Jack. "Because next week I'm going to Brazil."

Dana and Claudia erupted in screams of excited envy. Kyle looked across the table at Carly, sad to see her go and sad to see an end to their traditions. He felt Jack's hand on his thigh.

"Don't be sad, you big sap," Carly said, when he rose to hug her. "It doesn't change things."

But it does, he thought. *It does.*

After dinner, they retired to the living room, Jack and Kyle settling on the sofa with drinks, Claudia and Dana approaching the stereo.

"Enjoying yourself?" Kyle asked Jack.

Jack touched Kyle's bare foot with his own. "I always enjoy myself when you're around."

Kyle grinned with such ardor it was almost a leer.

And then Dana was grabbing Jack's hand and pulling him up before the fireplace with Claudia, who had placed a record on the turntable. *The Glory of Love.*

As the song kicked in, Jack and the two girls caroled, "You've got to give a little, take a little…"

Kyle raised his glass in salute.

When Carly curled up beside him on the sofa, he breathed, "Look at him," marveling at Jack's beauty, at his life. She said something in response, but he didn't hear, transfixed by Jack. When he asked her to repeat herself, she said, "You know G.K. Chesterton?"

"I know the name."

"Well, we had to read all about him this year. And this one quote really stuck with me. I'll paraphrase, but you'll get the idea: 'The way to love something is to believe that at any moment it could be lost.' Is that how you love Jack?"

"I couldn't have articulated it better myself."

A moment later, she said, "My God, he's fun," smiling at the singing group.

"What took you so long?" Kyle asked.

She gave him a pleased nod. "We approve."

"That's the story of, that's the glory of…"

"Dana and I give him eights," Carly said. "Claudia gives him an eight and a half."

"No tens?"

Carly pulled back, wrinkling her nose, as if he should have known better. "No, silly. If he were a ten, he'd be one of us."

Then they were laughing so hard they were falling on each other. It felt good to be in love with them again. And with Carly's impending departure, the night took on a nostalgic hue, as if it had already been steeped in sepia.

They left around one.

As Jack and Kyle undressed in Kyle's room, the radio quietly playing, Jack said, "Maybe you should call Trent."

"Now?" Kyle knew that wasn't what he meant at all. He was embarrassed Jack had known he was thinking about Trent. Behind them, the white curtains leading to the balcony rippled in the breeze. Late-blooming asphodel stood in lemon anguish in a vase on Kyle's dresser.

"No. Tomorrow—"

"Wait!" Kyle held up a hand to silence him. Then he went to the radio and turned the volume up.

"—what happened," the disc jockey was saying in his patented soothing voice.

A woman's voice followed, broken by sobs. "He's leaving me. I'll always be alone now."

"It's Veronica," Kyle said.

Her voice was tinny, coming across galaxies and years. "I want to dedicate *The Man That Got Away*."

The song began and all Kyle could do was look at Jack across the expanse of his room. He finally had verification. All those broken people were real. And that knowledge brought cold, desperate fear.

The grace of God.

"What smells so good?"

Kyle, in the living room of the McAllister house, heard Jack's voice and ran a quick hand through his long and unruly hair. He'd loaned Jack his car for the day so he could prepare his birthday celebration covertly. But when Jack came into the living room, it was Kyle who was surprised.

No, stunned.

Jack's hair had been—not cut, but shorn. The locks that had touched his spine, flirted with his shoulders, framed his face, had been mowed into a crew cut.

"Jack!"

Jack looked at him, not understanding. Then he realized. "Oh. Didn't I tell you? I get it cut every year on my birthday. That's why it was so long when we met. Can you believe it?"

Kyle couldn't speak.

"How did you remember it was my birthday?" Jack stepped over to the two card tables Kyle had set up before the picture window. One was laden with covered pots and pans. The other had two place settings, silver candlesticks with ivory tapers, and a large vase filled with red roses from Ann's garden. Beside the tables was a small pile of gifts wrapped in blue paper with gold moons and silver stars.

"I thought it was always long." Kyle couldn't stop staring at him.

"Do you hate it?"

"No!" He said it too quickly. "You're golden. I'm just..." Shocked. He got a grip and moved to where Jack stood. "You're still the most beautiful boy in the world." He embraced him, kissed his neck. He still smelled of sandalwood and that was reassuring. "Happy birthday, Puss. I love you."

"I can't believe you did all this!" Jack exclaimed. "I can't believe you remembered it was my birthday!"

Kyle slid behind him, arms around his waist, chin on his shoulder, so they were both facing the feast. "I remember everything."

Jack turned his head to the side and kissed Kyle's cheek. "So this is the reason you gave me your car?"

"I had to get you out of the way." He bounded over to the table and lit the candles with a wooden match, then pulled out a chair, looking at Jack in the hazy dusk. "Please. Sit. The food will get cold."

"I don't even have my camera!"

Kyle grinned and pulled a camera from behind one of the pots. "Luckily I have mine."

Jack grinned back. "Oh! I forgot about this." He held up a lock of his hair, eight inches long. "I wanted to give this to you to commemorate. I didn't know if it would be weird, being hair and all."

"No," Kyle breathed. He took the tresses, long and gold and silken. "It's perfect."

"I thought it could be a souvenir."

"You thought exactly right." He gave Jack a soft kiss on the lips. "But you always do."

He loaded Jack's plate with salmon, rice pilaf, cheese soufflé, carrots, potatoes, gravy and a roll. Jack gaped. "I can't eat that much."

"Eat as much as you can. We can always save the rest."

Lightning flickered in the dusk. "It's going to rain tonight," Jack said.

"All the better for snuggling." He reached beneath the table for a bottle of red wine. Opening it expertly with a corkscrew, he poured two glasses, then raised his. "'How many loved your movements of glad grace, / and loved your beauty with love false or true; / But one man loved the pilgrim soul in you, / and loved the sorrows of your changing face.' That man is me. So to your birth I make this toast and this promise: to love you and everything you will be no matter what is to come."

Jack was overwhelmed. "I—that's so beautiful. I don't even know what to say. Thank you."

"I was inspired."

They drank.

The food was brilliant. Jack gushed. "I can't believe you made this. I wouldn't have thought to have this catered, let alone to create it."

"This is our first birthday together," Kyle said. "It had to be special."

"How did you get it all here when I had your car?"

"Dana brought me. I bribed her with some of the food. The way to a woman's heart and all. She says happy birthday."

"She's the nicest of your friends," Jack said, spooning rice into his mouth.

"You really didn't suspect anything?" Kyle wanted his artfulness confirmed.

"I didn't have a clue."

Kyle gazed at him, still stunned by his hair.

"I'm sorry I didn't warn you," Jack said.

"No. I like it. I just need to get used to it. It makes you look so—masculine."

"So I looked like a fairy before?"

"Don't be cracked. You were—ethereal."

"Kyle."

"Really."

They ate for a moment, then Jack said, "Why do you call me Puss?"

Kyle looked stricken. "Do you hate it?"

Jack laughed. "Actually, I love it. I've never had a nickname before. But I want to know why you chose that. Knowing you, there's a reason."

Kyle hadn't anticipated how gratifying it would be for someone to understand. "My father used to call my mother that when I was young. So I think of it as the tenderest of endearments. I didn't notice until you came along that he'd stopped." He gave a sad smile and remembered the swan planter.

When they were finished with dinner, Kyle brought forth a package of praline crunch and a yellow birthday cake with blue icing. "The University of Michigan's colors," he said, lighting candles, the flames dancing across his shining face. The room was nearly dark. They could feel the rain.

Kyle held the cake up. Jack's eyes flashed blue fire in the candlelight. "Thank you," he said, his breath flickering the flames. Then he closed his eyes, made a wish, and blew.

Kyle set the cake down and revealed a bottle from beneath the table. "I even got a bottle of champagne so I can have my way with you." He gave a lascivious grin.

Once they each had a glass of bubbly, a slice of cake and a scoop of ice cream, Kyle presented the first gift. Jack, for posterity, set aside a small swatch of paper, then let the rest fall heedlessly around his feet. Within the packaging was a white box. Within the box were eighteen rolls of film. "One for each year," Kyle noted.

Within the second package was the soundtrack album to the film they had seen earlier that summer, when they'd met. "It's so you can practice that song you want to sing at the Eiffel Tower," Kyle said.

Jack looked up at him, moved. "How could you have thought about that? *I* haven't even thought about that since then."

"I think about you all the time."

The next box housed a French version of *The Little Prince*. "My God, where did you get this?"

"My dad brought it from the city."

"You have done way too much."

"There's just a little more."

"More!" Jack looked up to see a flashbulb explode in his eyes.

"That'll be a perfect candid."

And then Kyle presented the last gift. It was a tiny box, with room enough for only one star and half of one moon. Jack said, "I'm starting to feel like *I* should have brought something," as his fingers nimbly tore apart the paper. Within he found a white box, inside of which lay Kyle's ring resting simply and plainly on a cushion of cotton. He looked at it, his mouth slack in shock. It was moments before he could speak. His only reaction was, "I cannot accept this."

"Just don't let my mom see it." Kyle stood and took the ring from its container, the chain trailing after it like the tail of a comet.

"Kyle, I can't. Really," Jack protested as it was fastened around his neck.

"It was the only way I could express what you mean to me. The rest of this—" He motioned to the table, the food, the gifts. "—means nothing. But you know what the ring means."

Jack looked up at him, still hesitant. "Are you sure?"

"It's the only thing I was sure of."

"God. Wow." He grinned, then said, "Wow," again. "Does this mean we're going steady?"

Kyle laughed. "This is just the beginning of the pretty time."

Jack stood, snaking his arms around Kyle's neck. "Thank you, my gallant King Kyle."

His eyes were so enormous, so luminous, so dazzling, Kyle feared drowning in their depths.

"Happy birthday."

Later, after the rain, the night having grown heavy, they lay together on the porch, their patchwork home, slumbering, strains of crickets like sleigh bells coming through the screen. As the wind soughed in the wet willows outside, a presence entered.

Kyle's head jerked as he slept.

A shadow was in.

"Kyle." The voice was subdued, but firm.

Jack stirred.

The voice said, closer, "Kyle."

Kyle's head twitched once more, then he sat upright with a shout and his eyes popped open to find Dana standing in the doorway in a dark blue windbreaker. He jumped when he saw her, surprised to find someone actually there.

She glanced past him to Jack who had awakened. "Sorry. I didn't want to disturb both of you." Then she noticed. "My God, your hair."

"I got it cut." Jack ran fingers over his head.

"You scared me." Kyle could hear the wind rise in the trees, jangling the wind chimes.

"You need to come with me." Dana's black hair hung in limp, damp strings.

"What's going on?" He was thankful his boxers were on. The air was thick and he could feel it on his flesh, in his lungs.

"It's Trent."

"Is Veronica all right?" He felt a flutter of panic.

"She's fine."

Kyle let his head droop in relief for a second before squinting up at her again. Through the crickets and the wind, he could hear the insistent ticking of the clock. "Did he send you?"

"No. But he needs you."

He considered. He hadn't seen Trent in what seemed like a lifetime.

"Go to him," Jack said then. "He's your best friend."

"What about you?"

"I'm the love of your life. I'll always be here."

They took Dana's car, leaving the convertible for Jack; the following morning they were seeing Carly off. Dana drove, leaning forward, black-rimmed glasses on her face, hands gripping the wheel so tightly her knuckles were white. Kyle so rarely saw her in glasses, he always thought they looked odd, though she'd had them for years. Despite the seeming urgency, she drove a sure 40 miles per hour over the still-wet roads despite the speed limit being 45. "Driving's a very serious undertaking" she'd pronounced several times.

When they arrived at Trent's, they found him in the basement, seated sullenly on the sofa, a cigarette in his hand. On the end table beside him was an ashtray overflowing with butts and ashes. Claudia was seated on the loveseat opposite him, legs curled under her. Trent looked up in disappointed surprise when Kyle and Dana came down the stairs.

"I knew you weren't just taking Carly home," he said.

Kyle sat on the arm of the sofa beside him. "What happened?"

"What do you think happened? Veronica had an abortion."

"You were with her?" He hated not knowing.

Trent took a long drag from his cigarette. "Yes."

Kyle was impressed that Trent had done Veronica the honor of accompanying her. He'd hoped for but hadn't expected as much.

His next question was self-serving, and he felt a twinge of guilt thinking about Trey. But to him the friendship of Trent and Trey had reached epic proportions, spanning decades and continents. "Was anyone else with you?"

"One of her friends." Trent picked flecks of tobacco off his tongue.

Dana sat on the hearth, her legs stretched before her. In the middle of a prolonged yawn, she realized Kyle was looking at her over Trent's head. He mouthed the words *Is he drunk?* and she shrugged.

"It just—" Trent began, then stopped. As his cigarette waned, he lit another from it, before stubbing it out in the ashtray. "I know I did the right thing. But it bothers me. I mean—" His shoulders fell. "I forced her into it."

This was an epiphany to no one but Trent.

"What did you do when you were with her?" Kyle prompted.

"Deal with it. Chain-smoked. Ignored her, because I didn't care enough."

"You were with her, weren't you?"

"I didn't care enough to use protection. I didn't care enough to be good to her. I just didn't care."

"If it's any consolation," Kyle said, stroking the back of Trent's head. "She doesn't hate you."

"That doesn't mean I don't hate myself." Trent spoke simply.

Kyle didn't know what to say to that.

"I just—" He faltered, letting his head sag. Then he reached up and took Kyle's hand. "I'm glad you're here."

They were up a couple of hours later to bid Carly farewell. Kyle tried to rouse Trent, but he was out. Claudia slept in the car on the way there, the morning heat already oppressive. Carly's parents were carrying last-minute things to the car when they arrived. Inside, Kyle expected to see boxes piled in the living room and Carly running around frantically, but she was lying asleep fully dressed on her already-made bed, hair pulled back in a headband. Dana shook her awake and her eyes fluttered like she was a movie princess. "Wow," she said, sitting up. "I'm glad you're not my mother."

"What time are you leaving?" Claudia asked, sitting on the edge of the bed.

Carly looked at her watch. "Ten minutes ago."

"We're a little late," Kyle said.

Carly's mother stuck her head in the room. "We're leaving in two minutes, Carlene." She continued down the hall.

Carly rolled her eyes, grabbed her duffel bag and they trudged downstairs. All of her other things had been packed. When they stood outside in the colorless morning, she turned to Kyle, her eyes teary.

"Trent's unconscious," Kyle explained. "Or nothing could have kept him."

She gave a bittersweet grin. "Wild horses and all that, right?"

"Something like that."

She held him tightly. "Wow. I feel like this is the end."

"Remember what you said last week? Should we lose each other, we'll find each other when we're summering with our own families."

"Yeah. But from where we stand now that seems really far off."

"It's too early to be emotional," Claudia told them. "The rest of us will be affected because we're still vulnerable from sleep."

"Or the lack of it," Dana said.

"Take care of Trent," Carly softly told Kyle. "And tell Jack I said he's to take care of you." She hugged Dana and Claudia at the same time. All three were crying.

Carly's mother walked by carrying a small box and got into the car. Behind them, Carly's father was locking the door to the house.

"I wish y'all were coming with me." Carly swiped at tears that flashed down her cheeks. "I'll send postcards." She got into the backseat and poked her head out the window. "Once we get back I'll only have a couple of days to move into the dorm, so I probably won't see any of you until after school starts."

As her father passed, he clapped Kyle on the shoulder and said, "We'll see you all next summer, if not at Christmas."

"See you kids," Mrs. Salenger said from her open window.

As he started to pull away, Mr. Salenger honked the horn two short beeps. Carly called, "I'll find a Brazilian boy for each of you!"

They all laughed.

"I wonder what her parents are making of *that*," Claudia said.

They watched until the car rounded the curve of the coast, Carly still leaning out, waving.

Kyle never saw her again.

Kyle spent the rest of that day at the shore with Trent. The night before had acted as a catalyst to bring them together, though the strain of the argument had taken its toll. They lay in the sun, smoking, swimming, sleeping, talking very little.

It was mid afternoon when Trent said, "I think I'll visit her tomorrow."

Kyle watched two sandpipers at the water's edge. "She'd like that."

They crossed the hot beach, not rushing, letting it burn the bottoms of their feet, and went to stand at the shoreline, the water pulling sand from beneath them in small pouches. Above them, gulls, sharply white, scavenged, bobbing with the sure buoyancy of kites. Kyle dove into an oncoming wave, the water icy in a second of suspended time, his heart skipping, a gasp in his lungs, and then it was not cold at all.

They swam for so long that when they emerged, their fingers were crinkled, their senses of touch muted. Kyle's nasal passages hurt and his ears were plugged, obscuring his hearing. He lay on his towel, tilting his head first to the left then to the right to drain the water, but he was unsuccessful.

Trent sat beside him and said, "I'll soon pray."

His voice was muffled like underwater thoughts. Kyle didn't know what he was talking about. "For what?"

"Just to hang out."

Then he felt a warm, ticklish sensation in his ears, the water abating, restoring clarity. "Wait. You're praying?"

"No. I've seen Trey."

He decided he liked it better when he couldn't hear.

"I feel ridiculously guilty," Trent said.

"He's only trying to get to me through you."

"How do you mean?"

"I fucked around with him last summer, Trent."

Trent was stunned. "You had sex with Trey Shaw?!"

"You're not the only one who wants to get laid, you know."

"But I thought you were shy!" Trent found it hysterically funny and fell back on the sand, laughing.

Kyle waited until he was done, before asking, "Do you like him?"

"Trey?" Trent baited, still smiling.

"Who else?"

"He was someone to hang with since you weren't coming around."

"You weren't either."

"But I wasn't because you weren't." He was kidding.

"Yeah, well…"

There was a pause, then Trent admitted, "Part of me is relieved you're not as virtuous as I thought."

Kyle was silent for a moment, then he said, "I'm sorry."

"For what?"

"Everything. Anything. …Nothing."

"It's not your fault."

"It's not not my fault either." He fixed his eyes on the horizon. After a minute, he said, "Remember when things were simple?"

Trent turned to him for a moment, observing, then followed his gaze. "Things were never simple, Kyle."

Kyle got home about five. The house was quiet and cool. The deck curtains billowed in a soundless breeze. Scarlet-colored petunias were vivid in a vase on the kitchen counter.

The birthday party seemed like a hundred years ago.

He was about to ascend the stairs when a sound fractured the lull of the surf.

The door leading to the basement was ajar.

He pushed it open, the silence so complete again it was disconcerting.

He descended a couple of steps and bent down, looking through the rail with a total lack of preparation.

His mother knelt before the sliding glass doors, her green sundress trailing behind her so that, for a flash, he thought of her, ridiculously, as a mermaid. She was weeping with hard, ripping breaths, her head in her hands.

She still grieved.

Kyle stumbled back up the stairs, mouth agape, heart pounding. Her image was branded behind his eyelids. He felt sinful and guilty and ashamed, like he'd caught her masturbating.

He fled to his room where he sat on the edge of his bed, facing the door with fearful eyes, like he was seeking refuge in a horror movie. Blood rushed through his veins, roared in his head. He felt weak and tottering, like someone had pulled out a foundation card. He wanted to scream, he wanted to cry, he wanted to shake his mother and hold her gently.

He sat, wondering what in his life had been real, until long shadows fell across the room and he heard Jack downstairs.

When he emerged from the dark cocoon of his room, he felt like he'd slept a hard, sound sleep, his senses dull, his eyes unfocused. He found Ann cutting celery in the kitchen, Jack seated at the counter. The petunias were immoral in their garishness.

As his mother chattered amiably of amaranths and roses, Kyle, feeling pallid, a little nauseous and, having risen, very tired, surveyed her for proof, terrified he'd find a chink in her armor of day-to-day placidity and would have to take responsibility for the creation of a world he'd never questioned. That he would be to blame for having not cared enough to notice. The parties, the dances, the private schools, the island. It had all been for him. And he'd been so self-absorbed he'd never once wondered what price his parents were paying.

What did that make him?

But he found nothing untrue in her demeanor.

"Hey," Jack said, giving him a questionable glance.

"Hey." Kyle hadn't spoken for so long his voice was garbled.

"You okay, honey?" Ann gave a worried tilt of her head.

As much as he felt something akin to hatred for what he saw as betrayal, looking at her, he felt, in equal parts, almost paternal in his need to assuage her grief. Then he had the sudden urge to confront her, take her off guard, because maybe then he could get the truth. He stopped himself when he realized he wasn't sure he wanted it.

He finally said, "Yes."

When Graham came for the weekend, Kyle watched his parents to see if they made any reference to their secret. But there was nothing. They played their stoic parts for him flawlessly. Yet while observing them, he apprehended crow's feet, a sprinkling of gray in his mother's hair, the extent to which his father's hairline had receded. They were things he'd never noticed. His parents were suddenly strangers.

That Saturday, as Kyle passed his parents' bedroom, he glanced in to see his father struggling with a shirt button. The image struck him as immeasurably poignant. He stepped into the room and said, "Let me."

Graham held his hands up in surrender. "These damn buttons."

Kyle's slender, adept fingers deftly closed the shirt. "Don't you hate when you can't get them to close?"

"So it's not just my old age?" Graham chuckled.

At his father's words, Kyle suddenly became aware of the startling differences between them: firm, lean flesh compared to pliancy; quick, fluid grace contrasted with a thoughtful pace; youth and energy paralleled with maturity and history. How had Graham changed so much without Kyle seeing?

"No," he said, averting his eyes. "It's not about age."

Kyle obsessed over his parents until, one hot night in the tub, his skin clammy in the tepid water, crickets ringing in the dark, he knew what to do. They had always told him to be truthful; he had not been. Perhaps his admission would prompt their own, and they could deal with their pain, together. He needed to get back the peace he'd known for so many years. The peace he'd based his beliefs on. He needed to know there had been that tranquility once.

But what if it had never been?

With or without Kevin?

What then?

What then?

The dog days of late July were heavy and sticky. They made Kyle and Jack lazy so they killed their time alone at the McAllister place. They kissed and talked and ate and kissed and Kyle swam and Jack splashed, and when they came together, Kyle didn't know if the salt he tasted on Jack's lips was his sweat or the sea. They would kiss for hours, until they knew nothing else. The intimacy overwhelmed him, dizzying him, heightening his senses of smell, taste, touch.

Nights, they would lay together, Kyle behind Jack, his head on his shoulder, one leg nudging between Jack's. It was how they always slept. It felt like home, the contours of their bodies fitting, like ridges and valleys, Jack's spareness meeting Kyle's fullness, like they'd broken apart and, separate, were incongruous, but together, were unspoiled.

One day they lay under the mulberry tree on the front lawn, eating berries, picking dandelions, being silly. They'd whiled away the afternoon talking of the future, debating who would change schools, neither willing to let the other sacrifice but not knowing how to compromise.

Eventually their focus drifted to another kind of future.

"I wish we could get married," Jack reflected.

"We don't have to do it in a church. We could do it right here on the beach."

"Yeah? Be hippies about it?"

"You'd look super sexy in tie-dye."

Jack giggled.

"I don't wanna say 'I do,'" Kyle said then, as always serious about their life together. "I wanna say 'I will.'" He smiled, then reached over and took hold of Jack's wrist, his heartbeat, like a kitten's, so tiny it didn't seem it could be what sustained him.

"We'll have to plan a big ol' honeymoon for afterward." Jack's fingers and lips were stained with mulberry juice. "My grandparents have a place in Portugal. Can you believe it?"

"We could hitchhike around Europe."

"Wouldn't that be awfully dangerous?"

"Not with me there."

"My hero. I'll try not to get tied to any railroad tracks so you won't get your cape dusty."

Kyle laughed and squeezed Jack's wrist, nestling closer, the grass dense beneath them.

"We can never leave the island if you like," Jack said. "Our kids can be islanders."

Kyle sat up excitedly. "You want kids?"

Jack smiled. "Of course. Don't you?"

"More than anything." He reached down and touched Jack's face. "Except for you, of course."

Then, abruptly, the air turned icy. Wind whistled around them. They looked up at the silvery undersides of the mulberry leaves flapping in the breeze. Kyle sat upright and, over the heaving sea, saw storm clouds as black and tumid as a bruise rushing from the horizon toward the island. Lightning crackled along the undersides, followed so closely by the guttural growl of thunder that it seemed simultaneous. Two or three seconds later, the clouds were almost overhead. Kyle pulled Jack to his feet, suddenly fearing for their safety, and shouted, "Run!"

And they did, across the lawn, toward the house, past the front porch, the wind tearing at their clothes. By the time they reached the backyard and Kyle was jerking at the doors leading to the cellar, the gale was so strong Jack had to clutch the rail to keep from being blown away.

One of the doors flew open with a soundless crash. As Kyle let Jack precede him into the cellar, he braved a look up into the descending storm, fat raindrops just beginning to descend, remembering the sudden squall that had overtaken him and Kevin on the beach that day so long ago. And how Kevin had brought out the sun.

He turned and followed Jack into the darkness of the cellar, securing the doors behind them. When they reached the bottom of the stairs, the air was stale and chilly, the basement shadowy and ominous. They could hear the heavy pelting of rain above. Kyle rubbed Jack's arms.

"Where did it come from?" Jack asked.

"I don't know. Are you warm enough?"

"Yeah."

Kyle slipped off his T-shirt. "Put this on. You're cold."

Jack put it on. They sat on the steps, Kyle's arms around Jack, hands inside his shirts, fingers against his abdomen, and they listened to the destruction of the land. Jack couldn't stop shivering, and Kyle didn't know if it was because of the cool or nerves.

They both jumped to their feet when there was a deafening crack of thunder that seemed to come from within the house itself. "You okay?" Kyle reached for Jack's hand.

"Yeah. I just—I'm nervous."

"I know, Puss. It'll pass."

Later, after the storm, they stepped out of the cellar into the bright, wet, overcast day, their skin riddled with gooseflesh, Jack's face drawn, his enormous eyes the turbulent blue-black of a violent sea. The rain was over, but the air was still heavy with damp. Gutters ran noisily. Branches littered the lawn. The pear tree had been split in half, its trunk splintered, its lustrous head in a heap on the ground.

There would be no more fruit that summer.

The McAllister house had survived virtually intact.

But Jack's peace of mind hadn't.

Like a thunderhead, fear spread over Jack. They spent the remainder of the day on the beach, driftwood, dead fish and other debris having washed ashore. Gulls were loud overhead, scanning the rubbish. Jack was withdrawn, sitting on his towel, watching Kyle in the water, often looking to the horizon, though there was nothing there but white sky. It was like he could hear something and was waiting for it to materialize. Like there was the beginning rhythm of tribal drums, so low it could only be felt so far, but slowly becoming more intense, more insistent, like suspense, like his heartbeat.

When Kyle joined him, hair dripping, Jack said, "Something's going to happen."

Kyle lay beside him and rubbed his arm. "You okay?"

"I'm afraid."

Kyle smiled. "We'll be okay. Remember Bert the Turtle. 'Duck and cover.'"

Jack cupped his cheek but he was not consoled. "You're right, of course."

"Wanna go back to the house?"

"Let's stay here for a few minutes."

"Jack." Kyle was intent, grave. He wasn't sure he was strong enough to bring back the sun himself. "What can I do to stop it?"

Jack looked at him through big, apprehensive eyes, then smiled, sweetly, sadly. "You can't."

Jack never fully regained his spirit after the storm. He was more fearful of everything: the house, the weather, time. Things took on an air of urgency. Kyle did what he could to ease Jack's fears; Jack pretended to be soothed.

Concurrently, Trent, Claudia and Dana weren't the same carefree people they had always been either. Their rhythm was off, and sometimes Kyle got the feeling they were only biding their time, going through the motions until September when they could be free.

He tried to but couldn't fully attribute their change to Carly's absence. And he didn't suspect it was Jack either, because, though he had initially thrown off their balance, he had, essentially, become part of what remained of the group. A secondary part, but a part nonetheless.

One night he and Jack went to join them on the beach. It was one of those nights when there were so many stars the sky looked crowded, and, with the beach stretching endlessly in either direction and the sea reaching toward them from infinity, they made Kyle realize that he and his storyline meant nothing. Within a hundred years no one would know or care what had happened that summer. The choices made, actions taken, vows professed would mean nothing.

He and Jack and everyone else were inconsequential.

He had never felt so small.

He took Jack's hand to retain balance.

"Hey, fresh blood!" Dana called when she caught sight of them.

"She's blasting us," Claudia said.

The girls and Trent sat around a fire, playing cards. Beside them were a few empty beer bottles and a cooler. Low music played from the transistor that sat by Trent's leg.

They no longer played Truth or Dare.

And no one was challenged by "No secrets."

Kyle and Jack were dealt in at the next hand. There was virtually no wind. The water was calm. The group was still for maybe the first time in their lives.

They were on their second hand before Kyle voiced what was on his mind. "How was Veronica?"

Trent didn't look up when he said, "I haven't seen her yet."

Kyle was so surprised, he spoke without thinking. "Are you serious?" When Trent didn't reply, he followed up with, "You're fucking serious."

"Don't be so dramatic," Trent said.

"Fuck you, Trent."

"No, fuck you, Kyle."

Claudia gave a rhinestone smile. "Just another enjoyable evening at the shore."

"Fuck you, Claudia," Kyle said.

"No, fuck you, Kyle. We were having a swell time until you arrived."

Dana looked at Jack, who had set down his cards and was letting sand filter through his fingers. She shrugged and extended a pack of Lucky Strikes. He smiled and shook his head.

"Go, Jack," Trent said. "It's your turn."

"It's easier to ignore when I'm not around, isn't it?" Kyle demanded.

"Jack, it's your fucking turn."

"Don't swear at Jack."

"Fuck you, Kyle."

"No, fuck you, Kevin."

One of the logs in the fire broke, sending up a gasp of sparks.

The dark shifted around them.

"I didn't—I didn't mean that," Kyle stammered.

No one knew how to respond.

Trent dropped his cards and got up and walked away.

The day came when remaining coiled inside himself was more exhausting than the energy it took to come clean. And it seemed the perfect time was never going to present itself. So the following afternoon when Kyle found himself alone in the house—Ann working the garden, Graham mowing the lawn—he went to stand just inside his parents' bedroom, his secret bearing heavily upon him. A breeze fluttered the white, gauzy curtains to the balcony, bringing in the sharp-yet-soft scent of cut grass, the sibilance of the sea, the whisper of the willow's branches. A deerfly beat against the screen. The room was precisely as it had ever been—the bed against the south wall, parallel to the water, the bureau against the west wall, his mother's vanity against the north, the sliding glass doors and the deck against the east—yet Kyle couldn't remember when he had last looked at it.

And gazing at it then he felt tired.

He stepped to the vanity, remembering the many nights he had spent watching his mother prepare for an evening out. Atop the counter sat a framed photograph of him and Trent in their prep school uniforms, taken when they were twelve. Even then Trent had been beautiful. Far more beautiful than Kyle. Kyle could see the stunning man who would grow from the child. It unnerved him to see so clearly what was to come. Kyle himself looked almost exactly the same. That made him smile. He liked not having changed so much.

They'd been home from school that weekend and had found a caterpillar with dusty orange fur and black stripes. They had put it in a bottling jar, along with a stick and a handful of grass, to preserve it until it spun its cocoon and metamorphosed into regal adulthood. But it had died in the night somewhere between the building of a sheet fort and the wafting aroma of scrambled eggs.

Next to the photo was his mother's pill box. Pale green with an off-center rose and tendrils of thorny stems encircling it on the lid, it swaddled the tiny beads that assuaged Ann's despair, softening the edges so that she could think, so that she could speak, so that she could function. He thought they had stolen some of her youth, her vibrancy, her *joie de vivre*. Though, of course, in actuality, he knew Kevin had done that.

Next to the dispensary was his mother's jewelry box. It peeked out at him from behind a spray of white chrysanthemums. Lifting the lid, he saw, in its own little brown velvet square, his mother's charm bracelet. He held it up, the symbols he'd forgotten tinkling against each other. Their mystery and romance inundated his senses and consummate melancholy swept through him. The Eiffel Tower, the Golden Gate, the swan that reminded him of the planter at the front of the house. The planter was gone, but the emblem was still there. And then, there, among the chain of souvenirs, was the crown he had coveted, the crown that would never be his.

Because Kevin was king.

And that was when he knew it was time.

"The amaranths are dying," Ann said when he had called to her. She knelt in the garden and, looking at her, there, in the place she loved most, Kyle briefly felt nostalgic, and he thought again of the missing swan planter, before remembering that the present was what was crucial. He swallowed hard, suddenly terrified. Sweat tickled down his armpits. "It's important," he said.

Once in the living room, Ann sat beside Graham on the sofa, pulling her gardening gloves off. "The amaranths are dying."

Kyle's heart thrashed in its cage. He wished he'd rehearsed.

"So what's up?" Graham said.

"Um." His voice was feeble. "I've been thinking how there shouldn't be any secrets between us." He saw their faces become alarmed and realized that might not have been the best intro.

"Has something happened?" his mother gasped, unable to contain herself.

"No," he said, almost too fast. "This isn't anything bad. Nothing's wrong." How he had to assure them of that. "It's just something you've never known. And I think things like love and joy and fear and grief—" He dropped that in as casually as possible. "—are things we should be able to share with each other. Because if we can't trust each other, who can we trust, right?"

"Yes," his parents replied in unison, bobbing their heads, anxious.

"Please, Kyle," his mother said. "The suspense is painful."

He was making it melodramatic without even trying. Suddenly frightened, he turned toward the sliding glass doors. "It's really not that big a deal."

"Of course it is," his father said. "Or you wouldn't preface it like this."

"You're softening the blow," his mother told him.

Is it a blow? he wondered.

"Kyle." Ann smiled brightly, the wrinkles around her eyes scrunched together. "Whatever it is, it's okay."

Kyle gave a weak smile, though he did not face them. She was right, of course. Everything would be fine.

"Just say it," Ann said.

The top of his head prickled, and he felt big childlike tears well up. "Okay." But then he couldn't continue. He stood there for so long he began to wonder if they were even still in the room. When he finally said, "I'm queer," he wasn't sure if they'd know what he was talking about, as there seemed to be no context anymore.

But it was out.

He had to consciously control his body from springing from the room.

The silence became unbearable as he stood there, naked, coveting a response—a cry of disbelief, a scream of denial, a sigh of stolid resignation.

Something.

Anything.

Finally his father said, "Are you sure?"

He hadn't considered that reply. All he could do was nod. "Yeah." His voice was froggy. "I've known my whole life." He turned to find his mother standing before the fireplace, staring into its heart. He gave a half-hearted smile. "Surprise."

"I'm stunned." His father had paled beneath his tan. "I—" He fumbled and gave up. "I just don't know what to say."

"Nothing's changed." Kyle was hopeful. "Everything's precisely as it was a minute ago. I'm the same person I've been all my life."

No one said anything for a moment, and Kyle felt real fear sprout. He could hear wind chimes ringing on the deck. His only coherent thought was, *The amaranths are dying.*

His mother, he suddenly became aware, was gently crying, her back trembling. He took a step toward her, then stopped. "Mom?"

"Kyle." She inhaled loudly, her tears coming more freely. She spoke in a frightened and quiet voice, her words sad and slow. "I just don't want you to be lonely."

"No. I'm golden. I have Jack."

She turned to him in astonishment. "Jack, too?"

He couldn't help but smile. "Yes, Jack, too. He's the reason I'm telling you. When I met Jack I discovered what I'd been looking for without even realizing I'd been looking for something. Like I'd found something I hadn't even known I'd lost. He was like deja vu. Everything fell into place and the world made sense. It was like waking up to a dream instead of waking up to reality. But instead the dream was reality because it made sense." He was babbling. "I want to change schools."

"What!" his mother gasped.

"You've already been accepted to Princeton!" Graham cried.

265

"I know. But Jack's going to Michigan." A shameless lovesick smile spread across his face. "And we want to be together."

"*Michigan?*" Graham thundered.

"Michigan's not the issue," his mother said.

And then Kyle remembered the real issue. And though he hadn't expected their immediate surrender, he was still disappointed it hadn't come. He suddenly wanted to cry himself. "I just thought it was important you knew," he said, his voice imploring. "How can we support each other like *you* always say if we don't know the truth? You said you'd stand behind me no matter what."

"Of course we did," his father said. "And we will. We just…"

"What?"

"Do you think we're going to stand here and accept this as though you've told us you're having dinner at Dana's?" Graham demanded. "It's not that easy, Kyle!"

"I know! I don't expect it to be!" How had they ended up shouting?

Graham stood, turned away, ran exasperated hands through his hair. "God!"

"What? Have you finally decided there's no way I can live up to Trent's example? Or Kevin's promise?" A part of him knew he was only being vicious, and another part believed it to be true.

"What!" his mother gasped for a second time. Her voice shook with shock and anger. "Do you really think we expect you to be like Kevin?"

He didn't know.

"We have never asked *anything* of you," she said.

"Except that I be honest. And that's what I'm doing."

His mother gazed at him lovingly and her vexation crumbled. She went to him, taking his hands in hers and led him to the sofa, where they sat. "Are you in love with him, Kyle?" she asked.

He felt pink touch his cheeks. Suddenly the whole situation was so personal. "Yes."

"And he with you?"

"Yes."

"You'd give up Princeton for him?" his father asked standing before them.

Kyle wondered if dropping out of Princeton didn't distress his father more than anything else. "Yes," he said again.

His parents exchanged worried looks he loosely interpreted as, *Oh, shit.*

"You love him?" his mother asked again.

"Yes," he said again, and it felt empowering. "I love him." He stopped himself from blathering about it again.

His mother searched his eyes and he was unafraid because all she could see was the truth.

After a moment she said, "Then that's all that matters."

That night, Jack came in and closed the door to Kyle's room, leaning against it, out of breath. "You told them." He looked like he'd seen a specter and was pissed about it.

Kyle, pulling on a white T-shirt, looked over from where he stood in front of the dresser. "Yeah. Can you believe it?"

"Fuck you. It isn't funny."

"This way we don't have to be clandestine."

"That's not the point. You shouldn't have done it without telling me."

"Jack—"

"You could at least apologize."

"You're right. I'm sorry." He went over and gave Jack a chaste kiss on the lips.

"No, you're not."

"I am. I'm sorry I didn't tell you. Or warn you. But it's all right. They understand." He put his hands on Jack's hips, pulling him close so their pelvic bones bumped. "Don't worry. They're going to be more nervous than you are."

Jack sighed, not looking at Kyle for a moment. But then he couldn't not. He took him in fully for several seconds, then kissed his yielding lips. "I wouldn't bet on that."

Dinner started quietly. Kyle was anxious, but his sudden lack of weight made him feel giddy, like he had to hold on to something or he might float to the ceiling. The others, however, were quite grounded, avoiding each other's eyes and all conversation. They ate in silence for so long, Kyle began to wonder how long they could go without anyone speaking, until, finally, as he passed a plate of corn cobs to Jack, Graham said, "So. Kyle tells us you're in love."

Kyle almost laughed, hard and loud. He was surprised Jack didn't drop the plate.

Instead he set it down without taking an ear and looked across the table to Graham, his skin blotchy, eyes round and scared. He looked small. "Yes, sir," he said, and Kyle cringed. Jack had never called his father "sir" before. "We are."

He had a swath of milk on his upper lip, and Kyle thought it was the sexiest thing he'd ever seen. Despite the drama and the presence of his parents, he wanted to have Jack right then, right there on the dining room table.

"He's planning on giving up Princeton for you," Graham said.

"We haven't decided that yet!" Jack turned to Kyle, then back to Graham.

"Do your parents know?" Ann asked. "About you and Kyle?"

"No!" Jack cried. "I can't believe he told *you*!" He looked upset about everything, like he was unable to determine which feelings belonged where.

"You must know," Graham said, "it will take us some time to grow accustomed to this."

"Me, too!" Jack's voice was strident. "I'm not comfortable knowing you know. I could throw up right now!"

Before Jack decided to demonstrate, Kyle interjected, "Jack's parents don't know. Yet."

"Does Trent?" Ann asked.

"He—I just told him a couple of weeks ago."

"Is that why he hasn't been around so much?"

"That's more about me and him than me and Jack."

Graham gave Jack a soft expression. "Don't you think your parents are going to find out? Wouldn't it be better if they heard it from you?"

"We're working up to that, Dad," Kyle said.

"They'll understand, right?" Ann queried. "Like Graham and I do?"

Kyle thrilled that they were able to understand and accept. Good was already coming from his admission. Which meant that good would come from his parents' truthfulness too.

"I don't know," Jack said, his voice meek.

Ann and Graham shared a look over the table, then turned to their son, whose eyes were locked with Jack's. The boys looked at each other for several moments, assuring, affirming, pledging. Then Kyle squeezed Jack's hand under the table. "It's going to be all right," he said, to Jack, to all of them. "It's going to be all right."

But he wondered if they believed it.

Later they went to Carly's (the place to hang since the Salengers had left), finding Dana alone and into the alcohol. The night was dark and cool and breezy, the living room curtains fluttering in the wind. Dana made drinks for them in the kitchen. "I don't know where they are," she said in reference to Trent and Claudia. "They went to get pizza but I expected them back half an hour ago."

Kyle and Jack sat on the sofa. An ashtray, a bottle of bubbles, wooden matches and a box of cigars were on the coffee table. Kyle dropped a handful of yellow chrysanthemums his mother had cut beside them. "Maybe they got waylaid by Veronica."

"As opposed to getting *laid* by Veronica?" Dana came in and presented them with the drinks.

"You're cracked."

"I found these cigars," she said, holding up the box. "Aren't they great?" She handed one to Jack, one to Kyle and kept one herself. "I bet they're really expensive."

She was drunk. It wasn't apparent through slurred words or glassy eyes, but by the content and fluid way she moved. And it suddenly occurred to him that she'd changed when he hadn't been looking. When he'd been falling in love, fighting with Trent, losing his mind, she, who had always been the quietest of the girls—not out of shyness, but because she didn't crave the attention Carly did or have the smug conceit Claudia did—had grown into the one who took charge. If it hadn't been for her, their circle might not have survived. She'd been able to keep herself out of the turmoil and, hence, been able to bring each of them, Trent, Claudia, Jack, himself, in from their separate camps to some sort of neutral ground where they could reconnect.

He smiled at her as she bit a slot in her cigar. "You've been a good friend."

Sitting cross-legged on the floor, she cocked a brow at him, the unlit cigar between her teeth. "Thanks," she said, not sure what he was talking about.

"No." He was afraid he didn't sound sincere enough. "Really. Thank you."

"Sure." She took an Ohio Blue Tip and lit each of their cigars.

Jack puffed contentedly for a second, then choked, his face turning crimson. When he'd gotten his breath back, he reached forward and stubbed the cigar out. "These aren't as much fun as I pretended when I was a kid."

The wind suddenly fell and the curtains dropped back, lax. Kyle glanced to the sliding glass doors but could see only the reflection of the living room, like an alternate universe.

"We should play poker," Dana determined, pushing her black hair over her shoulder.

An hour later, the night air having become charged with electricity, the curtains springing in the air, they were tipsy from drinking on near-empty stomachs. Jack reclined on the sofa, legs thrown over an arm. Kyle sat on the floor, back against the couch, facing Dana across the coffee table. The flowers were sharp between them though they were already beginning to wane. Jack slapped at a mosquito on his neck. Kyle mindlessly shuffled a deck of cards. Dana slowly and intently maneuvered her forefinger through the flame of a large, white, flickering candle.

Out of nowhere, she crooned, "'Two drifters, off to see the world. There's such a lot of world to see...'"

"Why are you singing that?" Kyle asked, irritable. "It's forlorn."

"Only if you think you're going to end up lonely," Dana returned. "I think it's wistful."

Wind swept through the trees with a tremendous rush. Dana cocked her head, looking past Kyle to the balcony. "Sort of spooky, isn't it?" she said, when she caught him looking at her.

"Where can they be?" Jack was bored. He took his glasses off and placed them atop Kyle's head. Kyle reached up and hooked them over his ears, surprised to find that the world had disappeared. Jack was practically blind.

"Maybe we should go look for them," Dana suggested. She'd given up on the candle and was blowing streams of bubbles across the table, into Kyle's face and over Jack's torso.

"None of us can drive," Kyle replied. He gave the glasses back to Jack and lit another cigar. "We're too drunk."

"I wish you'd stop smoking those." The waiting had made Jack not just bored but peckish.

"I like it."

"You like it a little too much."

"What does that mean?" Kyle turned to face him, still supine on the sofa.

"It means you smoke too much and it's pissing me off."

"You said it didn't bother you!"

"I wasn't kissing you then."

"Oh, no," Dana said. "No nooky for Kyle tonight."

"Shut up, Dana."

Jack sat up suddenly, blood rushing to his head. "What? Do you tell them about our sex life? 'No secrets' and all that?" He stood and headed to the kitchen with his empty glass.

"No!" Kyle exclaimed. "I would never do that to you, to us." He paused. "This is about my parents, isn't it?"

"No." Jack stopped. "I don't know. I just can't believe you did it without telling me."

"I did tell you."

Jack turned to him. "You didn't tell me until after. When we talk about 'our' life that means a fusion of your life and my life. You didn't even warn me. I just drop by like always and there's your mother with a wounded look that says 'My God. You're having sex with my son.'"

"My mother adores you."

"But now she has to think of me as a son-in-law or something, where before I was just some kid. That's a huge deal for her. And for me to have to act on my feet when I'm confronted with it is unfair."

Kyle stood, suddenly feeling like they were facing off. "If I'd taken the time to confer with you, I'd have changed my mind."

"And telling them you're switching schools when we—"

"You're what?!" Dana exclaimed, aghast.

"—hadn't reached a decision makes me look stupid."

Kyle set his cigar in the ashtray. "But I wanted that to be a surprise. A gift. I wanted to make you happy!"

"I feel like you're tempting fate when you're so reckless."

Kyle wanted to explain, about Kevin, and his parents, and how his truth was needed so that they could heal. But instead they just looked at each other across an expanse of yards that felt like a chasm. The wind whispered in the boughs of the trees, flittering the curtains.

Then the door opened, creating a vacuum in the house, sucking the drapes to the screens, guttering the candle, and Trent and Claudia were there. Trent was stricken, face greasy, clothes rumpled, eyes red. Claudia was ashen and shaken.

"Oh, my God," Dana said, rising, a prescient note of panic in her voice.

Jack turned to them, his eyes growing large at their appearance.

Trent banged the door shut and the curtains relaxed into their prior fluttery nervousness. He sat on the sofa. Claudia went into the kitchen and stood before the sink swallowing glassful after glassful of water. Kyle gave a worried glance to Dana, then went to stand before Trent. "What happened?"

Trent fumbled in his shirt pocket for a pack of smokes and withdrew a box so crumpled Kyle couldn't imagine there being an unharmed cigarette inside. But there was. Trent removed it and lit it, tossing the empty pack on the coffee table, on top of the chrysanthemums.

"It's Veronica," he said, his voice low.

Claudia went to stand in back of Trent, facing Kyle. Jack moved so that he was behind Kyle, anticipatory. Dana stood farther back of them. They remained like that for many moments, as though freeze-framed. Trent and Kyle looked at each other like they were the only two people in the room.

Finally, Dana had enough. "What? She flipped out and wouldn't let you leave the restaurant?"

"Would you let me tell you what happened?" Trent snapped.

"Well, get to the point! You straggle in here an hour and a half late and then pussyfoot around!"

"Veronica," Claudia stated clearly and simply, "killed herself. Is that to the point enough?"

The meaning of her words took a second to sink in, lingering on the periphery of Kyle's consciousness before striking with a stinging viciousness that left him reeling. "What?" he eked out, after a lifetime, an epoch, an eternity. His voice was hollow and far away, like it had traveled across universes.

"Oh, my God," Jack and Dana said one on top of the other.

"We found out at the restaurant and went to see if we could do anything," Trent told them.

"How did she—" Dana started, then stopped, cut off by a sudden, painful sob.

"She cut her wrists," Claudia supplied.

A hum rang in Kyle's ears. He watched Trent speak, his voice muted, like sound through a wall. Kyle's face was hot, and he felt like he was going to vomit, and the sensation was so strong he reached out to steady himself on the coffee table. The hum was building, becoming a roar. He didn't recognize the person before him. He couldn't see the boy in him, the boy in the photograph on his mother's vanity. Had that only been that afternoon? What had become of that child? He had to blink rapidly to focus. The roar grew louder until it became distorted. His skin was clammy. His marrow tingled. Then, as the sound in his head reached a crescendo, his shock abruptly turned to rage, and what he thought would be an explosion, came out only a hiss.

"It's your fault."

They all looked at him.

No one spoke.

"Kyle—" Trent began.

"This is your fault!" Kyle pointed a finger, his voice powerful and shaking with furor. "I told you. I told you."

Jack cast a nervous glance at Dana.

"You killed her," Kyle said, a whisper that could have carried to the mainland.

Trent stood, exhausted, broken, and put out a steadying hand to Kyle, who lashed at him, striking a quick, flat blow across Trent's cheek with a cutting slap and a guttural, gasping moan. Long white ridges edged with red glowed against the tan backdrop of Trent's skin. He wasn't shocked, wasn't angry, wasn't even upset. He only looked at Kyle, his eyes sad, a simple defeat in the slump of his shoulders.

Then Kyle let out a shriek and began clawing frantically at Trent's face, heavy animal pants coming from his throat, fingernails ripping at flesh and hair. "React!" he screamed. "React! React!" sounding oddly like a prehistoric bird. Trent stood stoically, only bothering to close his eyes as self-protection. The flowers escaped to the safety of the carpet.

Neither Dana nor Claudia had their bearings to take action. So Jack stepped between the boys and shook Kyle so violently that his head snapped back.

Then they all fell still and silent again.

The star of Trent's neglected cigarette grew long and heavy in the sudden calm, until it broke under its own weight and dropped to the floor atop the yellow chrysanthemums.

Once Kyle was in the convertible, he fell asleep immediately, almost before Jack had shut the door. The wind had died. Jack circled behind the car where Trent stood, and stopped, wanting to say something. "I'm sorry" was the only thing that came to mind.

"You have nothing to be sorry for," Trent said.

Jack started to respond, stopped, turned away, then back. "You're not even angry, are you?"

Trent was composed, hands casually in the pockets of his jeans. "I can't be angry at Kyle," he said simply. "He's my conscience." He looked at Jack, openly, for a second, then averted his eyes to the dark trees around them.

AUGUST

The following days were sporadically tranquil and emotional. The most scorching image in Kyle's mind was the feral, desperate way Veronica had looked that night he'd fallen from her porch. Sometimes that was the only way he could remember her at all. It particularly troubled him because if he, too, knew, understood, was capable of that wild, primal despair, did that mean he was also capable of taking his life? Had Kevin been as crazed inside as Veronica had been? Had Veronica's friends or family had any idea? Had Veronica known it was coming to what it did? Or had she just, one moment, awakened?

His parents noticed his sorrow, though he couldn't sufficiently explain his mourning for an island girl he'd never mentioned. They watched him withdraw and, knowing only some of the circumstances of his summer, began to wonder if—and to fear that—their youngest son was going to be afflicted with the same demons that had preyed upon their firstborn.

None of the group came to visit, and he asked for none of them. He had no desire for communication—especially with Trent. His feelings for Trent were so sharply muddled, he mostly felt nothing.

Jack visibly relaxed once what he'd forewarned had come to pass. So as Kyle went under, Jack emerged, stronger, shinier, validated.

One day when Jack went to Kyle's, Ann met him at the door. Her gamine face was clouded with something like disappointment. She didn't hold the door open right away. She looked at him, intently, as if she were memorizing.

She was deciding.

"You could have told me," she said, and she sounded betrayed, by his lack of truthfulness, by his acceptance of their hospitality, by his having befriended her. Kyle was her son. But Jack was her friend.

She had different expectations from each.

Jack stammered. "I—I couldn't."

She didn't back down. "But you could have."

She opened the door wide to him.

It was late in the morning the day of Veronica's funeral when Kyle's dolorous mood began to change. He awoke before Jack and he lay, holding both Jack and the white stone he'd kept in his hand since they'd learned of Veronica, refreshed, lighter, hopeful, appreciating the sun, his life, the boy sleeping in his arms. Jack's presence kept Trent's and Veronica's ghosts at bay. He was the only thing that made Kyle optimistic for the future. It was difficult to remember why Princeton had excited him. The idea of living in a dorm, joining a fraternity, spending every moment, waking and not, with Trent bordered on distasteful. His dreams had changed, and drinking and getting stoned and skipping class, once things to anticipate greedily, suddenly seemed adolescent. He didn't begrudge anyone else pursuing those pleasures; he just felt too old for them. He was ready to get to the happily ever after.

When Jack stirred in his arms, he watched him coming back to life, appreciating the warm purity of love. "Hi."

"How you feeling?" Jack rubbed sleep from his eyes.

"Better."

"Yeah?"

"Yeah. I…"

"Yeah?"

"I was just thinking. About you. Us."

"And?"

"And the glorious life that lies before us."

"Glorious, huh?"

"Yeah. Once all this is behind us. The drama. This summer. Trent."

"You don't mean that. About Trent."

Kyle stroked Jack's face. He was suddenly clutched by a memory of a rainy day in the city. It was the perfect contrast to his time with Jack. He had never forgotten the experience, yet he had never told anyone about it either. It seemed shameful, and it made him sad, so he decided it needed to be exorcised. "Once, when Trent and I were fourteen, maybe fifteen, we were in the city at some store. He was really into this cologne he'd found, but he'd already spent his allowance, on a gift, for a girl. So after he moved on, I decided to buy it. For him. Because I still had my money. I waited the whole train ride back to school to give it to him. I couldn't wait to see his reaction. Once we were in our room, I went and sat at the desk in front of the window and turned to face him. He'd closed our door and was holding the cologne. I couldn't figure out how he'd gotten it out of my jacket. He came up to me and said, 'I stole it. I can't believe we didn't get caught.' I didn't know what to say. I was shocked, and I felt stupid, though I didn't know why. I just said, 'We were lucky.'"

When Jack didn't say anything, Kyle ended with, "That's just one of the stories I always remember about Trent."

Trent awakened late that morning. He thought it would be disrespectful to show up at the funeral, so he lay in bed, propped his hands behind his head and tried not to think of Kyle, or Veronica.

But their spirits would not be evaded.

He lit a joint.

He masturbated.

He showered.

He dressed.

He smoked another joint.

And then he went to town, cruising 70.

He parked on Main Street and was walking nowhere when he glanced into the diner to find Kyle and Jack breakfasting.

He hesitated.

Jack looked up.

Their eyes met.

Trent felt like he'd been caught.

He looked away and continued on.

He'd gone half a block before he heard his name.

He turned, tense, hopeful, to find Jack coming toward him.

"Hey," Jack said.

"Where's Kyle?" Trent couldn't stop himself from asking. He was stoned and wasn't expecting this.

"He's in the bathroom." Jack motioned toward the diner. "He doesn't know I'm out here and he doesn't know you are either. This is the first day he's been better. He doesn't need to see you." He spoke honestly.

Trent screwed his eyes up to the breezy brightness of the morning. He smelled fish and could imagine the fishermen coming into the marina for lunch. It made him nauseous.

"I just wanted to know what was up," Jack said. "What you were feeling. About...well, about Kyle."

"I think he hates me."

"He doesn't hate you," Jack said too quickly.

"The funeral was this morning."

"We know."

Trent noticed the use of the word *we*. As though they were one.

They looked at each other, like when they'd first met, assessing whether they were allies or adversaries. Somewhere they had switched places, though, and now guarded the interests they had formerly threatened.

"How did it go?" Jack asked then.

And Trent was ashamed.

If he were Kyle, he'd have gone.

But he was Trent.

"I don't know," he said. "I didn't feel like I belonged."

Jack gave him a searching look. "Kyle wasn't ready."

"That's to be expected." Then, "I'm glad you're taking care of him."

"It's not a sacrifice."

"I didn't mean it like that."

"I know what you meant."

"I bet you do," Trent ceded. "I have a feeling I could have any conversation with you that I could have with Kyle."

"Practically."

"I remember that first day he brought you to the beach. You were such a trouper to put up with our shit."

"You were always good to me."

"I was good to you for Kyle."

"I was there for Kyle."

"Touché." He grinned. "You're still one-upping me."

"Is that how you see it?"

"Don't you?"

Jack just looked at him, really seeing him for the first time. "I have to get back," he said. "Kyle doesn't know I've gone."

And he vanished, leaving Trent hanging with no sense of closure, or absolution.

A couple of days later Claudia came by. Kyle saw her from the living room of the McAllister house as she pulled up, the top of her silver Mercedes down. She took off her sunglasses and sat for a moment, thinking, her blond hair so bleached by the glare of the summer sun it was almost white. Presently she ran her fingers through her mane and got out.

When she appeared in the living room, she said, "Hey," breathily, like she'd sprinted from the back porch.

"Hey."

She sat beside him, too comfortably, on the sofa, and faced him. "How have you been?"

He shrugged. "You?"

"All right. You know. Considering."

He didn't look at her. "Yeah."

They sat without speaking. There were so many birds chirping and clattering outside, it sounded like a jungle beyond the confines of the house.

"I guess I fucked things up this summer," she said.

"You had nothing to do with Veronica."

She shrugged like there was so much more that not having had a hand in *that* hardly mattered. "We were surprised to not see you at the funeral."

"I didn't think I was ready for it," he said. "Or that I belonged."

"You weren't trying to avoid Trent?"

"I have no reason to avoid him." His voice was even. "Besides, who knew if he'd have the balls or the conscience to actually show?"

She let the remark slide. "So this self-imposed exile hasn't been to dodge him?"

"This 'self-imposed exile' has been for me to deal with some things within myself."

She looked long at him, her pale blue eyes probing. "We'd already lost you at Founder's Day, hadn't we?"

They regarded each other, her face soft, his hard, then he looked away, out the picture window. "I'm not lost."

"Aren't you?" she asked archly. Not expecting or needing a reply, she produced a pack of cigarettes and tapped it against a palm so that three displayed themselves. She took one, then held the pack to Kyle.

"No. Jack doesn't like it."

As she put the pack back, she smiled, raising her brows, innocently challenging. "Is this the boy equivalent of being pussy-whipped?"

"Actually, it's the human equivalent of respect."

"I see." She lit her cigarette and exhaled a hefty stream of cloud. "My point in coming over is to tell you that no matter how this ends with Trent, you're still our friend. Mine and Dana's." She smiled. "And Carly's, too, I'm sure, even though she doesn't know about all this yet."

All this. "Thank you," he said, wondering if she were done. For the first time he realized how easy it would be to move on, just leave them, be free of the grief, the games. He didn't think he'd miss it. Maybe Trent once in a while.

Maybe.

He sat, waiting for Claudia to leave.

"Where the goddamned bluebelly hell have you been?"

Jack and Kyle stopped in the foyer. Sheridan half stood from the sofa, facing them. "With Kyle," Jack said. "Where's Mom?"

"You knew she was going to the mainland. You were supposed to pick up syringes."

Jack blanched.

"I called and left a message with Kyle's mother when I realized you'd forgotten. I didn't know how else to contact you," Sheridan continued. "Where the hell do you boys go all day?"

"Take my car," Kyle said, diverting the conversation. "I'll stay here." He went to sit beside Jack's father on the sofa.

"Jack's head has been up his ass all summer," Sheridan said once his son was gone. "He's usually so sensible, but lately he just can't get it together."

Kyle said nothing, thinking he was probably the reason why. He hadn't realized Jack had shirked any familial duties. They'd spent a lot of time with the Averills, certainly more than he normally would have with Dana's or Claudia's parents.

Apropos of nothing, Sheridan said, "So Jack tells me you use a straight razor. Straight razors are classic. Real men use straight razors."

"Yes, my grandfather gave it to me."

"So it's an heirloom!"

"I…guess." He'd never thought of it that way.

"Jack never took to them or I'd have passed mine down, too."

"He likes the safety razors," Kyle said.

"Hell, sometimes I wonder if he's queer."

Kyle was startled by the suddenness of the statement. He didn't want to be in the conversation, but he had to know. "What if he was?"

"Things would change around here real quick, believe you me."

"Why?" His voice was quiet.

"*Why?* Why do you think?"

Kyle felt cold. "It's against your religion?"

"Because it's wrong, Kyle. I don't believe that free love bullshit going around."

He could think of nothing to say.

"You're the best thing that ever happened to Jack," Sheridan said then. "You've really helped him come out." He tapped Kyle on the knee. "You were better for him than finding love."

Not sure where he was coming from or where he was going, Kyle chose to simply not respond.

"You know... I should probably have something to eat. My blood sugar's low and it's making me crazy."

Maybe that was why he was changing topics so erratically. Whatever the reason, Kyle jumped at the chance to do something, anything, to get away. "Do you want me to make you something?"

"That'd be great. You're a better cook than Violet!" He laughed. "I've even daydreamed about paying you to stay on the island and be our cook when I retire. Violet can paint, I can sail and you can cook."

"Um...sounds good." Kyle stood and moved swiftly to the kitchen where he leaned against the counter for a moment, breathing into the quiet of the temporary refuge, and wondering where Jack fit into Sheridan's fantasy.

Once Jack returned and administered the injection, Sheridan went downstairs to sit in the cooler air and the boys went into the kitchen. "I hate that responsibility," Jack said, leaning against the counter. "I don't resent it, or my dad, but I'm terrified I'll fuck up."

"You okay?"

Jack nodded, arms hugging his body.

"You sure?"

"It's just that whether or not it really was, it seemed like a close call. It's not like he's not somewhat responsible or we'd have syringes on hand and he wouldn't be so squeamish and he wouldn't drink so damn much. But I can't mess up like that."

"I'll help you remember." Kyle touched Jack's forearm. "He's okay. You didn't fuck up. He's okay."

"It's just scary knowing you're responsible for your father's life. One wrong move and we become a Shakespearean tragedy."

He looked at Kyle, then they both laughed out loud.

When Kyle got home that night, he was surprised to find his father's Lincoln in the drive.

It was only Wednesday.

Scarlet and lemon geraniums called to him from either side of the porch as he entered the house. Mounting the stairs in the dark, a flicker of worry, like heat lightning, passed through him, so he rapped on the wooden rail to dispel any sense of doom. With the things that had happened already that summer he felt bracing for the worst wasn't paranoid, but practical. His hand was on the lightswitch at the top of the stairs when he paused, hearing a sound from his parents' bedroom.

His father was crying.

What now?

He took the remaining steps to his parents' closed door, ignoring the slight sense of shame that overcame him for eavesdropping.

"I thought I was fine," Graham was saying. "I thought I could deal with it. But whenever I'm in the real world, away from the island, it hits me." His voice quavered, bringing back to Kyle painfully vivid memories of the aftermath of Kevin's suicide.

"Should we talk to him about it?" Ann asked. "We could ask him where his ring has gone. Start that way."

"He'll think we don't support him."

"Which we do…"

"Yes, of course we do."

"But letting him know you're having a hard time isn't not supporting him, Graham."

"This is the end of our lineage, Ann. I can't put that on Kyle's shoulders." Then he was weeping.

Kyle jumped away from the door, his nerves so surged with electricity his skin itched. Afraid they'd heard him, he stumbled into his room and stood around the corner, back against the wall, trying to subdue his breathing and the booming of his heart.

When their muffled conversation continued he soundlessly closed his door, sat on his bed facing it, and folded his hands demurely in his lap. He felt like he'd suddenly and accidentally discovered he was adopted.

The next morning Graham explained his premature arrival by claiming he'd cashed in a couple of vacation days. Kyle accepted the story with a weak smile and averted eyes. He was so shocked by the seemingly bottomless well of duplicity from which his parents drew that he was unable to confront them.

Jack came at 11:30. Kyle tried to slip out as quickly and noiselessly as possible, but his father came up from the basement before he could make his getaway. "I thought it would be nice to have a talk with you two," he said.

Kyle looked over his shoulder at him, almost fearful.

"Why don't you join me at the club for a drink?"

They sat facing the water in the chill of the air-conditioned country club where the Founder's Day celebration had been held, each with a vodka tonic. Kyle found his father's summons curious. Something about it didn't ring true, and Jack could tell, too. They looked at each other for an uneasy moment, then away. Graham was discussing asters, and Kyle couldn't understand why.

Glancing out the window, he could feel the pounding of the surf, like some great engine moving the world. The air conditioning was so clear and so clean it had hurt to breathe when he'd first come in from the hot, dry atmosphere outside. Now, though, it was like there was nothing there. The club was claustrophobic, like a planet with dwindling oxygen.

Just as the lack of air was about to make him lose equilibrium, Jack touched his hand under the table and the status quo was redeemed, breath rushing back into the room like into a vacuum.

He chuckled because his father was chuckling.

Then Graham became serious, his smile fading. "Don't look so frightened," he said to his son.

"Tell us why we're here." The statement came with an edge.

"I want to talk to you. You haven't been around much this summer, so I thought by inviting both of you, we could spend some time together."

Kyle found it difficult to be understanding when he didn't know what the truth was anymore. "Can you get to the point so we can relax?"

Graham inhaled slowly and deeply. "I didn't realize how unbearable this was."

Kyle said nothing.

"Have you gotten the details about Michigan worked out?" Graham asked then.

"Of course." Kyle spoke confidently. But as he spilled forth the facets of their plans—his getting into the University of Michigan, their finding an apartment, embarking on a life together—he felt his youth like an albatross. The blueprint seemed immaterial in the harsh light of the sun and the antiseptic shininess of the club. It was so much more serious than it sounded. It was everything. But he didn't know how to make his father understand that, because he saw opening between them an abyss that grew wider each day. And he wasn't sure how to bridge it, or if he even wanted to anymore.

"What will you tell Jack's parents?" Graham asked.

"We don't know," Kyle said. "Possibly just that Jack won't be living in the dorms. Possibly more."

"What if they don't approve?"

"They won't!" Jack cried.

Kyle couldn't remember him speaking since they'd ordered. He said, "They'll have no say in the matter," sounding less sure than he'd have liked.

"I'm afraid." Jack appealed to Graham, his frightened voice making him sound small. "They're not going to take this very well."

Graham looked uneasy, but he offered, "Do you want me to talk to them?"

"No!" Jack shouted, attracting the attention of neighboring diners.

"Okay," Graham said. "Just a suggestion. I thought it might be easier if they saw Kyle's parents accepting of it."

Kyle didn't know if he should laugh, scoff or shout accusations. He was pissed that he'd fallen for their lies. Looking across the table at his father, he saw the same affable, polite, caring man he'd always known. Nothing seemed affected, and Kyle believed that was because his efforts were sincere. The problem was that there were efforts at all. He didn't want there to be walls, if only for the reason that all his life he'd thought there were none. Now they made him feel as claustrophobic as the club did.

That realization sparked something, a very strong memory he couldn't place. Walls or secrets or something. It felt so big he was terrified he'd lose it before he could recall it.

And then it came on its own.

The afternoon Jack had asked, "Do you ever wonder what your parents' secrets are?"

And he had been glib. He'd practically scoffed, No. His parents had none.

And now, now he realized he'd never had a clue. He'd been so arrogant, so assured, yet he'd never known truth in his life.

Not until Jack.

He was beginning to wonder how he'd ever respected his father at all.

He ordered a drink.

The temperature soared that day. Kyle and Jack spent the rest of the afternoon in the darkroom beneath the stairs, bathed in ruby light. Jack appeared cool as he went about dipping papers, the gold ring Kyle had given him resting on his back. He was so thin he didn't react to heat the way others did. As he hung a photo from a wire that stretched from one wall to the opposite, he said, "What do you think this is? I only took it yesterday but I have no clue."

It was a blue blur, like a stormy eye.

"What do you think it is?" Kyle responded.

"You go first."

"What if I'm wrong?"

"I'll just laugh at you." Jack was already laughing, and he leaned in and kissed Kyle on the side of the mouth.

Kyle's arms slid around him, and their lips met. Kyle's hands found their way under Jack's shirt, to his flat brown nipples. Jack pulled Kyle's shorts down over his hips. Kyle was immediately aroused. There was something freeing about having no pants on.

Flushed in scarlet, their kisses became hotter, deeper, serious.

They had sparked.

And then the door started to open.

Jack was quick. He let out a shout and slammed the door before anyone was shamed.

"Goddamn!" Sheridan was in the hall.

"Dad?"

Kyle pulled his shorts up, his bottom lip quavering. He felt like he'd been struck.

"Sorry about that, son," Sheridan said. "I didn't know you were home."

"Just developing some film."

Jack and Kyle looked at each other, blood pounding so hard their cells prickled. When Sheridan's footsteps receded, Kyle sat heavily on a box, his head in his hands.

"You okay?" Jack asked.

Kyle nodded, not looking up.

"That was almost the worst experience of my life."

"Mine, too."

They had a sticky dinner with Violet and Sheridan in their basement. Through the meal, Jack tried to work up the courage to broach the subject of September. But the golden moment either never presented itself or his timing was off.

When they were done, Violet made her hundredth remark about the humidity, then said, "Come upstairs with me, Kyle. There's something I'd like to show you."

On the dresser in Mr. and Mrs. Averill's bedroom, there was one of Violet's paintings. He had no idea what it was, so he just gazed at it, thoughtful. Then, thinking he should say something, he offered, "It's pretty."

"It's you and Jack," Violet provided.

And then he saw. They were on a porch swing. It was night. The swing was blue, the wall of the house behind them white. He was wearing a red shirt and looking to something beyond the rail of the porch. Beside him, Jack was in white and looking to Kyle's profile. It wasn't artfully rendered, but its modesty was sweet. For the first time, Kyle could see past Violet's lack of talent to the devotion behind her struggle to create beauty.

He was so surprised and so moved, he was speechless for a moment. "It's beautiful," he finally said, lamely. But the word hardly encompassed how deeply he was touched. To be so accepted by Jack's family was something for which he'd strove, and it suddenly appeared he'd been successful.

Fanning herself, Violet remarked, "Sheridan doesn't mean to be so hard on Jack."

He didn't know why she imparted that just then.

He waited, but she said nothing more.

Later, after Violet and Sheridan had gone to bed, the boys carried enormous pieces of watermelon down to the shore where they sat at the end of the dock, dangling their feet in the water, the boat rocking gently beside them. The waves lapped quietly against the sand, the August moon hanging, only half formed, above them, surrounded by a multitude of stars. Serenaded by a chorus of crickets, Kyle watched a leaf drift lazily, indecisively, on the wind before dropping consequentially into the water just beyond their reach.

He bit into the moist flesh of the melon, spat a succession of seeds into the dark, one, two, three, then turned to Jack and spat the final one at him. It hit his forehead, then bounced to the dock with a clitter.

Jack gave a bemused smile. "Where were you brought up again? The Midwest?"

"No, but that's where you're dragging me come September." He leered at Jack who was poking seeds from the melon. Then, without looking up, Jack drew his finger down Kyle's cheek, leaving a trail of dripping juice. "Hey!"

"Gotta problem?" Jack bit into the fruit, then looked at Kyle, nectar dripping down his chin, glimmering in the moonlight.

Kyle felt such a flush of ardor that his hair tingled. He kissed him, deep, long, probing, slippery, sticky, unable to control himself.

When he pulled back Jack was breathless. "You made my legs weak." He kissed Kyle again, quickly, hotly. "Do you love me, King Kyle?" he sighed into his mouth.

"My kingdom's worth," Kyle breathed back into him.

They broke apart, resting their foreheads together. Jack said, "I feel like we're tempting fate. Like the angels are envious."

Kyle looked at the moon, its coy half face mocking him sitting on the shore of a tiny island in the middle of an ocean beneath a trillion stars. He felt terribly insignificant.

They sat, looking at the water, listening to it, breathing it in. A subtle breeze roused the waning leaves of the trees. The boat swayed with the rhythm of the waves, its ropes groaning protest.

"I used to feel the call to the ocean everyone feels," Jack began, suddenly melancholy. "But something happened the summer I turned six. I was in the tub. I was underwater, looking up at the ceiling. I could hear drops splashing from the faucet. And, like it always is underwater, sound was muffled and slow. I remember waiting for each drop to fall, slower and slower, like a clock winding down. I don't know how long I was under before I heard it. Or how much longer before I became aware of it. I could hear its cadence, feel its vibration. It was shaking my sight. It was rippling the water. It was insistent and alarming, like a phone call in the night.

"And then I realized what it was." He looked across the water. "It was my heartbeat. I could feel it in my chest. I could feel it in my wrists and in my temples. And I suddenly became aware that it was the only thing keeping me alive. And what was to stop that tiny mass on which *everything* depended from giving out? It was like being held over a cliff by a shoelace.

"I panicked, and inhaled.

"I almost died. In some ways I feel like I did. Because it changed me. I feel like I'm a second draft. And I keep wondering who I was supposed to be."

He took Kyle's hand and looked him fully in the face. "That's why I'm afraid of the water."

A couple of days later Kyle was at home on the phone to Princeton. He'd been on hold for a number of minutes when he heard a noise at the door and glanced up to see Trent. Being unprepared for his appearance, Kyle just looked at him. There was no speech rehearsed, no decision made, so seeing him brought to the fore all the turmoil he'd pushed aside in the wake of Veronica's death. He hung up the phone and stood facing him through the screen, actually afraid.

"Can I come in?" Trent asked.

"What do you want?" he spoke quickly and warily.

"I'm not here to invade. I just want to see you."

Kyle considered his alternatives. He didn't want to see Trent right then. He was getting along without him very well. But he had a feeling that if he turned him away, he might damage the only chance they might still have, and until he'd decided whether he wanted to squander that chance, he wanted to protect it.

He pushed the screen door open and Trent entered with an intimation of autumn. Purple hyacinths stood in a vase on the mantel. The clock ticked ceaselessly forward in the kitchen. They stood, both uncertain. Kyle had the urge to offer a drink but resisted. He wasn't going to cave. This was Trent's tragedy. He needed to make it right.

So he was cold. "So?"

"How've you been?"

"Great."

"Great."

They looked at each other.

"May I sit?"

They sat, Trent on the sofa, Kyle in the armchair.

"You're still angry."

"No." It was the truth.

Trent gave a quizzical look. "Then why haven't we seen each other?"

Kyle felt the frustrated rage he'd buried surge again and when he spoke he spoke through lips tight as a spinster's. "What you did was so selfish, so thoughtless and so heedless of all the warnings I gave you that it says more about who you've become than you could ever hope to explain. So I've needed time to evaluate whether you're someone I want in my life." He was surprised and relieved he'd spoken as succinctly and eloquently as he had.

Trent stood, his anger as sudden as Kyle's. "God! I made a mistake!"

"Veronica is *dead*."

"Do you not think guilt is destroying me?"

"It was your choice. This is your burden."

Trent breathed quick, short breaths. "I am so sick of your sanctimony I could scream."

Kyle stood too. "If that's how you feel," he said, low and threatening, "get out."

"You always take this tack whenever I screw up. It always comes down to you being right, doesn't it?"

Kyle gave a smug smile. "No," he said caustically. "It always comes down to you being wrong."

They stood in heavy silence.

"Kyle—"

"Don't."

They faced off.

Then Trent exhaled deeply. "I don't want to argue with you. I came to find you again."

"I was fine until you showed up. Why couldn't you just leave me alone?" Kyle felt hatred for the disruption of the balance he'd established.

"Is that what you really want, Kyle?"

He was afraid he'd say what he was really feeling and then be unable to take it back, and, alternatively, he wanted to throw it in Trent's face because it was so ugly and black and stinging that it would scar him like acid.

"Do you want to end this, Kyle?"

"I don't know. I need time."

"How much?"

"I don't know! Don't pressure me."

"Summer's almost over, Kyle."

"Stop saying my name. I'm not four."

"We need to resolve this before we leave for school."

"Why?"

"Because I need you."

"*Why?*"

"Because! Because I haven't figured out how to feel good about myself without your approval!"

Kyle was so surprised by that, he looked at Trent with absolutely no understanding. "What?"

"I haven't been able to get your approval since Kevin died! I can't compare to him. I've tried, but I can't!"

Kyle was so shocked he had to sit down on the sofa. When he spoke, his voice was soft and level. "You have never had to live up to anything, Trent. You know that."

"No. I don't." Trent spoke quickly, liking the feel of the truth like the frenzied rush of a new addiction. "You have always held the brass ring just out of my reach. So I jump higher and I run faster and I swing harder, because I want it. I want to be good enough." And then he was hurt and on the verge of tears. "You've never known this?"

For many moments, the only sounds were the relentless ticking of the kitchen clock and the ageless roar of the surf. When Kyle spoke his voice was uneven with phlegm. "No."

"Then you've never known anything about me." Trent turned and walked out, letting the screen door slam behind him.

Kyle wanted to go after him, wanted to make things right, wanted to forgive, but the wound was still too fresh.

He let him go.

As Trey drove by Kyle's that night, he felt the twinge of the unrequited. The porch light was on, awaiting Kyle's return. His car wasn't in the driveway. Because Kyle was with Jack. That fact tormented Trey, every moment of every day, his jealousy having mutated into desperation.

There was so little time left.

His drive along the coast eventually took him to Trent's house, and, beyond that, Jack's. He'd known he'd come to it, and the idea had formed miles back. But it didn't gel until he saw that Kyle's car wasn't there either.

That was his luck.

Light burned in one of the windows.

That was his opportunity.

The opportunity to buy all the time until September.

But at what price?

Mrs. Averill didn't recognize him at first. She hadn't seen him since the dance. So he reintroduced himself and, though she still only vaguely remembered him, she let him enter when he said he wanted to talk about her son and Kyle Quinn.

Thursday.

They spent a lazy day at the McAllister house. The wind off the ocean was hot and did little to alleviate the sultriness that shrouded the island. They lay in the baking sun, drowsy and languorous and content.

This was Kyle's favorite time.

They said little, did less. Kyle watched as Jack drifted off, his glasses on the sand between them. His face was tranquil, free of the trepidation he'd felt earlier in the summer. His skin was smooth, brown, unmarred.

He's mine, Kyle thought, and it gave him a warm, solid feeling. He took Jack's glasses and held them safely.

Then he, too, drifted cozily into the slumber of the satisfied.

They had dinner in town. They didn't go to Olympus. They left about ten to head "home." They rode without speaking, Kyle's right hand covering Jack's left on the seat between them. The night was almost eerily still. Fireflies winked silently as they entered a Cimmerian forest, the same stretch on which they had run out of gas so long ago. Oleander struggled to flower by the side of the road. Thunder rumbled heavily, though there were no storm clouds. The moon was enormous.

"I guess the weather's changing," Jack said.

"We must be driving into it." Kyle squeezed his hand.

They shared a loving, knowing look.

And then it happened.

Jack sensed it first, quickly turning toward the windshield, shouting Kyle's name. Kyle reacted before he even saw it, hitting the brakes so that the car came to a screeching halt with smoking tires and a dull, solid thump.

Then the night was still again.

Kyle looked over at Jack and saw blood, in a thin, shiny streak, trickle from his right nostril onto his upper lip. "My God. Are you all right?"

Though he appeared a little dazed, Jack nodded. "Yeah. You?"

Kyle's chest felt tight and bruised from the seat belt, but otherwise he was fine. He nodded, then leaned over and wiped Jack's blood away. He was awash in guilt. "I'm sorry," he said at the same time Jack said, "What did we hit?"

They got out. One of the headlights was covered in spiderweb cracks, but both of them still worked. A few yards before the car, in the lit stage of the road, lay a fawn. The fur around its neck was matted with blood. One of its back legs twitched. Its eyes were hazed over, the lids half closed. It breathed with a labored, slurpy sound.

Kyle turned away, overcome with regret. He'd never imagined it might happen.

Jack looked at the back of his head for a long moment before speaking. "Kyle."

Kyle inhaled deeply, but the air felt thin. Pressure was intense in his chest.

"Are you sure you're all right? Do you need a hospital?"

"I'm just catching my breath."

Jack waited. Then he said, "Kyle. It's still alive."

The animal whimpered then, a high-pitched, painful sound, as if on cue.

"We have to do something."

"We don't have a gun."

Jack held the back of his hand to his nose to stay the flow of blood. "We don't need a gun."

He sounded so definitive, Kyle turned to him.

"We have to run it over."

Kyle looked to the animal, then back to Jack.

"I'll do it," Jack offered.

"No." Kyle's voice shook. "I can't ask you to do that." But cold, white cowardice took precedence, and he couldn't meet Jack's eyes.

"You don't have to. I'm volunteering."

Kyle started to back away, his face disintegrating with fear and shame.

"Hey." Jack reached out a quick hand and grasped his wrist. "Are you okay? I think you're in shock."

"I—" Kyle's eyes were attaining an edge. He couldn't conceive of the courage to kill the animal. His eyes darted from Jack to the deer, and back. "I can't do it," he said, a touch of delirium in his voice. "I can't do it. I can't take more death."

Jack pulled him by his wrist so that they were close and he could snake his arms around his waist. "You just stand here and wait. Okay?" He stroked Kyle's hair. "I'll take care of it. You might have hurt yourself more than you thought." Then he quickly jerked away. "God, I'm getting blood on you." It had dripped onto Kyle's shirt.

Kyle was hardly aware. "Hell of a king I am. I can't even take care of my own mess."

"That's why I'm here." He gave Kyle a light kiss on the lips, passing along the taint of fresh blood.

Then Kyle began walking up the road in the phosphorescent moonlight.

He didn't look back, stepping from the glare of the headlights into darkness.

He heard thunder rumble again, this time closer.

Then he heard Jack climb into the convertible, close the door and start the engine.

After a moment, there was a sickening thud, and then the car came alongside him.

He climbed into the passenger seat.

And Jack drove into the protective cover of oncoming storm clouds.

The porch was sweltering. A vase with two daisies stood at the head of the boys' bed. Both shirtless, they sat on the mattress, Kyle dabbing at the blood on Jack's nose with a sheet. He could see Jack's heartbeat through his chest. He stared at it, thinking about the water, Kevin, the deer. They all seemed connected somehow.

But Kevin and the fawn were dead.

And Jack was the most alive thing Kyle had ever known.

He didn't know where he fit in.

Jack watched him for a minute. "Love?"

He brought Kyle around every time. "Yeah?"

"You were aces tonight."

"I didn't feel aces."

"There'll be times you'll take care of me, too." He cupped Kyle's cheek. "There will be time."

His thumb parted Kyle's lips, and Kyle closed his mouth around it, their eyes meeting, Kyle's the dusky promise of Indian summer, Jack's glassy like a still pool of water, deterring intruders from its depths by distracting them with their reflections.

Kyle saw only Jack.

He had never wanted or needed him more. He lay him on his back, tasting his skin, hot and salty and wet. Chest to chest, Jack put his hands in Kyle's hair. Kyle's hands ran down the sides of Jack's legs, pulling them up around him. Without changing position they wriggled out of their shorts. Their kisses were sticky. Their teeth scraped. Kyle bit Jack's chin. Jack kissed Kyle's throat, the flesh that he owned. The smells of sweat, sea and sex mingled in the close, tropical sultriness. They fell into the cadence they had created, panting, laughing, moaning. They groped, shuddered, called out.

Then Kyle was falling, tearing painfully out of Jack, jarring his shoulder against the floor, aghast that the McAllisters had returned. He hurried to the bed to cover Jack's tiny form, and when he looked up, he was shocked—no, horrified—to see Sheridan standing above them, rage radiating from his twisted face so strongly that Kyle could look at nothing but him, like a tornado racing across an open plain. For a second, he actually feared for their lives.

"Dad," Jack said, peering from behind him.

"Mr. Averill." Kyle reached out a hand to tranquilize him, show that he meant no harm, but he couldn't move forward because Jack gripped his shoulder. He didn't want his father to see him naked.

Sheridan gaped at Kyle, then changed his focus to Jack's taut, slender fingers grasping his flesh. Seeing them touching so intimately caused something to break in him. He crumpled inward.

The boys waited, anticipating.

Then Sheridan stepped forward and raised an arm.

Kyle's mouth exploded as he fell onto the floor, his shoulder flaring. Darkness began to seep into his eyes. Blood coursed into his mouth.

He'd never been hit before.

"How dare you!" Sheridan raged.

Kyle crawled to his knees, spitting out a dense dollop of blood, his erection gone limp. The blackness receded, and he saw Jack clamber to the side of the bed to be next to him, despite his visibility.

"Dad," Jack said.

"Don't." Sheridan approached slowly, his voice tight. He stepped to the end of their bed and stopped, his eyes targeted on Kyle. When he spoke, the words were measured and concise so that each carried the weight of a threat. "Get. Away. From my. Son."

It was sinking in to Kyle that he had been attacked. His mouth throbbed. He had to spit again. He wasn't going to be able to speak around the blood. Jack's strained breathing was loud and hot in his ear. He wanted to throw a sheet over his quivering body but was afraid motion might instigate Sheridan into a frenzy.

He had never been so afraid.

"This isn't Kyle's fault." Jack began to cry, a soft, beautiful cry. "I was going to tell you."

"You are malignant." Sheridan's face contorted. "You have soiled my boy."

"That's not—" Kyle's voice was garbled with blood. "I love Jack."

There would be no righting this.

"I didn't want to believe it. I didn't want to believe."

"Dad." Tears slipped down Jack's cheeks.

Sheridan exhaled heavily, sadly. "Oh, Jack."

Jack looked to Kyle, his eyes the opaque blue of an iceberg. He swallowed, his fear so thorough there was no trace of humiliation.

He was hit, then, by his shirt. It smelled of sandalwood, of him. Sheridan squatted at the end of the mattress. After disentangling Jack's shorts from the sheets, he threw those to him, too. "Get dressed."

Jack dressed slowly. Kyle became aware that, at some point, the daisies had spilled and he was damp. When Jack was done, Kyle handed him his glasses, and he slipped them on, using both hands, like a child, to hook them over his ears. Then he stepped to the edge of their bed and went to the porch door, looking back around the threat of his father. His eyes met Kyle's, wet, dark, apologizing. They spoke, soundlessly, things they'd said thousands of times.

Then he was gone.

Sheridan still faced Kyle, his fingers pulsing like vicious hearts. He grappled to find words to articulate his contempt.

Kyle looked at him, sadly, sad that it had come to this.

They'd been so happy.

Then Sheridan spat, savagely, with malicious prejudice in Kyle's direction. But his aim was not true, and his saliva landed on the bed, amongst the soiled sheets.

Dana came by the next morning on her way to the farmers market. "What happened?" she asked as they stood in the foyer. She tentatively touched his mouth, which was swollen and red.

"I fell." He said it without conviction. It was the lie he'd told his parents, who were in the kitchen. "Let's go." He pushed past her into the sharply clear morning.

"What did you fall on?" Dana asked as she slid behind the wheel of her car. She started the ignition and put it in reverse.

"Mr. Averill's fist."

She had turned to look out the rear window before it clicked. She stepped on the brake and turned back to him. "What!"

Kyle couldn't help but smile, but it hurt his mouth so he stopped. "Mr. Averill walked in on me and Jack."

Dana was horrified, her mouth the shape of an egg. "Do you mean— what do you mean?"

"Could you die?"

Dana didn't think it was funny. She put the car in park. "He hit you?"

"Just once."

"And that makes it all right?"

Kyle didn't respond.

"What did he say?" Dana demanded.

He had to look away from her, out the window, to the willow and the sea. "He called me malignant."

"What!"

His words were small and hurt. "He said I tainted Jack." He swallowed heavily, then looked back at her. "I didn't taint him."

"Of course you didn't! You did *nothing* wrong! He doesn't understand that the basic principle of Christianity is to love." She hesitated then gasped. "Did he hit Jack, too?"

"No. I think he's safe." He looked toward his house, feeling a sudden, surprising swell of shame. He felt like he'd failed at something he couldn't name, something he hadn't even known he'd been trying to achieve.

Dana watched him, wondering, waiting.

When it was clear he was going to offer nothing more, she put the car in reverse and backed onto the road.

310

"They're gone," Jack said that night, studiously chewing his cheek. They stood in Jack's kitchen, Kyle's arms around his waist. A purple dahlia had been plucked from Ann's garden and rested on the counter beside a bag of groceries.

"Gone?"

"We came home last night and Dad was so upset he couldn't talk to me. Then he got up early and spent the day on the boat. My mom seemed normal. I don't know if he told her or what. When he came back, he wasn't feeling well, so my mom took him to the mainland." Jack unknotted himself from Kyle's arms, then turned back, hugging his own torso like he hadn't realized he'd miss Kyle's warmth. He let loose a heavy breath. "I'm afraid."

His words hung in the air before Kyle reached out a confident hand. "I'm sure it'll be fine."

"I don't know."

"What do you mean?"

"He was really upset."

"Jack. He'll be fine. And we will be, too."

Jack took Kyle's hand and pulled him to his side, nesting his face in Kyle's hair. He breathed deeply of his scent, salty and clean. "So what did you bring me to eat?"

They made cheeseburgers in the kitchen, because, surprisingly, the evening was too brisk to grill on the deck. Kyle stood watch over the sizzling meat as Jack sliced cheese and tomatoes. A firefly crawled up the screen, flashing, on, off, on, off. Outside, the wind violated the slumber of the leaves, bringing with it the sober reminder of autumn. And Kyle couldn't help but let a trickle of Jack's apprehension scuttle through him. He discreetly rapped his knuckles on the wooden counter as Jack leaned in front of him, placing cheese slices on the hamburger patties. The grease popped and spattered in the skillet, hitting the gas flame with a hot, violent *sssssss*.

Violet phoned. Sheridan would be in the hospital overnight but would be fine.

They would stay on the mainland until Sunday.

&

They ate in the living room, talking little. Afterward, they lay on the sofa, one at either end. Neither got up to turn on a lamp, so the only light they had came from the flickering images of the television, dancing over their faces like taunts.

During a commercial break, Kyle carried their plates into the kitchen. Jack rose and went to the window, pulling the cord of the blind. It dropped with a warning hiss and nerve-tightening clatter, and, not realizing he was on edge, Kyle jumped, the plates crashing to the floor.

They were living in suspense.

From the balcony they could hear the eerie tinkling of wind chimes.

"It's almost September." Jack went to the deck and slid the door shut, locking it with a wooden *tok!*

The hiss of static from the television was like the high whisper of ghosts, the light of whose images pulled and clawed vainly at Jack's and Kyle's slumbering forms. They lay together, facing the TV, Kyle's arms around Jack, protecting him from falling into the void.

The next day they slept in, ate a late breakfast, and sat on the deck in the stark white sun, the purple dahlia fading on the table between them. A sudden dry warmth, after the cool of the night, made them slothful and dull.

They dozed.

Later, Jack still dreaming, Kyle stood and pulled his shirt over his head and descended to the beach, the blazing sun so intense he felt like a mirage. He did a hopping walk on the blistering sand then broke the surface of the water so smoothly he left no trace.

As the sun began to set into a bleached horizon, Kyle leaned on the rail of the balcony, looking toward the place where the sea met the sky, the water stony in the light. A fog was moving in, slowly encroaching on their kingdom. Mimosa he had never noticed had bloomed, seemingly overnight, its rich pink pompoms loud in the bleakness of the day.

He stood, not thinking of anything in particular. It was an in-between time. He felt like a ghost, or a fetus.

Then he heard his name. He turned to find Jack standing at the door behind him. Jack looked at him for a very long time, like he was affirming, remembering, memorizing.

"Puss?"

Jack joined him at the railing and took one of his hands in his own. "I just wanted to be sure of you."

"Will this be what it's like when we're thirty?" Jack asked as he and Kyle stood before the bathroom mirror that night. He had on a white cotton nightshirt and held a toothbrush. Kyle was shirtless and brushing. In response to the question, Kyle just showed his teeth, foam dribbling down his chin, leaving a trail of white ooze.

They slept in Jack's bed, the windows open, the moon full.

Kyle awoke from a light sleep in the night, wondering if it weren't too still without the ticking of the clock at the McAllister house.

He waited for unconsciousness to overtake him again, but when it didn't, he slipped out of bed and went, naked, past the wild grass, to the cool, damp sand. He slipped into the water's chill and swam out deep, to where a light mist hovered above the surface, immersing himself in the sparkling brine.

It took a moment to get used to the underwater sounds before he heard it. It was the first time he'd been aware of the beating of his heart. It was like a drum, insistent as time. So conscious of it, he could feel it at the pulse points in his wrists, his neck, his feet. It made him feel both powerful and tenuous.

And then he missed Jack.

He broke the surface and swam with steady strokes back to the shore, where he turned his face, smoothly unyielding, toward the sky. "You can't have him yet, you know," he said evenly, the water forceless at his side. He did not smile. "You can't have him yet."

Then he returned to his lover, his hair ratty from the salt of the sea. He snuggled into him, their legs tangling like roots. Jack's back formed into Kyle's chest, their hearts aligned, and they were still.

ଛ

Kyle awoke at ten.

The overcast morning was shockingly bright and cool, the smothering heat of the previous day gone. Jack stood at the screen door, chewing his cheek. There were small, dark pouches beneath his eyes, an intimation of misgiving in the set of his mouth. He looked small framed in the door, the sterling sky and the aqua sea battling for precedence behind him. The purple dahlia had languished and lay withering on the bureau.

Today they come back, Kyle thought.

He propped himself up, the brown of his flesh in sharp contrast with the white ocean of sheets. He grinned, his bruise small enough now to be puckish. "Hey, stallion," he said in his best come-hither voice. "Want a ride?"

Jack turned and gave a bittersweet smile, the sweet winning out because he was happy Kyle was awake and they were together again.

They hung there for a second, enjoying their connection.

Then Jack climbed back into bed, settling into Kyle, and Kyle rested his chin on his shoulder, his breath hot in his ear. Jack was as delicately thin as he'd been at the beginning of the season, but now he had the color of health, the maturity of self-confidence, his gangliness, his awkwardness gone.

And Kyle had been justified.

At that moment, they were more themselves, no pretenses, no bartering, than they had ever been.

It was a moment of clarity, but it was a quiet moment, and they slept.

Jack awoke suddenly but not abruptly. The sky had turned a whiter shade of gray. Wind whistled through the screens. The air was cooler. The clock on the nightstand read 1:18.

He nestled back into Kyle's arms and slept.

Kyle roused himself around 3:30. Jack was already sitting up in bed and looking out at the leaden afternoon. The room was chilled and Jack's skin was rippled with gooseflesh. Kyle leaned up, kissing the underside of his arm.

Jack looked down at him. "Smell that mimosa."

"How long have you been awake?"

"Twenty minutes or so."

They watched the sea in silence.

Then Kyle squirmed out of bed and closed the sliding glass door. "I'll get ready."

When he was done, Kyle sat in the living room, hands folded in his lap, massaging the white stone he carried like a talisman. They hadn't discussed what to do when Jack's parents returned, both having thought of it tirelessly, yet each had reached the conclusion that Jack should face them alone.

Ten minutes passed before Jack descended the stairs. He went to the rear of the sofa and rested his hands on Kyle's shoulders. "I'll call you tomorrow."

Kyle turned around, kneeling on the couch, eyes level with Jack's sternum.

"I'm not compromising." Jack pulled him close. "That's how I know we'll win."

Head against Jack's chest, Kyle could hear the heartbeat that caged him in.

It made him sad.

He gave him a tight squeeze, then got up and went to the door.

"I love you, Kyle Ryan Quinn." Jack's voice made him hesitate. "You're a watermark on my life."

Kyle turned back, then stepped closer to touch the ring that hung around Jack's neck. "The Pretty Time is just beginning. We have tomorrow. And the day after that. And the day after that…" He trailed off, but Jack didn't pick up the line. Instead, he gave Kyle a pained smile, his eyes glassy and sparkling and wet.

"There won't be anymore saltwater kisses." Jack was crying, hard.

"I love you," Kyle said.

Jack's tears were hacking and fierce.

"I love you," Kyle said again.

And he left.

Kyle spent part of the evening with Dana, playing chess.

She won all four games.

Afterward, they went for a drive, Dana smoking behind the wheel.

The moon was nonexistent.

Dana dropped him off at home with a kiss.

He went to bed early and was still reading when he fell asleep atop the covers, the light burning, radio playing low. He dreamed he was fighting his way through inky blackness, to a surface, to light, to air. It wasn't a frantic, drowning feeling, but slow and warm, like he was being asphyxiated with kindness, or like he was being born.

He struggled and strove to attain freedom, to find peace, but when he finally burst out of the dark, the new world was so traumatizing that his eyes snapped open, his lungs gasped for air, and he was filled with a frantic wanting to return to the womb.

It had been the true peace.

Then he heard a rap on the door, giving him a start. Jack stood on the deck in a navy windbreaker. The night had turned stormy.

Kyle got up and pushed open the sliding glass door, reality taking hold again. He was grateful that his father naturally slept so soundly, and that his mother did so pharmaceutically.

He stepped outside and Jack wrapped his arms so tightly around his neck, Kyle felt suffocated, giving him a whiff of his dream in a flash of feeling. He held him close, his little body shaking like a frightened bird's. "Puss," he soothed. "You're here. You're safe. What happened?"

"You're going to think I'm stupid."

"Don't be cracked. I would never—"

Jack turned away. "Nothing happened. They came home, my dad seemed okay, we had dinner. I tried to bring it up while we were eating, but my father said they'd decided to deal with it."

A grin split Kyle's face. "That means we're golden."

Jack took up the ring that rested on his chest. "Maybe." *Something's going to happen...* was a vocal ellipsis. "It plucks at me."

"Oh, you."

"Don't patronize me."

"I'm not." He squeezed Jack's hands as if verification of his sincerity.

Jack gave him a limpid look in which the blue of his eyes caught the light at just the right angle so that they became translucent, depthless, and Kyle felt like he was being pulled into them, sucked deeper and deeper by an undertow, like a slow-moving vacuum, until there was nothing but blue. And he felt safe. And he was unafraid. And he knew then that Jack was his womb.

And then Jack began to cry. He put his face in his hands and wept, his body shaking with visceral despair. He let forth a lonesome, wounded sob that seared Kyle's memory and would come to torment him like memories of war.

He was at a complete loss. He realized he could dispel darkness from every aspect of Jack's life except where it reached into superstition.

It left him helpless.

So he took him in his arms again and murmured nothingness, hoping just his presence would salve. "Puss. Don't. Please don't cry. I love you. I love you. I love you." He knew nothing else to say, so he said it over and over, a mantra, until the words ceased to have meaning and they were only sounds, like a language he could speak but not understand. He was frustrated that *I love you* was everything. It needed more letters, more syllables, more resonance to reflect its power. *Love* was soft and kind and warm, but it didn't convey the truth, the conviction, the majesty, the glory, the freedom, the profoundness it also contained. Such a small word seemed inadequate to bear such weight.

When Jack's emotions subsided, he said, urgently, his voice raw, "You know I love you, right?"

"Of course, but don't say it like that. Like you're making sure I know for future reference."

Jack gave a pained, poignant smile. "I don't remember a time before us. Only us." Cool autumn wind shifted around them. "Tell me, King Kyle. How many years would you have to go back to change your destiny?"

His lips were puffy, his eyes red, his face anguished. But he was the most resplendent thing Kyle had ever known or imagined.

"I can't wait to grow old with you." He kissed him, tenderly, then fiercely and a little desperately. Then they broke apart, and he leaned his forehead to Jack's, and they shut their eyes, staying that way for many heartbeats.

"I have to go," Jack whispered too soon, the fear of the imminent in his eyes. "They might discover I've gone."

"They don't know?"

"I had to see you."

The wood of the deck was cold beneath Kyle's feet. The surf roiled. The wind hissed, seething through the willow's boughs. A mist had descended on the island. Both of them looked in the direction of Jack's house. Kyle put his arms around Jack from behind, nuzzling his face in his neck. Jack rested his hands on Kyle's forearms, leaning back into his strength. He breathed deeply. "I'm very afraid."

"I know," Kyle sighed into his hair.

They stood that way for countless moments, until Jack turned to face Kyle. "Kiss me."

Kyle leaned in and just as their lips touched, Jack stepped back. "All right. I'm off."

Kyle suddenly felt a pang of apprehension and the need to prolong the parting. "Want a ride?"

Jack backed slowly down the steps. "No. I love you." Then he was on the sand, still walking backward.

"Aren't you cold?"

"It reminds me of autumn." He smiled. "Your favorite."

"Jack—"

"Kyle, don't." Jack had stopped his backward walk and stood looking up at him. "I'll see you tomorrow."

Kyle just beheld him for a moment, hands hanging loosely at his sides. Then he nodded. "Tomorrow." The wind blew the word away as soon as it left his lips and he wondered if he'd even spoken.

"And the day after that," Jack recited, turning for home. "And the day after that…"

Kyle descended the stairs to the sand. "Jack!"

Jack halted, his shoulders tense.

"Look at me."

Jack considered, then turned, Orphic, his face appearing over his shoulder. That was the one moment Kyle remembered above all others when he thought of that summer—Jack's face, innocent and adult, fearful and accepting, his eyes sharply reflective, like a lake at sunset, black peeking below each wave.

Kyle faltered. *I love you.*

I love you.

I love you.

"I'll follow you like water follows the moon," he called, unable to keep from spouting clichés in his fear.

Jack, pregnant with sorrow, inhaled, slowly, painfully. "I know."

They absorbed one another for one last moment.

Then Kyle wasn't sure if Jack moved backward into the fog or if the fog came forward, swallowing him. All he knew was that one second he was there, and the next there was nothing but the oncoming mist.

He was awakened at ten by his mother.

He showered.

He ate no breakfast.

The day was hot. He helped Ann in the garden, purging the amaranths. The breeze was so strong that at one point he looked up, squinting into the sun. The wind was loud, like a rush of birds taking to the sky.

He heard the phone too late.

When his father suggested renting a boat that afternoon, he agreed to accompany him only if they stopped to fetch Jack. He wanted to see how things were panning out with his parents.

The first thing he noticed was that the shades were drawn. He got out of the car and went to the front door, anxiety gurgling biliously in his stomach. He didn't know how Sheridan would react to his appearance.

He knocked, and when there was no response, he knocked again, harder.

Still no response.

He tried to see around the blinds but could make out nothing.

He went to the garage and peered through a window, hands cupped around his eyes.

It was empty.

He spent the afternoon on the boat, roasting in the sun, thinking of the future, his father fishing on the other side of the deck. The soothing sway of the sea, along with the baking heat, lulled him into that area between sleep and consciousness, where he dozed, yet was still aware of the world around him. The day was quiet except for the infrequent buzzing of his father casting his line and the muted metallic coarseness of the water lapping against the hull.

His body glistening with sweat, he stood after two hours of simmering and dove cleanly into the water.

Dinner was to consist of tenderloin, garlic potatoes and grilled corn. He shucked the corn in the basement, a pail between his legs to collect the husks. Above, he could hear his parents talking, their voices vague but pleasant as they moved from the kitchen to the balcony where the grill was.

He was thinking how stark his day had been without Jack when, his stomach still singing to the rise and fall of the water, he was abruptly seized with dizzying nausea. The ear he held fell into the bucket of husks with a hushed thump. He put his head in his hands, the coolness of his fingers welcome on his feverish face.

Then the sickness departed as suddenly as it had come.

He finished shucking the corn and, feeling surprisingly normal, took the bucket and the naked ears upstairs to the kitchen. He was squatted beside the oven extracting a pot from a cupboard when his mother said, almost affronted, "You didn't tell me Jack was leaving today."

He didn't even deviate from what he was doing. "That's because he's not."

Then something snapped and broke.

"Brenda Fairweather saw him and his parents getting on the ferry," Ann said.

The empty garage, the drawn blinds, Jack's silence. He knew it to be true in a sudden, terrific pain that knocked all conscious thought out of him.

His mother said his name, then stopped, suddenly afraid.

He stood on unfeeling legs. "I'll call." He went to the phone and dialed the number, familiar as his name. Ann leaned against the counter, hands forming a worried steeple under her chin.

The phone at Jack's house rang.

Six times.

Nine.

It was ringing for the eighteenth time when he replaced the phone in its cradle. "I'm going over there." He was feeling the diluted panic of dreams.

He turned and headed toward the door.

"I'm coming with you!" his mother shouted behind him.

He waited in the driveway. Monkshood flared through the dusk. The shadow of twilight deepened around him. Numbness robbed his extremities, his cheeks, even his lips of life. He absently wondered if he were having a heart attack.

He looked to the sky where the new moon was just an aloof sliver of pearl through the haze of sunset.

Take my youth, he thought. *Take my money. Take my kingdom.*
Just don't take Jack.

The Cheshire moon mocked him.

"I'm driving!" his mother cried, the screen door slamming behind her. As she rushed past him, she added, "And you are going to tell me exactly what is going on!"

He told her about the McAllister house. He told her about Sheridan and his wounded mouth. He told her about their weekend of worry and Jack's unannounced visit the night before. He told her all of it in a voice devoid of emotion, looking out the open car window at the shore rushing by. *If I left a trail of bread crumbs would I be able to find my way back to where I was this afternoon? To who I was long ago?*

"I can't believe you were trespassing!" Ann snapped. "What if the police had found you?"

He felt dazed, like he might not be able to complete a sentence.

Presently he said, "I'd still have Jack."

The house and yard were filled with murky shadows when they pulled into the driveway. Ann turned the ignition off, and he sat, letting the sounds of the oncoming night penetrate the car. His throat was dry as sand. "I should go alone," he said, eyes on the dashboard.

His shoes crunched on the gravel as he got out. He looked to the sky. The moon had been obscured by a low cover of clouds.

He was alone.

The journey from the car to the door stole a lifetime. The house rose before him, black and threatening. His flesh so recently anesthetized by terror slipped so quickly into a different sort of deadness, this time of cold, that he was unaware, until he stood on the porch, that he was freezing.

When he rapped on the door, the noise was startling in the stillness.

He listened for noise from within.

There was none.

He laughed, wondering at the insane way it sounded in the hushed twilight.

He knocked again, this time more insistently.

No answer.

There was a clamor as his fist crashed through a pane of glass in the door. His wrist was slashed shallowly in several places. Heedless, he unbolted the lock from inside. His mother scrambled out of the car screaming his name.

The front door swung open. He stepped into the darkened foyer. The house looked the same, but it felt forsaken.

His mother appeared, a silhouette in the doorway behind him. "You can't break in!" she demanded. Then, "Your hand!"

Rivulets of blood trickled down his fingers, onto the carpet. She reached out to inspect his cuts, but he was already moving away, his heart pounding, a movie monster's footsteps. He could see ghosts, hear their malignant whispers. He headed for Jack's room upstairs. Ann followed, turning on lights in his wake.

The room, when he got there, was dark. Leaning against a wall was the framed painting of Jack and him on the swing.

He went directly to the dresser and pulled a drawer open at the same moment that his mother entered and turned on the light.

The drawer was empty. The drawer below that was empty as well. The drawer below that held a white pair of undershorts. Jack's remains. Drops of blood sprinkled them, tainted their crisp chill, glistening in quiet crimson menace before being absorbed.

"Honey, he's gone."

He felt his mother's hand on his back. He turned, shirking her, ridiculously pissed off she was there.

She reached out again, went to speak, stopped, withdrew her hand. "Your wrist…" she offered.

He went back to the first level, to the room beneath the stairs. When he reached for the doorknob, he felt the same crescendo of horror he felt every summer when they opened the beach house, knowing what to expect, but fearing, hoping it would be different.

The darkroom was empty.

He could do nothing until morning, when Jack and his family would arrive home. So he sat on the deck, watching the dark water, helplessly hating the moon and, not knowing if it would still be there, desperately awaiting the rise of the sun.

By next morning, anxiety had built from a drizzle to a typhoon, accelerating so slowly, yet often in such violent surges, that it had chipped away at his resolve, leaving him frayed.

At noon his mother prepared a light lunch. The sight of the food made him nauseous, so he sat in the living room while his parents ate on the balcony.

The phone call he'd missed the day before plagued him, taunting him like a bored schoolyard bully. What if it had been Jack phoning for help?

He focused on nothing tangible for half an hour before, no longer able to bear the suspense, knowing that if he waited one second longer he'd think about it and not be able to act, he stood and went to the telephone and dialed Jack's home number.

As the phone began to ring he heard his father laugh on the deck.

A bead of cold sweat trickled down his back.

His heart beat an arrhythmic, panging pulse in the scabs on his wrist.

The phone continued to ring until it was apparent it would not be answered.

He replaced the receiver in its cradle, his head drooping like a long-lasting bloom weighted under the first snow.

Dana came by that afternoon to say good-bye. She joined him on the balcony, beaming with good health and hopefulness. Her exuberance turned to dismay when he told her about Jack. She gripped his hand. "I wish I could stay to help."

"It's just waiting now. There's not a whole lot you could do."

"I could be here."

"I'll go to him in Michigan," he told her valorously.

Dana chewed her bottom lip. Her black hair was pulled into a ponytail that jigged in the breeze. "He didn't even call you?" she queried.

At the mention of the call, he felt panic and had to struggle to keep intact the lid that minded his sanity. It stirred, rattled, twitched, but he steadied, secured it.

For many moments she watched him thinking of Jack.

Presently she said, "You know how we always talk of coming back here with our children?" She stood, releasing his hand, and went to the rail, leaning toward the full, reflecting water. "A lot's happened this summer. We're not together anymore. We're not a group." She turned back. "And I'm afraid we won't stay in touch and when we run into each other, in the future, we won't know each other anymore." There was a tremor in her voice.

He sat for a second, amused. "Why, Dana, are you becoming sentimental?"

"Yes! Before there was no reason to be. ...We had the rest of our lives."

They looked at each other, nostalgically.

He wondered if he'd ever see her again.

She sat next to him then, told him of her plans for school, what classes she was taking, what she had to buy, when she had to be there.

He could tell her only that he was going to find Jack.

They talked of summers, past and present, but not so much of the future. Dana seemed to not want to leave, lingering before the last ferry.

Eventually she stood and squeezed his hand. "I'll show myself out. It'll only make me sadder if you walk me to the door. It'll be so formal."

Summer's end didn't feel much like New Year's Eve that year. He looked up into her face, but he found it difficult to concentrate, difficult already to remember.

"Are you still going to put me in your book?"

"You'll be part of my coming-of-age years." She leaned down and embraced him tightly, whispering hotly into his ear, as if she'd come solely to say this but hadn't been able to summon the courage until then: "The first love isn't necessarily the brightest. Know that." She gripped him as if imparting strength, then kissed his cheek and stood back, looking down at him plainly. "You know how I knew you loved Jack?"

He smiled, his heart thrilling at Jack's name. "How?"

"You wouldn't have left us for anything less."

He went to collect their things from the McAllister house. Once there, he turned the car off in the driveway and sat listening to the buzz of the cicadas.

It made him feel hotter.

The god of silence cautioned him from above the porch. Between them stood the mulberry tree he and Jack had sprawled under before the tempest.

It ridiculed him with its silent serenity.

Time passed. At various junctures, he considered moving, walking, crawling to the door.

But he sat for half an hour before eventually stepping onto the gravel. He sized the house up, feeling, oddly, like it was something to overcome, and, for the first time, like he was trespassing. A window in the attic caught his attention and he started, wondering if he'd seen something move. But the sun reflected so brilliantly on the glass that, as he squinted into the light, he realized he couldn't have seen anything behind the brightness.

The house was musty and stale. As he went from the kitchen to the living room, he was aware of ghosts fluttering ephemerally around him. They didn't frighten him.

He was one of them now.

On the porch the air was not so heavy, but there was the residual scent of sandalwood. One of the pictures he had taken of Jack in the darkroom was on the table. His face was uncomfortable and shy. He had not yet blossomed.

He put the photo in his pocket.

Beside the mattress he found Jack's copy of *The Beautiful and the Damned*. He flipped through it, remembering when Jack had first mentioned it, that day in the theater lobby.

That day seemed so long ago.

The last night he'd seen Jack seemed like another century.

Under the table he saw the lock of hair Jack had given him on his birthday. The hair had separated and lay in a jumbled pile.

Suddenly, he was weeping with such sorrow and such tenderness and such ferocity, it was pretty. Sticky, salty tears wet his cheeks, slipped into his mouth, his features warped. His body rocked with despair as he keened. He didn't think his chest was big enough to contain his broken heart.

His eyes were already haunted with the broken look he would never lose.

He clutched the novel to his chest and, kneeling before their empty, disheveled bed, grieved.

In his dream he stood on the shore of a river. Jack was ankle-deep in the water, his eyes the exact blue-brown of the churning current behind him. Holding something white in his hand, he wore red shorts and a crimson polo shirt with a large bleached circle at the bottom. Behind him the river became a lake. From beneath the water, something—big, long, scaly—touched the surface, its wetness flashing in the sun. When Jack moved his head, the trees and the sky at the opposite side of the water were visible through them. Suddenly Trey, also holding a white object, appeared, dressed in white shorts and shirt. The backdrop became a glistening, rolling sea. Drops fell from Jack's shirt, speckling the water, the bleached spot diminishing. And the dreamer knew, like dreamers know, that the shirt had once been white, but blood, someone's blood—Jack's, Trey's, his own?—was steeping the material, weighting it. And it was then that what remained of the white circle, at that point no more than a centimeter in circumference, was tinged pink, then fully scarlet. Through Jack's eyes he could see the sea monster, just below the water, scales gleaming, rushing toward shore, toward Jack, drawn by the blood. Unable to run, like dreamers find, he was also unable to shout. Jack was laughing, beckoning him to join them in the water, the monster moving with amazing speed, closing in, its target within reach. Jack and Trey shared a secret, knowing smile, then lifted the eggs in their hands, the shells cracked in hundreds of crisscrossing, patternless veins, and swallowed them whole.

His eyes popped open. The sun was not as blinding as it had been when he'd gotten to the McAllister house. *The Beautiful and the Damned* had fallen to the floor. He lay, waiting for the terror of the dream to fade and his heartbeat to decelerate. He vividly remembered the way the eggs had been swallowed. The memory of Jack's soulless eyes stilled him.

"Did I scare you?"

He jumped and that was when he became aware of Trent's presence.

"Did I scare you again?" Trent asked.

"Yes! Why are you here?"

Trent was too surprised to mask his hurt. "I just wanted to see if you were all right…"

"I didn't expect you."

Trent ran stray fingers through his hair then looked to the ground. Through the screen they could hear the leaves of the willows. "Dana told me what happened." He forced himself to make eye contact.

He averted his eyes. "I'm afraid." He was embarrassed he couldn't be stronger.

"That's what Dana said."

"She could tell?"

"When have you ever been able to hide your emotions?"

They both smiled, but neither laughed.

"What are you going to do?" Trent asked.

"Go to Michigan."

The plan of action was presented for judgment.

"I'll go with you."

"I don't need a chaperone."

"I'm worried."

"About what?" he snapped, suddenly defensive.

"About you, if he's not there."

"Of course he'll be there."

"Don't pick a fight with me."

Trent's shadow was elongated, stretching across the bed where he sat. He felt small and shriveled in its tenebrous clutches. He was weary. "I didn't know how lonely I was until I found him, Trent. Now I can never not know. I can never not miss him."

In the hush that ensued, the ticking of the clock grew unrelentingly assertive.

"I'm sorry—" Trent began.

"Don't." He was quick.

Trent exhaled loudly to show his annoyance. "I'm trying to apologize because I hurt you and I let you down."

"Apology accepted. I don't want to talk about it ever again."

"Why is it you always get to explain yourself, but now that I want to it's unimportant?"

"It's not unimportant. It's just too painful, and I don't think I can deal with it right now."

Hands in the pockets of his shorts, Trent went to the screen door. Beyond it lay the willows, and, beyond them, the reeds and the shore. In the deadness of the late afternoon he could see the red sun sparkling on the water. Presently, he said, "What if he's not there?"

As quickly as it could swallow up his words, quiet reinfested the porch and sat there rotting.

Then the emphatic hammering of the clock took precedence again, and he could no longer stand it. He seized it, beating it, pounding it on the stone floor, smashing it until there was no hope for repair. When he was done, his breathing was heavy, but the act had alleviated a sliver of oppression. He looked up at Trent, his response smothered immediately by the ancient silence of the house. "I will find him."

Trey called on him once.

His mother told him that he wasn't there. That he was sick. To please not come back.

Watching from an upstairs window, he saw Trey's hurt, surprised expression.

He laughed, but it was harsh and humorless and sounded oddly maniacal in his head so he cut it off, curtly. It wasn't just his emptiness, it was the lack of fullness around him that caused everything he said or did, every voice or noise he heard, to echo. Sound bounced off the walls of his mind, coming back at him from all directions, attacking, pummeling, mocking.

The burden of waiting turned him both listless and restless, so he spent hours wandering the house with too much energy to sit, not enough to find direction.

His parents tried to comfort him, soothe him. They talked to him like to a fresh widower. They repeatedly asked if he was okay and he repeatedly told them yes, but both question and answer were so scripted and the performances so mechanical he wondered if any of them believed.

Since there were only a few days left until September, there was very little time for Jack to prepare for school.

He and his family would have to return home soon.

He would keep a vigil over the phone.

He would catch them.

He was in the kitchen staring into
the fridge thinking about nothing when he heard Claudia pull up. Through the
window over the sink he saw her get out of her car in white shorts and a white
tank top and push her sunglasses onto her forehead. She held a daisy. Her tan
and sun-bleached hair gave her a look of vigorous health. She saw him and
gave a fluttery wave with the flower.

He met her at the door and she swooped in, enveloping him in a tight
embrace, giggling. "This is it," she said into his hair. "Until the holidays."

"You're in such a good mood," he replied as she pulled back, looking
him up and down.

"You're losing your color."

They killed their time talking, much as he had with Dana. It made him feel like
a shut-in. He listened to her anecdotes with a smile but was so far away he felt
guilty being on automatic pilot. It all came easily and believably because they
had known each other for so long.

She looked at him near the end of the afternoon, a thoughtful
expression on her face. "Do you think Jack knew that it was going to end?" she
asked. "And he didn't know how to tell you?"

He gave her a look that said he'd expected as much. "He loves me."

"That's not what I asked."

"We had plans." He was firm. "He loves me."

She smiled.

He didn't like her attitude but kept himself from becoming defensive.
It was hard to tell when he was overreacting lately, so he'd taken to assuming
he always was.

"Did Jack ever tell you I warned him?"

"About?"

"When you came to Carly's for dinner. I told him if he broke your
heart, I'd break his back."

"What did he say?"

"He told me if I continued to act like a bitch he'd make sure I never
saw you again."

Kyle smiled, then laughed out loud.

"We were both trying to protect you," she said.

He believed her.

"I could tell you were whipped. And I didn't want the breaking of our circle to have been in vain." She looked at him, not challenging, but unafraid to place blame.

Evenly he met her gaze. There was a moment of competition, then he smiled, graciously, if not warmly. "You knew from the start, didn't you?"

"Not until Jack."

They looked through each other, thinking their own thoughts.

Then Claudia stood and smoothed her unwrinkled shorts. "I should leave." She still held the daisy.

He followed her to the door where she turned for a last hug. She gave him an extra-tight squeeze.

He felt like he should apologize, for breaking the circle, for letting them down, for whatever. He didn't know for what.

But he wasn't sorry.

And he wasn't sorry to see her go.

The day before they were to leave he went to a cemetery on the other side of the island. He had never been there, but he found it effortlessly. He meandered through the graves, content to pass his time among the dead. Theirs was a tranquil place, where, for the first time since Jack's capture, he felt a buffer.

The headstone, when he found it, was simple: a white granite marker with a rose chiseled beside the name and the dates. The plot, situated before a dormant black locust tree, was covered with thick, dark sod. A clay pot of marigolds and a purple hibiscus reminded him he'd neglected to bring recompense.

He stood for several minutes, content to have found the site. He had no idea what, if anything, he wanted to say. He'd never done it before. Not even with Kevin.

Presently, he said, "I understand," then looked away, guiltily, ashamed, as if she could see him.

He stood there, inhaling the sea, which seemed very far away, and considered what Claudia had suggested: What if Jack had left of his own volition? Which would haunt him more tenaciously: the duplicity or the abduction? Which would make him less unhappy?

He envied Veronica her option.

When he went home that afternoon he called Jack's house again.

This time the phone had been disconnected.

He went to the beach where he had first seen Jack. He was surprised by how roughly the expanse of sand gripped him, how inexorably its beauty and its sadness were linked. But the wind had edited the dune on which Jack had appeared. It wasn't the same dune that had proffered the Boy at all.

It was time to leave the island.

SEPTEMBER

As the summer waned, he and Trent flew to Jack's town.

They took a cab to his house.

When they got there they found it empty.

They took another flight, bound for Michigan.

On board, his light on, Trent sat beside his slumbering friend. He had had a vicious argument with his parents about missing the first few days of school. But because it wasn't his place to divulge another's secrets, he could only tell them that he had to. So he was on a plane to a state he'd never seen and never imagined he would, trying to ease an unsalvable pain by tending someone else's wounds.

It was too late to tend his own.

He wondered if his actions were pure enough to save his friend, though, because in the deepest, blackest pit of his heart, when no one was looking, he allowed himself the freedom to admit he was glad Jack had gone. Jack's disappearance had given them a bridge that Trent wasn't certain they'd've built on their own. He found it tragic and fitting that Jack's absence was restoring the friendship his presence had nearly destroyed.

When he allowed himself the luxury of freeing that demon of truth, it fouled him until he had to pin it down and cage it again, so tightly it hadn't a chance to escape.

He hated himself for finding sustenance in another's grief.

But it was the first time he was the strength.

And it felt good to be needed.

He looked back down the empty aisle behind him, as if sensing a presence, as if the demon truth inside him was being surveilled, then reached up and turned off his light, so that they were both in darkness.

They checked into their hotel, and while he went to the university's registration office, Trent went to the pool and swam from end to end so many times he lost count. He flirted with the bartender but bought no drinks from her. He fell asleep poolside, his flesh drying under the September sun.

He awakened with a start as an enormous cloud passed between the earth and the sun. Gathering his bearings, he determined he'd been asleep for roughly 45 minutes. The lapse of time disconcerted him. He felt like a sentry who'd fallen asleep under imminence of war.

He showered in the room, head directly under the spout.
    He didn't know how long he'd been there when the ringing of the telephone startled him back to life. He ran into the suite, naked and dripping.
    Silence stopped him.
    Water trickled down his chest, his arms, his thighs, to the floor.
    He waited.
    The stillness was disquieting.

He showered again, but when he emerged he still felt unclean.

He waited.

Trent was seated on the side of the bed when the door opened and he was there with news that Jack had withdrawn from school. Trent could see blackness curling soft, deceptive tendrils around his friend's edges, the pain feeding on itself.
    Trent consoled him, as the cold aura of autumn enveloped them both.
    Eventually exhaustion shut his body down and he slept.

He dreamed of eternally descending stairways in the dark. There were no rails, but he was unafraid of falling. His energy was unflagging in his quest for something he couldn't name or even feel. It never occurred to him to turn around.

He just descended.

He slept for two days.

When he awoke on the third, he realized he'd been expecting the world to stop, because he was surprised to find that it hadn't.

He rose and stepped into the shower. To keep his mind clear he bit his lower lip so hard he could taste the warm, salty tinge of blood. It was imperative that he keep from breaking down. The slashing drops of water helped him pretend he wasn't crying. This gave him a sense of strength.

Emerging, he shaved and dressed in jeans and a sweater. It was, after all, September.

Trent was sitting up in bed when he came out of the bathroom. They looked at each other, seemingly surprised the other was there. They spoke at the same time.

"You're awake."

"What day is it?"

"You slept so long."

"I was tired."

"Friday." Trent rubbed his face in an attempt to wake up. "Are you ready to go home?"

He moved to his open suitcase at the end of the bed. "I'm not going home." He turned to Trent with an even look. There was no need to lie. "I'm going to find him."

It took a second for the words to make sense to a sleepy Trent. When they did, he jumped up, scrambling to the end of the mattress, where he hesitated on all fours. "You're going after Jack."

"Yes." He went to the bathroom and gathered his scattering of toiletries, then returned and dropped them with a short clatter into his suitcase.

"You'll never find—" Trent began.

"Don't." He raised a warning hand. "I was hoping to be gone before you awakened."

"You were going to leave without me?" Trent sat back on his haunches, a forlorn *David*.

He snapped the valise shut. "I was going to pay the bill," he said, like it mattered.

"I'm coming with you."

Then he was annoyed. "No. You're not."

"How long do you think it'll take to find him?" Trent hopped off the bed.

"You're not coming."

"I won't let you go alone."

"Why not?"

"Why?" Trent demanded back.

"Because I don't want you there."

"Do you really think we'll find him?" Trent snapped his suitcase open on the bed and began tossing things into it in a jumble. When he didn't receive a response, he turned and repeated the question.

"I'm not talking about it," came the reply.

"What do you mean you're not talking about it?"

He hesitated. When he spoke his voice was faint. "I'm afraid I tempted fate by being heedless and that's why Jack's gone." Finally admitting what had been torturing him, he was humiliated. He turned toward the dresser to collect loose change that sat there, but Trent was fast.

"Don't talk that way!" he exclaimed, jumping before him.

"What way?"

"About tempting fate. I won't let you become like him."

"You can't help it. You can't help me, Trent. You don't know what I fear."

Trent grabbed a handful of coins. "Do these scare you now?" He threw the change at him. "See a penny, pick it—"

Before the currency even hit him, he was smashing Trent up against the bureau. They grappled. Trent pushed. He punched. "I hate you!" he screamed. "I hate you!" He rammed his shoulder into Trent's chest, and they fell to the floor in a heap, the struggle over almost before it began. Trent, gasping, could hear nothing but his own breath for a moment. Then, very quietly, he made out, "I can't face life without him. I can't do it alone..."

"That's why I'm here," Trent said, though he was in pain. "You're not alone."

He never got a response.

☙

Later he sat on the bed, watching Trent pack. There was a scratch above his left eye from the clash. "Why are you doing this?" he asked.

Trent, at the dresser, paused and looked to his reflection in the mirror. "I'm atoning."

Ann and Graham didn't approve. But seeing how distraught he was, they were afraid to forbid. All they could say was that they loved him.

Trent had an enormous row with his parents. They threatened to cut him off. In the end, they allowed it only in exchange for his requisite year of travel after college. His *wanderjahr*.

He had two destinations.

Jack had talked about a cabin, in Minnesota. He had never specified where, but one night at the McAllister house, the weather too sultry to sleep, he had mentioned a lake. Outside St. Cloud.

If that didn't bear fruit, he was heading to Portugal. Jack's mother's parents had a house there. He didn't know where. He had never pressed for details, because, at that point, he and Jack were going to be together forever.

There would be time.

And suddenly there was.

So much time.

So he ran.

Information gave them the address of the camp where he surmised Jack and his parents had rented their cabin, and they flew to Minneapolis where they caught another, smaller flight to St. Cloud where they leased a car.

Trent drove, as would become his role in the months to come. They traveled mostly in silence, watching the sun-dappled fields, the farms, the towns slip by. Rust, gold, bronze leaves eddied in their wake. When they entered a forest of enormous maples and oaks and elms, shadows infiltrated the car, insidious as envy.

Along with the paling photograph of Jack in the darkroom, he carried two seashells and the white stone Jack had given him that first day on the beach. He thought of them as amulets, since he no longer possessed the ring. But somehow, away from the sea or the island, the shells were colorless in his hands, the stone had lost its luster.

He feared this made them powerless.

After traveling for what seemed like days, they turned down a narrow dirt road, at the end of which was a fence that blocked farther progress. A sign, looking like an arts-and-crafts project, was nailed on a wooden arch over the gate:

Camp Care-A-Way
Where you can camp your cares away!
Open May–August
Smile! God is watching!

They cringed at the presence of so many exclamation marks.

They stopped in the nearest town where he put forward Jack's photo. No one knew anything. Or they weren't telling.

They flew to Lisbon. He remembered Jack saying his grandparents lived in a place where there weren't many tourists. But did that mean a small town, or simply that Portugal was a jewel undiscovered by the bourgeoisie? He didn't know, so they were to look everywhere. The country wasn't large. It was smaller than Indiana.

He would catch them.

He didn't know Violet's maiden name, so the details he could furnish people were minimal as he provided the photograph of the boy whose sad eyes had prophesied this.

In the weeks they were in Lisbon, they found no clues.

They rented a car and they drove, the windows down, sea breezes taking up the space their voices would have filled. The weather was turning cooler. First they went north, toward Porto. There were many towns along the way, many opportunities for kismet.

He phoned home every day. He needed to know if Jack had called. He needed to know if the endless supply of letters and postcards he'd been sending, writing on the road, mid flight, in hotel rooms, had been returned. Whoever answered the phone, his mother or his father, would tell him, *No, Jack hasn't called. No, your letters haven't been returned. How are you? Do you need anything? We love you. Come home. We love you.*

As the days, and then the weeks, passed, Trent came to enjoy their intervals on the road, those stretches of time that seemed to contract and expand, giving him the peculiar sensation that they'd been driving forever—beside the same rushing river, toward the same misty mountains, across the same rolling plain—and that they would never reach the horizon. This did not instill a flutter of panic in him, as he felt it should, but a sense of silent serenity. There was nowhere specific to be, no one expecting them, no actual time constraint, so there was no urgency in getting to the end of the road. He sometimes wondered what would happen if they actually did make it to the hazy horizon.

He wondered if there would be anything there.

They became proficient at procuring hotel rooms, reading maps, grasping the essence of a city and the grid of its streets. They learned enough Portuguese to relay pertinent information. *A avó. A casa. A família.* Living out of suitcases became so normal it ceased to be a burden. They learned how to pack and unpack with amazing efficiency. Every town was different, but they were all easily wooed, seduced and left behind.

He became adept at surveying rooms for those slender limbs, those brilliant eyes, that hair of indeterminate length. He adapted the skill quickly because they needed to be as many places as possible in as little time as possible because he didn't know how much time he had.

There were moments when he was certain he'd seen Jack, and he'd hurtle down a half-deserted street after a glimpse of a swatch of white. Or he'd chase a departing train for a face in a window. Or he'd burst through a crowded restaurant, chasing a scintilla of sandalwood.

And he'd be freshly devastated.

He didn't understand how three people could simply vanish.

This time there wasn't even a note.

The blow came in late November. He stood in a phone booth, the Portugal sun setting in a fiery twilight around him.

"Your letters are being returned," his mother said over the wire. "The Averills have moved. There's no forwarding address."

He was quiet for a very long time. He stood in the booth, looking at nothing, eyes glassy, gleaming, empty in the light. The roar of aloneness had robbed him of voice. That was the moment he learned how to feed off the solid, dull emptiness he'd already learned to endure.

"You can come home any time," his mother said. "You know that."

He felt cold and forsaken like the sun had gone away. The loss was searing, leaving a bitter hollow in his stomach. The unreturned letters had been his only hope. Maybe Jack was getting them, reading his words of love and reassurance.

"Come home," his mother beseeched.

He wondered if she still left the porch light on.

"Come home," she repeated, gently.

Home. It made him think of Christmas lights and "Anchors away!" wallpaper and a sense of security. What had it felt like to feel safe?

It reminded him most of all of sleep. Deep, restful slumber.

But now?

Now he would only pass time there. If he kept on the move, at the very least he had purpose. Home offered the warmth of nostalgia, but it couldn't offer hope.

He found his voice, only a croak. "I can't."

That night he took his straight razor and slashed his face. It didn't hurt as much as, but the blood was hotter than, he'd anticipated. He'd hardly had time to process that realization when Trent opened the door. He gave a look of almost comical shock, his lips in a wide O. Then, as he approached in a panic, his sock-covered feet slid on the linoleum, and he was falling, back, so that his tailbone cracked against the door molding. He crawled to his knees, his back flaring, and reached for the razor.

He surrendered the blade, already sorry he'd caused grief.

He should have locked the door.

He turned the faucet on and began splashing water onto his gash, causing it to sting. Trent, still on the floor, glowered at him, then began pounding on his legs. "What are you doing!"

He tried to kick him away, afraid Trent might accidentally cut him with the razor, but Trent was stubborn. "God *damn* you!" he shouted, hitting with hard fists. Watery blood spattered his face, his arms, the white of his tee. Then he stopped punishing, tears springing fresh and hot as the blood. "Damn you."

He stooped and helped Trent to his feet. "I think I need to go to the hospital."

He received eighteen stitches, and they moved on.

He atrophied.

He felt like he'd been ripped from scrotum to skull. The pain had the stinging, silvery feel of a fresh, clean cut, and it burned.

It was so unadulterated that it maintained a sense of purity and became his only connection to Jack, a comfort by its sheer steadfastness.

Some days it consumed him until he knew nothing but it.

Some days it was the only thing he could still identify as real.

Some days it was so inviting he felt like he was coming home when it changed from a dull ache to a welcoming roar. He began to wonder if he fed off it or if it fed off him. Which was the parasite?

It wasn't simply that part of him was gone. It was that he was left gawking in horror at the bloody stump that remained. He had to adapt to living without being whole again. He would never be able to perform the simplest action without being reminded of what it was to be complete.

One evening in the Sagres region of the Algarve, at the southernmost tip of Portugal, when they had nearly exhausted the country, he walked along the sea, scanning the furthermost reaches of the inky Atlantic. The stars blinked and winked in the water. He looked as far as he could, to the place where the sky touched down, wondering how far he could see. Could he see all the way to the other shore? Could he see all the way to the island? Could he find his way home again?

When he went home for Christmas, his parents were panicked to see the scar on his cheek, taking it for a suicide attempt. They had aged. His mother's face was papery and tight. His father's hair had grayed. They looked at him like a paper doll they'd found in the rain.

He wished he could explain the wound but he was embarrassed that he despaired so sheerly he'd wanted to disfigure himself.

He went to his room and fingered it in the mirror, liking the feel of the soft, fleshy ridge. He enjoyed playing with it like the spongy crevasse of a missing tooth. It drew him compulsively.

He marveled at his reflection, at how new he was. He didn't know what had become of the boy who'd grown up in his room. He'd disappeared, as ephemeral as a dream in the light.

On Christmas, after the gifts and the food and a subdued celebration, he slipped to his room to escape the endless, echoing desert of the day. The hours were infinite with his panic forced to simmer. No one had anything to say though their minds roared.

He sat on the bed, staring at the wall and its "Anchors away!" paper but seeing Jack's face as it had looked back at him, over his shoulder, that last night. He missed him so much that his limbs ached.

Presently, his mother came in and sat beside him. She wondered where his gold ring was but was afraid she'd push him further away by inquiring. It was precious. But not as precious as her son and his sanity were. So she let it go.

They were silent for a few moments before she offered: "Would you like a pill? Just to help you sleep?"

He didn't turn to her. "I have to keep the pain fresh."

Her lips were thin and pursed. She took his hand. "We'd like you to see someone."

He still didn't turn to her, thinking how frantic he'd become trapped in one place. "What did you do with the swan?" he blurted, thinking, without reason, that she would understand.

"What swan?" she asked, exasperated.

"The planter that used to sit outside the beach house."

"I don't know!" she exclaimed, angry he was digressing. "I threw it away! It was old!" She wasn't prepared for the way his face crumpled. "You never told me you were fond of it!"

"I didn't realize it wouldn't always be there." He withdrew, pulling his hand loose. He wanted to lash at her, demand to know why she had never told him she still grieved. Instead, he tried to comfort her with, "I didn't try to kill myself."

She looked away from him, away from the subject.

Then, unable to refrain from twisting the knife, he added, "But don't you think I hate Kevin for cursing me to this?"

She burst into tears at verification of her fear.

And then he felt guilty and wanted to console her. He reached for her hand and she let him hold it. "I'm sorry."

Through her tears, she said, "Just get better."

That night Trent received a call.

"I'm leaving tomorrow. I can't stand the waiting."

Trent didn't ask for what he was waiting.

They spent the new year in Portalegre.

And that was where they caught their break.

On a blustery day, they stopped into a small Baroque church to chase the chill from their bones. The nave was dark and drafty. Candles that had been lit for the dead wavered with gusts of wind from outside. The priest on duty greeted them, then took the photo of Jack and lowered himself heavily into a pew. After studying the image for a moment, he said in heavily accented English, "I know this boy."

The shells from that long-ago day scattered on the floor with a clatter.

Trent audibly gasped.

"He used to visit his—" The priest faltered for the word.

"Grandparents?" Trent supplied.

The priest smiled and nodded. "Si. Yes. O avós. But he hasn't been here for years."

"Can you direct us to them? To the grandparents?" As he spoke, he could feel Trent's hand on his back, its reassurance familiar. "It's imperative."

The priest looked up at them with kindly, wrinkled eyes of the softest blue. "They moved to Romania."

"Romania!" Trent was stunned.

"If I recall, she had family there."

"Do you know where they went?" His thumb stroked the stone, siphoning its strength. "Specifically?"

"I don't. If they said, I don't remember."

"Their names," Trent demanded. "What are their names?"

They went to Romania by train.

Seated beside Trent, looking out at the rolling hills of Spain, he felt the traitor hope buoying him. He didn't want to give in to hope. The flip side of hope was despair. He just wanted to keep moving forward, enduring through faith without anticipation. That way there could be no disappointment, there was nothing to be lost.

So he tried to oppress yellow hope.

But yellow hope would not be denied.

All he had was a lead.

But the lead might take him to Jack.

He would catch them.

Somewhere in the night, speeding through the dark, as Trent tried to doze in his seat, he beheld a specter: Jack staggered down the aisle with the pitch of the train, opened the door at the end of the car and proceeded into the next, leaving Trent gawking after him, his heart pounding so hard it hurt.

Turning to the slumbering form of his friend and his own reflection in the window, Trent was disconcerted. He looked haggard and tired and...old. Was he dreaming?

He stood, not willing to accept ambiguity, and passed into the next car. The people there were resting. Most of the overhead lights were out.

He began making his way into the shadows, searching the face of each person he passed. He was midway up the banks of seats when the train lurched and he was nearly thrown onto a tall, thin young man.

He looked down and saw Jack's match.

But it wasn't Jack.

Trent peered down the aisle toward the next car, then back the way he'd come, then back to the boy.

He almost didn't believe it wasn't Jack.

The boy said something in Dutch.

Trent looked at him, openly, rudely.

It was so important that he not be wrong.

When he returned to his seat, he was unnerved, as if he'd had a near-death experience.

He never mentioned the boy to anyone.

Part of him was never sure.

The train abandoned them in Bucharest. The city was gothic and gray. They wandered for weeks in the biting cold, but they got no leads.

When they advanced into the rest of the country in a rented car, the terrain was rough, the weather snowy, the people friendly, but poor. Romanian was harder to acquire than Portuguese. It was more sensual, yet harsher with its blunt consonants.

But the slowly fading photograph spoke volumes.

And melancholy was universal.

They drove through deep, dark forests, the forests of fairy tales.

They traversed plains through fathomless snowfall.

At points, dense fog billowed soundlessly around them, a passive saboteur.

It got so cold they couldn't get warm. The chill invaded their bones. They became hushed and cool, like corpses.

Sometimes as they drove, particularly at night, the silence that enveloped them seemed also to permeate them, staying that part of them that did still live. That was when Trent would feel Jack's substantial absence the most.

Sometimes, driving through nothingness into more nothingness, he feared there was nothing beyond the roar of the road.

Sometimes he feared that if he opened his mouth, no sound would come out.

Sometimes he couldn't even remember what his voice sounded like.

And sometimes, during those moments, his heart pumping cold silence, Trent would look at his passenger and see him conversing with, conferring with, conspiring with Jack's ghost.

And he would wonder if there was any way back.

Or if Jack had shaped all that was to come.

He dreamed he was running through a shadowy labyrinth of bleached stone. The muted light of the moon came from within the walls. He ran, barefoot, harshly, chasing something that always stayed a turn ahead. He rounded corners, descended flights of steps, reversed back on himself, not knowing what he was pursuing or why.

It didn't occur to him to stop.

Then he turned a corner and was horrified to find that his prey was lying in wait where the hall dead-ended.

His hands flew up, flat against the surface of the gilt-edged mirror.

He awakened screaming because he couldn't remember, and Trent comforted, soothed, pacified him.

The forgetting was more alarming than the remembering.

As the bleakness of winter began to give way to the tenderness of spring, they realized they were running out of options.

There was nowhere left to go.

Some days he didn't recognize the ashen, brittle face that confronted him in the mirror.

Some days he was startled to discover that he wasn't looking back at himself.

And some days he would wonder where he had gone.

It reached the point where he could remember no time before the search.

Only the search.

Spring arrived in full with its humid, sultry days, and he became anxious. The air was fresh and gentle and hopeful. His spirit stirred like the dormant buds of the lilac bush as they passed fields of burgeoning, grasping shoots of wheat and corn.

Soon they'd be back on the island.

When they returned it was a mid-May afternoon, as gray and thin as he had become.

In the preceding weeks a hopeful anticipation had grown like a cancer inside of him. He wouldn't allow himself open optimism, so his spirits had been confined to a hesitant lightness that lingered, tingling at the base of his heart. Sometimes a smile or a giggle would wriggle through his wall of gravity, but he would quash it before it could reach fruition. So his expectancy rose and fell like the tides with amazing frequency, sometimes within seconds. It reminded him of the maelstrom he'd endured when he'd first met Jack, the terror of allowing himself to even imagine a happy ending combined with the joy of reveling in the notion that it was actually an option. His mixture of eager hope and paranoid restriction made him feel like he was two people fighting for the same body.

But he would not give in.

He could not bear disappointment.

So for all he'd done to temper his expectation, he was still surprised at the grimness he felt as Trent drove from the ferry toward their side of the island. His trepidation and stifled enthusiasm had combined and metamorphosed into a dull dread that stole what color remained in his flesh and left him shaky and withdrawn. He peered out at his familiar summer haunts through large eyes, as if through a keyhole, as if from a hiding place, or a prison.

When he opened the door to the beach house, he thought, that year, instead of Kevin, of Jack. The aroma of the place hit him, and within it was Jack. He was suddenly so alive he could taste him, his breath, his skin, his sweat. He could feel him, his energy, like a ghost, move through him. As he threw wide the windows and uncovered the furniture, the sounds of Jack's cries on that last night were more real than ever, like those of a stillborn child.

When he was done opening the house, he went onto the deck, into the warm grayness, the wings of the willow welcoming him. He leaned into the sea breeze and inhaled. The view was the same he'd known since he was a child. But it had been idealized, so it wasn't really the same at all.

Daily, he walked up the beach to Jack's house, scrutinizing it from behind a striped barricade of reeds. The two window-eyes reflected back the sea and the sky, letting nothing out and nothing in as he knelt in the sand, scouting for signs of habitation, equally terrified he would find nothing and that Jack's parents would divine him.

But the days passed with no indication of life.

His sixth day on the island he screwed up the courage to approach the house. He stepped onto the lawn, advancing slowly, feeling painfully visible without the shelter of the reeds. When he came to a window, he cupped his hands to shade his eyes from the light and peered through, discovering with horror that the house was empty, devoid of furniture and trinkets and life.

He turned and sat hard on the ground, back against the wall. His mouth formed a serrated oval, his right hand absently clawing at loose dirt so that tiny sprinkles of blood appeared beneath his fingernails. He tore at the soil, gouging, until he raised his hand over his head and let the earth sift between his fingers and scatter over his head. He scratched for more, turning his face up, letting it rain across his forehead, down his cheeks, into his mouth, clinging to his lips, coating his tongue, gritting in his teeth. He lifted handful after handful until he was sated.

But he didn't cry.

His parents arrived, noting his pallor, his lethargy, his hush. Neither mentioned any of these things. He read it in the lilt in their voices, their hooded, probing eyes.

He found it better that way.

If they didn't ask, he didn't have to lie.

After being on the move for so long, it was difficult for him to stay in one place. He thought of the time that was roaring past and had to talk himself out of jumping into the river to be carried along.

When he traveled he had purpose.

On the island he simply existed.

The only thing that kept him from fleeing was the knowledge that no matter what happened, Jack would know where he was.

So, for the summer, he restrained his ardent, yearning wanderlust.

Dana came, flush with youth and vibrancy. Their first night on the beach she spoke so animatedly and so ceaselessly about school that he wondered if she'd really had that much fun or if she were trying to make up for Trent's and his dearth of it. He envied her exhilaration, but it also saddened him, because he could remember when he had felt it, too.

He noted that Trent flickered with life as Dana told her collegiate tales. He saw the envy in his eyes. And he realized that he didn't want Trent to become what he, himself, had.

Dana brought news that Carly was going to Padre Island off the coast of Texas with a friend, and Claudia was spending the summer with her boyfriend on Martha's Vineyard. He was disappointed, but also a bit heartened. That way there were two people out in the world who might run into Jack. It made him wonder if he wanted Trent with him when he started his pursuit again in the fall.

Trent, on the other hand, having no conception of how things changed in one's first year at college, was resentful. He felt like they'd been deserted.

All in all, the beach seemed emptier.

Each night the little transistor radio sat beside them, playing the same songs they had heard every year, but, as the waves lapped the sand and the breeze intimated sultriness, somehow they were sweeter. Every word, every melody, every sweep of bow across string quivered with emotion.

The music brought back Jack, but Jack was too intimate.

So often those nights with Trent and Dana on the beach, he would have to walk away, up the waterline, to where the music could not flay him. Where he could not be laid bare publicly.

One evening at the shore, when he had sought solace in solitude, the almost-full moon was shining, reflecting in the water, bathing everything silvery green, reminding him of that night after the Founder's Day dance when he and Trent had fought. Funnily, he was beginning to think of those as golden days.

"So that's the scar that's not a suicide attempt."

He turned to see Dana standing a few feet away. He hadn't realized he'd been fingering his cheek. "I sort of like it," he said. "It gives me character."

"You always had enough character for all of us."

They smiled comfortably at each other, then turned to the undulating sea.

They stood without speaking for many moments. Then Dana took his hand and said gently what had been needed for months. "Hon', someone can only disappear if he wants to."

Some early mornings when it was still dark, he'd jerk awake in bed, terrified, listening for the phone, certain he could hear the echo of its ringing. But past his furious breaths, he could never ascertain another sound. So he'd lay back, his body and mind taut with anxiety, and there, in the deepest part of the night, he would be incapable of fighting the demon doubt. Had Jack purposely misled him?

Panic would surge until he could talk himself down, remembering Jack's touch, his voice, and those magnificent eyes that had memorized him.

And, if he were lucky, that panic would subside before the sun broke, and he'd be able to rest again.

He took walks.

He sat on the beach.

He learned to hear the surf.

He was lonely.

He joined his mother in tending the garden. He got down on his hands and knees, working loose the earth, pulling the weeds, giving the plants—dark geraniums, bright petunias, benevolent bluebells—room to breathe. He liked the texture of the soil, the way it smelled, how it crumbled under his fingers. It felt good to be part of something so base, so simple, so real.

When he was alone, away from his friends, his family, where he could give in to his torment, music was his only comfort. Heartbroken lovers mourning their losses, lamenting their loneliness, were all that salved him.

The music brought his pain to such a precise agony, it made him feel closer to Jack. By making him feel at all, it made him think that maybe he was still alive.

So he sang along with the passion of the bereft.

But when the music stopped, he could think of no way to quell the echoing silence.

What remained of his life was so overwhelmingly long without Jack.

He wondered what he would do with all his time.

"What about this fall?" Dana asked Trent one day in late May. They were on opposite sides of her tennis court, both in whites.

Trent served the ball. "Mom and Dad told me I had to go to school."

Dana volleyed. "Will he go on without you?"

Trent ran, swinging, but his racket whistled through the air. He stopped, panting in the afternoon sun, and looked at her, severed from him by the net. "If he stops, I think he'll die."

One afternoon he and his mother sat on the deck, each on a chaise longue, eyes closed. After a long while, Ann looked over and asked tenderly, "What will you do this fall?"

Just by being there, his parents saddened him and saddled him with guilt they didn't mean to administer. He felt like he was letting them down. But at that point it was a struggle to not just walk into the ocean. So he couldn't do more.

Without opening his eyes he said, "I'm going to find him."

There was an extended respite. He eventually cocked his head toward her, past a posy of purple cardamine that stood in a vase on a table between them.

She faced the sea, concentrating on something internal, something very far away.

She never responded.

He happened to be alone one day when there was a knock on the door. He opened it, not expecting, but also not surprised, to find Trey. Trey's frame had filled out. His shoulders and chest had broadened. But his long mouth still curled up around the edges in a seductive I've-got-a-secret half-smile. "Hi," he breathed. He was nervous. "I heard you were back." Behind him, snapdragons flamed in brazen slashes of lemon and scarlet and orange.

"Hey, Trey."

"I'm sorry about Jack."

He grimaced, then recovered. "Would you like to come in?"

Trey was hesitant. "Would that be all right?"

"Didn't we resolve everything last summer?"

They spent the afternoon together. He found Trey to be more at ease with himself than he'd been before. He wasn't the spiteful, self-centered boy he remembered. He was clever, intelligent, warm. He even found himself laughing with him.

Mid afternoon they decided to go swimming. He loaned Trey a pair of red swim trunks and, while they changed, he was unable to keep from watching him, surprised at just how much his body had matured. He wasn't big, like a jock, but toned and tight. A patch of dark hair in the middle of his chest crossed his stomach and disappeared into his swim trunks.

"Ready?" Trey asked.

He looked away and took his own shirt off. "Ready."

That night, they walked four miles along the shore to town, ending up at Olympus. Not even a frisson of Veronica remained. Like she had never existed. She wasn't even a ghost.

Once they'd eaten, they sat in easy silence, Trey lounging comfortably against the window facing the street, one foot on his seat, his knee lazily peaking above the table. He gazed across the remains of their pizza, his voice low, and said, "Tell me about Jack."

He was shocked to hear the words come out of Trey's mouth. He wasn't sure he was prepared.

"Only if you want to," Trey said. "Or need to. And only when you're ready."

He hadn't realized how much he'd needed to talk until he started. The story nearly burst out of him as they headed back along the shore. Every sigh, every spoken word and unspoken feeling. He had thought about fragments of their story incessantly, but to relive it in its entirety brought the pain into sharper focus than it had been since the previous autumn.

And in relinquishing it he felt relief.

When he concluded, they sat on the beach in front of his house.

They had come full circle.

"There was one midsummer morning. One of those mornings that's soft and full of promise. One of those mornings where you know all is right with the world. Jack was standing on the balcony when I woke up. I went out and embraced him from behind, putting my chin on his shoulder. We didn't speak. There was nothing to say. We were living the dream of every single person in the entire history of the world. Our sweet hereafter had been determined, our destinies defined. We would be sustained through famine and war. It was the most concentrated moment of bliss I've ever known." He looked to the water, focusing on something intangible. "But now I wonder if it was *the* moment of bliss. Like maybe you're supposed to understand that at the time. But how can you possibly take yourself out of such rapture to conceive of the apocalypse?"

They were quiet for a few moments.

Trey was sincere when he said, "I think sometimes you need to just appreciate that you had that. Even for only one brilliant shining moment. Some people don't even get that."

He turned to Trey who was looking at the sand. He understood what Trey was saying, but he wasn't willing to submit to it. "Well, I'm not one of those people. I'm going to find him and I'm going to live my life in that moment."

"You're going to continue searching?" Trey's astonishment was evident.

He was surprised Trey was surprised. "Of course. I'm only here until September."

Trey shook his head in disbelief. "You're astonishing."

He didn't respond at first, his voice hoarse and his throat aching from so much talking. "It's all I know."

They looked at each other deeply, and he knew that Trey understood.

Trey searched his eyes intently. Then he said, "I'm sorry," in one quick, hot breath, and turned away.

Trent's and Dana's surprise when he showed up with Trey at the beach the next night was apparent, and almost comical.

Dana recovered first. "Hey, Trey. You look fabulous."

He smiled that killer grin as they sat around the fire. "Thanks. So do you."

"No. I look good. You look fabulous."

He gave her a bashful look. "Thanks."

And it was then, looking at Trey with the firelight dancing across his features, humble, accessible and—for once—real, that he was at last unable to deny his beauty.

Trey, like Trent, was breathtaking.

Nerves tickled inside his stomach.

"So this is how you've been spending your time," Trent said with a satisfied smile.

He realized then that Trent thought Trey's presence meant the search was over, and he was surprised that didn't anger him. Instead it only saddened him that Trent had been his sole companion the past year and yet he still didn't understand.

The garden became his prize. He worked and reworked it, extending it toward the sea with harebells, windflowers, poppies, altheas, daffodils, primroses. He got on his hands and knees, hoeing and rooting and pulling and patting. The yard blazed with colors: cherry, honey, indigo, periwinkle. He planted trees, huge black locusts, for shade. They added a seclusion the yard had never had. It made the house seem cozier.

Safer.

To look out and see the colors, vivid in the summer sun, made his heart thrill. He collected prince's feathers and zinnias and pincushions and left them in nosegays on the mantel, by his bed, above the kitchen sink.

The flowers were the only things except the water and the music that gave his heart rest.

He found a planter in the shape of a swan at the weekly flea market.

His mother was taken aback when she saw it.

"It's just like before," he said.

He placed stars-of-Bethlehem inside.

He and Trey spent a lot of time together. Sometimes with Trent, sometimes with Dana, sometimes with both.

They had fun.

But something was missing.

So most of the time they were alone, swimming, sunning, talking. He felt he had nothing to hide from Trey, because he hadn't really known who he was before. Trey couldn't see how he'd changed, because he had never known any different.

It took some of the pressure away.

His parents thought of Trey as a savior. They practically fell over themselves attempting to make him feel part of the family. They thought they had found a substitute for Jack because Trey showed an interest in the garden, in conversing with them and, most importantly, in their son.

They clung to the idea that everyone eventually is consoled.

But their son would not be consoled.

Trent's relief at Trey's appearance soon turned sour. While he also saw him as a replacement for Jack, he came to realize that Trey was his own replacement as well. And just like the summer before, he couldn't figure out a way to crack that circle.

So he withdrew, though he wasn't sure if his absence was even noted. His presence was rarely requested.

One day near the end of June, he and Dana, without Trent, went biking. The sun was scorching, and before they'd gone two miles they had to stop and jump in the ocean to cool off. Once they emerged, he knelt to fix a slipped gear and Dana mounted her bike, casually saying, "I'm going to join Carly."

He looked up at her in surprise. "What!"

"You have to understand that it's different for all of us without Carly and Claudia here, but it's most different for me. And you're not even really here this summer. And Trent's not the same. He's jealous of Trey and he's become so quiet. I'm not blaming anyone. I'm only telling you all this so you'll understand." She gave a quick smile and self-consciously pushed a lock of hair behind an ear.

"I can't believe you're leaving," was all he could say. "I'm shocked."

"Spend some time with Trent," she replied. "And give Trey a chance. He wants to be everything for you. Every declaration of love is an act of heroism. Both yours and Trey's. And in the long run, we'll look back on last summer as the best one. Because it's the one where the most was lost."

Dana left.

He missed her more than he would have anticipated. Just the fact that she had been there had been reassuring in some way he couldn't name. He had come to depend on her.

He went to Trent's the afternoon she departed. Trent looked at him with censuring eyes like it was his fault she had gone.

He decided to not attend the Founder's Day dance.

That Saturday he went to Trey's. He'd never been there. The house was in town, set into a hill overlooking the marina. Catchflies burst forth at the base of the porch, like they had at Veronica's. The place was big and airy with a view of the sea and an oncoming storm that was moving in with alarming speed. Tendrils of lightning raced along the bottom of ominously black clouds.

With Trey's family at the dance, they sat on the sofa with beers, dried purple chrysanthemums in a vase beside them, as the squall descended. The rain was heavy and plodding. Thunder cracked and pounded around them. Geysers of white foam shot up from the sand as waves crashed. The lights flickered, then went out, and stayed out. The festivities were more impressive in the dark.

"It's like the Twilight of the Gods," he said.

And then Trey kissed him.

He was surprised, but found himself responding hungrily. Trey straddled him so they were groin to groin, his soft, insistent lips covering his cheeks, his forehead, his eyes. Then he stopped and looked down at him.

Lightning flashed in their eyes.

"You know I'm in love with you," Trey breathed.

Their breaths were short and fast.

Thunder rumbled, making their world tremble.

He put a hand against Trey's chest, feeling the urgent pound of his heart.

Trey put a hand over his, holding it to him.

"Yes," he said.

Then they were kissing again.

They kissed for what felt like hours before Trey knelt before him and worked his penis out of his shorts and took it into his mouth. He was astonishingly adept, throat muscles contracting, tongue slathering, lips tight, working it the way he'd practiced on the boys at school, anticipating this moment.

Finally, when he could take it no more, he pulled Trey's shorts down and knelt before him, eyes level with his genitals. He inhaled deeply his male scent, feeling his bristly hairs against his skin.

He cupped the balls, tenderly.

He was hungry.

When he took him in, Trey gasped. He was gentle, savoring the texture, the heat, the tang. His throat muscles opened, and he took it all in.

Trey kept saying his name like he had so many times when he'd been alone.

When he got close, Trey pulled himself out and took his hand. "Come to my room."

Upstairs, they disrobed, and Trey lay on his bed, pulling his legs back, beckoning.

He stood over Trey, his penis erect and wanting. He leaned in, using his hand to guide himself inside. Trey heaved and shuddered at the pleasure of the pain, gripping his buttocks, aiding in the penetration, legs tightening around his waist, arms around his neck, pulling him closer so their chests ground together, so that he was entirely inside him.

Grunting into each other as they came, it was over quickly, because neither could hold back.

When they were sated, Trey looked at him reverently, still trying to catch his breath, and gasped, "Thank you."

They spent the majority of their time together through the next month. Mostly they made love or sat without speaking. Trey wasn't proprietorial, he wasn't needy, he never said more than he thought permissible. He accepted just being with him, kissing, tasting, touching, just being the one he made love to.

It wasn't how Trey had imagined it would be.

But it was enough.

They had sex two or three times a day, he to attain peace, Trey to atone.

When they were fucking, he knew that Trey wanted, more than anything, to look into him in their final seconds, to be bonded in that moment of oneness. But he wouldn't relinquish that part of himself. He'd close his eyes, locking himself away in his Ivory Tower, so that his spirit could not be touched.

He would prostitute his body, but his soul, or what remained of it, was still sacred.

When they made love, Trey labored to initiate the most astonishing sex either of them had ever had. If he could offer nothing else, he could offer sex.

It was something.

It became a lifeline.

The more semen he ingested, the more of him he possessed. Like a desperate woman scheming to get pregnant, he sensed each orgasm with a conscious awareness as the one that might tie them together forever. He expected that, when it happened, the orgasm that connected them, he would know, he would perceive the moment when he had succeeded in exorcising Jack's ghost.

So he consumed orgasm after hot, slippery orgasm. And with each ejaculation he felt fuller, more complete, as if soon he'd be able to chase the shadows from his lover's eyes.

Ann was astonished to see her yard bear such splendor. The colors stretched from the garden toward the sea, and along the driveway toward the road like tentacles. They were vibrant, vivid…alive. There was life there that she hadn't been able to cultivate herself. She looked at her son kneeling in the dirt and raved, "It has never looked this beautiful."

Digging among the amaranths, he gazed up at her with a softly blank expression and said, "I feel closer to him here, you know."

One day in mid July, they lay in bed, he on his back, gazing toward the gray beyond the balcony, Trey on his stomach, face in his pillow, sleeping. The morning was already heavy and sticky with the threat of unbearable swelter. It was the kind of morning that reminded him of summers as a child, when each day materialized out of the early haze like a mirage, or a promise that could be fulfilled only if he rushed headlong into it.

He turned and watched the steady rise and fall of Trey's smooth back.

After a minute, he placed the flat of his hand on it.

It took a moment, but eventually, past Trey's body heat, he could feel his heart, beating through his ribs, through his skin, from the inside out.

He jerked his hand away as if he'd been scalded.

But he could still feel the thunderous pulse in his fingers, on his palm, in his joints.

As July turned into August, he became restless.

He talked less than he had, becoming virtually silent.

And the more withdrawn he was, the more forced and animated Trey became.

He tried to play along for Trey's sake.

But his heart wasn't in it.

His heart longed to move on.

One night, unable to sleep, he rose, slipping from under Trey's protective arm, and went to the balcony. A mild breeze came off the water. Something akin to wanderlust tickled just beneath his flesh and, in a flash, he was consumed with an urgency that time was running out. Every second, every moment, every day was time without Jack, and he suddenly had the impulse to run, not just to Jack but from something.

Trey became quieter. He no longer made suggestions or pointless conversation.

He came to enjoy the silence.

But it didn't take long for him to admit to himself that the hush between them was not the contentment of stability, but the fact that they had nothing to say.

A couple of days later he came home to find Trey standing at the open closet in the upstairs hall. In his hand was Violet's painting of him and Jack.

The shock of finding him there, like that, was like a razor slash. He strode down the hall, grabbed the art, dropped it into the closet and slammed the door shut.

Trey was so surprised by his sudden appearance he stepped back, almost frightened. "I—I was looking for a jacket."

He looked at Trey, his heart pounding irrationally. "That's just really personal."

Trey went to see Trent a few nights later. "How do I win him?" he asked as they stood on the balcony, Trent smoking a cigarette.

"Haven't you already?" Trent was not unkind.

"No. That's why I'm here. It's almost September. I'm running out of time." He sighed. "I just want him to love me."

"Do you think that's simple?"

"I can't think of anything simpler."

They were silent, the waves loud on the sand.

"What did he have?" Trey asked then. "What did Jack have?"

"I've been trying to figure that out since day one."

Trey looked at him gazing at the black sea. "I have to try, you know."

Trent didn't turn from the horizon. "And for his sake I hope you win."

That night Trey discovered him kneeling at the open door of the upstairs hall closet, holding the painting of himself and Jack, weeping.

He looked up at Trey, accusing, condemned, the vacuum seal ripped away.

He still grieved.

Trey fled.

He went downstairs half an hour later and found Trey sitting on the sofa. He sat beside him, their legs touching. He took Trey's hand in his, interlacing their fingers, and held it in his lap. His thumb stroked the flesh between Trey's thumb and forefinger.

Trey rested his head on his shoulder.

Neither spoke.

The next morning he prepared breakfast, as usual, and placed it before Trey who had come to the kitchen table in a pair of boxers and a T-shirt. They sat but neither ate. The morning was cloudy and cool.

Trey didn't look at him or the food. When he spoke he was expressionless. "I will devote the remainder of my life to you. But I must know if you think you could ever love me. Because if you can't, I have to extract myself. I cannot bear the pain." He stopped speaking and it seemed like he'd ended with a question.

The response, when it came, was soft yet unyielding. "I'm leaving. Next week. To look for him."

Trey sat for a moment.

It looked fleetingly that he would burst into laughter, then hysteria. He restrained both.

Then he stood and, not looking back, walked out the door.

Trent came by a few days later. He looked peaked and worn and more than a bit sad. They sat on the sofa, each with a bottle of beer, and he realized he knew what Trent was going to say before he said it, and he was relieved.

"I'm going to school in September."

He was sincere. "I'm glad. Really."

They sat in prolonged silence.

Trent focused on the bottle in his hands. He was quiet when he said, "I did the best I could."

He wondered if he were losing Trent that very moment.

Or if he'd already lost him when he wasn't even looking.

Standing at the deck door that evening, he heard, above the roar of the surf, the opening strains of *My Funny Valentine* coming from the stereo. He turned, tilting his ear to the music. A clutch of purple asters sat on the mantel. The willow wept with the wind. The song was almost over before he was moving to the telephone and dialing the number he never knew he knew.

After, he poured himself a cognac and went back to the deck, looking through the screen into the dark. He didn't know how long he was there—five minutes? twenty? thirty?—before his voice was being played back, hollow and distant. He heard something familiar in his inflection, recognized the catch in his throat, the timbre of his tone. He wasn't surprised, yet he also hadn't known.

As his voice faded and the song began, he realized that he was just an echo from another time, a repercussion in a story no one would ever know.

                              Enter Claudia.
She phoned the day before he was to set out.
A friend had gone to a party at the University of Virginia.
She had taken photos.
Jack was in the background of one.

The leaves were vibrant and the air warm in Charlottesville.

He missed the admissions office by 10 minutes.

He got a hotel room.

He called information.

There was no listing under Jack's name.

He took to haunting campus with Jack's photo.

When he returned to the admissions office, no one would furnish any information pertaining to the university's students. This did not diminish his burgeoning joy. It shot up, grasping at the sun so long denied it, basking in its warmth, its sustenance.

He was consumed by blissful anticipation. He smiled at strangers on the street. He strode with purpose. He had direction.

It felt strange, life. He'd forgotten what a rush it was. He wanted to laugh. And to dance. And to hope. Or at least he began to think he might be capable of those things again one day.

Being mistaken for a student, he was welcomed into their lives. He was invited to parties. He was flirted with by girls. He was asked to rush a fraternity. He entertained the idea for the following year, when he would actually be a student, when he would have Jack, when he would be normal.

The idea of normal buoyed him.

He made plans.

He got an application to the school.

He explored neighborhoods to determine where they might like to live.

He turned in job applications at bars and bistros and bookstores.

He felt like a ghost who had regained his soul.

Oxygen prickled in his lungs.

His scalp tingled.

He was shining.

The Friday of his fourth week there, dusk descending, he chanced upon Jack.

He knew it was him.

To not know would be to not know his heart.

He didn't see physical details. Only an integral part of him that had been lost. Like he'd stumbled across his inspiration or imagination, something without which he was not complete. And after so much time, in the middle of his path, as simple as love, there it was.

His senses turned on. He felt the subtle chill of the coming evening, tasted the gritty exhaust of a passing automobile, heard voices and laughter, smelled pastries and coffee. It was as though he'd been living in a black-and-white film that had been suddenly draped in Technicolor.

But it wasn't fireworks he felt.

He felt relief.

He felt light.

It was a quiet thing.

Because it was right.

It took a moment for Jack, sitting at an outdoor café with his inherent grace, to look up from the book he was reading. Then he stood, wary, an array of emotions culling his face. "Kyle?" he queried. "Kyle Ryan Quinn?"

He was still thin, but his eyes weren't as blue—they seemed to have faded, but gently, like a memory. His hair was butch and had lost some of its golden sheen, having matured into a darker, dishwater blond.

He looked older.

He didn't look like the photo Kyle had carried for so long.

But it was Jack.

Then Jack was going to him, embracing him, and a grimace of happiness cracked Kyle's mouth, dour for so long. A veil of sandalwood, Jack's aroma, enveloped him, and it, for the first time, brought back the feeling, not just the memory on which Kyle had survived all that time, of that summer. It transported him. To the McAllister house and the glitter and the goldenrod sea. He could feel the sand and smell the paints.

He could remember what it was to be pure.

Jack held him for a moment then pulled back and took his hand. "Kyle. You shouldn't've come."

Kyle thought he heard his heart crack above the sounds of the city.

But he couldn't take his eyes from Jack long enough to think about it.

He never wanted to look away again.

Jack led him to the table and they sat. There were so many things Kyle wanted to ask, to tell, to share. He wanted to know what had happened, if he'd been well, if he was still afraid of the water. He could practically taste the saltwater on his lips.

"What happened to your face?" Jack's question was gentle.

Kyle fingered his scar, self-conscious of it for the first time. "I had an accident."

"It makes you look rugged."

He smiled, irrationally uncomfortable with the compliment, like an unsure 13-year-old, because he knew the real story.

Jack smiled back, encouraging. "It's a story."

Is that all it's become? "What happened to you?"

Jack turned gray. "Oh, Kyle."

"What?" He spoke too quickly.

"I wasn't expecting you."

"I finally found you, though. I'm here. I'm here."

"But it's too late."

"What?" He heard his voice go up.

"I was going to call you when we got to the mainland, but—" Then he was crying. "My father had a heart attack on the boat."

Kyle blanched. "You should have called! I would have come. I would have…" He could think of no other words. "I would have come."

"You have to understand: It was my fault. I was right. Something *did* happen."

"Jack—"

"So I dropped out of school and stayed with him. For months. I read to him, I talked to him, I tried to atone. Then, right before Christmas, he had another heart attack. …And he died."

"No… Jack. I…would've come."

"I couldn't call you."

"But you could have."

"I couldn't. I couldn't have you near me. I couldn't have anyone near me. I could hardly bear to *be* me." He looked across the table with a stony expression. He had completely removed himself.

Kyle understood then.

He didn't want to, but he did.

Jack reached across the table to grasp his hands. "You will always be the most beautiful man who ever loved me."

Which meant there would be more.

"I still do." The words came though his lips did not move, his brain did not think; his heart was acting for him.

"You have the most beautiful phrase for when things are good. 'Golden.' All is right with the world. Well, nothing will ever be right with my world again. I can't have golden people around me anymore, Kyle. I have no more golden days."

Kyle blinked twice in succession. He hadn't realized he'd forgotten the term. "You're still golden to me. You're my sun."

"I don't think two people could have been happier."

"We can still be happy."

"Oh, Kyle. Sweet, sensitive Kyle." He gingerly touched his cheek, his scar.

"Come with me. We can go back." He saw a distance in Jack's eyes. "We can go back."

"Tell me, how is Trent?"

"He's—he's good. He's well." *We can go back.*

"You two always had eyes like twins."

"He was never what you were."

"How're your parents?"

"They're well." Then he thought about the truth in a sudden drowning crush of remorse for the anguish he'd caused them.

"My gallant King Kyle," Jack breathed. "We had such fun that summer." He looked into his eyes, serious and deep. "And I was in so much fear. Of my parents. Your friends. That you'd find out about Clay."

"Clay?"

"That guy who was in love with you."

"Trey?"

411

"Trey. He was so jealous, I was afraid he'd tell you. About us. I didn't want you to hate me."

Kyle wasn't sure he understood. He wanted to not understand. His heart hurt. He put icy fingers to his forehead and the flesh there was so hot it felt as if they left marks. He was reeling. "You had sex with Trey?" The words came out stripped.

"Only before you came. I'd have never hurt you that summer. You were my world. You are my first love."

Kyle started to speak, but his tongue was thick, his lips numb.

"I guess he never told you because he knew it would hurt you," Jack said. "And as much as he wanted you to hate me, he didn't want to hurt you."

Kyle felt weary, old. He wanted to sit before remembering that he already was.

Then Jack said, "And you were so terrified that he'd tell me about the two of you."

"You knew about us?" Kyle blurted. He couldn't even pretend.

"I figured it out. Why else would he be sniffing around?" Jack reached over and put his hand on Kyle's arm. "I never expected to see you again, Kyle Ryan Quinn."

"I searched everywhere..."

"I need you to let me go, love."

"But I love you."

"I need you to let me go."

"But, Jack..."

"Damn it, Kyle, he was my father!"

"I—" He had no idea what to say. "I'm sorry." He looked down at the table. Hot, hot tears burned his cheeks.

A student, tall, thin, bookish, stepped out of the shadows. "Jack?"

Jack stood then, Jack the man, not Jack the Boy.

Kyle looked at both of them and was suddenly ashamed.

He wasn't supposed to be there.

He rose, his knee banging against the table.

He heard a snatch of violin, laughter from the sidewalk, the impotent pop of a cork.

The city lights were just starting to come on.

"I miss you," he said, his voice cracking. "All the time."

The moon shone weakly in the old light of the sun.

"I miss you, too," Jack said.

Kyle looked deeply into the sorrows of his changing face. He wanted to demand he take back what he'd said, leave with him, love him again.

But he had no power over him.

"Jack…"

"Oh, Kyle," Jack said hotly. "No one will worship me now."

Then he turned and was gone.

WINTER

He moved to the island.

He felt complete, there, with his ghosts. He atoned for his hubris as the flowers—red clover, purple vetch, glorious goldenrod—withered, the days grew short, the shadows long, in the one place Jack would know where to find him.

The hours left were daunting in their blank, boundless emptiness. So he took the clocks down—the one above the fireplace, the one in his bedroom, the one in the kitchen—and he put them in the basement.

The clockless house was more silent and still than it had ever been, but eventually he grew accustomed to its creaks and its sighs. The noises of his home, in concert with the purr of the sea, far away and unreal, like its echo in a shell, slackened to a slower rhythm, a rhythm that he understood, a rhythm that he created.

That was when the house became his.

It didn't happen immediately, but he fell in the habit of leaving the porch light on, so if Jack came to find him, he would know he was home.

He'd inherited his mother's superstitions.

Then, her pale-green box with the off-center rose on top began to beckon. The tiny beads it held, that had assuaged her despair, offered to pacify the cacophonous voices that sneered at him, mitigate his roaring self-hatred, temper his misplaced guilt. They tempted to soften his edges, allowing him to rest, even if he had to awaken to the vacuum of his life again in the light.

He thought of the ring, the golden essence of all he'd been destined for and all he'd been denied, wondering if Jack would stumble across it in a drawer, or remember it packed away in a box, or touch it at home against his heart, and awaken.

He spent his twilights on the balcony, watching the water, the horizon, the silent, steadfast willow. Shadows lengthened over the house, over the balcony, over him.

He waited for nothing.

ॐ

The days turned into weeks.
The weeks into months.
The months into years.
And yet he waited.

It was another era when I returned to the island.

Just as Jack was stained in him, he was stained in me.

And I, too, had to return to what I remembered happiness to be.

The lilacs were dying the week we ran into each other in town.

We seemed unsurprised.

Resigned.

Like we'd known it had been destined and it had finally come to pass.

When he sighed "Trey," it felt like an autumn blast.

I don't recall who suggested a drink at Olympus.

But we went.

And I listened.

As I had always listened.

We'd been living with ghosts for so long we could no longer remember being without them. We understood that in each other. Like we remembered the same war. And no matter which side we had been on, now we were comrades.

Yet his haunting was more devastating than my guilt.

I was prepared to let him go after that first night. His presence flared the regret I had so carefully worked to extinguish.

But the next day, he came to me.

We stood, looking at each other through my screen door.

I wanted to run.

But it was what I'd always wanted.

Somehow I had won.

So I opened my door wide to him.

It happened effortlessly.

We'd find each other in the afternoon, out of boredom, or loneliness. One of us would show up at the other's door, a bottle of wine or summer berries in hand. An ostensible reason for our appearance. We'd drink, walk the shore, watch the sun set. Our days were fawn colored, like perpetual dusk. Twilight would come late, and we would sit in our easy hush. An intimacy grew between us, an intimacy of which we never spoke. Perhaps we knew all we needed to know about each other. Perhaps there was nothing more that could deepen our bond.

I felt like a seagull, though, wanting to scavenge what I thought to be mine. I wanted all of him.

Instead, I valiantly bore my guilt, pretending I had none, so that we could be happy together.

Happy.

When summer came to a close, we had nowhere else to go. We had the money to do nothing, so, though an explicit choice was never stated, we segued into autumn along with the island. The nights grew cooler, but we continued in the pattern we'd established, mornings alone, afternoons finding our way into each other's orbit, evenings on the veranda, his place or mine, drinks in hand, comfortable in our seclusion.

The nights grew longer, and darker, and our evenings on the balcony watching the sun set, dusk paling to twilight, began to swell, and, where, prior, we had been companions in our exclusive silences, mine mirroring his in a grim pas de deux, we became more ourselves. We relaxed, and laughed, and he yielded the dimness that stained and sustained him. As if our shadows, so apparent in the day, evaporated into the obscurity of night.

But, as his loneliness seemed to dissipate, my guilt expanded, magnified in the light of his acceptance.

Winter came, suddenly and fiercely. Mid January the worst blizzard in a quarter century hit and we were trapped in his house for two weeks. We had food and wine, and we, mostly, had heat.

I liked the isolation, it being just the two of us, the idea that there was no world outside the one we shared. And as the white wind howled, I allowed myself the luxury of pretending we were happy.

Then, one afternoon, the storm screaming around the house, I awoke from an unexpected nap in the living room. He had lain a light gray blanket over me. The fire crackled softly. Ice had formed on the sliding glass doors and cracked in spiderweb veins. They looked like shattered mirrors. The house was eerily quiet despite the maelstrom without.

I called his name, then went to the foot of the stairs and called again. Then I noticed something. No matter how high we turned the heat, no matter how roaring the fire, we were unceasingly chilled. So I was surprised to see the door to the unheated basement ajar. I said his name again, more quietly this time. I wasn't sure why, but I was suddenly fearful he'd hear me.

I moved to the top of the stairs and was grateful when I pulled the door to and it moved silently. The stairs were aligned with the door; they too did not utter a sound. The silence was so complete it was thunderous. I stopped a third of the way down and looked through the rail with absolutely no expectation.

He knelt before the sliding glass door, weeping in harsh, rasping sobs. His grief was so all-encompassing, I felt it choke in my throat. He wasn't weeping for Jack. I knew this. But I didn't understand for what or for whom he *was* weeping.

I staggered up the stairs. I felt guilty and embarrassed and vulnerable and keenly aware of my heartbeat over the shrieking of the storm.

I was breathless at having escaped.

Mid May, he took to walking in the afternoons. I'd watch him from the living room, heading down the same stretch of shore until he disappeared around the bend. Sometimes he'd be gone briefly, sometimes hours. He never told me where he went, and I never asked. He didn't seem to be hiding the knowledge so much as simply not sharing it.

Though, deep down, I knew.

He went only a couple of times a week at the beginning, but by mid June he was going every day. My hysterical panic born of guilt and the terror that he might someday go away made my cells scream to follow.

But as terrified as I was that he might go away, I was even more terrified that I would be the catalyst for his doing so.

So I remained steadfast, and silent.

He became more insular, settling into himself in small but significant ways, and it seemed to exclude me. Like he had some other companion he was sharing his jokes with.

I didn't know if he noticed.

If he knew.

But that was when his ghosts began to become mine.

When I came to understand that we were ghosts, too.

He never seemed to miss Trent, the girls, his family.

He seemed content.

Some years Trent came to visit. It was a study in perpetual awkwardness, like someone had died.

I think Trent was happy when it came time to leave.

I know we were.

Once he was gone, we could slip back into our tranquil, monotonous routine.

Dana came once.

Neither Carly nor Claudia did.

Eventually their houses were sold to new families so that different children could dare their childhoods away.

It wasn't until later, years later—Ann and Graham had passed, my parents were gone—that I finally gave in to the impulse to follow him down the beach.

It was late summer. The day was gray, the beach white.

I felt shame for intruding upon the sanctity of his vigil.

Yet I had to know how ardently he still mourned.

I followed, slowly, afraid to be caught yet relishing the anticipation that soon I would know all of him.

I finally crested a dune and stopped short. He was sitting on the sand, legs crossed, hands lying limply in his lap, gazing not at the ocean, but at Jack's house, an open, almost joyful look on his face, as if he were there again, that classic summer, when he had learned to kiss, to love, to be loved, by the Boy, shining in his white. The memories were warm, like their hearts still beat. The chill stillness of death that had permeated his own flesh (he was incessantly cool, as though someone perpetually danced on his grave) had not robbed them of breath.

Each day he lingered for the golden boy whom he loved.

But Jack was never going to come to him.

His image seared onto my corneas.

I turned and started running, back, home, to who I had been before this knowledge.

And then a realization stopped me dead with the sudden impact and total incapacitation of a heart attack: It was my fault. My schemes, my machinations, my betrayal had stunted and warped and perverted him.

I doubled over and wept with such wrenching sobs I feared my heart would burst. I keened, my vision flashing black, unable to vomit the depthless, poisonous bile of self-hatred that would make me clean again.

I might have stayed there, prostrate, forever, but the thought of him discovering me in my degradation dwarfed my shame and made me rise to my feet.

I ran.

And ran.

I am still running.

I will never be able to stop.

Just as Kyle will never be able to stop chasing.

A note from the author

I hope you were moved by Kyle's summer of love. Please leave a review if you were. Your kind words can only help others find this story. And if you have friends you think would appreciate it, please share. I would be humbled and honored.

If you'd like to follow my adventures or if you'd like to share stories of your own first love, you can find me at:

FB: facebook.com/UntilSeptemberBook/
IG: @harker_j
Email: HarkerJones@gmail.com

Cheers!

Harker Jones

Made in the USA
Middletown, DE
24 June 2022